Michelle Douglas has been writing for Mills & Boon since 2007, and believes she has the best job in the world. She lives in a leafy suburb of Newcastle, on Australia's east coast, with her own romantic hero, a house full of dust and books, and an eclectic collection of sixties and seventies vinyl. She loves to hear from readers and can be contacted via her website: michelle-douglas.com.

Being an author has always been **Therese Beharrie**'s dream. But it was only when the corporate world loomed during her final year at university that she realised how soon she wanted that dream to become a reality. So she got serious about her writing, and now she writes the kind of books she wants to see in the world, featuring people who look like her, for a living. When she's not writing she's spending time with her husband and dogs in Cape Town, South Africa. She admits that this is a perfect life, and is grateful for it.

ESCAPE WITH HER GREEK TYCOON

MICHELLE DOUGLAS

FINDING FOREVER ON THEIR ISLAND PARADISE

THERESE BEHARRIE

MILLS & BOON

First Published in Great Britain 2022
by Mills & Boon, an imprint of HarperCollins*Publishers* Ltd,
1 London Bridge Street, London, SE1 9GF

www.harpercollins.co.uk

HarperCollins*Publishers*
1st Floor, Watermarque Building,
Ringsend Road, Dublin 4, Ireland

Escape with Her Greek Tycoon © 2022 Michelle Douglas

Finding Forever on Their Island Paradise © 2022 Therese Beharrie

ISBN: 978-0-263-30214-1

03/22

MIX
Paper from
responsible sources
FSC C007454

ESCAPE
WITH HER
GREEK TYCOON

MICHELLE DOUGLAS

MILLS & BOON

To Brad and Felicity,
for the Friday night catch-ups, tea and whisky,
and weekend barbecues.
The next round of orange whips are on us.

CHAPTER ONE

MJ PEERED AT the imposing façade of the Constantinos residence and blew out a breath. The house was on Grosvenor Square in Mayfair, no less. As if the Constantinos family was important landed gentry.

'This is the address, miss.'

The cab driver's voice made her start, but with a quick smile she paid him before forcing herself to step down to the footpath. The Constantinos family might not be landed gentry but, whenever anything happened to remind her father of where his sworn enemy lived, it was still a fact that never failed to rile him. The current generation were 'only' second-generation British. She shook her head. As if that made an ounce of difference to anything.

The Mabels, however, could trace their ancestry back to the Restoration. Such things mattered to her father—he was forever telling Siena and her that they should be proud of such a heritage. He wouldn't trade the family's Knightsbridge mansion for any other property on the planet, but the fact the Constantinos family lived in prestigious Grosvenor Square still rankled.

While MJ couldn't give a flying fig about how far back a family could trace their ancestors or who lived where, she suspected it mattered just as much to Nikos Constantinos as it did to her father. And that meant she was the last person he'd be interested in helping.

'Which means the next half an hour is going to be fun,' she murmured as she marched up the stairs, seized the polished brass knocker—her father had one very like it in Knightsbridge—and rapped smartly on the dark door.

'Ms Mabel to see Mr Nikos Constantinos,' she said, sweeping past the butler into the grand foyer as if she were entitled to—as if she were the Queen herself. She had no intention of allowing the man to slam the door in her face or keep her ignominiously waiting on the doorstep.

'Is Mr Constantinos expecting you, Ms Mabel?'

'No, but assure him he will want to hear what I have to tell him.'

She planted herself on a hard-back chair and stared at him blandly, the picture of patience while still managing to emanate impatience. It had taken her a long time to perfect this particular attitude of entitlement. It made people edgy; made them clench their jaws and start to simmer. She rarely pulled it out of her arsenal, as it was mean-spirited, but she'd use every trick at her disposal today if she had to.

For a moment she thought he might lose his composure, but he was too well-trained. He inclined his head with a 'Very good, miss.' But his sniff told her he considered her presence in these hallowed halls a bad omen. She watched him stalk off down a hallway to the right. The direction of Nikos's study, no doubt.

She counted to twenty and then followed. Normally she'd never do anything so rude, but necessity was the mother of invention. And she wasn't leaving until she'd spoken to Nikos. Her stomach clenched. She couldn't fail. There was too much at stake.

You have time. There's still time.

Yeah, well, time had a habit of running out.

'If she wants to see me, tell her to make an appointment.'

There was no denying the hard, dark tones of Nikos

Constantinos coming from the open doorway just up ahead. He had a voice threaded through with velvet and steel. She'd always found it rather attractive.

Not that she'd ever admit as much to a living soul.

She walked into his study with a confidence she was far from feeling, but in this instance it was better to show no weakness. 'How ungallant of you, Nikos. Rest assured, I won't take up much of your time. I believe you'll find what I have to say in your best interests to hear.'

His lips thinned. 'MJ, I presume?'

He was one of the few people who could tell her and Siena apart.

He waved away his man, who left on silent feet, closing the door behind him.

'Though, as you're actually dressed more like your sister, I can't help wondering if you were trying to fool me.'

'When you find out why I'm here, you'll realise what a stupid assumption that is.'

Her pale pink capri pants and flamingo print blouse had been a present from Siena. That was why she'd worn them today. She'd wanted—*needed*—to feel close to her twin.

His lips thinned even further. He hadn't stood when she'd entered the room—not that she could blame him, as he'd made it clear he didn't want her there—so she folded herself into the chair opposite his desk without an invitation. She had no intention of standing before him like a naughty child.

His lips twisted. 'Please, take a seat.'

'How kind of you.' But just for a moment she had to fight the urge to laugh at the absurdity of their barbed fake politeness.

He blinked, as if he'd read that impulse in her face, and then leaned towards her. She became aware of the tightly leashed masculinity contained in that impeccably cut business suit. Not that she was afraid he'd ever hurt her—not physically, anyway. 'What are you doing here, Marjorie? What do you want?'

She and Nikos had barely exchanged words one-on-one before. Oh, they moved in the same circles, attended many of the same parties and exchanged the briefest of courtesies when they happened upon each other in the interests of greasing the wheels of social intercourse. But that had always been in the presence of other people. She and Nikos had never actually been alone together before.

Well, except for that one time when she'd been sixteen, but that didn't count because *he* hadn't said anything. Oh, and there was that other time when she'd been nineteen, but it'd been in a noisy nightclub and they certainly hadn't been alone. She swallowed and pushed that particular memory as far from her mind as she could.

It was just…she'd always wondered how they'd address each another if—when—they finally did speak one-on-one. Her use of 'Nikos' had felt instinctive, while him calling her 'Marjorie'…

She swallowed. It sounded completely natural, but something about it made her mouth dry. Most people called her MJ, short for Marjorie Joan, including her father. Her twin called her Jojo. Nobody called her Marjorie. Did he hope to annoy her by using it? He'd be sadly disappointed, because she found she liked it. She liked the lilt in his voice when he said it.

For a moment she wished the two of them weren't sworn enemies. Suddenly the fake politeness, the pretence—the hate—wasn't funny. None of it was funny. Not in the slightest. She and Nikos didn't even know each other. You shouldn't hate someone you didn't know.

She lifted her chin. Well, she had every intention of ridding her family of that hate. But that wasn't the reason she was here today. She wished she could find a smile, wished she could be casual and confident. But face to face with him she couldn't feign any of those things. 'Why am I here and what do I want? Why, Nikos, I want your help.'

She half expected him to give one of those harsh, ugly, triumphant laughs her father was so adept at. He didn't. His eyebrows lifted and he eased back in his seat. 'And how, I wonder, do you think I can help you?'

At least it wasn't a straight-out *no*. But only because he was probably playing a deeper game—just as her father and his father before them had done. And his grandfather and her great-aunt before that. She bit back a sigh. Just because she didn't want to play this game any more, it didn't mean Nikos was of like mind. She'd be a fool to forget it. His questions would merely be an attempt to find a deeper and more damaging weakness, one he'd ruthlessly be able to exploit if he could.

So that he could ruin her family through her.

She refused to let her chin drop. 'My sister has gone missing. I want you to help me find her.'

He blinked, the surprise in his eyes quickly masked, but she'd been looking for it. She nodded gently. So he didn't know.

'Why do you think I should know where Siena is? And, even if I did, why do you think I would help you?'

Because she had something he desperately wanted.

'I don't think you do know, but Christian does. And I'm hoping you know how to find your little brother.'

Although it didn't look as if he'd moved a single muscle, everything about him grew harder, tighter and more forbidding. With his dark hair, dark eyes and olive skin, he looked like the Prince of Darkness himself.

She frowned. Except, his nose was a little bigger than the devil's would be if he were ever made flesh. It was certainly too large for perfection, but it added a certain stateliness to his face. It was a nose that had character. Perfection bored her. She had a feeling Nikos would never bore her.

She stamped the feminine appreciation flat. She might want to end two generations' worth of anger and resentment, but *that* wasn't going to happen.

Nikos and her an item? She couldn't imagine having an affair with someone she didn't trust. Oh, who was she trying to kid? Of course she could. She had a good imagination. It'd probably be terribly exciting—thrilling, even—but far from comfortable. She'd never be able to let her guard down.

She tried to shake off the weight that wanted to settle over her. If she succumbed to his charms, Nikos would chew her up and spit her out. She was pretty certain that wasn't the way to find the peace she so desperately sought for their families. Besides, the only thing she ought to be focusing on at the moment was finding Siena before her twin did irreparable damage to herself.

'What makes you think my brother knows where your sister is?'

It was her turn to raise an eyebrow. She hoped it would raise his hackles. 'Clearly you've been working too hard. I've been told you're a man with his finger on the pulse.' She made a little moue. 'But maybe I've been misinformed.'

Those dark eyes narrowed. 'What game are you playing now, I wonder, MJ?'

He didn't look the least enraged, not even a little put out. It occurred to her then that she didn't actually want to see him angry, but she did want to fire him to action. 'It appears our siblings have been secretly dating for...well... at least two months, though I suspect it's been longer.'

His nostrils flared. 'What proof do you have?'

Sucking her bottom lip into her mouth, she gnawed on it for a moment before releasing it. He stared at her mouth, and in the depths of his eyes something flared—something warm, inviting and terribly intriguing. But then he raised a mocking eyebrow and it startled a laugh from her. Did he think she was trying to disconcert him with her wiles and *seduce* him?

If she'd had the time, she'd have thrown her head back and laughed until fat tears rolled down her face. Bad, bad move. Nobody liked being laughed at.

Focus. How much should she tell him? If she wanted to find Siena, she was going to have to take a risk or two. And she'd risk everything for her twin.

Uncrossing her legs, she planted her feet firmly on the floor and folded her hands in her lap. 'Two weeks ago Siena and my father had a huge row. And when I say huge, I mean a row of truly monumental proportions. Ugly things were said on both sides.'

Things that could never be unsaid. The kind of things that not even MJ, in her role as family mediator, was sure she'd ever be able to help smooth over. She understood them both so very well—understood why they didn't get each other—and loved them with all her heart. If only they'd stop being so stubborn!

'And in the heat of the moment she told your father that she's dating Christian to get a rise out of him, because she knows it's the one thing he'd most hate to hear.'

That surprised a laugh from her. 'If she really wanted to outrage him, she'd have said she was dating you. You are, after all, CEO of the Leto Group, not your brother.'

The Constantinoses and the Mabels owned rival five-star hotel chains. The Mabel Group of hotels was known for its old-world charm and understated elegance, while the Leto Group's was pure glamour and over-the-top glitz.

Dark eyebrows rose and the bump on the bridge of his nose grew more pronounced. She wondered how he'd broken it. She'd love to ask and...

Stop it!

Focus. She needed to find Siena. 'So...ugly fight,' she

repeated. 'I tried to smooth things over, which of course backfired. What's the saying—no good deed goes unpunished? Anyway, the upshot of all that is Siena is now no longer talking to me.'

'And why should I care about your petty family dramas, Ms Mabel?'

'Heavens! We've gone from Marjorie to MJ to Ms Mabel. What's next? Madam?'

She could've sworn his lips twitched.

'No, that's all just background context for you.' She wrinkled her nose. 'I'm not especially proud of what I did next. Long story short, I pretended to be Siena and met with a couple of her girlfriends.'

She'd dropped into the bar they frequented most Thursday nights. 'They wanted to know how come I hadn't left with Christian yet, how romantic it all was, how handsome he is—though I won't sport with your patience by giving a blow-by-blow account of your brother's physical virtues. And they also wanted to know if she'd confided in me yet, her nearest and dearest twin.'

He leaned towards her. 'Are you telling me they couldn't tell the difference between you and Siena?'

She spread out her hands. '*That's* what you want to take away from what I just told you?' Rather than the fact that it sounded as if Siena and Christian had eloped. He raised an eyebrow and she shrugged. 'People see what they expect to see…what they want to see.'

'Which means you maybe saw what you wanted to see too. It's possible Siena's girlfriends played you.'

'I've had twenty-seven years to study my sister, Nikos. My impersonation of her is pretty damn good.' Better than Siena's was of MJ. 'You also need to understand that Siena's friends are arty types, not…'

'Not cut-throat businesswomen used to dealing with subterfuge and deceit.'

Was that what he thought she was—a cut-throat businesswoman? She shook the thought away. 'Once I heard Siena's and Christian's names linked, I visited my godmother, Lady Charlotte Hamilton.'

His lip curled. 'Tottie Hamilton is the biggest gossip in London.'

'She certainly keeps her ear to the ground. And she doesn't tell half of what she knows either, which makes the mind boggle. But she confirmed Siena and Christian *have* secretly been seeing each other for the last two months.'

'And you now want my help to bring an end to their relationship.'

She should've realised that was what he'd think. And what he'd want to do. 'No.' She said the word as gently as she could. 'Siena is twenty-seven years old, and Christian is what…twenty-eight? They're adults. I'm not going to tell my sister who she can and can't date.'

'Let me be clear, Marjorie. I won't allow a union to occur between our families. Do I make myself understood?'

'Excellent!' She beamed at him. 'We're back on a first-name basis. It's so much friendlier, don't you think?'

'Do you hear me, *Marjorie*?'

He made it sound as unfriendly as he could and it was all she could do not to roll her eyes. His vehemence and the darkness that gathered on his brow had her stomach clenching, though. 'The sentiment doesn't surprise me.' After all, it was a sentiment her father shared. 'Though I confess I'd hoped for better from you.'

His eyes narrowed. He looked as soft as granite. 'I wonder, then, what it is you *do* want from me.'

'I've already told you. I want to find Siena. I've searched in all of her usual haunts, as well as the unusual ones. She's nowhere to be found. Which means she's with Christian.'

'And you think I can find them?'

'Yes.' She put on her bravest front. 'And I want you to take me along with you when you do it.'

His jaw slackened and so did his spine. Only fractionally. *Finally*, she'd surprised him. She only noticed because she'd become so adept at reading people since she'd started working at the Mabel Group. *Not* because she was a cut-throat businesswoman.

He folded his arms. 'No.'

'I've reason to be concerned about my sister's health.'

Neither Siena nor their father would easily forgive her if she divulged the nature of Siena's illness. It wasn't her place to discuss Siena's health with anyone. Her twin guarded her privacy jealously. Normally MJ wouldn't have mentioned as much as she already had. But…

One shouldn't take chances with polycystic kidney disease! If only Siena would return MJ's calls.

She pulled in a breath; let it out again. There was still time. As soon as she spoke to Siena, she'd know where her sister's head was at. She'd know what she needed to do and how to fix everything.

'No,' Nikos repeated.

She inched forward and rested her arms on his desk. 'Even if I tell you I'm talking about a possible life-and-death issue?' She locked eyes with him. 'Do you really hate us that much?'

CHAPTER TWO

MJ's WORDS SENT ice surging through Nikos's veins. He had to fight competing impulses. The first was to remain in his seat with a carefully bland expression on his face like a civilised man. The other was to grab her by the upper arm, physically frog-march her to his front door and toss her onto the street as if he were a bouncer. Or a hoodlum.

Damn it. He was a civilised man, and he had no intention of allowing a member of the Mabel family to provoke him into doing something he'd regret.

Do you really hate us that much?

The short answer was *yes*!

It was an ugly confession to make, even silently to himself, but the Mabels had brought nothing but misery and wretchedness to the Constantinos family. When Joan Mabel had tricked his grandfather into believing she loved him, her perfidy had sent the older man into a spiral of self-hatred that had resulted in him exiling himself from the world and becoming a hermit.

And when MJ's father, Graham Mabel, had seduced Nikos's mother… Nikos's hands clenched. It had destroyed his parents' marriage. He'd witnessed the fallout from that with his own eyes—the anger, the anguish, the despair. The ugliness. It had been a blight on his childhood.

While he might not be able to hate MJ personally—he didn't know her well enough, thank God—

he could still hate the idea of her. He could hate the harm her family had inflicted on his. He could hate all the Mabels had taken from him and his. He could hate that she'd profited at his family's expense.

So, yes, he supposed he did hate her that much.

'Your silence speaks volumes, Nikos.'

Good.

But, when he glanced into her eyes, it wasn't hatred that filled his veins. Her eyes looked so deep, honest and true. All a lie, of course, but right now he found that hard to remember.

'Such a progressive attitude,' she teased. 'I can see there's no thoughts of burying the hatchet in your world view.'

There was real amusement in her voice beneath the deeper thread of worry for her sister. He wanted to respond to it but he'd be a fool if he did. She was only toying with him, as her father had with Nikos's mother and her great-aunt had with his grandfather. He wasn't falling into that trap.

He shouldn't need reminding how dangerous MJ was. There'd been that incident in a nightclub eight years ago. He'd been twenty-four—old enough to know better. She'd only been nineteen, and already a siren. If he was being honest, he'd been far too aware of her that evening, had found it difficult to drag his gaze away from her.

Which had proved lucky for her. She'd been making her way to the dance floor when a drunken lout had lurched into a waitress carrying a tray full of drinks. Before he'd realised what he was about, Nikos had leapt to his feet and yanked MJ out of harm's way before five cocktails in fragile glasses, a tray and a drunken lout could crash into her. Instead the glasses had shattered to the floor around them and the tray had rolled away, while the drunk had regained his balance and kept weaving through the room.

'Oh, wow. Thank you, I…'

And then her gaze had collided with his and her words had stuttered to a halt, but the impact of her gaze had nearly felled him. She'd half-lain in his arms, her eyes huge and the beginnings of a smile trembling on her lips, and he'd been held spellbound.

Some measure of common sense had eventually kicked in. He'd forced himself to right her and set her back on her feet. She'd smoothed a hand down her orange silk blouse and had shaken out her hair, which looked softer and shinier than the silk of her shirt. 'Thank you, that could've been nasty.'

'A pleasure.' Their gazes had caught and clung and in that moment he'd felt that he knew her, deep down in his bones, in a way that made no sense. The air had shimmered as if electrically charged.

Music had started to throb around them and she'd drawn in a ragged breath and gestured towards the dance floor with an unsteady hand, her gaze not leaving his for a moment. 'Would you like to…?'

He'd nodded, not wanting the moment to end, knowing he was being offered something precious. But before he'd been able to take a single step, his date's scarlet-tipped fingers had wrapped around his upper arm and she'd pulled him back from the brink.

'I don't think so,' Cynthia had said. 'Back off, MJ.'

MJ had blinked and then lifted her hands in the universal sign of non-aggression, thanked him again, before turning and walking away. He'd watched her go, feeling he'd missed out on something momentous. He still woke in the middle of the night sometimes, remembering it.

That proved exactly how dangerous MJ could be. He'd known who she was that night and yet he'd still been prepared to follow her onto that damn dance floor, and probably anywhere else she'd wanted to lead him.

Idiot! He would *not* repeat the mistakes of past. He refused to inflict that kind of pain on his father and grandfather.

As for her worry for her sister… He hardened the places inside him that were in danger of softening. It wasn't his problem. No matter how much he told himself that, though, he couldn't make himself feel it.

She leaned towards him, all amusement gone. 'Doesn't it exhaust you, carrying around all of this animosity?' Her brow creased. 'Do you really mean to pass that burden onto your children?'

He stiffened. He would *not* allow the Mabels to harm so much as a single hair on the head of any children he might be lucky enough to father one day.

'Maybe a match between Siena and Christian would be a good thing,' she mused. 'Maybe it would help heal old hurts.'

He stabbed a finger on his desk. 'Over my dead body!'

She stared at it then grinned. 'You've no idea how tempted I am to turn this conversation into a gangster movie and say, *That can be arranged.* Except I'm afraid you might actually believe me.'

Her grin was a lopsided affair that had mischief dancing in her irrepressible eyes the colour of laurel leaves—too dark for emeralds but not dark enough for a pine forest. His heart gave a giant kick. They promised shade. And rest. And relaxation.

Damn it! Who cared what colour her eyes were? Besides, her mouth was too wide. A fact that grin only highlighted.

Ha! He might want to find that a flaw, but it was only a flaw in the same way Julia Roberts' mouth was flawed. Which meant it was gorgeous and almost impossible to resist.

Therein lay the fatal flaw. Apparently certain members

of the Constantinos clan found certain members of the Mabel family temptation personified, and it was startling to discover he wasn't exempt from their number. Despite all he knew about them. Despite the destruction he'd witnessed them wreak on people he loved.

Except he was made of sterner stuff. His hands clenched. He *would* resist. He'd resisted eight years ago. And he'd resist again now.

She glanced at his hands and the fists they formed. Her shoulders and chest lifted as she dragged in a breath and then dropped as she released it. Not a sigh, but something deeper and more heartfelt.

She's toying with you.

He hardened his heart.

She eased back and crossed her legs. 'Very well, I'll speak to you in a language you'll respond to, rather than attempt to appeal to your better nature. I know you must have one buried deep down, but I can see you're not going to dust it off for me. So, Mr Constantinos…'

He ground his teeth together, forcing himself to focus on her words rather than the lips uttering them.

'Consider, if you will, the headlines that would appear in the papers if Siena were to fall seriously ill—or worse— in the company of your brother.'

It took a moment for her words to sink in. When they did, he found himself on his feet, everything clenched so hard he'd started to shake.

'Don't look at me like that. It's something I'd like to avoid as well.'

He strode to the window. It looked out on the quiet elegance of the square, but none of the square's peace or orderliness could work its magic on him at the moment. The feud between the Constantinoses and the Mabels was well known—notorious, even. If Siena were to fall ill while with Christian, there'd be allegations of foul play—as if

Christian had somehow orchestrated her illness as some form of dastardly revenge.

His brother couldn't have found his way out of a wet paper bag, let alone plan such a thing, but that wouldn't stop the rumours, the innuendos. Graham Mabel and his daughters would milk it for all they could too, no doubt. His family had suffered enough. He would *not* allow his kind, hapless brother to become the latest in a line of victims. He wouldn't allow the rocky relationship between his father and brother to disintegrate even further.

He swung round from the window.

'And yet he continues to look at me as if I planned this whole thing,' she said to the bust on his filing cabinet.

'It wouldn't surprise me to discover you had!' He regretted the words the moment they left his mouth. They were too unbridled, too childish.

'Wow.' Her whispered word seemed to fill the room right to its very corners. Not a trace of amusement stretched in her eyes now or lurked at the corners of her mouth. She tilted her chin, everything about her hard and determined. 'If I refuse to let my father's hate control me, you can rest assured I won't let yours either, Nikos.'

He blinked. He almost believed her.

'So,' she said when he remained silent. 'Are you going to help me find them?'

'You can rest assured that I'll find them, MJ. You needn't doubt that for a moment.'

'So far, so good.'

'But you won't be accompanying me on my search, tagging along like a—'

He broke off. He was a civilised man. He refused to descend to insults.

Those damned eyes danced again, reminding him of a shady inlet on his grandfather's Greek island, the sea dancing in the sun as a breeze ruffled its surface. 'Were you going to say, like a piece of unwanted baggage…or a bad smell…a thorn in your side, perhaps?

Whatever she saw in his face had her throwing back her head and laughing. He shifted. He didn't understand this woman at all.

She swiped her fingers beneath her eyes, her merriment slowly fading. 'That, however, is not such excellent news.' She cocked her head to one side. 'I could be an asset, you know.'

He seriously doubted that.

'I know my sister better than anyone else on the planet. I'm hoping you know Christian just as well. Are the two of you close?'

He strode back behind his desk. 'None of your business.'

Those green eyes weighed him up. 'So that's a yes, then.'

She said the words almost to herself and he could've kicked himself for being so transparent. Except he hadn't been. He'd kept his usual armour firmly in place.

'Which means if we put our heads together we should be able to predict where they are and what they'll do. And how they'll react in any given situation.'

'If I need your input, I'll call you.' The less time he spent alone with this woman, the better. Nothing she could say would convince him to change his mind.

'So implacable,' she mused. 'And yet I still think I can convince you to let me tag along.'

'I think not.'

'Nikos, if you personally help me find my sister—and that includes allowing me to tag along as a piece of unwanted luggage—then you have my word that I will give you the Ananke necklace.'

His heart kicked so hard against the walls of his chest that for a moment he couldn't breathe. Had she just said…?

'You lie.' The words scraped out of him, leaving his throat raw. 'It's not yours to give.'

Those green eyes didn't falter. 'My great-aunt gave it to me on my twenty-fifth birthday.'

He slashed a hand through the air 'The word of a Mabel is worthless.'

But...*the Ananke necklace*. The heirloom his grandfather had given to Joan Mabel fifty years ago when they'd embarked on their whirlwind affair—when he'd asked her to marry him and she'd said yes. The heirloom she'd refused to return when she'd betrayed his grandfather with another man.

The Ananke necklace belonged to *his* family.

'You might not trust me, but do you trust Bayard Crawford?'

He glanced up at the name of the prominent London lawyer. Not her family's lawyer, nor his family's lawyer either. The man had an impeccable reputation.

'I had him draw up a contract.'

If he could win the necklace back for his grandfather before the old man died...

She reached into her handbag, drew out several folded sheets of paper and handed them to him.

'As you'll see from his attached note, the necklace is currently in his keeping. So you can drop any of your nasty suspicions that I'll simply make the necklace disappear.'

Her words made him feel petty. No doubt a result of one of the many tactics she had in her arsenal. She remained silent as he read over the contract. It was above board and water-tight, though there were provisions protecting her from him giving her the slip, abandoning her or otherwise misleading her.

His lips twisted. Whose suspicions were petty now? He was a man of honour. When he entered into a contract, gave his word...

He stilled. A Mabel would no sooner believe a Constantinos than a Constantinos would a Mabel. She no more trusted him than he did her. He glanced at her. Over the years he'd demonised her family—he knew that. But maybe she *was* a woman of her word.

It didn't change the fact that he'd love to cut her dead. Every instinct he had warned him against spending any time alone with her. But the image of the Ananke necklace dangled before him, a provocative prize. If he could win it back, nearly any price would be worth that. Even being forced to spend time in the company of a Mabel.

His gut clenched. But she needed to learn that *he* was boss. The sooner she understood that, the better. In two strides he was in front of her, his hands slamming down to grip the arms of her chair, locking her in as he drew his face close to hers. 'Why would you give me the Ananke necklace?'

'I'm not *giving* it to you. I'm *buying* your co-operation. I want to find my sister.' Her eyes flashed and she lifted her chin. It angled her lips towards him in a way that had his heart thudding too hard against his ribs, but he sensed she was entirely unconscious of that fact.

'The necklace is a curse, Nikos. It's brought far more pain than joy. I don't want it. I never wanted it.'

He didn't believe that for a moment. 'Then why haven't you got rid of it?'

She hesitated. 'My intention was to donate it to a museum.'

Did she expect him to believe that? 'And now you mean to give it to me?'

'As long as you keep your side of the bargain.'

'Your father will never forgive you.'

That determined chin lifted a notch. 'Yes, he will. I'll make sure of it.'

'How?'

She eased her spine from the back of her chair and leaned in close, so close their breaths mingled. He called himself every kind of fool for having played this game in the first place, for drawing near in an attempt to intimidate her. She didn't look alarmed or cowed, merely intrigued. And now he was in a hell of his own making because, if he wanted to maintain face, he had to remain exactly where he was. That was what he got from trying to be tyrannical. And it served him damn well right.

'Love.' She said the word clearly.

He wanted to scoff, but his throat had drawn tight and an ache started up at the centre of him.

'I love him and he loves me. He'll be in a temper—there's no doubt about that. He might not understand why I've done it, but he'll forgive me in the end. Because he knows in his heart how much I love him.'

She moistened her lips and he couldn't help but follow the action. She had pretty lips—not too full and not too thin; they looked soft and firm in exactly the right proportions. When he glanced into her eyes again, they'd widened, and he could read the surprise in their depths. Had she recognised the desire burning at the back of his own eyes?

His hands clenched so hard on the arms of her chair, his fingers started to ache. He wanted her to be as apprehensive as he was. 'Do you really want to spend that much time alone with me?'

'Needs must,' she whispered.

Her sudden breathlessness told him she wasn't as unaffected as she'd like to appear. The spectre of her in his arms eight years ago rose in his mind. His heart pumped too hard and fast. The ache that had flooded him then burst back to life now. 'What would you do if I kissed you?'

Very gently she placed a hand in the middle of his chest and pushed him back, rising to her feet, ensuring there was at least three feet between them before she drew her hand back to her side. 'Why, I'd slap you, of course. It's what all the best heroines do in those old classic movies.'

She spoke lightly as she moved to the window and he couldn't contain a rueful smile. The woman had class—he had to give her that.

She turned back to face him. 'My sister is worth a hundred Ananke necklaces. So, Nikos, do we have a deal?'

'Yes.'

'Excellent.' She pulled in a breath. 'I'd like to get started on the search as soon as possible. While you haven't bothered to enquire after my sister's health, she could be dangerously ill. Time *is* of the essence.'

Shame hit him then. Shame and guilt. Siena might be a Mabel, but she was also a human being. Where the hell was his common decency?

Where the Mabels were concerned, he had a feeling he had none. For the first time, he wondered what the hell he was in danger of turning into.

He dragged in a breath. 'Then let's not waste time. Let's get started immediately.'

CHAPTER THREE

MJ REMAINED SILENT as Nikos punched a number into his phone. 'Christian, it's Nikos. Give me a call as soon as you get this. Something has…' he glanced at MJ '…come up.'

He slipped his phone into his top pocket and it drew her attention to the breadth of those shoulders and the hard height of him.

'Right. It'll be quicker to take a cab than to drive.'

She started, had to shake off the strange lethargy threatening to steal over her. *Focus.* She'd wanted to fire Nikos to action and, now that she had, she needed to rise to the challenge.

Hooking her handbag over one shoulder, she worked at making her face politely bland. 'I guess that depends on where we're going.'

'Christian's flat.'

'In that case, it'd be quicker to take the Tube.'

He didn't answer that, just started the shutdown procedure on his computer.

'But if we did that,' she continued, 'someone might see us together, and the sky would fall in, right?'

He threw her an irritated glare. She seemed to do that a lot—irritate him. She wasn't sure how she felt about that. Not that it mattered, of course. All that mattered was finding Siena. Once that was done, she and Nikos could go their separate ways.

Unless Siena and Christian had fallen in love and were planning to marry. In which case she and Nikos would be thrown together at family events. Hmm…could she imagine Christmas dinner, all of them one big happy family?

'What's so amusing now?'

She shook her head. 'As you won't find it the least bit funny, I'll spare you the details.'

'No, no,' he said with chilling courtesy. 'By all means share the joke.'

She lifted her chin. He'd asked for it. 'I was imagining all of the family Christmases that would feature in our future if Siena and Christian marry.'

His mouth dropped open, and then his brow grew progressively darker as he came from behind his desk. 'Why didn't you put a stop to their relationship?'

She took the two steps that brought them toe to toe and she squared off. 'You want me to forbid my younger sister by forty minutes from dating someone? Seriously? Has that approach ever worked for you in the past with Christian?'

He stared back, an arrested expression on his face, and then he wheeled away.

They caught a black cab to Christian's flat.

When they arrived, she was tempted to say she'd wait for him in the car. She already knew this was a wasted journey.

She made sure to remain hidden behind him when he rang the doorbell.

'Señor Constantinos.' Luisa, the Spanish housekeeper, greeted him. 'Señor Christian is not in.'

'Do you know what time he'll return?'

'I'm afraid not.' She caught sight of MJ. 'Señorita Mabel. He has not returned since you were here last.'

MJ sensed Nikos stiffen. 'I didn't think he would've, but we thought it best to check.' She hesitated. 'How long has he been gone?'

The older woman glanced at Nikos, who gave her a nod. 'Ten days.'

Ten days! They'd been gone longer than she'd thought. It took a super-human effort not to reach out and wrap her fingers around Luisa's arms. 'Did you see my sister prior to that? Was she here with him?'

Again, Luisa glanced at Nikos. Again, he nodded. *'Si,'* she said.

MJ's heart pounded so hard it was difficult to get her words out. 'Can you tell me how she looked? How she seemed? I understand it's only an impression,' she added quickly when the other woman started to turn away, 'but Siena has been unwell and I'm worried about her. It's why I need to find her. I want to make sure she doesn't become any sicker.'

Nikos shifted his weight to the balls of his feet. 'We'd appreciate any information you can give us, Luisa. I'm concerned that Christian might be unaware of Siena's condition.'

'Si. Yes. I have seen her,' Luisa finally said on a sigh. 'She stayed here for several days.'

MJ could feel Nikos tensing and bristling, but he didn't say anything.

'How did she look?'

'She…was pale. It was clear that when she first arrived she'd been crying.'

MJ's heart clenched. Crying? Pale? Dear God, please let her sister be okay.

'Señor Christian, though, cheered her up and made her laugh.'

She managed to find a smile at that, though the shoulders of the man beside her became even more rigid, if that were possible. Rubbing a hand across her chest, she said, 'Thank you.'

'The two of them, they are good friends,' Luisa added. It sounded like a warning.

'If Siena was here for several days...' MJ bit her lip. 'Did you happen to overhear any snippets of conversation that might—?'

'Absolutely not!' The housekeeper drew herself up to her full height with a glare.

She knew asking had been a risk. She gave a wan smile. 'You can't blame a girl for trying.'

'Luisa, can you tell me where I might find my brother? Where he has gone?'

'No.'

'But—'

'It is Señor Christian who pays my wages. Not you and not his father. I'm sorry, sir, but I cannot help you any further.'

MJ stepped in before Nikos could explode. 'I'm glad Christian has such loyal staff. It speaks well of him. Thank you for talking to us, Luisa. I really appreciate it.'

Luisa surprised her by reaching out and squeezing MJ's hand. 'He's a good man, señorita.'

She met Luisa's gaze and nodded. 'I believe you. My sister is a great judge of character.'

'I do not think you need to worry about her so much.'

That was impossible under the circumstances, but MJ found a smile for the other woman anyway.

They returned to the waiting cab. 'Why didn't you tell me you'd already been here?'

Everything about him seemed hard and unyielding. 'Because you wouldn't have believed anything I reported to you. I figured it'd be quicker and would save an argument if you checked for yourself. Besides, it's been a few days since I dropped round, and things might've changed. I also thought Luisa might tell you more than she did me.'

He sat back with a huff.

She stared out of the window, biting the side of her thumb. Pale and crying... Over ten days ago... That would've been just after the row with their father. Just after MJ had tried to patch things up between the two of them.

'If Siena is with Christian, MJ, he will look after her—take good care of her.'

The assurance was uncharacteristic, the attempt at re-assurance kind, but...

'I've no doubt your brother is a good man.'

His eyes weren't black, as she'd originally thought, but a dark brown that reminded her of the finest Swiss chocolate.

'Why, I wonder?' He spoke softly. 'Given all the history between our families, why would you think well of Christian?'

'Luisa's loyalty is a fine reference, and I trust Siena's judgement.'

'Just not her judgement in relation to her health.'

She ignored that. 'Why shouldn't I have a good opinion of Christian? Or of you, for that matter? Neither of you have done anything to injure my sister or me. This ridiculous feud between my great-aunt and your grandfather is...well...*ridiculous*. Why should it impact us? My great-aunt is dead now, and I'm of the opinion the feud should've died with her. My father and your father should never have got involved, and I don't see why we—you, me, Christian and Siena—have to buy into it either.'

Those dark eyes narrowed and his jaw firmed. 'You can't be serious.'

'Why not?' Why was he so intent on keeping the feud alive and perpetuating the enmity between their families?

A frown lowered over his face. 'You can't be serious,' he repeated. 'You don't...?'

'What?'

Before he could answer, the cab pulled to a halt outside an exclusive London club. MJ had been here too.

'Want me to wait, sir?'

'No, thank you.' He paid the driver and then turned back to MJ. 'This is Christian's club.'

She blew out a breath. 'Far be it from me to point out the obvious, but it's only just gone midday. It's not exactly what I'd call club hours.

He waved that away. 'Christian often lunches here. He sometimes even works from here.'

That sounded like something her research should've uncovered.

Unlike his brother, Christian hadn't gone into the family's hotel business. Instead he was making a name for himself as an up-and-coming fashion designer. It was one of the things he and Siena had in common, MJ supposed— their creativity. Rather than being a clothing designer, though, Siena was a mixed-media artist. She'd had a couple of small exhibitions and had won a couple of commissions. Her sister was wonderfully talented and MJ didn't doubt that she'd make her mark in the art world.

The interior of the club was pure tradition, and as far from *avant garde* as one could get with its wood-panelled walls, high ceilings and lush Axminster carpet. MJ made her way to the bar and hiked herself up onto a stool. 'Hi, Big Dave.'

The bartender nodded. 'What can I get you, MJ?'

'The usual.'

He glanced at Nikos. 'Sir?'

'I'll have what she's having.' Nikos settled on the stool beside her. 'So you've been here too?'

'I'm a cut-throat businesswoman, remember? I do my due diligence.'

His lips twisted. 'Naturally.'

Had he honestly thought he'd been her first port of call? Fat chance. He was her plan of last resort. 'This is Christian's brother, Nikos,' she said when Big Dave placed their drinks in front of them.

Big Dave rested his forearms on the bar. 'I haven't seen your sister.' He shifted his gaze to Nikos. 'Or your brother in here for over a week. I checked with the other lads and none of them have either.'

She nodded. It was what she'd been expecting. 'Thanks, Big Dave.'

Nikos sipped his drink, then shot her a surprised look. 'Lime and soda?'

'It's a little early in the day for me to be drinking anything heavier.' She didn't tell him she was a teetotaller, and therefore it was always too early in the day as far as she was concerned. He'd probably take it as a sign of weakness. 'What were you expecting?'

'I had no idea.'

She found herself suddenly grinning. 'For the first time ever, I wish my usual was *crème de menthe*.'

His lips actually kinked upwards. It felt like a win.

'Big Dave.' He called the bartender back over. 'Are Raymond Diaz, Freddy Smythe or Solomon Golding here by any chance?'

The bartender nodded. 'If you don't find them in the reading room, then try the billiards room.'

'I'll wait for you here,' MJ said. 'I suspect you'll have more luck without me in tow.'

Across the bar, Big Dave gave a chuckle and Nikos raised his eyebrows.

She wrinkled her nose. 'My last meeting with them didn't go so well.'

Nikos returned fifteen minutes later. 'Any joy?' she asked.

He thumped down onto the stool beside her. 'None.'

He pulled out his phone and dialled a number—Christian's again, she suspected. This time when it went to voicemail, he didn't leave a message. Instead he ended the call with a savage punch of his finger.

'At least you didn't yell at them,' she offered. 'Apparently I could be heard all the way in here.'

'You yelled at them?'

'They were being *seriously* irritating. All fake ignorance and holier-than-thou platitudes—but beneath it all ran a whole swathe of "I know more than you do, but I'm not going to tell you" superiority that really got up my nose.' She shrugged. 'And I was tired.' She'd barely slept for three days.

Big Dave laughed. 'Which is why you tipped your drink into Freddy's lap?'

'*He* was being the most irritating. He's never forgiven me for turning down a drunken pass he made at the Davenells' silver wedding anniversary party.'

'You tipped your drink in his lap?' Nikos asked. She couldn't work out if that was surprise or admiration in his voice.

'And then I was asked to leave and escorted to the door.'

Nikos swung back to Big Dave. 'You kicked the lady out?'

Big Dave raised his hands at the dangerous edge in Nikos's voice. 'Not me. I wasn't on that day. I heard about it second hand. I'd never ask MJ to leave.' He stroked his jaw. 'I'd be tempted to give Freddy Smythe a clip around the ear, though.'

'You and me both,' Nikos muttered, draining his drink and setting the glass on the bar before turning back to MJ. 'Ready to go?'

She slid off her stool with a wave in Big Dave's direction and followed him to the door. 'Where to now?'

'Devon.'

Devon?

'Something Diaz let slip informed me my brother is

no longer in the city. Freddy kicked him before he could reveal any more, and he recovered beautifully…and they thought they'd got away with it.'

But he was a cut-throat businessman who could smell weakness at fifty paces. It would never do to underestimate this man. 'So we're going to your family estate in Devon.'

He hailed her a cab and gave the driver her address before handing her into the car. 'I'll collect you in an hour. It might be wise to pack for a couple of days.'

She nodded and then met his gaze. 'I'll pack my passport too. Just in case.'

He hesitated and then nodded before closing the cab door behind her.

Nikos pulled the car to halt in front of the Georgian manor house his maternal grandfather had gifted to his daughter as a wedding present, and glanced across at the sleeping woman beside him.

With her face in repose, the pallor of MJ's skin and the dark circles under her eyes that the force of her personality and ever-present humour had masked were now evident. As he stared at her, something in his chest shifted. MJ's worry for her sister was no longer academic, but a real and vital concern.

Ice crept across his skull. What *was* wrong with Siena? And what kind of mess had Christian landed himself in?

They were questions he hoped to find the answers to by day's end. A glance at the clock on the car's dashboard informed him there were still a few hours left. And sitting here staring at MJ wasn't going to help him find the answers.

He doubted she'd thank him for letting her sleep, and he had no intention of carrying the damn woman into the house. An armful of warm, sleepy MJ…

He cut the thought dead.

Reaching across, he went to touch her forearm, but halted. Her arm was bare...and in her lap. Too close to her legs, breasts and things he didn't want to accidentally brush if she moved. Instead he gave her shoulder a soft shake—a shoulder covered in the cotton of her slightly silly, holiday vibe T-shirt—but even the brief touch had her warmth filtering from his fingertips into his bloodstream and told him how delicate and fine were the bones there.

Her eyes opened and she blinked a few times before glancing at him. And then she smiled. The force of it punched the breath from his body.

Her smile wasn't a sultry, seductive invitation. There were no come-hither overtones. It was simply her default expression.

And it was the sexiest thing he'd ever seen.

'We're here.' The words croaked from him.

She straightened, stretched. 'What time is it?'

'Four-thirty.'

'Wow, we made good time.' She turned to the house and stilled. 'It's beautiful.' She glanced back at him. 'This is where your mother lives, isn't it? Is she nice?'

'So many questions.' His words were meant as an admonishment, but that was not the way they emerged. He shook himself. 'Of course my mother is nice. Why do you ask? Unfortunately—' or perhaps he should have said 'fortunately' '—she's not here at the moment.' His mother was currently living in New York with her second husband.

'Well, that's a shame. I've met your father and Christian, of course, but never your mother.'

She wouldn't have. His mother shunned London. She spent as much time away from England as she could. He frowned. Was MJ really ignorant about what had happened eighteen years ago? Did she really not know about the torrid affair between her father and his mother...and the painful fallout that had resulted?

She pushed out of the car as if she was looking forward to stretching her legs, checking her phone as she did so. 'Has Christian called you back?'

He swung away to collect their bags from the boot, his gut clenching. 'Not yet.'

'*Nada* from me too.' She sighed.

The familiar sounds of Rufus's and Seth's barking greeted him as the dogs raced from the house, and he knew Mrs Digby would be waiting for them on the threshold with the door wide open. He smiled in anticipation of the hot drink and shortbread or cake that would be imminent.

'Were you expecting otherwise?' It was clear to him that Siena had gone into radio silence.

He didn't know what alerted him that something was wrong. Maybe the fact MJ hadn't answered him. Or perhaps it was the unnatural stillness that seemed to emanate from her and descended around him, even though he couldn't see her, as she was currently obscured by the raised boot of the car.

He stepped round and took one look at her face—eyes fixed on the dogs, her face bled of colour and her muscles clenched so hard she'd frozen to the spot—and he was galvanised into action.

'Sit!' he instructed the dogs before they could reach her. She couldn't know that they'd have rushed right past her in their eagerness to greet him. They skidded to a halt. MJ didn't even flinch at his shouted command.

Two steps brought him to her side. Her eyes were so wide and wild it looked as if the sky could have fallen into them. They never left the dogs. He stepped in front of her to block them from view.

'MJ?'

Nothing.

'MJ, look at me.' He lifted her chin, forcing her to meet his eyes. 'You're frightened of dogs?'

'B-b-big dogs…. T-t-terrified,' she stammered between chattering teeth. 'Attacked. Six.'

Attached when she'd been six years old, or had there been six dogs? He wanted to swear.

He ran his hands down her arms, wanting to offer her the comfort of human touch, aching to rid her of her gut-wrenching terror.

Her fingers lifted to dig into his forearms, as if to anchor herself. Words fell from her lips. 'I have a s-s-scar.' Her laugh held a hysterical edge. 'Sienna too. They…' She gulped. 'It ran so fast at us.'

It? There'd only been one dog, then. He sent up a prayer of thanks. But it had obviously hurt her. And Rufus and Seth had run at her the way it must have, forcing her to relive what looked to be her worst nightmare.

'Oh, lass, they won't hurt you.' Mrs Digby appeared at his side. 'This pair are lambs.'

But he knew MJ was too far gone to heed her words.

'Would you take them into the kitchen, Mrs Digby?'

Without another word, the housekeeper returned to the house with the dogs. With a smothered oath, Nikos pulled MJ against his chest, running his hands up and down her back to warm her up, but she simply stood there frozen as if lost in her nightmare memory. Beneath his hands she felt so small and frail. He lifted her into his arms and strode into the house, through to the drawing room. Setting her on the sofa, he poured a brandy and then sat beside her and forced a mouthful of the amber liquid between her lips.

The moment it hit the back of her throat, she coughed. And coughed and coughed. Colour flooded her face. 'What are you trying to do? Kill me?' She pushed his hand away. 'That stuff is ghastly!'

He feigned indignation. 'This is my finest brandy.'

'Then *you* drink it.'

He brought the glass to her lips again, dodging her hand when she tried to push it away again. 'One more sip.'

'No, thank you. What I need is tea—sweet, hot tea.'

'Mrs Digby will be on it.'

'Tea fixes everything.'

'One more sip, MJ. I'm going to insist. You've had a nasty shock. This will help put the fire back in you.'

'I have plenty of fire, thank you very much.' She glared, but he refused to back down. Grumbling, she took the tumbler and had another sip, grimacing as it went down, then thrust it back into his hands. 'I'm fine now. Stop fussing.'

She obviously wasn't a fan of brandy. He downed the rest in a single swallow, finding he needed fortifying too.

And then he moved to the sofa opposite, because MJ smelled like apples and vanilla, and he was starting to feel hungry. Ravenous, actually. Now that she'd started to recover from her scare, the memory of her in his arms tugged at the edges of his consciousness. He did what he could to banish it.

Mrs Digby arrived, bearing a tea tray with a pot of tea, two cups and a sponge cake.

'Oh, that looks wonderful,' MJ said. 'Thank you so much, Mrs Digby.' Pressing her hands together, she glanced at them both, her nose wrinkling. 'I'd like to apologise. We're in the country. I should've expected dogs, but...'

But her mind had been on other things.

'I had a bad experience when I was a child. And I have a checklist of things to go through whenever I see a large dog—focus on my breathing, isolate five separate sounds, things like that. But because I was off with the fairies...'

She meant because she'd been worrying about her sister and his brother.

'Well, I just looked up, and they weren't on leads, and they were running towards me, and I'm ashamed to say I froze.'

'You'd just woken up,' he said, his voice gruff, wanting to ease the distress and embarrassment he sensed simmering beneath her apology. 'You weren't properly awake. It's only natural that you were taken off-guard.' He only wished he'd been aware of her fear so he'd have been able to prevent the episode from happening at all. 'You don't need to apologise.'

'And you don't need to worry, Miss Mabel. I'll keep the dogs in the kitchen with me.'

MJ smiled her gratitude, and the way her body sank into the sofa spoke her silent relief.

And then he realised Mrs Digby had addressed MJ by her name. Her surname, admittedly, but still... 'Is Christian here, Mrs D?'

'No, Mr Nikos. I haven't seen him in...' She cocked her head to one side. 'It'd be six weeks ago when he came with a small house party.' The older woman hesitated, glancing at MJ.

'Go on,' both he and MJ said in unison.

'Well, it was a house party that included Miss Mabel here. Though I have to say you didn't seem to take so badly to the dogs then, though I noticed at the time you kept your distance.'

MJ smiled. 'That would've been my sister, Siena. I'm MJ—short for Marjorie Joan. And I'd much prefer it if you'd call me MJ instead of Miss Mabel.'

The housekeeper's eyes widened. 'You're the spitting image of each other.'

'Identical twins.'

Nikos frowned. It was true that MJ and Siena looked alike, but in other respects they were chalk and cheese. It amazed him that people found it difficult to tell them apart. Besides the different way they dressed, MJ moved with far more energy and purpose than Siena. Her smile was also quicker, and her answers to questions slower.

'Well, that's a surprise and there's no two ways about it. Welcome to Sedgewick House, Miss MJ. Will you be staying long, Mr Nikos?'

The housekeeper's question pulled him back. 'For the night.' He had no appetite whatsoever for a three-and-a-half-hour return journey to London this evening. And MJ looked wiped out. They'd need to put their heads together and decide where to search next. But MJ needed a decent rest first.

'Your room is ready for you.'

As it always was.

'Should I make up the Rose Room for Miss MJ or…?'

Did she think MJ and him might be an item?

'Thank you, Mrs Digby, the Rose Room sounds wonderful,' MJ said before he'd recovered his equilibrium.

Did that mean Christian and Siena had shared a room when they'd been here six weeks ago? It wasn't a question he could ask. He'd never invade his brother's privacy like that.

Seizing his phone, he sent his brother a text demanding he call ASAP. When he finished, MJ handed him a cup of tea and a slice of cake.

His stomach rumbled and she laughed. 'Sounds like you skipped lunch too.'

He should've stopped for lunch! He should've made sure MJ had some sustenance in her belly.

'Thank you for being so understanding and…' she hesitated '…kind.' She nodded, as if that was the exact word she'd been looking for. 'About the dogs and everything.'

She sipped her tea, her eyes on his face. Now that he'd seen her weariness while in unguarded sleep, he couldn't un-see it.

'I know you feel you have no reason to show any kindness or consideration to any member of my family, and you probably took no joy in having to leap to my aid like that. I'm sorry if that caused you any discomfort.'

His gut churned. The fact she was a Mabel hadn't even crossed his mind when he'd seen her frozen in terror. All he'd wanted to do was make her feel safe again.

He forced himself to eat a mouthful of cake. 'I'm not a monster, MJ.'

'Far from it,' she agreed. 'What I'm trying to say is that I'm very grateful to you. And I'm sorry I abused your brandy,' she added, with a gravity that made him laugh. 'That's better,' she said with a smile of her own. 'You've been looking far too grave and serious, and I didn't know if it was due to my dog phobia or Christian's absence.'

That wasn't a question he wanted to answer. Instead he said, 'Tell me what happened—about the dog attack when you were small.'

She settled back against the sofa and sipped her tea. 'Siena and I were six and had gone to stay with Aunt Joan in the country for the summer. It was idyllic…until Siena and I decided to scale the wall that bordered our great-aunt's estate with her neighbour's grounds.'

She glanced at him, wrinkling her nose. 'We were young and fearless and eager to explore everything. Unbeknownst to us or Aunt Joan, her neighbours had recently acquired a guard dog to go with the expensive racehorse they'd bought. I don't rightly remember how long it took for him to find us, but it felt as if suddenly this enormous dog—and he was truly huge—started barking really loudly and running towards us. We, of course, took off as fast as our pudgy little legs would carry us.'

He grimaced. 'Except dogs run faster than people.' And they'd only been six. He bet she'd been the cutest little kid.

'Exactly.' She set down her mug. 'He caught Siena around the thigh and latched on.'

Her throat bobbed and his hands clenched.

'I didn't know what to do. There was a rake lying on the ground so I picked it up and hit him with it as hard as I could—over and over. Eventually he let go and grabbed me round the shoulder instead.'

He swore.

She blinked and straightened, seizing her tea again. 'Luckily, we'd run towards the house rather than away from it, and we were screaming loud enough to wake the dead. People came running from everywhere. The gardener reached us first and he pulled the dog off me.' She smiled. 'It was all over in the quickest of flashes.'

She paused, her eyes begging him to smile. So he smiled. 'Injuries?'

'Minor. We both had a couple of puncture marks and some bruising, and we needed a few stitches each. We were lucky.'

Yet the incident had scarred her in other ways.

She shrugged, as if it was no big deal. 'So I don't wear singlet tops and Siena doesn't wear short skirts.'

'Your scars bother you?'

She kept sipping her tea. 'No. My scars don't bother me.'

But they bothered Siena. He was starting to see that MJ would do pretty much anything for her sister—including keeping her scars hidden and giving him the Ananke necklace.

He wanted to find Siena and shake her for causing her sister so much unnecessary grief.

CHAPTER FOUR

'I'VE BEEN TO your flat and spoken to Luisa. I've been to your club and spoken to Raymond, Freddy and Solomon—and on a side note, little brother, I can't believe you're still friends with Freddy Smythe—the man's a toad. And now I'm at the house in Devon. I understand you're with Siena Mabel. Her sister is worried about Siena's health—there's a medical issue and Siena needs to see a doctor.'

He blew out a breath. 'Nobody has seen hide nor hair of you in over a week, and you're not returning my calls. If you don't ring me by morning, I'm reporting you to the police as a missing person and hiring a private detective.'

MJ winced from her seat on the sofa as Nikos ended the call with a vicious stab of his finger and threw his phone onto the coffee table, his back rigid as he paced across the room.

'It doesn't have the same effect, does it?' She nodded at his phone when he turned to pace back towards her.

'What doesn't?'

She was almost proud of him for the way he held his temper in check, careful not to direct any of it her way. 'When I was a little girl, I once saw my mother slam down the phone.' The image had stayed in her mind. She'd never seen her mother so angry. 'It was one of those old-fashioned phones with the receiver attached by a cord. You know the ones?'

He nodded.

'It looked so *satisfying* to hang up on someone by slamming the receiver down like that. Jabbing one's finger at a tiny screen is nowhere near as gratifying.'

He dropped into the sofa opposite, the storm on his brow not clearing, but his shoulders lost some of their stiffness. 'You think they've left the country, don't you? It's why you brought your passport.'

'I don't know.' She forced herself to hold his gaze, even as her cheeks heated when she recalled the sense of security that had stolen over her when she'd been in his arms, paralysed with fear.

It reminded her of that time in the nightclub eight years ago when he'd pulled her to safety. She'd simultaneously felt safer than she'd ever been and more alive than she'd ever thought possible. Something warm, sweet and laced with excitement had passed between them. She'd never wanted a man the way she'd wanted Nikos in those few short moments. The memory disturbed her.

As did this new one. The fact that, even through her terror, she'd sensed Nikos would keep her safe. It was a false impression, of course. The man hated her. Which wasn't entirely true. Nikos was beginning to realise that he only hated the idea of her. He didn't hate her personally.

She crossed her fingers in her lap.

'Marjorie?'

She shook herself. 'I can't help thinking that if they were still in the country we'd know about it. But I hope I'm wrong.'

England was a big enough area to search as it was. Once you added in the rest of the world... She closed her eyes. If she could just *talk* to Siena.

'Can you afford to take time off work like this? Last I heard, you'd been promoted to Vice President of Mabel's.'

She opened her eyes. 'I've taken a month's leave.' She

was hoping it would spur her father into rethinking… things. 'As the Leto Group's CEO, can you?'

'I'll make time. Would you like a drink?'

She'd refused wine at dinner and he gestured now to the drinks cabinet. She shook her head.

'You don't mind if I…?'

'Not at all.'

He poured himself another brandy and moved back to the sofa, nursing it. A fire crackled in the fireplace. It wasn't a cold night, but the fire was cheerful, cosy, and though it was early, she found herself fighting a yawn.

'You told me Siena is angry with your father. And you. What does she usually do when she's angry? Does she party hard in defiance? Or hide away somewhere quiet to lick her wounds?'

Her chest clenched. 'Given those two options, I'd say the former. But Siena isn't angry—not really…not any more. She's hurt.'

'What does she do when she's hurt?'

It depended on whether her hurt had turned to despair.

'Usually she'd throw herself into some project to try and take her mind off it—like her art. And talk things out… with me.' She tried to smile. 'We're sisters, so obviously we've had arguments and disagreements in the past, but they've only lasted a couple of days at most, and usually not more than a couple of hours. We've never had one that's lasted this long.'

He leaned forward to concentrate more fully on her and her words. His forearms rested on his knees, brandy balloon hanging negligently from his fingers. While the room was large, and the space between them more than generous, it felt as if the room had shrunk and that the air she was breathing was full of him.

She reached for her water, her hand shaking slightly.

'Christian adds a wild card element, and until I talk to her I can't predict what she'll do.'

'Wild card in a good or bad way?'

She needed to tread carefully. She didn't want Nikos getting his back up or jumping to unnecessary conclusions. 'I'm hoping she's turned to him the way she'd normally turn to me. From what I've heard about Christian, he's kind and sensible.'

Nikos's lips twisted. 'He's certainly kind.'

No, no, no. She wanted him to be sensible too. Siena *needed* sensible.

'He's been taken advantage of in the past.'

She wanted to swear. Really loudly. She needed Christian to see past Siena's usual tricks.

Nikos's knuckles whitened around his glass. 'What are you *not* hoping for?'

He saw too much. She bit the side of her thumb, worrying at the nail. 'I hardly know.'

Before he could call her a liar, she rushed in with a question of her own. 'Tell me a classic story about you and your brother.' It might give her a clue as to Christian's real nature and tell her how he and Siena might act—and react—together.

'What do you mean, a classic story?' He sat back and crossed his legs, seemingly at ease, but some sixth sense told her it was a pretence. 'Give me an example of one involving you and Siena and then I'll know what you mean.'

She gave a mirthless laugh. He just wanted to hold all his cards close to his chest and not share any of them. She rose. 'I think I might retire and have an early night.'

'No.' The word seemed to leave him involuntarily. 'I'm a man of my word, MJ. Quid pro quo and all that—you give me a classic story about you and Siena and then I'll give you one about me and Christian.'

'Except you've given me nothing so far.' The way he'd

handled her fear of dogs, the way he'd dealt with that situation during and after, rose through her mind now. She battled the urge to sit and tell him everything he wanted to know. 'Tell me how Christian reacts when he's in love.'

The brandy in his glass rocked wildly. 'He's not *in love* with Siena.'

Just because he wanted that to be true didn't make it so. 'I never said he was.'

His glare would have incinerated a lesser person.

'Fine, then tell me how he reacts when he's smitten... infatuated.'

He slammed his brandy on the coffee table. Leaning over, he dragged both hands back through his hair. Eventually he straightened, picked up his glass and downed what was left in it in one swallow.

He glanced up at her. She sat.

'He makes the woman the queen of his world. He'll do anything in his power to make her happy.' His gaze turned sharp, mocking. 'What does that tell you, Ms Freud?'

'He sounds like a real sweetheart.'

He leaned towards her, his eyes hard. 'But what does it *tell* you?'

'You're saying he lacks moderation,' she said slowly.

He gave a nod.

'If Siena, for example, wanted to do something reckless, would he encourage her? Or would he be the voice of reason and talk her out of doing anything silly?'

'Between those two options,' he forced out between gritted teeth, 'my money would be on the former.'

Damn, damn, damn.

'Are you telling me Siena is reckless?'

She chose her words carefully. 'Siena is an artist with an artist's temperament. In art and in life she'll sometimes seize on an idea and will follow it blindly, without thinking through where it might lead.'

Nikos nodded. 'Christian's the same.'

'Whereas I'm a thinker and planner.' She suspected Nikos was too. It was what made them so good at their jobs. 'I'm usually her voice of reason. I want Christian to be that voice of reason for her now.'

Dark eyes met hers. She reluctantly forced the words from her lips. 'From what you've told me, I'm worried Christian will become so caught up in her enthusiasm he'll follow her wherever she leads.'

'You think she'll twist him around her little finger.'

'I'll tell you two classic stories—two sides of the same coin. When Siena and I were six, we stayed in the country one entire summer. We heard rumours of an amazing apple orchard in the grounds of the castle next door. It wasn't really a castle, of course, but we pretended it was. So it follows that the apples were likewise enchanted because everything about that summer was enchanted.'

She smiled, remembering that long-ago summer. 'Neither of us had ever picked an apple straight from the tree before, and Princess Siena wanted to so very badly. But how could she get over the eight-foot stone wall that surrounded the castle?

'Well, this is where Princess MJ comes into her own. She turned her mind to the problem and worked out that, if they climbed the old oak tree on their side of the wall and walked along the wall for a way, they could then climb down a maple on the other side and be in the castle grounds.'

'You could've broken your necks!'

'Instead we found a guard dog who didn't take kindly to two little trespassers.'

He pursed his lips. 'Siena came up with the idea and you found a way to make it happen. And it ended badly.'

'Story two. When Siena and I graduated from university, Siena was obsessed with the idea of travelling to Africa. She wanted a first-hand look at African art and to practise some of the techniques for herself with a local artist. Nice idea, except her travel plans sounded haphazard at best. So I explored some options and discovered a non-denominational charity that was building schools in Africa. We decided to volunteer in Cameroon for two months. Siena didn't get to see as much art as she wanted, but the colours and impressions of the place continue to inform her work today.'

'And you, MJ? What did you get out of it beside baby-sitting your sister?'

'It was one of the best experiences of my life. I not only had the chance to encounter a culture vastly different from mine, but have also made lifelong friendships.'

Very slowly, he nodded. 'She had the idea, you made it happen…and it ended well.'

'Like I said—two sides of the same coin. I just don't know which way the coin will land with Christian in the picture.'

His jaw clenched.

Before he could get too caught up in angry thoughts and blame Siena for his brother's current status as a missing person, she said, 'Your turn now. You promised a classic story about Christian.'

His gaze returned to hers and his brows lowered. For a moment she thought he might make an excuse and put her off, but then he shook his head and opened his mouth. She leaned towards him…

His phone rang, the piercing ringtone making them both jump. He jerked forward to snatch it up. 'It's Christian.'

'Put him on speaker phone,' she begged. 'I'll be as quiet as the proverbial mouse.'

After the briefest of hesitations, he nodded. It felt like another win—a sign of trust.

'Christian,' he said, answering the call. 'It's a relief to

find you haven't been abducted by aliens and that I don't need to report you as a missing person.'

She resisted the urge to roll her eyes at his sarcasm.

'Very funny, Nik. Since when does it become a national crisis if I don't return your call within twenty-four hours? You better have a damn good reason—'

'Since I received a visit from MJ Mabel desperate to get hold of her sister and convinced you're the key.'

Christian remained silent.

'Is it true?' he barked.

'Actually, Nik, it's none of your damn business.'

'I'm worried about you.'

'I'm capable of looking after myself.'

'But are you capable of looking after Siena?'

'What the hell is that supposed to mean?'

For the first time, real anger entered Christian's voice and it made MJ's heart beat faster.

'You listen to me, Nik. I'm twenty-eight years old. You need to stop sweeping in like the cavalry every time I make a decision you don't agree with. I'm not the idiot you think I am.'

Nikos blinked. 'I don't think you're an idiot.'

'I might not be the paragon you are, but I refuse to put myself in the same damn straitjacket you wear. I'm entitled to live life on my own terms. If I make a few mistakes along the way, well, I can live with that.'

Nikos massaged his temples, and MJ ached for him. Couldn't Christian see how much his brother loved him? He shouldn't be so resentful of Nikos's concern. It was obvious he'd do anything for his little brother.

Christian gave an ugly laugh. 'What you're really worried about is me tarnishing the family name and giving Father even more grief and worry. Not once has it occurred to you that he deserves the grief and worry. If he'd made different decisions…'

Nikos swore. 'You need to listen to me—'

'No!'

'MJ has offered me the Ananke necklace in exchange for me finding Siena.'

Silence greeted this announcement.

'Tell me you refused,' Christian finally said.

'Of course I didn't refuse!' Nikos exploded. 'What did you expect me to do?'

'You're just like father and grandfather!'

Nikos gripped the phone so hard his entire body started to shake. 'And what's wrong with that?'

'You don't see it, do you?'

She had to agree with Christian there. Nikos was oblivious to how destructive this feud between the families continued to be.

'What I do know is that Siena is ill and—'

'Siena is no concern of yours.'

And then the line went dead.

Nikos turned pale. The lines bracketing his mouth deepened and his eyes flashed. He flung his phone down and paced around the room calling his brother every kind of fool. Eventually he rounded on MJ. 'What has your sister done to him?'

She shot to her feet and slammed her hands to her hips. 'Oh, right, it's all Siena's fault, is it?'

He advanced, his face twisting. 'What is wrong with her?' His nostrils flared. 'If she's on drugs…! If she gets Christian hooked on drugs, I swear I will destroy everything you love.'

MJ's eyes widened at his words. She swung to address the painting above the mantelpiece. 'And then he goes and ruins it all, just like that.'

Ruined what? Nikos ground his back molars together.

There was nothing here to ruin. It was already ruined by two generations of bitterness and betrayal.

'One moment he proves he's a flesh and blood man—kind, smart, reasonable—and then…'

'And then what?' He couldn't stop from asking.

She swung round, her eyes flashing. 'And then you turn into a jerk. And a bully.'

He recoiled, but she had a point. He shouldn't have lost his temper like that. He couldn't remember the last time he'd lost it so completely. But his grandfather's stooped shoulders had risen in his mind, along with the deep lines etched into the skin around his father's mouth and the dead light in his mother's eyes. He'd do anything to prevent Christian from the kind of pain they'd suffered. Pain suffered at the hands of the Mabels.

'I'm afraid it'd keep you awfully busy, Nikos, destroying everything I love, because I love a lot of things.'

He fell onto the sofa, raking both hands back through his hair. 'Then you're a fool, MJ, because love makes you weak.'

She poured a brandy, but she didn't drink it as she walked round the room, studying the paintings on the walls. Eventually she set the brandy in front of him and left the room without another word. She didn't even bid him goodnight.

He didn't deserve a good night.

He was on his feet and in the hall before he knew it. MJ was only a quarter of the way up the stairs. 'I'm sorry I lost my temper.'

She halted but didn't look at him.

'And I'm sorry for what I said about Siena. It was unfair…out of order.'

She turned her head. 'How much did that just hurt—having to apologise to a Mabel?'

His temples throbbed. 'A lot.' But she deserved an apology.

'Good.'

The shadow of a smile touched her lips and something in his chest unhitched.

'Apology accepted. Goodnight, Nikos.'

'Goodnight, MJ. Sleep well.'

He hoped she'd have colour in her cheeks when she woke in the morning and that the dark circles beneath her eyes would have started to fade.

For the briefest moment their gazes caught and clung, and then MJ swung away and took the stairs two at a time and he forced himself back into the drawing room to drink his brandy.

The next morning Nikos found MJ hovering at the top of the stairs, peering down at the hall below. He halted and then backed up a couple of silent steps, before starting forward again with a heavier tread so as to not startle her.

She swung round, a smile in place. His gut clenched. Except her smile wasn't *in place*. It wasn't planted there as some kind of fake assurance or civility. It was real. Despite him being a bad-tempered jerk who'd tried to bully her more than once yesterday, she still sent him the kind of smile that could make the blood surge in a man's veins.

He didn't deserve her good-natured generosity. And she deserved better than his continued curmudgeonly ill humour. They'd made a deal and she'd submitted to it with grace, even though sacrificing the Ananke necklace had to be a blow. He needed to act with grace too, and not just because the necklace was a prize worth winning. He needed to prove, if only to himself, that he could be mature and reasonable in this situation.

The Constantinoses and Mabels would never be friends, but that didn't mean he and MJ couldn't behave with common courtesy and dignity. In fact, it felt imperative that they did, though if pressed he couldn't have explained why.

He dragged in a breath, suddenly aware that the silence between them had stretched for too long. 'The dogs will be locked in the kitchen.' His chest clenched. How long had she been standing up here, gathering the courage to venture downstairs? 'It's safe to go down.'

'I know I'm being silly.' She pushed a lock of hair behind her ear. 'I know they wouldn't hurt me even if I did accidentally stumble across them. It's just…'

Phobias weren't rational. She knew it and he knew it. But knowing it didn't necessarily change anything. He didn't want her feeling bad about it, so he steered the conversation to safer channels. 'Are you hungry? Ready to go rustle up some breakfast?'

'Ooh, yes please!'

Her enthusiasm made him smile. 'I take it you're a breakfast person, then?'

'I'd eat breakfast three times a day if I could.'

Her cheerful confession eased some of the tightness in his chest.

'It has all of my favourite foods—bacon and eggs, sausages, toast, porridge, croissants…even black pudding.'

She glanced up, her eyes dancing now without a trace of fear to darken their depths. He wondered where she found her good humour and optimism. She seemed to have an endless supply of both.

'What about you?' She gave a mock-groan. 'Please tell me you're not one of these paltry people who make do with a cup of black coffee as they rush out the door?'

'Not a chance. I skip lunch too often to miss breakfast. But my favourite food would be steak and potatoes.'

She rolled her eyes. 'Typical man.'

And yet she was far from a typical woman. 'And my mother's baklava.'

'Pastry, honey and nuts…' She sighed. 'Hard to beat.'

He paused outside the kitchen door. 'Wait here while I take the dogs out.'

Her hands twisted together and… Was that guilt at the back of her eyes? 'They'll be fine outside, MJ, I promise. They love to run around and play.'

'It seems hard—unfair—that they get banished because of me.'

He stared at her for a moment. 'Do you want me to leave them in?'

Fear flashed in her eyes and she shook her head, giving a funny little hiccup. 'I know I'm being a coward, but…'

'Nonsense.' He made his voice crisp. 'It's no drama and no bother.'

A few moments later he and MJ were seated at the big oak table drinking huge mugs of tea while Mrs Digby busied herself at the range, cracking eggs into a frying pan and laying rashers of bacon alongside them, the room filling with the most delicious aroma as the food sizzled and spat. Outside the windows the dogs gambolled in the garden.

'They're rescue dogs,' he said, spying her watching them. 'When Mr Digby died a few years ago, Mrs Digby thought it might be nice to have a couple of dogs here.'

Mrs Digby turned from the stove. 'It'll be four years this September that Mr D passed, God rest his soul. And with Mrs Constantinos remarrying and spending less time here, and the boys up in London more often than not…' She plated their food. 'Well, it got to being a bit lonely, like.' She set a plate in front of MJ. 'They're good company, Miss MJ. And they keep me fit.'

'And you're also giving a home to animals who need one, which is nice.'

MJ bit into a piece of toast, her eyes half-closing with bliss. It made Nikos want to laugh. She evidently hadn't been exaggerating when she said she loved breakfast.

'But why choose dogs that are *so* big?'

Her expression made them both laugh, which he suspected had been her plan.

'They're harder to place,' he said.

'And we have the room here for them to run around in.'

MJ gestured to her plate. 'This is delicious, Mrs Digby. Thank you so much.'

'There's plenty more if you want it. Just give me a yell. I'll be in the laundry room if you need me.'

Mrs Digby left and MJ's gaze returned to the window.

'Rufus was found half-dead in a ditch.'

Her knife and fork hung suspended above the food on her plate as she stared at him.

'He hadn't just been dumped. He'd been thrown from a moving vehicle. When he was found, he had a broken leg, broken ribs and multiple abrasions. For a while they weren't sure if he'd make it.'

'*What?* How could…? The poor thing! How could anyone do that to another living creature?'

He shrugged. 'Beats me. Seth's story isn't any happier. He was found tied to a post on a short lead in a deserted yard without any shelter, half-starved and covered in sores. He's frightened of strange men. It takes them a while to earn his trust. We think a man used to beat him.'

Her cutlery clattered to her plate and her eyes filled. 'I don't believe in corporal punishment, but if I did it'd be people like that I'd…'

He nodded. 'Seth's previous owner was charged, which is something, I suppose.'

'There's no excuse for that kind of cruelty. To deliberately hurt someone or something weaker than you…' She broke off. 'It's unforgivable.'

And yet she didn't seem to view her great-aunt's behaviour towards his grandfather as either cruel or unforgivable. Though, even Nikos had to admit that, despite the fact Joan Mabel had taken advantage of his *pappoús*, the power dynamic between the couple had at least been equal.

A different kind of ice settled over him. If MJ ever found out about it, would she find what had happened between their parents unforgivable?

'Nikos?'

He shook himself. 'Sorry, what were you saying?'

'It was nothing.'

She arranged her cutlery into a neat line on her plate and pushed it away. She hadn't finished her breakfast and he wanted to thump himself. In trying to make her less afraid of his dogs, he'd robbed her of her appetite. *Way to go, Nikos*. He'd organise croissants for morning tea.

In the meantime... 'Any thoughts about where we go from here? I spent some time last night—' *when he'd been lying in bed, staring at the ceiling, strangely restless* '—trying to pinpoint where Christian might retreat to. He has friends in Paris and loves the city.'

'Siena loves Paris too—loves the art galleries.'

'We also have an apartment in Switzerland.'

'It's not ski season.' She tapped a finger against her lips. 'Which doesn't mean they haven't gone there, of course. Siena won't have retreated to any of the family's places— the villa in Spain or the apartment in Paris—because she'd worry the staff would betray her location to my father.'

She glanced at her watch. 'But the smart money is on her ringing me this morning.'

'What makes you say that?'

'She and Christian would've spent last night working out what to do—about us—and one of those things would be getting me to back off.'

Her words made sense, and no sooner had she uttered them than her phone rang. She turned it towards him so he could see the name on the screen.

Siena.

'Are you psychic?'

His words made her smile. She answered the call and put it on speaker phone. 'Thank you for calling, Siena, I've been worried sick.'

Siena sighed—a great, heaving sound that rolled down the line and made MJ wince. Nikos's hands clenched. *Seriously?* Didn't Siena have a clue what she'd been putting her sister through?

'Look, Jojo, I only have a couple of things to say and it won't take long.'

'I have a couple of things to say too. Promise me you'll hear them before hanging up on me.'

Silence followed MJ's request. If he could, he'd like to reach down the phone and shake Siena. He'd like to shake Christian too, who was no doubt sitting beside her.

'Siena?'

'Is any of it about Dad?'

'No.'

'Okay, fine.'

He doubted Siena could have been more grudging if she'd tried.

'First off, Jojo, I want you to give me some space. It doesn't seem an unreasonable request. I don't hold you responsible for anything Father said, so you can stop fretting about that. The thing is, I can't be what you want me to be either.'

'I don't want you to be anything other than happy!'

MJ's teeth worried at her bottom lip. Nikos wanted to tell her to stop it, that she'd hurt herself.

'And healthy, of course,' she added. 'That's all I want for you, Sisi.'

'It's not *all* you want. You want me to play happy families and I can't do it. Not at the moment. Have you heard about learned dependence?'

MJ's brow wrinkled. 'What's that got to do with anything?'

'I've relied on you for too many things over the years and it's time it stopped. I want to stand on my own two feet.'

A bad taste stretched through Nikos's mouth. That refrain sounded all too familiar.

MJ briefly closed her eyes. 'When you say you want some space, how long are we talking? A week? A month?'

Siena remained silent.

'Longer?'

The panic in MJ's voice made his chest ache.

'I don't know. I'm not like you. I don't have everything plotted on a graph and every detail worked out to the nth degree.'

MJ's head rocked back.

Nikos glared at the phone. The ungrateful little witch!

'Jojo, it's not fair to use me to make you feel better and less alone because Mother's no longer here!' Siena burst out.

MJ went so white, he reached out to grip her hand.

'That's just about the meanest thing you've ever said to me,' MJ choked out.

'I don't mean it to be,' Siena said in an almost identical choked whisper, and it made MJ's eyes fill.

She gripped his hand so hard, it almost hurt. 'I haven't meant to make you feel bad, Sisi.'

Siena didn't say anything for a moment. 'If you and Nikos hire a private investigator to track us down, neither Christian nor I will forgive you. Do you hear me?'

'Loud and clear.'

There was another hesitation. 'Dad will never forgive you if you give the Ananke necklace to Nikos.'

Her chin lifted. 'Yes, he will.'

'Your faith in him is astounding. He's going to break your heart, Jojo.'

'Or maybe he'll surprise you instead. But we promised not to talk about him.' She pulled in a breath. 'Sisi, your doctor told me your test results.'

'*What?* But that's… It's an invasion of privacy!'

'To be fair, I was wearing the gypsy skirt you gave me for my birthday, so it was an understandable mistake to make.'

'And you didn't set her straight? You pretended to be me?'

'I bumped into her at our Chelsea hotel—she'd been lunching with a guest. It's not like I planned the meeting. Anyway, all she said was that she'd been trying to contact you, that you needed to come in for more tests, and she briefly mentioned why.'

Siena remained silent.

'Why haven't you returned her calls?' MJ shot back with some of her old fire. 'You can't take risks with your health like this and—'

'My health, my life, Jojo. I'm capable of making my own decisions on the subject.'

Nikos winced at her tone.

'But you've involved Christian. Does he know what you've dragged him into?'

'That's what you and Nikos want, isn't it? To break us up. Well, it's not going to happen!'

Then the line went dead, and the devastation on MJ's face wrung his heart dry.

And then a sudden thought left him reeling—a brutal, ugly thought.

MJ and Siena were twins. Siena had some kind of health issue that scared the hell out of her sister. They were twins, identical twins—identical DNA.

His mouth dried. Did that mean MJ was sick too?

CHAPTER FIVE

MJ STRODE ACROSS to the window to stare unseeingly out at the garden, her heart stretching thin and everything aching. She'd been so convinced that after speaking to Siena she'd know exactly where her sister's head was at, and therefore would know what to do. She'd been convinced she'd know whether Siena had real feelings for Christian or if she was using him as a kind of sticking plaster.

But she *didn't* know.

She didn't have a clue.

And it scared her senseless.

She hadn't lied when she'd told Nikos that she loved a lot of things, a lot of people. But the person she loved above all others was Siena, and if anything were to happen to her...

She closed her eyes and pressed a hand to her chest.

'Marjorie?'

She opened her eyes and forced herself to turn and meet Nikos's gaze. 'After that phone call, I'm none the wiser, Nikos. None at all, I'm afraid.'

And she *was* afraid.

He looked as if he wanted to ask something, but she didn't have the heart for any more talk. She wanted—needed—to do something. She needed action. Needed to feel in control again.

Swinging back to the window, she watched the dogs. Rufus walked around with a big stick in his mouth looking ridiculously pleased with himself, while Seth nosed a tennis ball and then went for a run, before racing back to the tennis ball. Their antics made her smile. They looked perfectly happy. And then she remembered their sad histories and straightened. Well, there was at least one less thing she could be afraid of.

Wordlessly she moved to the back door, stepped outside and closed it behind her. Both dogs stopped what they were doing to look at her, and she faltered. She was alone in the garden with two ginormous dogs. In that moment, if Nikos had opened the door behind her she'd have leapt into his arms.

Don't be a coward.

Besides, this fear of dogs, especially of this pair who were clearly far from vicious, paled in comparison to the fear that knotted her stomach whenever she thought of Siena. She forced knocking knees forward and lowered herself as steadily as she could to a stone bench.

Rufus, the braver of the two, started towards her with his stick still held in his mouth. She watched him and held her breath.

He halted and turned his head away.

Oh! 'Was I…was I eyeballing you, Rufus?' She forced her gaze to her lap, though it felt alien to be this close to a dog and not minutely tracking its every movement. 'I'm sorry, that was rude. I don't like being stared at either.' She kept her voice low, though she couldn't always keep it steady. 'The thing is, you see, I don't really know how to act around dogs and…'

His head came into view and her words jammed into her throat. What should she do? Would he let her pat him? Did she dare?'

Very carefully he laid the stick at her feet, the gesture absolutely melted her heart. 'You're giving that to me? Oh, what a big sweetheart you are.' Reaching out, she touched his head, ran her hand down his shaggy fur to scratch his shoulder. He leaned into her touch, his bottom half-wagging in time to her scratches in an ecstasy that made her laugh. 'Well, I seem to have got the hang of making friends with you.'

In response, he laid his head in her lap and gazed up at her in undiluted adoration. 'Oh, sweetheart.' Her throat thickened and she gently tugged on his ears. 'You don't know me. I'm not sure you should be so trusting.' Now, where was Seth? Had he run away and hidden? She wouldn't blame him if he had.

She found him standing a little way to her right, watching her and Rufus. 'Hello, Seth.' She held her hand out towards him. 'Would you like a pat too?'

He started towards her, halted, took another step forward and stopped again. All the while she stroked Rufus's head in her lap and kept up a stream of what she hoped was soothing chatter. For the last few yards, Seth dropped to his tummy and almost cowered, crawling to her. Tears burned the backs of her eyes. 'Oh, Seth baby, I'm not going to hurt you. C'mon, boy.'

The moment she stroked his head, and then the tummy he promptly presented to her, he bounced up again, all excited energy. He licked her hand, her arm and her face when it got too close, making her laugh. He jumped up on the bench beside her and tried to crawl into her lap.

Not to be outdone, Rufus leapt up on the other side. She wanted to give them both big, squishy hugs. The moment felt like a gift. An unlooked-for one. Because it wasn't what she'd envisaged when she'd woken up that morning.

'Rufus, Seth—down.' The command came from behind her. Rufus jumped down immediately. 'Seth, down,' Nikos ordered again.

Seth moped to the ground with a reluctance that made her want to laugh.

'Sit.'

Both dogs sat. Nikos threw a ball and they immediately tore after it. He lowered himself to the bench beside her and she was suddenly achingly aware of the breadth of his shoulders and the power of the muscles bunched in his thighs—all the life contained within his denim jeans and thin jumper.

A thousand butterflies filled her chest. Before this morning, she'd never seen Nikos in anything but a suit. He looked great in a suit—powerful, sexy, gorgeous…. He looked great in jeans too—approachable, sexy, gorgeous…

She tried to stamp out the feminine appreciation that welled up inside her, craning its neck for a better peek. It would do her no good. She suppressed a shudder. He'd see it as a weakness he could exploit.

He reached out and clasped her hand. 'Are you okay?'

She stared at the picture of her hand in his. 'Yes.'

'That was just about the bravest thing I've ever seen.'

She glanced up. 'That wasn't brave. Brave would be saving a child from a pack of wild dogs or—'

'Nonsense. That kind of bravery is just gut instinct—hurtling into the fray to help someone in trouble. What you did was calmly and knowingly face a fear that has crippled you for most of your life.'

He released her hand to throw the ball for the dogs again. She missed the warmth. She tried placing it in her other hand, but it wasn't the same as being held by his.

'I merely faced two dogs who I knew wouldn't hurt me—who had more reason to fear me than I them. I'd hardly consider myself cured. I'm always going to be wary around dogs I don't know.'

'That's wise. Everyone should take care around dogs they don't know.' He turned to meet her gaze. 'My heart was in my mouth when they jumped up. I'm impressed you didn't panic.'

She shrugged, trying not to let his admiration affect her. 'By then I knew it was nothing to be afraid of. Other than maybe being smothered by too much affection.'

That made him grin. He threw the ball again. 'They forget their manners when they get excited. Their education is a work in progress.'

That grin... *Oh!*

She had to look away. 'Given their histories, it must be hard not to spoil them.'

'What made you do it? What made you come out here and make friends with them?'

His voice had sobered, so she risked glancing at him. The light in his eyes didn't slow the racing of her pulse. She lifted one shoulder. 'I got tired of being afraid.'

He nodded as if her words made perfect sense. The sudden accord she felt with him shocked her.

'After that disastrous conversation with Siena, it felt like everything was starting to spin out of control.' She wrinkled her nose. 'I guess I just wanted to gain an illusion of control back again.'

'Maybe I need to find something I'm afraid of so I can conquer it.' His lips twisted. 'Perhaps it'll help me get a handle on things.'

She slapped her hands to her knees. 'Well, as you're afraid of me, you needn't go far for inspiration.' The words shot out before she thought better of them.

Very slowly, he turned more fully on the bench to face her. His gaze lowered to her lips. A tic started up at the side of his jaw. 'And do you want to be conquered, Marjorie?'

The way he said her name turned her insides to molten caramel. It took an effort to wrench her gaze from his. 'Conquering me and conquering your fear of me are two very different things.'

She stood. This conversation was getting out of hand. She swung back to him, hands on hips. 'You're implying that in sleeping with me you'd be conquering me. Why do men do that—view women as conquests?'

'Actually, I don't—'

'So often sex has to be framed as a man winning something and a woman losing or surrendering something. It's chauvinistic and damaging, and I—'

'And it's not what I truly believe, MJ.' He spoke over the top of her. 'I was just being facetious. I'm sorry.'

Heat rose in her face. 'Sorry,' she mumbled. 'It's one of my soap boxes.' She folded her arms. 'Why were you being facetious?'

'Because you hit a little too close to the bone when you said I was afraid of you.'

She wanted to cry. She made herself smile. 'I know you're not afraid of the real me, Nikos. But it doesn't stop you loathing the idea of me. The only way to overcome your antipathy is to get to know me and drop your prejudices.' But she didn't think he'd ever let that happen. He'd keep his barriers firmly in place. 'For what it's worth, that—' she gestured to the dogs '—felt like a gift.'

His lips twitched. 'You're telling me now that you're a gift?'

The thought made her smile for real. 'You bet your sweet patootie I am. It's better than being a conquest, right?'

He nodded. But he stood then, sobering. He leaned down to peer into her eyes. 'Aren't you the slightest bit afraid of me?'

His proximity made her breath stutter. She gripped her hands together so hard, they started to ache. Letting out a breath, she forced them to relax. 'I've watched you. Over the years. I mean, we move in the same circles, attend many of the same parties and business functions. I've seen the way you do business. I've even seen how you conduct yourself when a romantic relationship has ended. You work hard, you have high standards and you demand loyalty, but you don't ask for anything you can't give yourself.'

He blinked and snapped upright.

'You're ethical and you have a sense of honour. You'd never physically harm a woman, even if she is a Mabel. So no, Nikos, I'm not afraid of you. I think you're a good man.'

'You…'

He looked at a loss for words and she nodded. 'I'm worried about what you might do if you don't manage to gain a sense of perspective where our families are concerned. But as for the rest of it?' She shook her head. 'I'm not afraid of you.'

Though she was beginning to become afraid of the feelings being near him had started to engender inside her.

'Aren't you worried about giving away so much? Being so unguarded around someone who could be your enemy?'

His words confirmed what she already knew deep in her heart. He would view any attraction she felt for him as a weakness. And vice versa. If he found himself attracted to her, he'd consider it a fatal flaw.

'How do you think you can use anything I just told you against me? Besides,' she continued when he remained silent, 'I didn't say I was worried for *myself* or *my* family if you didn't gain that perspective.'

'Which only leaves me and my family.' His eyes narrowed. 'Why would you worry for us, I wonder?'

He didn't believe her. It shouldn't surprise her. She pointed a finger, stopping short of touching his chest. 'Because I want this feud to end. And, from where I'm standing, I think you and I are our families' best hope of making that happen.'

His head rocked back. '*That's* the real reason you offered me the Ananke necklace.'

'No, that was an act of desperation. I really did want to donate it to the Victoria and Albert Museum. And, if you do help me find Siena, when I hand the necklace over to you that's what I'm going to ask you to do with it.'

He opened his mouth, as if to tell her *Over my dead body,* but she rushed on before the words could drop from his lips. 'I'm dying for another cup of tea. What about you?'

Ten minutes later they nursed fresh mugs of tea, the dogs dozing beneath the table. The warmth of a soft body against her feet felt strangely comforting. Could she get a dog? Did Nikos have one in London?

She started to ask him, but he spoke first. 'What *is* wrong with Siena, MJ? How ill is she?'

Her heart lodged in her throat. If she told him, would he use that information to hurt Siena? Or their father, or her? He could circulate rumours, discrediting MJ's ability to lead the Mabel Group into the future. If clients and business partners thought her in danger of becoming seriously ill, opportunities could be lost. Big ones. Would he stoop to such tactics?

Her stomach gave a sickening lurch. If she told Niko, but Siena hadn't already confided in Christian, would Siena ever forgive her?

She recalled the expression in Siena's eyes when she'd had that dreadful fight with their father, and her heart plummeted. Siena could act tough and uncaring, but beneath the bluff she was sensitive and easily hurt. And she'd *always* preferred make-believe to reality. If she decided to bury her head in the sand now…

Acid burned her throat. If her sister continued to put off the tests she needed, she could lose a kidney. She could lose both kidneys. *She could die.*

'You don't want to tell me.' He stared at her, his eyes turning murky and his mouth hardening. 'You think I might use it against you and your family.'

'Would you?'

He opened his mouth, as if to utter an instant denial, but shut it again with a snap that had an ache stretching through her chest. He would—if it would give his family the upper hand over hers. The fact that the notion seemed to bring him little joy was no comfort at all.

'It's Siena's private information. It's for her to decide who should know. Not me.' Her heart pounded so hard it took a moment for her to push the words out. 'Would you…?'

'Would I…?'

'Would you give me Christian's mobile number?' Christian's volatile relationship with his father was well known. If he cared about Siena…well…surely that meant she could trust him to keep Siena's private information private? With Siena refusing to speak to her, she had left MJ little choice. 'I'd like to text him all he needs to know about Siena's condition—what he needs to know to keep her safe.'

He gave her the number without hesitation.

She composed a text to Christian—a long and comprehensive one—and sent it.

Please, God, let Siena forgive me.

She set down her phone. 'Thank you. No one else was prepared to part with his number.'

He nodded, then drummed his fingers against the table. 'What did Siena mean when she said that thing about your mother? About using her to make you feel better and less alone now that your mother's no longer here?'

MJ's stomach shrivelled to the size of a pea. Out in the garden they'd found an accord that had seemed auspicious, but that now felt like a lifetime ago. Suspicion and distrust once again reigned supreme. 'What did Christian mean when he said you were just like your father and grandfather?'

His lips pressed into a thin line.

He had no more intention of answering her question than she did his. 'Quid pro quo, Nikos,' she said softly.

Her words had his gaze spearing back. Slowly he nodded. 'I haven't shared the promised story about Christian yet.'

He hadn't.

'I don't know if it's a classic story, but have you finished your tea?'

'Yes.'

'Then follow me.'

He led her all the way to the upstairs attic. Although it was piled with boxes and discarded bits of furniture, it was still well kept and ordered. Sunlight filtered in from the rows of dormer windows that marched the length of the room, making the corners of the room appear shady rather than dark and sinister.

He led her across to the furthest corner and there, behind a couple of big wardrobes, she found a battered velvet sofa sitting on an old rug, and three mismatched occasional tables—one holding books, one displaying a collection of feathers and shells and the other one marked with coffee rings.

A large chest sat opposite the sofa beneath the window. Nikos nodded when she silently asked if she could look inside. It held a collection of boyhood treasures—a beaten up and evidently much-loved toy truck, a collection of bird eggs, comics, a football cap...

Her heart caught. *Siena's favourite scarf.*

Each item looked as if it'd been placed there in a certain order and with absolute precision, and she didn't have the heart to disturb a single thing. She lowered the lid and sat on it, and stared at Nikos, waiting.

He stared at the floor and she sensed he was miles away. She kept her hands folded in her lap and her mouth shut.

She had no intention of rushing him, not when she could tell he was already half-regretting bringing her up here.

He gave a start and thumped down onto the sofa, waving a hand around the room. 'In the lead up to my parents' divorce, the family retreated here—away from the prying eyes of London.'

She nodded, understanding their need for privacy.

'During that time my parents…argued a great deal.'

He chose his words with care and she nodded again, reading the subtext. The Devon house had become a battlefield. 'I'm sorry.' She couldn't help it. Her heart ached for what Nikos and Christian must've suffered. She knew her father viewed them as mortal enemies, but she'd never been able to share his feelings…hadn't wanted to.

'It was especially hard on Christian. I was fourteen and understood what was going on. Christian was only ten, still a little boy. I was angry, hated what was happening to my family, but he…'

She rubbed a hand across her chest as pain flashed through his eyes. To witness the disintegration of his parents' marriage must have been so gut-wrenchingly distressing. Especially as a child.

'Christian was confused. Scared. Hurt.' He gestured around again. 'He created this little spot up here as a kind of haven. Surrounded himself with all of his favourite things and tried to forget what was happening downstairs.'

His favourite things? Siena's scarf now resided in the chest MJ sat upon. That had to be significant.

'It must've been the most awful time for you all. But Christian still managed to fashion this safe place for himself.' Good for him. If he'd been ten and Nikos fourteen… She worked it out. She and Siena would've been nine.

Was Christian now making a safe place for Siena somewhere? She crossed her fingers. 'This must've all been happening around the same time my mother died.'

His head came up. He stared at her with a strange expression in his eyes. 'Your mother died just before we came down here.'

'Worst year of my life,' she whispered. She thought of Siena and shivered. 'I had no idea you were going through an *annus horribilis* of your own.'

His gaze sharpened. With a smothered oath, he dropped his head to his hands, scrubbing his fingers back through his hair. Her heart thumped. She ached to go to him and put an arm around his shoulders. He looked so solitary and alone. But he wouldn't want her sympathy. He didn't want her friendship, and she couldn't force it on him, no matter how much she might want to.

Nikos bit back a curse. MJ didn't have a clue how her mother's death and his parents' divorce were related, did she? How the hell had her father managed to shield her sister and her from that knowledge? Even Christian knew part of it, if not the whole.

He pressed his fingers to his eyes. Not a lot of people had known about Graham's and Tori's affair. And nobody outside of their two families would know that, on the same day she'd had the car accident that had killed her, MJ's mother, Diana, had been driving to Graham's and Tori's rendezvous location to discover if what she'd been told that afternoon was true—whether her husband and Tori were having a torrid affair. It *had* all happened a long time ago. MJ had only been nine.

He lifted his head and forced in a breath. Over the years, in idle moments, he'd sometimes wondered how MJ had dealt with the knowledge, how she'd coped with it. He'd wondered about how much she must hate his parents—his mother for the affair and his father for telling Diana about it. That seemed almost laughable now. She hadn't coped because she hadn't had a clue.

If he wanted to hurt her, he now had the perfect weapon.

An image of MJ with Rufus and Seth in the garden rose through him. The determined chin that hadn't quite hidden the tremble of her bottom lip, the tears that had risen in her eyes when he'd narrated the dogs' histories of abuse and neglect.

He didn't want to hurt her. *Damn it!* She wasn't the hardened nemesis he'd created in his mind. She wasn't the kind of woman who'd stop at nothing to contrive his downfall. MJ was savvy and smart, but she was also kind and brave. And she loved too many things. A corner of his heart trembled for her. He had no intention of being the one to reveal the ugly truth. It'd probably be best all round if that particular truth remained buried.

'I'm sorry you had to go through all of that, Nikos. I'm sorry it was so hard.'

'It wasn't your fault, MJ.' And for the first time he felt the truth of that right down to his very bones. She was no more to blame than he was. He'd scoffed when she'd said she wanted to bring the feud to an end...

But he wasn't an idiot. He knew his father, his grandfather, her father—none of them would ever let it go. But the previous generations couldn't live forever. He couldn't imagine a time when the Constantinoses and Mabels would ever be friends, but he was starting to envisage a world where they weren't mortal enemies either.

'You've gone very quiet.'

He snapped out of his thoughts.

She glanced round again and smiled. 'Christian made a pleasant nest up here.'

He had. 'It was supposed to be his secret spot, but I found him up here one day.' When he'd been searching for a place where his parents' fighting wouldn't reach him. 'He'd found a clutch of baby starlings that had been blown from their nest. He'd been keeping them up here in a box with towels and a hot-water bottle, feeding them on condensed milk.' He bit back a sigh. 'They died of course. Damn near broke his heart.'

Her lips parted. 'What did you do?'

'We buried them, and the next day I searched high and low until I found a rabbit kitten. I gave it to him and told him how to look after it.'

'Did it survive?'

'It did, much to Mr Digby's disgust. He had no use for wild rabbits, but he built a hutch for it all the same once it grew too big for us to keep locked up in the attic.'

She laughed and it lightened something inside him. 'What a lovely big brother you were.'

They stared at each other for a long moment and he felt the same strange pull he always felt whenever he looked at her—as if something in him recognised something in her. Up here in the dim intimacy of the attic, the pull grew keener, stronger.

He stood and paced to the window. It'd meant drawing closer to her, but at least he'd been able to break eye contact. Down below Mrs Digby pegged laundry on the line. He drew the scent of vanilla deep into his lungs. 'This room served its purpose, but I doubt Christian ever comes up here any more.'

'Then you'd be wrong.'

He swung towards her.

She stood and lifted the lid of the chest, gesturing for him to look. 'See that blue and pink scarf there? That's Siena's favourite scarf. It's pure silk, hand-printed, and cost her an absolute packet. She treasures it. It's not the kind of thing she'd ever accidentally leave behind.'

His gaze drilled into hers. 'You think Christian took it?'

She rolled her eyes. 'No, Nikos, I don't think your brother is a thief.'

Of course she didn't. 'Sorry, I—'

'I suspect she gave it to him.'

'Why? It's not like he can wear it.'

'For an extremely clever man, you can be really dense sometimes.'

He wanted to take offence, but her smile removed any sting.

'It's obviously a love token. Haven't you ever done that?'

'No.' He frowned. 'Have you?'

'Of course I have.' She stared at the scarf. 'But not as an adult. I hardly think giving Bertie Stevens my princess ring and tiara set really counts. Though he did give me his red fire engine. With hoses that actually worked. So maybe it was true love after all.'

He snorted at her nonsense. A love token? Reaching into the trunk, he pulled out the scarf.

The air whistled between MJ's teeth. 'That's...it's an invasion of privacy.'

She could bet her life it was, but a Constantinos and Mabel sharing love tokens was an absolute disaster. He needed to nip this little romance—if that was what it was—in the bud ASAP. He held the scarf but made no move to unfold it. 'There's something wrapped in it.'

MJ pursed her lips and rolled her shoulders. 'Go on, then.' She nodded, gnawing on her bottom lip.

Very carefully, he unwrapped it. MJ said the scarf was precious to her sister. He didn't want Siena and Christian forming an attachment, but that didn't mean he wanted to treat MJ's sister's property with disrespect either.

MJ craned her neck. 'What is it?'

He held the photo frame towards her. A picture of Siena and Christian beamed from it, heads close together and arms around each other. She took it and ran a finger over Siena's face. 'She looks so happy.'

His throat tightened. So did Christian.

She nodded at the velvet ring box clenched in his hand. 'What do you have there?'

'This is the box that holds my maternal grandmother's engagement ring. I have a similar box with my paternal grandmother's engagement ring. They're family heirlooms. Meant for our future brides.'

'Engagement ring?' MJ took Siena's scarf from his unresisting fingers. 'Is the ring still inside?'

He didn't want to depress the little silver latch. He didn't want to know. He wished he'd left the scarf where it was. He wished they hadn't come here. Steeling himself, he opened it…and then held it towards her.

'Empty.' She tottered over to the sofa and sat. Lifting the scarf to her face, she inhaled, as if searching for a trace of her sister there. 'Well, that changes things.'

'How?' His voice sounded harsh and angry in the still air, but he couldn't temper it.

'Because they're obviously in love.'

He strode across to the sofa and sat too, choking back the torrent of savage words clamouring at the back of his throat. She didn't deserve his anger. 'This can't happen, MJ. A marriage between Christian and Siena would tear my family apart. I *won't* let that happen.'

'You're saying your father and grandfather would sooner cut Christian off—disown him—than accept a Mabel into the family?'

That was exactly what he was saying.

'But surely when they see how much Christian loves her…? And when they actually meet Siena…'

'You're deluding yourself if you think your father will be any different.'

'You're wrong. We can make them all see sense and—'

'Just because you want that to be true doesn't make it so!'

The force of his words echoed into every corner of the

vast space, bouncing off every box and item of discarded furniture. Her head rocked back and the shock in her eyes had his hands clenching.

'This doesn't have to be a tragedy.' He did what he could to moderate his voice. 'We'll find them and talk sense into them. It's that simple.'

'Not a tragedy?' Her voice rose. 'You have to be joking, right? Our two families have Shakespeare written all over them.' She shot to her feet, hands clenched. 'I'm not going to let your father or grandfather—' she hesitated '—or my father destroy Siena *or* Christian.'

Damn, she was magnificent.

'If my father forces me to choose between him and Siena—' her throat bobbed '—I'll choose Siena, because she and Christian have done nothing wrong. Who will you choose, Nikos?'

A stone lodged in his chest and he couldn't speak.

Her eyes widened at whatever she saw reflected in his face and she took a step back.

He didn't want her looking at him with such appalled disillusion. He was a Constantinos! What did she expect? He forced himself to his feet. 'My father and grandfather have both suffered enough. I'll do all I can to protect them from further heartache. They have made many sacrifices for our family already. It's Christian's turn to make a sacrifice.'

'Do you not care about breaking their hearts?'

'Of course I care!' He slashed a hand through the air. 'But broken hearts mend.'

'Do they *really*?' That pointed chin hitched up, angled in challenge. 'Tell that to your grandfather and my great-aunt because I doubt they'd agree.'

Her words chilled him.

She sat again, folded the scarf, set the frame on top and plucked the ring box from his fingers.

'What are you doing?'

She snapped a photo of it all with her phone. 'I think we should let Siena and Christian know what we found, don't you? It's the decent thing to do.'

His stomach clenched even tighter, but he gave a curt nod. Hopefully the shock of it would pull Christian from his current romantic haze and make him realise the futility of continuing an engagement with Siena.

'Oh, and look.' Her phone buzzed and she turned it towards him. 'I have an incoming call from Freddy Smythe. This should be good.'

What the hell...?

She pressed her phone to her ear. 'Hello, Freddy.'

She listened to whatever he had to say and then her eyebrows rose. 'Hold on. I'm putting you on speaker phone.'

CHAPTER SIX

'REPEATING FOR THE benefit of your companion's ears,' Freddy said with an archness that set MJ's teeth on edge. Could he have made the word *companion* sound any more suggestive? 'I know where Christian and Siena are.'

She and Nikos shared a look as she set the phone on top of an abandoned chest of drawers. His distaste matched hers.

'Playing games again, Freddy?' Nikos folded his arms.

'Dastardly ones,' Freddy agreed with infuriating cheerfulness. 'And, just so we're clear, the information doesn't come free.'

'Of course it doesn't,' she drawled. What a piece of work he was. 'What's the asking price these days for selling out one's friends?'

If her dig perturbed him, he didn't let on. Nikos's scowl turned ferocious.

'My two cousins, Joey and Merrilee Withers, are currently between jobs. I want you to find placements for them somewhere in your oh-so-vast business empires.'

His request made her frown. Merri was a sweet girl, and MJ could find a place for her at Mabel's easily enough if she was serious, but...

Nikos raised an eyebrow. 'Why would you ask for something so selfless, Freddy?'

Exactly! How on earth could she and Nikos be so in

tune in their reactions to Freddy and so at odds in relation
to Christian and Siena?

'It's not selfless!' Freddy snorted. 'Let's just say it
would suit my purposes to have my uncle feeling warmly
towards me at the moment.'

Nikos raised an eyebrow and MJ nodded, pointing at
herself and mouthing, "Merrilee."

'Very well,' Nikos said. 'Have Joey visit my office on
Monday, and Merrilee visit MJ's.'

'Make it tomorrow and you have yourself a deal.'

MJ rolled her eyes. 'Fine, Freddy, it's a deal. Now tell
us where Siena and Christian are.'

'Switzerland.'

Nikos pursed his lips. She stared at them. An indenta-
tion rested above the cupid's bow of his top lip. The bottom lip swelled fractionally fuller. Her mouth dried. Those
lips looked firm and generous. They looked like the kind
of lips that knew how to kiss a woman.

She wrenched her gaze away, her pulse echoing in her
ears.

'They've gone to some medical clinic or health farm.'

Her head snapped up.

'What's the name of this facility?' Nikos demanded.

'Haven't a clue.'

Damn.

Nikos glared at the phone. 'You said you knew where
they were.'

'I do! In as much as it's a medical centre in Switzerland.' He hesitated. 'Geneva, I believe. All it'll take is a
bit of research on your part to track them down. You're
now closer to finding them than you were before my call.
So don't forget the deal!'

Nikos waved an impatient hand in the air. 'Yes, yes.'

'So what's the skinny? They both looked healthy enough
to me. Is someone trying to dry out or—?'

'Goodbye, Freddy.' MJ ended the call.

Nikos paced to the window and back. 'The man is a worm.'

'He's worse than a worm. He's an amoeba on a worm.'

'Looks like we're going to Switzerland.'

'It does indeed.'

They drove back to London that afternoon and were booked on flights first thing the following morning. A medical facility... Had Siena gone to a clinic seeking treatment?

The knots that twisted MJ tight loosened a fraction. While Freddy obviously didn't know what was wrong with Siena, surely this must mean that Christian did? That he hadn't just deleted her text without reading it.

She crossed her fingers as she marched through London's Gatwick airport. If Siena and Christian were in love, then surely her sister had confided everything to him anyway? Wouldn't she do everything she could to ensure they had a rosy future full of promise ahead of them and not throw it all away in a blaze of glory?

She spotted Nikos across the concourse. Despite her best efforts, her pulse did a funny little dance. *Deep breaths*. It'd be foolish to trust him or expect too much from him.

While he might be a man who kept his word, she knew now what Christian had meant when he'd accused him of being just like his father and grandfather. Nikos gave too much credence to their families' feud, gave it too much power. The fact he had every intention of rupturing Christian's and Siena's relationship told her that.

How much influence did he have with his brother? Would his pressure and emotional blackmail succeed? Her heart quailed at the thought. If Siena loved Christian...

She set her jaw. She'd promised him the Ananke necklace. Nothing more. He sure as heck wasn't getting her co-operation in breaking up Siena and Christian, and he'd discover she could be a formidable opponent. She *would* bring all of her powers of persuasion to bear on their siblings. They *would* get her support. She wouldn't stand idly by and let anyone break Siena's heart.

'You're looking particularly martial today, MJ,' Nikos said when she reached his side.

If she hadn't already come to a standstill, she'd have tripped and stumbled at the expression in his eyes. They held real pleasure. Was that at seeing her? Her stomach turned to mush in the space of a heartbeat.

Oh, for heaven's sake. She swallowed and forced her lips into a semblance of a smile. 'Just eager to finally clap eyes on our pair of fugitives.'

'We're boarding at gate eighteen. I suggest we head straight on through and grab coffees on the other side.'

'Excellent plan. I—'

'Ms Mabel and Mr Constantinos?'

They both automatically turned and a camera flash immediately went off in their faces. The press. MJ bit back a rude word and smoothed out her features. Beside her Nikos did the same, but she sensed the tension coiling him up tight.

'Rumour has it the two of you have been spending a lot of time in each other's company recently. Would you like to comment?'

'No.' Nikos took her arm and started marching her towards the nearest check-in counter.

'Aw, have a heart. It's a slow news day and my editor is busting my—'

Nikos swung round. 'Mind your language around the lady!'

The reporter raised both hands in surrender and a shaft of mischief trickled through MJ. Mischief and something a little darker. She gently disengaged her arm from Nikos's grasp. 'Mr Constantinos and I are currently in secret negotiations.'

The reporter's eyes lit up at that juicy titbit. 'What kind of negotiations?'

'If we told you,' Nikos inserted smoothly, 'They wouldn't be secret any more, would they?'

He marched her through check-in with a speed that had her fighting back a laugh.

'Damn it, MJ! What the hell were you thinking?' he bit out when they were finally out of earshot. 'You made it sound like…'

She raised an eyebrow.

He raked a hand through his hair. 'My father is going to have a fit when he hears about this.'

Her grin widened. 'Mine too.'

His hand dropped back to his side. 'That's why you…?'

She nodded.

'You could've warned me,' he grumbled, following as she led the way to the business-class lounge.

'I could hardly warn you when I didn't know such an irresistible opportunity was going to present itself, could I? Besides, you've dealt with the press before. You're a man who can think on his feet. Don't worry, you looked as debonair and sophisticated as ever.'

His scowl deepened and she realised she'd pushed him a bit further than she'd meant to.

'I don't care how I looked,' he ground out. 'I care—'

'About your father,' she finished when he broke off. 'And your grandfather,' she added. 'And you don't want them catching wind of what we're up to. Or what Christian and Siena are up to.'

His silence spoke volumes.

She hauled in a breath, but he spoke before she could.

'You seem to think my wanting to spare them anxiety is a crime.'

'What I want to know is why they should be spared any worry whatsoever when it's they who continue to cling to this stupid feud. I'm starting to think the feud matters more to them than anything else—more than Christian and Siena's happiness, for example. Doesn't that seem wrong to you?'

She wanted to stir them all up—her father, his father and grandfather—and make them face the ugliness of being at daggers drawn, for bequeathing that *hatred* to their children.

'We're not going to agree on this, MJ, so just drop it.'

Something flashed in his eyes, something she didn't understand. It sent unease spiralling through her. Was there something she didn't know?

Was his father in bad health? In which case she certainly understood his desire to shield the older man. She passed him her hand luggage. 'Find us somewhere comfortable to sit. I'll grab us coffees while you ring your father and make up some story about me simply trying to create mischief.'

MJ ticked off the last of the clinics that Siena's doctor had recommended she check out—ones the doctor thought might be of use to her sister. Her stomach clenched. Siena wasn't in any of them.

'What now?' Nikos asked.

'We head back to the hotel, I suppose.'

Neither of them spoke during the twenty-minute drive back to their hotel.

He followed her into her suite, his face a study in frustration. She fell onto the sofa, her shoulders slumping, and waved him to the bucket seat opposite.

Those dark eyes burned as they surveyed her. 'Don't

give up, MJ. We'll find them yet. I made you a promise, didn't I?'

This was their second full day in Switzerland, tonight would be their third night but, despite their best efforts, they were no closer to finding Siena and Christian than when they'd started. What was more, none of Nikos's or her combined contacts in Switzerland had uncovered any news of note, and that in itself was astonishing.

Where on earth could Siena be?

Nikos had promised to help her find her sister, and he'd been trying. Hard. They both had. But it was becoming increasingly clear that their siblings didn't want to be found. And the trail was going cold.

She snatched up her phone when it rang, and then bit her lip as she read the caller ID. 'It's my father.'

Nikos immediately rose. 'I'll give you some privacy.'

'Nonsense,' she returned as crisply as she could, though her heart had started to hammer against her ribs. 'I don't expect this to take long, and we need to come up with a new plan.'

She lifted the phone to her ear. 'Hello, Father.'

'What are you up to?' The older man exploded.

'I'm fine, thank you,' she sing-songed. 'And you?'

She could practically hear his teeth grind together. 'Listen to me—'

'Have you made things right with Siena yet? I told you I wouldn't speak to you until you did. And I meant it.'

'Is it true you're with Nikos Constantinos?'

She let the silence stretch for a beat too long. She wanted her father anxious and uneasy. 'Have you spoken to Siena?' she repeated.

'Listen to me, MJ.' A new urgency entered his voice. 'There are things you don't know about the Constantinos family.'

'There are things you don't know about Siena,' she shot

back. She knew which of those two issues he should be paying attention to.

'Do not trust Nikos Constantinos!'

She wasn't playing this game. She ended the call without uttering another word and sent all her calls to voicemail.

Nikos winced. There wasn't an ounce of triumph in his eyes. 'I'm sorry. That didn't sound as if it went well.'

'Drink?' She rose and lifted the brandy decanter, but he pointed to the mineral water instead. She poured two glasses, added ice and lime.

'He told you not to trust me, didn't he?'

'Of course he did. No doubt the same way your father told you not to trust me.'

She sipped her water. He did the same.

'He told me there are things I don't know,' she said.

His gaze immediately slid away and her heart thump-thumped.

'Right, so that's obviously true then, but...'

Nikos met her gaze again.

'I don't care. These hostilities—all of this bitterness—it has to stop.'

Nikos stared at MJ, at the resolution in those clear green eyes and the jut of her chin, and a burn started up at the centre of him.

She'd meant it when she'd said she wanted to bring an end to their families' hostilities, but her father was right. There were things she didn't know. Things that would hurt her.

Things that would make her as bitter as his father and hers.

Things that would make her as bitter as Nikos himself.

The thought of her disillusionment, of all of that warmth and light diminishing...

He paced across the room.

'Nikos?'

'This resolution of yours to fix things between our families.' He swung around. 'It could backfire, you know.' He pressed his lips together so hard they started to ache. 'Don't sacrifice yourself for it, because it won't be worth it.'

For the first time that day, she smiled. A real smile. One that slid in between his ribs and had him wishing for...

He didn't know! But he had to battle an entirely inappropriate and overwhelming tenderness—a sweetness and warmth that was as seductive as a blazing fire in the hearth on a cold, cold day. A warmth that wanted to possess him wholly and completely.

'Careful,' she teased, 'or you'll find yourself friends with me before you know it.'

He shook his head, unable to hide his smile. Despite his best intentions, it felt as if he and MJ were already friends. The woman could make him laugh when he least expected it. And the last four days had shown him that they were on the same page in so many ways. It was strange how so many of their values aligned. His lips twisted. Except the people who mattered. Such as their families.

A friendship might be forming, but the moment he separated Christian from her sister any amity between them would end. He'd seen enough evidence of her devotion to Siena to know that.

He braced himself against the weight that settled on his shoulders. It was an effort to fight the urge to close his eyes and sleep for a week.

'You know what, Nikos?'

He jerked his attention back.

'Freddy Smythe is a real weasel.'

'He is.' He moved back and planted himself in his seat. She was right. They needed to come up with a strategy to move forward. He needed to start thinking smart again, not mooning for impossible things.

'What was it you called him before—a toad?'

Her meaning sank in and he bit back something rude and succinct. 'You think he lied and sent us on a wild goose-chase?'

'Don't you?'

Damn the man. 'When I get my hands on him…'

'I think Siena and Christian put him up to it.'

He leaned forward. *'What?'*

'Think about it. The only part of Freddy's information that lent it any validity whatsoever was the mention of the medical clinic.'

'That and the fact he extorted something from us in return for the information.'

'But it wasn't something that would harm him personally if we were to renege.' She cocked her head to one side. 'I'll still trial Merri. I know why she was let go at her previous job and I don't like it. Her manager passed the buck and she took the blame.'

He stared at her. 'Are you a one-man crusader?'

'Woman,' she corrected.

'I suppose you want me to give Joey the promised trial too?' He scowled. 'What do you know of him?'

'He's young…been partying too hard and giving his father headaches. I suspect he just needs a bit of direction.' She suddenly grinned. 'If he doesn't pull up his socks, you could always have him cool his heels at your Reykjavík hotel.'

That made him laugh. 'Okay, fine, I'll trial him, but I'm making no promises beyond that.'

Her grin was the only thanks he needed.

She sobered again. 'Back to my original point, though. Siena had to have told Freddy what to say to throw us off the scent.'

She was right.

'There is one silver lining in all of this.'

'I can't see it myself, MJ. You might need to help me out.'

'Freddy might be a toad, but at least he didn't betray them. I hate to think of either Siena or Christian's friends selling them out.' When he didn't say anything, she frowned. 'Don't you?'

This woman was going to be the death of him. He rubbed a hand over his face. 'Were you born an optimist?'

Something sad floated through her eyes before it was blinked away, replaced instead with her natural smile. 'I think being aware of the things in your life you should be grateful for is more conducive to happiness than brooding about everything that's wrong.'

Like the feud?

Still, he had to admit she had a point. 'Are there any other silver linings to this situation you'd like to share?'

Her eyes filled with mischief. 'Getting to know you has been mostly fun. And definitely interesting. I always knew I'd like you.'

He wanted to laugh the words off, deflect them, but beneath her teasing he sensed she was deadly serious and it knocked the breath clean from his body. Something fierce, hot and sweet pooled in the space left behind, and he didn't know what to do with it. 'Marjorie...' He halted, not sure what to say.

'Ooh, Nikos Constantinos at a loss for words?' Her lips kinked upwards and those mossy-green eyes sparkled almost emerald. 'I bet that doesn't happen very often.'

It took a super-human effort to fight an answering smile.

She sobered. Shadows replaced the sparkles. 'So, in your world view, not only can't Siena and Christian become romantically involved but we can't be friends either?'

He rubbed that hand over his face again, wishing he'd

chosen a brandy instead of mineral water. 'I thought you had enough friends already.'

'Oh, Nikos.' She stared at him with the kind of pity one normally reserved for stray dogs and crying babies. 'One can never have too many friends.'

She leapt up and strode around the room. He followed her movements, finding them oddly and soothingly hypnotic. Some critical inner voice told him she didn't move with any more grace than other women he knew, that her figure wasn't finer or her hair shinier, but the sight of her held him spellbound. And the longer he watched, the greater was the hunger that started gnawing at the centre of him.

He and MJ friends?

It shocked him how much the idea appealed. Maybe once the Ananke necklace was where it belonged—in the Constantinos family vault—he and MJ could become friends. Maybe between them they could start to heal the breach that two generations of hate and hostility, betrayal and bitterness, had created.

'There's another silver lining, of course.' MJ spoke quietly, but when she spun back to face him her eyes had grown serious and full of intent. 'Freddy's mention of the medical clinic, even though he used it as a blind, has to mean Christian knows about Siena's medical condition. Either Siena has confided in him, or he read my text.'

What the hell was wrong with Siena? And was MJ unwell too?

He scanned her for signs of illness and fatigue. Admittedly, she looked a little tired, but her colour had improved over the last couple of days. And her energy levels hadn't flagged until this afternoon when she'd realised they'd been duped. His had too, though.

His hands clenched and unclenched. He'd not seen her touch so much as a single drop of alcohol. Although she'd said she loved bacon and eggs, toast and pastries, she'd not eaten anything like that since leaving Devon. She mostly ate vegetables, salads and a little lean meat. She drank tea relatively freely but limited herself to one cup of coffee a day. For the rest of it she drank water—still and sparkling.

Things inside him pulled tight.

'Nikos?'

He blinked.

'Wouldn't you agree?'

'About what?'

She rolled her eyes, as if realising she'd been talking to thin air. 'If Christian knows about Siena's condition, he'll do everything he can to take care of her?'

'Not a doubt in my mind,' he said immediately, because she needed the reassurance.

He flashed back to the empty ring box. If Christian loved Siena, he'd move heaven and earth to make sure she had everything she needed.

Pressing fingers to his eyes, he counted to three before dragging them away and meeting MJ's gaze. 'What's wrong with Siena, MJ? How serious is it?'

She stared back with bruised eyes. Striding across, he closed his fingers about her shoulders, careful to keep his touch gentle. 'You have my word I will never use this information to hurt you and your family, but you're identical twins—identical DNA. Are you ill too?'

Should he be seeking medical attention for her? Was she risking her health not only to find her sister but to bring their families' feud to an end?

The feud wasn't worth that kind of sacrifice.

She chewed her bottom lip. 'Perhaps we should sit.'

How bad was this?

He led her to the sofa but, rather than returning to his original seat, he eased down beside her. He might be crowding her—the sofa was only small—but he refused to relinquish his hold on her hand.

'First of all…' She dragged in a breath and sent him the smallest of smiles that would've felled any remaining barriers he'd still had in place. 'Identical twins' DNA is identical at the moment of conception—same egg, same sperm—but, the moment the fertilised egg divides, slight changes in each twin's environment means our DNA is no longer identical. Similar, yes, but not identical.'

He mulled that over and nodded. 'Okay.'

'Both Siena and I have polycystic kidney disease. It's a hereditary condition and we have the recessive type, which is less common.' One slim shoulder lifted. 'The severity of the disease varies from person to person. It's possible I could go through my whole life without it ever causing me a problem.'

He caught a slight stress on 'my' and 'me'. 'What happens when it doesn't remain dormant?' Was that even the right word?

'Worst-case scenario is kidney failure.'

Hell! That meant…

She winced and with a start he realised how tightly he gripped her hand. He immediately loosened his hold and worked hard to keep his voice gentle. 'Are Siena's kidneys failing?'

'I don't know. Her last round of test results threw up some early indications that all might not be well—higher than normal blood pressure, traces of blood in her urine.'

'She's aware of this?'

She swallowed and nodded. Tears welled in her eyes.

He wrapped an arm around her shoulders and pulled her against his chest. How could Siena be so thoughtless? She had to know how much her twin would worry. 'We'll find her, MJ. I promise.'

He could see now why she'd been prepared to trade the

Ananke necklace for his assistance. Besides her sister's health, its importance faded into insignificance.

She softened against him and her perfume rose up all around him in a sweet cloud that had his every sense sharpening—making him minutely conscious of the warm weight of her against his chest, the softness of her hair against his cheek and the strange sense of *déjà vu* that settled over him. As if she'd been in his arms exactly like this, and nothing had ever felt quite so right.

He swallowed and made his voice as matter-of-fact as he could. 'If Christian is aware of Siena's health issues, he will look after her.'

With a sigh, she lifted her head, and he immediately missed the weight and warmth of her. 'Except we're not a hundred per cent sure he does know. And you think him gullible and easily manipulated by a woman he considers himself in love with.'

It was true. 'While you're worried the news of her latest test results has sent Siena into a spin and made her reckless.'

She hadn't said as much, but he realised that was what she'd feared from the very first. His heart burned—for Siena and Christian, but mostly for MJ.

'There's something I haven't told you,' she whispered.

He brushed her hair from her face and let his hand linger against her cheek a moment longer than he should've. 'What's that?'

Had he imagined that she'd arched into his touch?

'I think Siena deliberately picked that fight with my father. They're opposites—he's practical, she's artistic; he's focused, she's dreamy; he's hard-headed, she's soft-hearted. You get the picture. They love each other but struggle to understand one another.'

While MJ understood them both. And was devoted to them both.

'I think she deliberately enraged him as much as she could, and then I think she picked a fight with me.'

Frown lines marked her brow and he wanted to smooth them out. MJ was the kind of woman who deserved sunshine, sweet pastries and smiles, not this gut-wrenching worry and heartache.

'She knew I'd try to play peace maker, and I think she made a deliberate decision to act as offended and outraged as possible by it.'

It was his turn to frown. 'Why would she do that?'

'To alienate us both.'

He still didn't understand. A single tear spilled onto her cheek and a groan rose through him. 'MJ, please don't cry.' He wasn't sure he could bear it.

She forced her lips into the semblance of a smile. It didn't help. Had he ever seen a sadder smile?

'My father is a match. His kidney was always going to whichever one of us needed it first. Of course, he's only allowed to give one, so…'

When her meaning hit him, his heart stopped. 'You think she's run away so…?'

'She always credits me with saving her life against the dog that day. I think this is her returning the favour.'

Siena had run away so that she wouldn't take the kidney MJ might one day need. While MJ… Nikos saw in that moment the sisters' devotion for each other.

She pulled in a ragged breath. 'I bet she hasn't told Christian that.'

Resolve crystallised inside him. 'Marjorie, I promise you we'll find them.' He'd move heaven and earth to make that happen.

Her breath hitched as if she'd read that thought in his face. And then he realised he'd been cradling her face and tracing her bottom lip with his thumb, his body unconsciously betraying his desire for her.

He should move away, apologise.

Reaching up, she pressed her hand to his cheek. 'Dear Nikos,' she whispered, a matching desire flaring in her eyes. No fear accompanied that desire, even though he was a Constantinos and the last man she should ever trust. Instead, awe, wonder and a building excitement turned her eyes a brighter shade of green. He found himself drowning in them and never wanting to surface. 'Such a noble face,' she murmured.

He knew what she was really telling him was that she thought *him* noble. In that moment he was helpless to stop his mouth from descending to hers. Their lips instantly shaped themselves to the other's in a fit so perfect it sent sensation roaring through every nerve ending.

Dear God.

Her mouth opened and so did his. It felt as if he stood on the edge of a cliff about to take flight. He was glorying in the freedom of it, the sense that anything was suddenly possible, when a shrill ringing tore through the moment and had them jumping apart.

Dazed eyes met dazed eyes. Mere seconds had passed but everything had changed.

With a muttered oath, he grabbed his phone and glanced at the caller ID. Blowing out a breath and grimacing, he brought it to his ear. 'Grandfather.'

CHAPTER SEVEN

NIKOS SWUNG AWAY to take his phone call and MJ did what she could to get her breathing back under control. She didn't have a hope in Hades of tempering the wild race of her pulse, though. That kiss had been…

She marched over to the bar fridge and poured herself another mineral water, more aware than ever of the bedroom behind the nearby closed door.

The moment had been so brief, it barely qualified as a kiss, and yet its impact reverberated through her like an earthquake, shifting the ground beneath her feet.

She turned to find Nikos surveying her. His gaze immediately slid away. She knew that barely nothing kiss continued to reverberate through him too. He'd been just as dazed as she when they'd broken apart.

She gulped her mineral water but it did nothing to cool the fevered, half-formed hopes that whipped through her like wisps of cloud scudding before a spirited breeze. In ordinary circumstances, if she'd ever experienced something like that she'd be breathless with excitement, anticipation…hope.

But circumstances were far from ordinary.

And she'd never imagined sharing a moment like *that* with Nikos Constantinos. She'd be a fool to let it happen again.

Oh, she liked him well enough, and to a certain extent she trusted him. For years now she'd surreptitiously watched him whenever she'd found herself in the same room, read whatever the newspapers printed about him, undeniably fascinated with the man. But she'd always put it down to the bad blood between their two families and her fantasies of finding a way to heal the breach.

Had she been lying to herself all these years? Had her fascination been due to something more primal? Had it been due to an attraction she hadn't wanted to acknowledge?

She strode to the window and stared out at the street below—part of Geneva's old town, its cobblestones and quaint old-world shop fronts looking like something out of a fairy tale. She pressed her glass to her cheek.

She and Nikos had so much in common. They shared the same work ethic, took the same joy in their careers and found the same sense of satisfaction in it. He wasn't a playboy and she wasn't a party girl. Neither one of them was a player. And they were both devoted to their families.

On paper, they were perfect for each other.

If not for the feud.

If not for him buying into the feud, she told herself with blunt ruthlessness. She'd be an idiot to hide from that fact. If Nikos refused to tolerate a union between their siblings, he sure as hell wouldn't allow himself to fall for her.

That was the thing to remember.

And, even if the world turned upside down and he had a road-to-Damascus moment and wanted to embark on a romance with her, what if things didn't work out? What if it went bad? That would only cement the poor relations between their families, not heal them. And she wasn't risking more bad blood between the Mabels and Constantinoses.

'MJ?'

She turned, heat flaring in her cheeks when she realised it wasn't the first time he'd called her name. *Focus.*

He hesitated. 'About that kiss.'

The expression in his eyes almost broke her heart. She could challenge him, force him to acknowledge the attraction between them, but what good would it do?

She made herself smile. 'It barely deserves the title of a kiss. If we'd blinked we'd have missed it, it was so brief.'

He stared. 'So…you're okay with it?'

She frowned. Did *he* want to talk about it? 'Are you? Okay, I mean?'

'Of course.'

That was a no, then. He was just being polite. 'Emotions have been running high, Nikos. It's no excuse, but…'

His shoulders unhitched a fraction. 'I guess it's natural to search for a release valve when things get tense.' He grimaced. 'But that's not the ideal way to…'

'Heavens, no.' At least they agreed on that.

'I'm sorry, MJ. I—'

'Do you remember stumbling across me in the gardens at the Wallaces' golden anniversary party?' It had been noisy and crowded inside and she'd sneaked away to sit by the fountain. 'I was sixteen, so I guess you'd have been twenty-one.'

He hesitated, though whether it was because she'd thrown him with the change of topic, or because he had no idea what she was talking about, she couldn't tell.

'I knew who you were, of course, but it was the first time we'd ever come face to face.' She dragged in a breath but couldn't find a smile. 'I introduced myself to you and held out my hand, but you refused to shake it. Instead you turned on your heel and went back to the party without saying a word.' She rubbed a hand across her chest. 'You've no idea how much that hurt my feelings.' She'd gone home and cried. That was when the feud between their families had finally felt personal.

'I didn't mean to hurt your feelings, MJ.'

She glanced up. So, he did remember.

'Put yourself in my shoes. I was twenty-one and you were sixteen—' his lips twisted '—and looking an absolute picture.'

Had he thought her pretty?

'Besides the fact that our fathers were sworn enemies, no twenty-one-year-old should be found in what could be construed as a compromising situation with a teenage girl. If your father had seen...'

He broke off with a shake of his head.

She blinked. She hadn't thought about it in those terms. She'd just thought he'd hated her so much he'd refused to engage with her on any level.

'I'm sorry I hurt you. If I could go back to that day, I'd shake your hand and tell you it was nice to meet you and then leave. I'm sorry I didn't do that.'

Suddenly she could smile without any effort at all. 'See, that's an apology I'm happy to accept. But, as for the kiss that was barely a kiss, none is necessary.' She nodded at the phone in his hand. She didn't want to talk about the kiss any more. 'That was your grandfather?'

'I've been ordered to report for duty. He wants a face-to-face meeting.' His lips briefly twisted, but he schooled them almost immediately, as if he hadn't meant to betray his impatience.

'A face-to-face meeting?' On his private Greek island? Aunt Joan had been scathing about her former swain's romantic retreat, his dramatic exile from the real world. While he might have shunned society, he'd continued to be the puppet master controlling the strings of the Leto Group, nursing his sense of injury like some tragic Greek hero of old.

The very thought of him made MJ lose all patience. Another thought struck her. 'Christian and Siena aren't there, are they?' Was it possible they'd found an unlikely

ally in Vasillios Constantinos? Now, that would be an interesting twist to the tale.

He shook his head. 'But—quote—' he made air quotes
'—he has information.'

'Then why didn't he just give it to you over the phone?'

He remained silent and, while not a single muscle
moved in his face, a shadow passed behind the dark brown
of his eyes.

Slowly she nodded. 'He wants to impart to you, face-to-
face, the importance of ensuring this thing between Siena
and Christian doesn't develop into anything permanent.'

'Family is everything to my grandfather.'

'Not everything,' she returned. 'His love for his family
isn't greater than nursing his sense of injury and resentment towards my family.'

'Which only makes him want to protect his family all
the more. They're intertwined, MJ, and nothing anyone
says will have him seeing that differently.'

'And so...what? You must be a slave to it as well?' She
slashed a hand through the air. 'The man is as stubborn
and wrong-headed as my great-aunt was.'

Nikos blinked and straightened. Behind the darkness
of his eyes, she sensed his mind racing. 'Would you like
to accompany me?'

She had no hope of hiding the way her eyes started
from their sockets, but she immediately nodded in case
he should change his mind and take the offer back. 'Yes
please.'

One broad shoulder lifted. 'It was part of the deal we
made—that I wouldn't ditch you somewhere or give you
the slip.'

He was trying to justify the invitation, and she could
see that was the line he meant to give to his grandfather,
but what was his real reason?

And would she be able to discover it before they reached the island?

'You did,' she agreed. 'It would be contravening our agreement if you were to travel to your grandfather's without me.'

'And I've no intention of giving you the smallest loophole for not handing over the Ananke necklace at the end of all this.'

A stone lodged in her chest. Did he really care so much about the necklace? 'So, what's the plan?'

His eyes narrowed. 'What do you mean, *what's the plan*? I love my grandfather. I've no intention of betraying or manipulating him.'

But he had an agenda. She sensed that much.

'Nikos?' She started to lift her eyes to meet his gaze, but her attention snagged on his lips. Everything inside her pulled tight. How she ached to...

The white line of his mouth pulled her up short. A pulse in his throat pounded and his eyes had gone too dark. She jerked herself back. What had they been talking about? *Oh, that's right.* 'I merely referred to our travel plans.'

'Oh.'

His gaze dropped briefly to her lips, heat gathered beneath her breast bone and she swore perspiration gathered between her breasts.

'We'll leave for Athens in the morning and I'll charter a yacht to the island.

She gave a nod because she wasn't sure she could speak.

'Have you sailed before?'

She took a gulp of lukewarm mineral water. It did nothing to dampen the heat rising through her. 'I sailed once, a long time ago, on Lake Windermere.'

'The island is only three hours from the mainland. I've made the trip on my own more times than I can count, so you won't be called on to crew. I was just curious. Can you swim?'

'Like a fish.' If she fell overboard, he wouldn't need to dive in to save her.

He rolled his shoulders. 'Did you want to go out for dinner tonight?'

He wasn't asking her on a date. They were simply stuck in the same city together, and he was being polite. 'I'm a little tired after all of our traipsing around. I was planning on ordering room service and getting an early night.'

For a moment she thought he might argue, but then he nodded. 'That's probably wise.'

All the fine hairs on her arms stood to attention at the way the words left his lips. Lips that looked as if they yearned to…

'I mean, it'll be a big day tomorrow, and we'll want to be fully rested. Plus, there's some work I need to get done.'

She didn't say a single word when he turned on his heel and left. She wanted nothing more than to fall face first on her bed and groan into the eiderdown. Instead she forced herself to fetch her phone. 'I need you to arrange for a courier to deliver a package to Athens airport,' she said to her PA. 'You'll find it in the safe.' She gave a description of the parcel. 'I'm afraid I need it first thing in the morning.'

Once she'd ended the call, she opened the door to her bedroom, fell face-down on her bed and groaned.

MJ didn't sleep well that night. Nikos didn't look any better rested the following morning either, which didn't help. She'd not been able to stop her mind from drifting to all the things they could've been doing instead—things that would have been far more fun. At least then she'd have felt she'd earned her sleepless night.

But they were foolish things, the things she and Nikos could've been doing, she told herself for the millionth time.

They couldn't lead to anything permanent. And, with the best will in the world, those sorts of foolish things could lead to hurt feelings.

She'd vowed to her Aunt Joan and herself to do everything in her power to heal the rift between their two families. She couldn't do anything now that might jeopardise that. It'd be selfish and self-defeating. Besides, if Siena did truly love Christian, then MJ would do everything in her power to smooth the way for her sister, not make matters worse.

'I thought you said you were on a leave of absence,' Nikos said when she collected her parcel from the airport the next morning.

'I am.'

A smile touched his lips. 'And you call me a workaholic.'

'You are.'

'Pot.' He pointed to her and then himself. 'Kettle.'

She laughed. She couldn't help it. There was a subtle change in Nikos today. His step was lighter and his eyes brighter—and she couldn't prevent it from infecting her.

From the airport, they headed straight to the marina. He turned his phone towards her and pointed to a storm front showing on the screen. 'There's a storm forecast for this evening.'

She wrinkled her nose. 'I'm definitely a fair-weather sailor. I don't want to be tossed around like a cork on big seas in gale-force winds.'

'We'll be at my grandfather's island enjoying a cool drink by the time this hits.' Keen eyes raked her face. 'But I'll check with more experienced heads before we leave, just to make sure.'

'I'd appreciate that.'

Fifteen minutes later, he returned from the marina's

main office. 'Common wisdom claims the storm will miss us completely.'

'I like the sound of that.'

'We might get a shower later this evening, but that's probably the worst of it.'

'Excellent.' She gestured to their yacht. 'What do you want me to do?'

He helped her on board and then pointed to a seat. 'What you can do, MJ, is take the weight off and enjoy the ride.'

She realised then the reason for his good mood—Nikos loved to sail. And, as she watched him navigate the boat out of the harbour, she discovered that she loved to watch him sail.

He looked at home on board this small yacht. At one with the elements. Who would have guessed that beneath those immaculate business suits beat the heart of a man at home on the sea?

A brisk breeze filled their sails and they clipped along at a playfully brisk pace. She lifted her face to the sun and closed her eyes, enjoying the sound of splashing water, the cry of a sea bird and the scent of salt that seasoned the air.

'What do you think?' Nikos asked, turning from the wheel to smile down at her.

'It's glorious! It feels like...'

'Freedom.'

She nodded. 'I need to take up sailing.'

He grinned up at the sky. She stared at the strong, tanned column of his throat and a deep ache burrowed into her chest. He glanced back at her and very slowly he sobered, his eyes darkening. She didn't want the moment to end...

Don't be foolish.

She dragged her gaze away. Swallowed. 'Shouldn't you be keeping your eyes on the road?'

He didn't speak for a long moment, but she didn't dare

glance at him again. 'There are drinks and a packed lunch down below if you want anything,' he finally said.

She nodded, but didn't speak, trying to find her earlier sense of serenity.

'Can I ask you something, MJ?'

She glanced up and gave a cautious nod.

'Why would Siena get sick now? You said there are slight differences in your DNA, that environmental factors play a role.'

She fought a frown. Why did he want to know?

'For example, is being out here in the elements, or taking an unexpected dip in a cold sea or air travel likely to cause you any issues?'

Her heart turned over in her chest. She'd known he was a good man from the years she'd spent observing him, but those words confirmed it. He wanted to keep her safe, to prevent her from falling ill.

Nikos could feel the ticking of his heart as he waited for MJ to answer. If she caught a cold or chill would it set off her illness? What about stress? Or a shock—such as a bump on the head or unexpectedly falling off a yacht into the sea?

'When we were babies, Siena got a UTI that went undiagnosed and developed into a kidney infection. That's how we were initially diagnosed as having polycystic kidney disease in the first place. She suffered damage to her kidneys then.'

Damage MJ hadn't suffered.

'Our parents were always ridiculously vigilant after that, never letting the slightest high temperature go uninvestigated.'

He didn't blame them. He couldn't imagine what it would be like to have something like that hanging over one's children's heads.

'We've had six-monthly check-ups ever since. My doctor assures me that I could go to annual checks, but the six-monthly ones give my father some peace. And it seems such a small thing to do.'

She might be leading her father a merry dance now, but he could see she'd spare him any unnecessary anxiety about her health that she could.

His hands tightened on the wheel. How the hell could Siena frighten her family like this? He recalled what MJ had said to him yesterday about Siena not wanting to take their father's kidney in case MJ should ever need it. He rubbed a hand across his chest. What would he do in Siena's place?

She reached across and briefly clasped his arm. It was all he could do not to lift it to his lips. 'Stop looking so serious. Polycystic kidney disease can't be cured, but it can be treated.'

A kidney transplant was pretty extreme treatment!

'And, like I said, it might never become an issue for me.'

Having something like this affecting her had probably given her a very different view of mortality—about what was worth clinging to and what was worth letting go.

Such as the feud.

And maybe she was right. For so long, he'd had such a rigid view of the antagonism that existed between their families. There were reasons—strong reasons—for bitterness on both sides. But, between them, could he and MJ begin to heal that breach and prevent it from impacting future generations?

If he had the Ananke necklace, it might be possible for him to reconcile his grandfather…

His fingers tightened on the wheel. If Christian truly loved Siena, *truly* loved her, nothing Nikos did or said would convince him to give her up. It would cause a rupture in their family unless Nikos found a way to reconcile his father and grandfather to the match.

But he needed to find his brother first before he raised any of that with the older generations. Christian and Siena could just be enjoying a harmless fling, a bit of fun that would eventually burn itself out. His lips thinned. Or it could just be Siena doing her best to estrange her father.

'And you don't know exactly how ill Siena is? Or if her kidneys are failing?'

A shadow passed over MJ's face and he wished he hadn't asked. She'd already told him she didn't know. 'All I can tell you is that the poor test results are an indication that something *might* be wrong, not that something *is* definitely wrong. She'll need further tests to know for sure. If something is wrong, though, she needs to start treatment ASAP.'

'Instead she's tripping the light fantastic with my brother and giving you and your father heart attacks.'

'My father doesn't know about Siena's recent test results.'

Hadn't MJ told him?

'And if they were living the high life we'd have found them by now. No, they've gone to ground. Siena can do a brilliant job of ignoring reality. I have visions of them living in some wonderfully rustic farmhouse in Tuscany or the south of France, far from everyone and everything. I just hope their phones aren't lying at the bottom of a lake or well, or smashed into a thousand pieces. My worst nightmare is Siena collapsing and Christian not having a clue why.'

Things inside Nikos clenched tight. He knew Christian had said he'd never forgive him if he hired a PI, but...

'Quid pro quo?' MJ asked, before he could develop that line of thought further.

He glanced across. For someone who'd hardly ever been on a yacht, she looked remarkably at home.

And she'd felt utterly at home in his arms.

He did what he could to squash that unwelcome thought. He needed to cut all memory of their kiss from his mind. Which was easier said than done. That brief kiss had rocked the foundations of his world.

Which was exactly why he had to block it from his mind now.

'You want to ask me something?' *Please God, don't let it be about the kiss.*

'What's the real reason you invited me along to visit your grandfather? And does he know I'm accompanying you?'

Ah. 'I haven't told him you're coming,' he said carefully. 'But he has a lot of…friends.'

He watched her mull that over. 'So someone from the marina has probably already reported in to him.'

Probably.

'That answers my second question, but what about the first?'

When he didn't answer immediately, she turned to stare out at the water. Evidently, if he didn't want to answer, she wasn't going to press him.

'Besides the fact that I enjoy your company?'

She swung back, eyes wide.

'And God help me…' his lips twisted '…but I do.'

She didn't laugh at him. Her eyes became warm and somehow gentle. 'And that's a bad thing? Because I'm a Mabel?'

He shrugged. 'That's how I once thought, but it's not how I feel now.'

A man could fall into those eyes.

He wrenched his gaze away. 'Obviously, I now realise you're not some scarlet woman out to destroy me, my family or my family's empire.' It seemed ludicrous to think he'd ever suspected such a thing.

She rubbed her hands together and sent him a teasing smile. 'Ooh, we're making progress.'

'I'd fallen into the habit of taking as gospel all that my father and grandfather had to say on the matter.' He scraped a hand across his jaw. 'They've fallen into the habit of believing the worst of your family and expecting the worst—and constantly bracing themselves against attack.'

But the Mabels hadn't made any such attack, and he could see now that they had no such intention. The death of MJ's mother had made them lose their appetite for such hostilities. And MJ didn't have revenge on her mind.

She wanted to mitigate and conciliate.

Because she doesn't know the truth.

A band squeezed his chest, making it hard to get air into his lungs. It was a truth better buried for everyone's sakes.

Better for whom?

He clenched his jaw. It wasn't his truth to tell.

'You're hoping that, in meeting me, your grandfather will get a different perspective on the situation?'

Her words came slowly, haltingly, and all he could do was shrug. 'I don't know if that's even possible.'

'You know what?' One corner of her generous mouth lifted. 'That sounds like a challenge I'm definitely up for.' With a smile, she rose. 'Would you like a drink?'

She headed below deck to get drinks. 'Hey, it's really cute down here!'

But when she started up the ladder again, she halted, her smile freezing on her face. She said an unladylike word that had him swinging round, and he nearly swore himself. He caught himself in time. He didn't want to alarm her. The sky in the east had darkened to every shade of charcoal, black and dark green on the colour chart, and on cue a wind whipped up into his face. If he'd been on his own he'd have tried to outrun it, but a glance at MJ and the way she gnawed on her bottom lip put paid to that idea.

'I love disaster movies.' She handed him a bottle of water, her voice wobbling the tiniest bit. 'But at moments like these I wish I hadn't watched quite so many of them.'

That made him laugh. 'We're not going to run into disaster, MJ, I promise.' He took a swig of water before screwing the lid back on. 'As you're still finding your sea legs, we'll sit this one out. I don't want to give you a nasty bout of seasickness.'

'For which I'm grateful, but...' She glanced at the clouds that were rapidly advancing. 'How does one *sit it out* on the open sea?'

He handed her back the bottle of water and reached beneath the seats for life jackets. He carefully placed one over her head and did up the ties. 'This is a precautionary measure only.' He pulled the other over his own head.

'Precautionary, huh?'

He curved his hands round her shoulders and squeezed lightly. 'Don't look so nervous. We're going to be fine. The weather was supposed to be coming from the south, not the east, so it's caught me on the hop.' He should have been paying more attention. 'See that island over there? We're going to anchor in its leeward side, which will protect us from the wind and let us ride out the storm in relative comfort.'

She followed the line of his finger. 'Can that little pile of rocks actually be called an island?'

He lifted his eyes heavenward. 'First a kiss isn't a kiss because it's too brief. And then an island isn't an island because from this distance it looks too small.'

Damn, he shouldn't have mentioned the kiss, but the consternation in MJ's eyes disappeared as her gaze lowered to his lips. Without thinking, he bent his head and captured her mouth in another blistering kiss.

Her mouth opened under his, not in surprise but in hunger. She tasted of honey and heat and felt like silk and springtime. Her fingers dug into his forearms and he nearly lost his mind then and there.

'Any dispute that was a real kiss?' he rasped out when he finally lifted his head, his breath sawing in and out of his lungs.

She touched her fingers to her lips, her eyes huge. 'None whatsoever.'

'So when I say that's an island…' The finger he pointed towards the island was far from steady.

'Then we'll agree it's an island.' Then she laughed, and he wanted to hear that sound again and again. 'What can I do to help?'

'I'll be quicker on my own but, if you want something to do, I can find a job for you.'

She glanced at the advancing storm front. 'Sometimes the wisest and most strategic move is to get out of the way and let the experts get on with it.'

Her words shouldn't have surprised him. He already knew she wasn't one of those people who needed to constantly prove themselves. And, although he knew she'd much rather keep busy, she refused to allow her fear to override her common sense.

'I'm guessing the best place to stay out of the way is…?' She pointed below deck and he nodded. 'And you'll shout if you need any help?'

'I promise. But, MJ, in half an hour we're going to be at anchor with the kettle on.'

Without another word she disappeared below deck and Nikos set sail for the little island, the wind whipping them along at a great rate of knots. He made minor adjustments here and there, trying to choose the easiest, least bumpy route, but the entire time that kiss burned in his mind.

Why the hell had he kissed her?

He shouldn't have kissed her. It'd been a stupid thing to do.

And yet he couldn't find it in himself to regret it, not in the slightest. That kiss hadn't felt stupid. It had felt like a promise.

CHAPTER EIGHT

TRUE TO HIS WORD, within half an hour Nikos steered them into a sheltered cove and the noise of the wind and the bumpy seas gave way to a strange silence and odd calm.

MJ peered out of a porthole and huffed out a laugh, but whether in genuine amusement or despair she didn't know. It was just that the outside conditions perfectly mirrored her emotional state—tempestuous and wild, but momentarily encased in a pocket of calm.

Nikos had kissed her. *Again*. And she'd barely been able to think straight since. Maybe that had been the point. Maybe it'd been a deliberate strategy to stop her from worrying about the storm outside by creating an even greater storm inside her.

Her solitary half-hour had given her a chance to lecture herself. Remind herself how foolhardy it would be for Nikos and her to act on the attraction flaring between them. Neither of them entered into sexual relationships lightly. If they threw caution to the wind and acted on impulse, feelings would become engaged.

And there was no room for her in Nikos's world. His loyalty to his family would always prevent it. Feelings *would* get hurt.

She gnawed on her bottom lip. Yet she sensed he'd started to consider the possibility of a ceasefire between their two families. For his own sake, or for Christian's?

Siena and Christian...

She pondered again Freddy's mention of the medical clinic. Maybe her sister wasn't being as reckless as she feared. Maybe Siena was seeking the treatment she needed.

If a truce could be brokered between the families—for Siena's and Christian's sakes—then maybe she and Nikos could become friends. Her breath hitched. If they could find their way to a friendship, maybe they could find a way to *more*.

How much more do you want?

Her heart started pounding. The air squeezed from her lungs, making her breathless.

She'd never met a man she'd wanted so *fiercely*. Sometimes she looked at him and all she could think about was making love with him. She had *important* things to think about. Siena's health, the Mabel-Constantinos feud, her father and Siena's relationship, Siena and Christian's relationship. And yet one glance at Nikos had all of that fading to nothing.

And when he stared at her with smouldering eyes that told her he felt the same...

She leaped up, fanning herself. She had to stop thinking about this. She and Nikos made no sense.

Why does it have to make sense?

If they started anything, it couldn't go anywhere.

Why does it have to go anywhere?

She was trying to form a friendship with the man, build trust.

Maybe it'll help.

'Oh, and now you really are scraping the bottom of the justification barrel.' Practically wrenching the door off its hinges, she stuck her head above deck. 'Time to put the kettle on?'

'You bet!'

She followed Nikos's voice and found him at the bow,

dark hair glistening with sea spray and eyes alive with energy and satisfaction. Her mouth dried. Had he ever looked more perfect?

She cleared her throat, not entirely sure it'd work. 'You enjoyed that, didn't you? Man wrestling the elements and all that.'

His grin did the craziest things to her pulse. 'Sprung. Sorry if the ride was a bit bumpy. I hope it wasn't too harrowing.'

'Nothing disaster movie-ish about it all.' She did what she could to keep the smile on her lips and the lust from her eyes. 'It was a little anticlimactic, if the truth be told. In the best possible way,' she added in double-quick time, in case he decided they ought to bounce all the way to his grandfather's island. She wanted to be at her best when she met Vasillis Constantinos, not look like a dishevelled mouse.

'You don't look the slightest bit green.' He studied her face so intently that even from this distance she had to swallow. 'I swear, MJ, you don't have a single hair out of place.'

Was that good or bad?

'You're obviously a natural sailor.'

The warmth that flooded her almost undid her. To hide the depth of feeling his words created, she pointed at the rain clouds. 'Looks like things are about to get wet. Is there anything I can do?'

'I'm nearly done.'

She disappeared back below deck. The galley kitchen and seating area were small but well-equipped. In no time at all she had tea brewing and had cut several slices of the fruitcake she'd found among the provisions, arranged them on a plate.

The moment he clattered down the steps, the tiny cabin shrank. He collapsed onto a seat, seized a piece of cake and devoured it in two bites, before draining half a mug of tea. Without a word she topped it up, glad she'd made a large pot.

He smiled his thanks and gestured back the way he'd come. 'It's hungry work.'

Evidently. She wrapped her fingers around her mug and tried not to stare. It was as if, out here on the sea with the wind in his hair and salt on his lips, some hidden part of him had come alive. She had to fight the urge to reach out and touch it…touch him.

He pulled out his phone. 'Let's see how long it'll take for the storm to pass.'

She watched him tap away with long, lean fingers and had a sudden vision of those fingers on her body—teasing, tantalising, exploring…giving her pleasure…

Jerking her gaze away, she seized a piece of cake and bit into it. A pointless exercise because no amount of cake could fill the ache yawning inside her.

'Looks like we could be here a while. See?'

He angled the phone towards her and she saw the storm front moving across the screen. She fingered the hem of her shirt. One leg started to jig. 'How long is a while?'

She was stranded on what suddenly felt like a tiny boat with the hottest man in the history of hot men and her hormones were acting out like a raging, seething, defiant teenager. As if that wasn't a recipe for disaster!

Lean lips pursed…

Don't think about the lips.

'It's still a good two-and-a-half hours to my grandfather's island, and it doesn't look like this storm will pass until eight o'clock.'

Eight o'clock tonight? She felt suddenly hot and then suddenly cold. Both legs started to bounce.

'There's a smaller front coming behind it too. It'll probably miss us, but…'

He trailed off. Outside, rain lashed the windows.

She forced a breath in through her nose and out through her mouth. She would *not* freak out about spending the night in a floating bathtub with Nikos. *She wouldn't*. She was an adult woman. *Be cool, MJ*. She needed to aim for unflappable. 'Looks like we're here for the night, then.' If her voice squeaked at the edges, well, who could blame it?

All the energy that had sparked him to life drained out of him. 'I'm really sorry, MJ. I should've planned all of this better.'

MJ topped up his mug with a shrug. 'You're hardly responsible for the weather, Nikos. You took the advice you were given at the marina. It sounds like this storm will have caught everyone on the hop.'

She pushed the plate holding the last piece of cake towards him and sipped her tea. Was she really as relaxed as she looked? Hadn't that kiss tied her up in knots?

He raked a hand back through his hair. He was strung tighter than a mainsail in a hurricane. Ever since he'd come below deck and found her so capably presiding over the teapot—with cake, no less—his awareness of her had grown until his entire body throbbed with it. He'd had to gulp down cake in an effort to regain a semblance of equilibrium. So far he'd only found the semblance, not the real thing.

Up on deck, when he'd been focussed on finding shelter and making sure MJ felt safe, he'd been able to push away the memory of the kiss, even as its aftermath burned in his body and lent him an energy both strange and invigorating.

Now, seated so close to her, heat and need pierced him. He couldn't look at her without wanting to haul her into his lap to kiss her again. To spend the next few hours...

Stop it!

He could do this. She didn't deserve to have him panting all over her, lusting after her. He *would* keep his wayward desires under wraps. Glancing up, he opened his mouth to say something—*anything*—but her gaze skittered away and the words, meaningless anyway, died in his throat.

Shuffling round the table, she stood and explored the small passage leading deeper into the hull. Two doors stood opposite each other and she peered into both. 'There are sleeping quarters.'

Separate sleeping quarters. 'We'll be snug as bugs,' he assured her, trying not to wince at his descent into cliché.

She hovered for a moment and then slid back into her seat, as if aware she had nowhere else to go. Outside thunder crashed and she jumped. Rain lashed the boat. Did she feel trapped? He clenched his hands beneath the table. 'We'll be fine, MJ. I swear, you're perfectly safe.' From the elements and from him.

For a moment he could have sworn disappointment flared in her eyes, but then she blinked and they turned opaque. 'I know. I trust you.'

No Mabel had ever had reason to trust a Constantinos, or vice versa. When they'd been enemies, he'd had a script to follow. Now that they weren't, he didn't know what the hell to do. This yacht might be safely anchored, but he felt cast adrift on a vast, unknown ocean.

Unknown oceans should be terrifying. Why, then, was he filling with energy, anticipation and a mystifying sense of adventure?

'So…'

Her voice, oddly strangled, snapped him back to reality.

'This is probably where I ought to confess that I can't cook.'

He shook himself. What did that matter?

'I mean, it's hardly a fair distribution of labour, is it? You found us shelter and yet I can't even make you a meal in return.'

He leaned towards her.

Dear God, don't draw too close.

He leaned back again. 'You don't cook at all?'

'I can…uh…toss a salad.'

'How do you survive?' She didn't live in the family home. She had her own apartment. She wouldn't have a housekeeper or cook.

Her chin lifted. 'If you work similar hours to me—and I suspect you do—then tell me, when do you find the time to cook?'

She had a point, but he sensed she was also deflecting the question. Some instinct warned him to tread carefully. He speared a leftover crumb of fruitcake and popped it in his mouth. 'I have a housekeeper. That's how I survive.'

His self-deprecation made her smile. 'There are several restaurants close to my flat who'll all make me a meal to go whenever I want. Fresh ingredients, beautifully cooked.'

'Win-win,' he agreed.

'But I don't outsource all my chores. I wash my own dishes and wipe the kitchen counters down. I even take out the rubbish.'

'So what you're saying is, if I cook, you'll clean?'

'That's *exactly* what I'm saying.'

He laughed. The jut of her chin made him to want to…

Jumping up, he slammed his knee against the top of the table. *Hell!* Rubbing it, he glanced around the kitchen, down the hallway and at his knee—anywhere but her. 'Which cabin do you want? The beds won't be made up, so I'll do them now rather than later when I won't feel like it.'

'My bag was put in that one.' She pointed to the left. 'And I'll make my own bed.'

'I don't mind.' He wanted to keep busy, keep his hands occupied with something mundane and innocuous. 'It can be tricky manoeuvring in such confined spaces, and I promise not to short-sheet your bed.'

'*I* mind.'

She didn't want him intruding on her space. Smart. It'd be wise to keep to their own dedicated areas and enforce no-go zones.

'I'm not some pampered princess you need to wait on hand and foot. If anything, *I* should be making *your* bed, as you steered us through the storm so ably.'

She smelled like every good thing a man could want—vanilla, a hint of salt and spiced rum. And she stared at him as though he was a hero. He wasn't a hero. He was a low-down, dirty creep who couldn't get thoughts of her naked body out of his mind.

'You're not making my bed, MJ.'

The words rasped out of him on a hoarse growl, and her eyes widened. She edged away. 'Okay, then. I'll just… um…go and make mine.'

She practically fled to her cabin. He stood in the middle of the galley, staring at the spot where she'd been, his hands clenching and unclenching. He *would* get a grip of himself. He would *not* lose control.

Striding into his designated cabin, he closed the door and leaned back against it. He was thirty-two years of age, for God's sake, not a horny teenager.

It took no time at all to make the bed, but he strung it out for as long as he could. Eventually, though, manners forced him to move. She was his guest. Glancing at the rain-slicked glass of the porthole, he shoved down a sigh. If only the damn rain would stop, they could sit out on deck, maybe even eat out there.

On deck, with all the sea before them and all the sky above them, they wouldn't feel so confined. He might be able to focus on something other than MJ's lips, or burying his face in her neck to inhale her scent, or imagining what she'd look like lying abandoned beneath him.

Don't think about that.

He shot out of his cabin. MJ shot from hers at the same

time, with much the same haste, and they crashed into each other. He grabbed her upper arms to stop her careening back and colliding with the wall.

'Sorry, I…'

She glanced up and her words stuttered to a halt. She moistened her lips and he could have groaned out loud when her gaze lowered to his mouth with a hunger that sent sparks firing through him.

'Why did you kiss me before—up on deck?'

He fought to draw air into cramped lungs. 'It seemed like a good idea at the time.'

'Did it? I wonder why?' Her brows drew together and she almost glared. 'I haven't been able to stop thinking about it.' Her hands slammed to her hips. 'You don't strike me as the kind of man who goes around kissing strange women on a whim.'

'I don't think you're strange, MJ.' She felt like a… Damn it, she felt like a friend, a kindred spirit! 'And it wasn't a whim. I haven't been able to get the thought of kissing you out of my head since…'

'Since my hotel room in Geneva.'

'Since the moment you walked into my office five days ago.'

Her throat bobbed and her eyes grew huge. 'It's madness.'

'Total,' he agreed.

'I'm not even sure you like me.'

The vulnerability shining in those eyes nearly gutted him. His hands slipped up to curve around her shoulders. 'You sure about that?'

'You're still afraid to trust me.'

It was true, but only sort of. 'Not because I don't trust you, MJ, but because I don't trust myself. I know what I owe my family.' And yet, staring into those green eyes that promised refuge, hope and a safe haven, all his reservations dissolved to nothing.

'So...' Her breath hitched. 'You're saying you think I'm a nice person and that...that maybe you like me.'

'That's exactly what I'm saying.' He gave a single hard nod. 'But I can't make you any promises, and you deserve more than that.' A woman like Marjorie Joan Mabel deserved the very best a man had to offer. She deserved *all* of a man's allegiance, not merely a fraction of it.

She reached up and touched his face. 'You say it as if it means nothing when it means everything.'

A loud crack of thunder sounded overhead and she gave a low laugh. 'I once likened our families to a Shakespearean play.'

She'd meant *Romeo and Juliet*, with its tragic, star-crossed lovers.

'But personally, I've always been more partial to *The Tempest.*'

And then she stood on tiptoe and kissed him.

MJ hadn't meant to kiss Nikos.

Correction. She hadn't *planned* to kiss him. But, when they'd barrelled into each other coming out of their rooms at exactly the same time... Well, it had felt a lot like fate.

It wasn't just that he set her pulse on fire. Though he did.

It wasn't just that she could see in his eyes that he wanted her every bit as much as she did him. Though she did.

And *that* was headier than vintage champagne.

It was because he held himself on too tight a leash— a leash called duty and responsibility. He didn't want his actions to cause pain to anyone—not to his family, and not to her.

Because he finally saw her. The real her.

It was frightening and exhilarating in equal measure. He'd had the courage to look past first impressions and their families' prejudice and history. While he initially might have wanted to believe her to be a treacherous Mabel, playing some deep game to gain an advantage, he'd ultimately judged her...justly.

Despite the volatility of their initial meeting, he'd treated her with courtesy. He hadn't mocked her fear of dogs or exploited it. He hadn't bad-mouthed her great-aunt or father to her face. He'd remained true to their deal. Nikos Constantinos was a man of honour and he made her feel cared for, protected and safe. He made her feel smart and beautiful. He made her feel cherished.

She wanted to make him forget duty and responsibility for a little while, to give him a holiday from it. And she also wanted to make him feel beautiful and cherished.

That was why she'd kissed him.

But the moment their lips met, all rational thought fled. Sensation flooded her as his lips opened to hers and he kissed her back with what felt like all of himself. All MJ could do was wrap her arms around his shoulders and hold on.

One large hand cradled her head and the other splayed across her hip. Tongues met in an erotic dance, teeth nipped playfully as he backed her against the wall behind and they moved against each other until it wasn't possible to get any closer while fully clothed.

Fierce need and heat pummelled her. She hooked a leg around his waist and he held it in place, his hand splayed across her buttock, fingers digging into her flesh with an urgency that made her tremble. He pressed against her more intimately exactly where she wanted.

She moaned his name, low and needy.

He stilled, resting his forehead on the wall beside her

head, but the quivering of his muscles told her how much discipline it took.

'MJ, if you want me to stop...'

Her answer was to reach down and open the door to her cabin and they fell inwards. Only his strength and balance stopped them from tumbling to the floor. Not that there was enough floor space for them to fall to. But the bed was plenty big enough for two.

'Don't you dare stop, Nikos. I want this. I want you.' And then she kissed him—with passion and urgency, unable to hide just how much she wanted him.

She didn't want to stop. She didn't want to think. All she wanted to do was feel.

A low growl rumbled from his throat, thrilling her every nerve ending. He took charge of the kiss, cradling her face, angling it and holding it still so she couldn't move. Then he laved every millimetre of her lips with attention until her fingernails dug into his arms and her body arched into his, silently begging for his attention.

Tearing the shirt from the hem of his trousers, she explored the smooth skin of his back and the bumps of his spine, before dancing her fingers down and around to his abdomen. He sucked in a breath that made something inside of her sing. With more eagerness than grace, she hauled his shirt over his head, and her breath caught as she stared at him. 'You're beautiful, Nikos.'

She reached for the waistband of his boxers, but he batted her fingers away, lifted the hem of her shirt and pulled it gently over her head. With a flick of his fingers, he released the catch on her bra and drew it down her arms.

His gaze darkened and he reached out to caress her breasts, his thumbs grazing her nipples. Her quick intake of breath sounded through the cabin and she arched into his touch, unashamedly wanton. With someone else she might have felt self-conscious, but Nikos gazed at her with such open approval she felt she could do no wrong—not here, not now, not in the privacy of this haven they'd created for themselves.

Her capri pants and knickers followed the rest of her clothing, but he again dodged her fingers as they reached for the waistband of his boxers. 'I'm keeping these on for the moment.'

'But—'

'I'm going to explore every inch of your body, MJ. I'm planning on giving you the most mind-blowing orgasm of your life, and I don't want to be distracted. But, once I've done that, *then* I'm going to get naked and do it all over again.'

Her breath jammed at his words. Her pulse went ballistic at the hunger flaring in his eyes. He laid her on the bed and tears pricked the backs of her eyes at his tenderness. And then he proceeded to show her exactly what he'd meant.

His hands and mouth moved over every inch of her, exploring, worshipping…making her gasp and arch into his touch as he built and fanned an inferno inside her. It burned, raged and demanded until she could no longer think, only feel. She urged, begged and pleaded for him to go faster, but he refused to rush. It was as if he was taking as much relish in her building pleasure as she was. She gave herself over to it until finally she found herself flung into a vortex of sensual delight greater than any she'd ever experienced. Sensation sparked along every nerve ending, the reverberations reaching every part of her body.

She floated back to earth to find herself cradled in Nikos's arms. When she'd caught her breath and could make her limbs work, she lifted up on one elbow to stare down at him. 'That was incredible.'

He laughed, gently pushing a strand of hair behind her

ear. 'If you keep looking at me like that, Marjorie, you're going to give me a swollen head.'

'You deserve a swollen head.'

But there was something more than his ego on her mind. Reaching down, she palmed him through his boxers. The hard length of him pulsed against her hand and he sucked in a breath. A tic started at the centre of her, and her body tightened again, hungry for him once more.

'Can we now dispense with the rest of your clothes?' She'd wanted to make her voice playful, but it came out breathless, impatient...needy.

'MJ?'

'I want to see you naked,' she whispered, meeting his gaze.

Without a word, he rose and shucked off the rest of his clothes. And then swore. 'I'll be right back. I...'

She held up a hand to stay him. She'd been in the process of rising to her knees to study him better, but she diverted to the bedside table and plucked a box of condoms from her handbag.

A slow grin spread across his face. 'You're my kind of woman, MJ. You know that?'

She didn't answer, except to pull him back down beside her to press kisses along his chest and explore his magnificent body as thoroughly as he had hers.

All too soon, though, he'd rolled her over, his clever fingers and mouth making her breathy and needy all over again. 'Please, Nikos, please,' she found herself begging.

Covering her body with his, he brushed her hair from her eyes. Her gaze found his and he joined their two bodies in a single fluid stroke.

She gasped at the spine-tingling pressure, at the sense of fullness and completeness...at the perfection. Neither of them moved or breathed for several long seconds.

Wonder that was no doubt echoed in her face spread

across his. And then they were moving in unison and it didn't feel as if they were merely touching each other's bodies, but something deeper and more important, more essential. Before she could work out what it was, sensation and pleasure fogged her mind and took her over completely. Their cries mingled as they found release and rapture together.

Nikos didn't know how long he lay there, stunned at the intensity of making love with MJ, relishing the afterglow and the feeling of her wrapped against his side. She didn't speak, but her fingers trailed an idle path across his chest, as did his on her back. He had a feeling she was as shocked and awed as him.

Making love with her had felt like making the world right when he hadn't realised it was wrong. It was as if something inside her counterbalanced something inside him. When their bodies had been joined, she'd felt essential to...

He frowned. To what? His happiness? His success? His life? It was too much too soon, and he had no idea how to temper any of it.

Or how to re-establish the boundaries they'd smashed when they'd given into temptation.

A weight bore down on him. Where on earth did he think this thing between them could lead?

'I'm getting the distinct impression you've started over-thinking things.'

Her soft admonishment shouldn't have surprised him. She was so attuned to him it should scare him. He turned his head to meet her gaze. 'I would hate you to regret what just happened.'

'I don't regret it.' Small white teeth worried her bottom lip. 'It was more intense than I expected.'

He nodded, went to say something and then hesitated.

'Go on,' she urged. 'What were you going to say?'

His lips settled into a grim line. 'I can't help feeling we're going to have to pay the piper for scaling such heights, MJ.'

She reached up and touched his face. 'Maybe we will. And maybe the price will be worth paying. Nikos, neither one of us knows what the future holds. But we won't have to pay up just yet. It's only late afternoon—we have the rest of the night and tomorrow morning before the world intrudes on us again. I vote we relish it while we can.'

How could any man resist this woman? He pressed a quick kiss to those eminently kissable lips. 'In which case, we need to keep our strength up. Hungry?'

Her smile filled his soul. 'Ravenous.'

CHAPTER NINE

Nikos made a simple meal of stir-fried vegetables and noo-
dles that they devoured. And then they made love again.
And, when they woke in the wee small hours, they turned
to each other and made love once more with a dreamy kind
of reverence that almost undid her. They fell asleep in
each other's arms and woke to a still, cloud-free morning.

On deck, sipping coffee in their tiny sheltered cove, it
felt as if they were the only people in the world.

Nikos sent her a smile that heated her from the inside
out. 'Ever been skinny-dipping?'

She choked on her coffee. 'It's daylight!'

He gave a lazy shrug. 'Who's to see us? We're all alone
out here, MJ. You, me and this perfect sea.'

Standing, he lifted his shirt over his head and tossed
it to the deck, his eyes sending her a sensual challenge as
he pushed his shorts down his hips. He stood in front of
her, completely naked and her mouth dried. Dear Lord,
the man was magnificent.

'Chicken?' he taunted with another devilish grin.

She'd have shot back a sassy retort, but he chose that
moment to turn and walk to the rear of the yacht, and the
words dried in her throat as she took in broad shoulders,
lean hips and taut buttocks. She leaned forward with a
frown. There were marks...

Heat scorched her cheeks. The marks on Nikos's buttocks had been made by her *fingernails*. In the throes of passion when he'd sent her hurtling over the edge…again and again; when she'd held him as close to her as she physically could.

She blinked when both his feet left the deck and he arced through the air, barely making a splash as he executed a perfect dive. She raced across to peer over the side and held her breath. His head broke the water a short way away. The grin he sent her as he shook water from his eyes was pure sin and playfulness. 'Come on in, the water's fine.'

She bit her lip. 'I've never skinny-dipped before.'

'Then you haven't lived.'

She glanced around. Not another boat was in sight. And a completely relaxed, grinning Nikos was impossible to resist. Shucking off her clothes, she jumped in the water and resurfaced with a gasp. 'It's freezing!'

In two strokes Nikos was in front of her and his arms slid about her waist. 'Maybe I can warm you up.' His teeth tugged gently on her ear, making her boneless. And then he dunked her.

She bobbed up a moment later, laughing. They swam and cavorted like children for a glorious half-hour before climbing back on board to dry each other off. Where, of course, they became distracted again, before finally indulging in a hearty breakfast.

They'd planned to set off for Vasillios's island immediately after they'd eaten, but Nikos saw her gazing at the tiny island and he nodded. 'It'd be fun to explore.'

The man could apparently read her mind now.

He shrugged, a roguish twinkle lighting his eyes. 'It wouldn't make much difference if we set off after lunch instead.' Sobering, he reached out to touch her cheek. 'I can't seem to get enough of you at the moment, Marjorie. I want to hold on to this moment for as long as I can.'

Her heart thundered when he pulled her in for a kiss. She felt exactly the same. Taking a moment to catch her breath, she gestured to the island. 'Will we swim to it?' No matter what Nikos said, she wasn't walking around that island naked.

He laughed as if he'd read that thought in her face. 'We'll use the dingy and row across. We'll need our shoes.'

His powerful arms and shoulders made short work of the journey. Hand in hand, they explored the pebbly beach and then trekked up the rocky rise. She hesitated before they could crest it.

He sent her one of those grins that could turn her insides to warm marshmallow. 'Worried we might bump into someone?'

'Of course not.' The island was deserted except for seabirds and the occasional small lizard. It was just...once they crested the hill, they'd see the rest of the world again, and it would start to intrude. Everything inside her protested at the thought.

She turned away with a frown, pretending to admire the view of the beach below and the yacht at anchor. Her heart protested it far too vehemently, and that couldn't be good. They hadn't planned this to happen, and they'd not made any promises.

It'd be crazy for either one of them to invest too much in what had happened here in this gorgeous place, and yet it felt crazy not to. She had no notion of what the rules were for such a situation, though. They were going to have to make them up as they went along, which was going to be interesting, when she suspected he was as befuddled by all this as she was.

Damn it. That kind of 'go with the flow' attitude was more Siena's province than hers. She liked forward planning and knowing what to expect.

What to expect?

A hollow laugh sounded through her and her heart dropped to the soles of her feet. What on earth was she thinking? This thing between her and Nikos…it was fleeting. It was always going to be fleeting.

Still, did it have to be *this* fleeting?

'MJ?'

She turned back and made herself smile, reached up and took the hand he offered. 'Just catching my breath.' She gestured back the way they'd come. 'It's beautiful here.'

Another half a dozen steps brought them to a meadow of golden grass dotted all over with blue and white wildflowers. She laughed when she realised the meadow was ringed on three sides by a rock cliff. They were still cocooned in their own little world and it felt like an omen. A good omen.

Rosemary scented the air and, with the sun warm on her arms, MJ felt as if they'd stumbled on Eden. She squeezed his hand. 'What a perfect place for a picnic.'

'What a perfect place to pitch a tent.'

'On a clear night the stars must be amazing here.'

They strolled around the perimeter, found a small spring to drink from and then sat on a large, flat rock, MJ seated between Nikos's thighs and resting back against his chest, his arms circling her shoulders. 'What an utterly idyllic morning,' she murmured. 'I've never been more grateful for a storm in my life.'

He pressed a kiss to her temple. 'I'll second that.'

Questions bombarded her. Would they ever make love again once they left this place? How did Nikos want them to act around his grandfather? Did he want to keep what had happened here a secret? When all this was over, would he want to see her again? She didn't ask a single one, refusing to break the spell. There'd be time enough to ask them once they'd set sail.

Not that she had any intention of asking that last question. He'd make it clear if he wanted to see her again.

A sigh whispered from her. 'I guess there aren't any more storms forecast for this afternoon?'

His arms tightened about her fractionally. 'Afraid not.'

Had he checked?

Of course he'd checked. As their skipper, it was his job to know the weather forecast. It'd be foolish to read too much into it.

They sat there for as long as they could, silently soaking each other in—at least, that was what it felt like. As if they needed it to shore themselves up for what was to come. Eventually, by mutual consent, they silently rose and made their way back down to the beach, holding hands when they could.

While Nikos busied himself readying the dingy, MJ bent down to collect a pink-hued pebble washed smooth by the tide. She slipped it into the pocket of her shorts. A memento. A talisman. Her fingers closed around it—a good luck charm.

For lunch they ate a salad of tomato, cucumber, red onion, olives and feta cheese in a delicious dressing that Nikos made. She wiped her bowl clean with pitta bread, shaking her head when he offered her more. 'That was delicious. Compliments to the chef. You're an excellent cook, Nikos.'

Her words made him chuckle. 'I threw together a salad, MJ, not a three-course meal.'

'You made that dressing—which was exquisite, I might add.'

He set his plate aside and eyed her over the rim of his glass of sparkling water. 'Why do I get the impression there's more to your "no cooking" story than you're letting on?'

The question was asked gently and she knew that if she

brushed it away he'd let the matter drop. But they'd shared so much, and it felt right to tell him something she'd never revealed to another soul. 'It's a bit silly,' she said, biting the inside of her cheek.

'I doubt that.'

His gaze never left hers but she found she couldn't look at him as she told the story. She stared down at her feet instead, fiddling with the laces on her tennis shoes. 'When I was nine, I developed a real bee in my bonnet about learning how to cook. Siena's thing at that time was painting. My mother arranged for Siena to attend art classes two afternoons a week and promised me that, on those afternoons, she'd teach me how to cook.'

'What happened?' he asked when she halted.

The gentleness in his voice had tears prickling the backs of her eyes. Because, yes, something had obviously gone wrong or she'd have been quite happy and capable of whipping up a meal for ten.

'We had three lessons, and I can't tell you how much I loved them.' And then had come that angry phone call that had had her mother slamming down the phone and directing Alice, their housekeeper, to finish the lesson.

'And?'

'My mother was called away before our cake had finished cooking. I never saw her alive again.'

His quick intake of breath speared into the centre of her. 'Oh, sweetheart.' He reached out and gripped her hands, and his endearment gave her the courage to lift her head. 'You don't cook because it reminds you of your mother and makes you miss her more.'

His understanding shouldn't have surprised her. 'I told you it was silly. She wouldn't want me to not cook because of her, but whenever I've tried I just… I get sad.'

His eyes darkened and the corners of his mouth turned down. 'I'm sorry you lost your mother, MJ.'

'It's not your fault she's gone, Nikos.' It was the fault of that angry voice on the phone. 'It's crazy, isn't it? She's been gone for nearly twenty years and yet I still miss her every single day.'

The moment the words left her mouth, the jangling of ropes and snapping of sails off to their right had them swinging to stare as a large yacht journeyed past, so close she could make out the people on board.

They waved. She and Nikos waved back, and watched silently as it rounded the far end of the island and disappeared from view. But the image of it remained like an aftershock.

She glanced back at Nikos and winced at the lines bracketing his mouth. 'And so the real world finally intrudes,' she murmured, her heart sinking.

'Yes.'

The single word was blunt, uncompromising, and answered more of her earlier questions than she wanted it to. Her chest grew heavy, and for some ridiculous reason her eyes started to burn. 'I'm guessing that what's happened here isn't something you want to share with your grandfather.'

He hesitated.

'Don't worry, Nikos. I understand.' She'd be his dirty little secret.

He swore. 'I'm starting to think this wasn't a good idea.'

Her head rocked back, but before she could form a lucid response he said, 'I'm not talking about what's happened here over the last twenty-four hours!'

The sharpness of his tone reassured her. She searched his face then let out a slow breath. 'Good.' Because as far as she was concerned the last twenty-four hours hadn't just been a revelation, they'd been a gift she'd treasure forever.

'I'm talking about taking you to my grandfather's island. My grandfather...'

She watched him struggle to find the words to describe Vasillios without making him sound like an ogre. She took pity on him. 'Your grandfather hates anyone with the same surname as mine.'

He neither confirmed nor denied it, but he didn't have to. 'I don't want his attitude to hurt you.'

'I don't want his attitude to hurt you either.' Her words made him blink and she shrugged. 'It'll take too much time to return me to the mainland now. Besides, I feel we're set on this path, don't you? It feels too late to turn back.'

He raked a hand through his hair, indecision rife in his eyes.

She reached out and touched his arm. 'I didn't ask you to shield me from anything, Nikos. I'm a big girl and I can look after myself. I'll hold my own against your grandfather—you'll see.'

She gestured to their yacht. 'Come on. Haul anchor or cast off, or whatever the lingo is, while I go and clean up the lunch things.'

Three hours later, on a spectacularly beautiful Greek island, MJ and Nikos entered Vasillios's beautiful but remote villa. She glanced around the interior, taking in the general splendour. While Vasillios might have shut himself away from the world, he'd not forgone his creature comforts.

She turned to Nikos. 'So your grandfather is a modern day Mr Havisham, sitting around in the last suit he ever wore when courting my great-aunt and nursing his heartbreak and bitterness?'

'Not quite,' a wry voice said from the staircase behind her.

She closed her eyes and grimaced before turning round. 'Mr Constantinos Senior, I presume? You weren't supposed to hear that.'

He moved to stand in front of her, but didn't proffer his hand. 'And you're one of the Ms Mabels.'

'Marjorie Joan, otherwise known as MJ.' She held her breath. She wanted this man to like her and the realisation shocked her. Did she want that because of her great-aunt or because of Nikos?

'You look like her,' he finally said.

'So few people see the resemblance.'

'You have the same mouth.'

Her lips twitched. 'Are you referring to its shape or what comes out of it?'

Dark eyes twinkled briefly. 'I'm a gentleman. Of course I meant the shape.'

His words made her laugh. 'I knew I'd like you. Even though your stupidity, stiff-necked pride and pig-headed stubbornness broke my great-aunt's heart…not to mention your own.'

Vasillios's head reared back. Nikos gaped at her. 'You can't talk to my grandfather like that!'

She shot him an apologetic grimace. 'Ordinarily, I'd agree with you. As a rule, I think the older generation should be treated with respect. But that doesn't give them a free pass.' She wrinkled her nose. 'If it makes you feel any better, I accused my great-aunt of exactly the same things. The pair of them were both utter idiots.'

Nikos stared, as MJ strode across to the backpack she'd refused to hand over to his grandfather's staff, and pinched the bridge of his nose. Bringing her here had been a *bad* idea.

'What is the meaning of this, Nikos?' Any amusement his grandfather might have harboured had disappeared. 'Why would you bring a Mabel—' he spat the name out as if it tasted bad in his mouth '—here to my island, my haven…my refuge?'

MJ came back, a package clasped in her hands, and Nikos could have groaned out loud at the way her lips twitched. 'You live in splendour here, sir, so I refuse to feel sorry for you.'

She was a force of nature and he had no idea how to stop her.

'Your grandson had no choice because I blackmailed him.'

His grandfather's face darkened. Nikos didn't know whether to laugh or cry, whether to try and wrest control of the situation or to let things run their course.

'But you're going to need to offer us refreshments before we embark on that particular story. In the meantime, I have something for you. If you have the courage to read it.'

She held up the parcel and his grandfather's eyes flashed. 'I am no coward.'

The laugh she gave made Nikos wince. 'Excuse me for contradicting you, but rather than trying to win back the woman you supposedly loved you focused instead on trying to win back a trinket you'd given her.' She shook her head. 'That doesn't sound like the actions of a brave man to me.'

'The Ananke necklace is no mere trinket!' his grandfather roared. 'It's an heirloom worth millions!'

Her quick intake of breath and the small step she took away from Vasillios made Nikos ache. A burn started up in his chest.

'Did the necklace matter more to you than my great-aunt's heart?' she whispered.

She held the parcel to her chest and stroked a hand over it, as if to give it—or herself—comfort. The expression on her face—a mix of sadness, vulnerability and loneliness—had Nikos wanting to drag her into his arms and give her whatever comfort he could.

Just as he'd wanted to when she'd spoken of her mother

earlier. He bit back an expletive. This was why he needed
to stay the hell away from her, and why he should never,
never have let things between them become so explosively
intimate! If MJ found out the truth, she'd hold his family
responsible for the death of her mother.

His heart clenched. What was more, he wouldn't blame
her.

'I spent a lot of time with my great-aunt in her final
months. She knew she was dying and had time to prepare.
We often talked about you and the Ananke necklace, Mr
Constantinos. You accused her of cheating on you, but she
never did. She remained true to you until the day she died.
She left both the necklace and this diary to me—to do with
as I thought best. She knew I had hopes that fences could
be mended between our two families.'

Nikos's heart beat harder. He wanted to mend those
fences too. Between them, could he and MJ make that
happen?

'I think you ought to read her diary—to see for yourself
and understand the heart of the woman you spent most of
your adult life battling.'

The older man pointed a shaking finger. 'If what you
say is true, why did she never tell me this herself?'

'You got married.'

Vasillios abruptly turned and strode to the window.

'She thought you'd forgotten about her, that she'd read
more into your love affair than she should have. Of course,
your marriage ended badly, and you blamed her for it. But
she merely considered herself a convenient scapegoat so
you could cast yourself in the role of tragic hero and exile
yourself from the world.'

Vasillios swung round, his face darkening. 'You know
nothing of these events!'

Her face softened, as if she empathised with the older
man, and Nikos had to brace his hands on his knees. MJ

was caught up in events she didn't fully understand, events that had the ability not only to hurt her but to crush her.

He struggled to get air into suddenly cramped lungs. He had to prevent that from happening.

'I know. I'm merely narrating how my great-aunt interpreted events. Unfortunately, she had her pride too, of which you're undoubtedly well aware. She was every bit as stubborn as you. Why on earth should she be the one to make the first move…blah-blah-blah?' She shook her head. 'But, as I told her often enough, stubborn pride won't keep you warm at night.'

The heightened colour faded from the older man's face. He gestured at the package MJ held. 'You want to give the diary to me? You want me to read it?'

'Yes.'

'Why?'

'Because she loved you. And I think you loved her. Reading her diary will prove that to you and I think it will bring you peace. And, Mr Constantinos, that's all I want for our two families—peace.'

His grandfather's eyes flashed. 'There will be no peace until the Ananke necklace is once again in the hands of the Constantinos family. I notice you do not offer *that* to me.'

'With the greatest respect, sir, my generation may have very different thoughts on the matter.'

'What do you plan to do with it?'

She glanced at Nikos briefly and everything inside him drew tight. 'It's a valuable art deco necklace designed by a celebrated artist who died before his time, which makes it rare. I think the best place for it is the Victoria and Albert Museum.'

'Over my dead body!' Vasillios roared.

She gave an involuntary laugh and Nikos knew she was thinking of that moment in his office when he'd said those exact same words to her.

'You mock me?' he roared, his white hair vibrating with outrage.

'No, I don't, but you're impossible.' She said it as if speaking to a recalcitrant child, and he had a feeling she did so deliberately to enrage the older man further.

'You should not have come here, Ms Mabel. You know our history. What if you were to meet with…an accident?'

Before Nikos could intervene, she laughed again. 'You and your grandson have much in common, but I'm not afraid of either of you. You can both be fiery and passionate, and no doubt cold and calculating too…and, yes, you both hate my family.'

Her words rang in Nikos's ears and shame pooled in his gut. He wanted to fall down into the nearest chair and cover his eyes, avert his gaze…try to un-hear her words.

'But neither of you would ever physically harm a woman. And, if you did actually manage to frighten me, the shame of it would burn in your soul far longer than my fear would last.'

The older man's eyes dropped. He took a step away before glancing at Nikos. 'See that Ms Mabel is shown to one of the guest rooms and then join me in the library.' Without another word, he turned and strode away.

MJ watched him go. Blowing out a breath, she turned to Nikos with a shrug. 'I think he likes me.'

Her deadpan delivery had him fighting an entirely inappropriate laugh. 'You didn't think to clue me in about—' he gestured to her and then to where his grandfather had been standing '—that?'

'That had nothing to do with you, Nikos. Or me. It had everything to do with him and her.'

'You didn't tell me because you don't trust me.' The words left a bad taste on his tongue.

She took a step closer and stared up into his face, those green eyes intent. 'Should I trust you?'

He wanted to roar that of course she could trust him. But he couldn't. Not when he was keeping from her a vital piece of the puzzle surrounding their families

You're not keeping it out of spite or to hurt her.

And yet it still left him feeling as if he had a stain on his soul.

'Are you going to tell him about the deal we made?'

Her question made him blink. 'That if I help you find Siena you'll give me the Ananke necklace?' He rolled his shoulders. 'He's my grandfather, MJ. All his life he's loved and cared for me. He saved my mother's life once. I'm not going to keep secrets from him.'

She touched a finger to her lips in a pose of exaggerated deep thought. 'So does that mean you're also planning to tell him what happened last night when we were stranded by the storm?'

Hell, no!

She laughed softly. 'So you pick and choose your secrets, then?'

He had no response for that because it was exactly what he was doing. Without another word he led her upstairs to the best of the guest rooms.

She barely glanced around. 'How long do you think we'll be here?'

'Only overnight.' He suspected the less time she and his grandfather spent together, the better. He turned to leave, halted and turned back. 'While we're here, MJ...' *Damn it. The words shouldn't be so hard to get out.* 'I mean tonight...'

She glanced up, waited for him to continue and then nodded, as if realising what he was trying to say. 'You won't be visiting my room and you'd prefer it if I didn't make any midnight forays to yours.'

A light in the back of her eyes went out, and he felt like an utter heel. But she straightened, both hands clasped at her waist. 'Nikos, let me make this easy on the both of us. What happened last night and this morning was lovely, and to be cherished. But we both know it was a moment out of time.'

Was she calling a halt to this thing between them?

Everything inside him roared a protest.

'It can't happen again, unless...'

He found himself leaning towards her. 'Unless what?'

She met his gaze squarely. 'Unless we're both prepared to take the next step.'

His mouth dried. He wanted to. He wanted to take that next step with an intensity that made his hands tremble. But she knew how things stood between their families. How could they ever make things work?

He pressed thumbs and forefingers to his eyes. How could he contemplate hurting his father and grandfather like that?

He pulled his hands away, darkness gathering beneath his breastbone. Even if they could overcome his father's and his grandfather's objections, and her father's... Even if by some miracle they could reconcile them to it...

His heart started to thud. He'd need to tell her what had happened between their parents. Nobody but his father and him knew the full story. And Nikos had promised never to tell.

He would have to break his word. Or ask his father to release him from that promise.

His heart thumped harder. There might be a way...

'MJ, I know that in an ideal world you want the necklace donated to a museum, but just think for a moment. If having the necklace would bring my grandfather peace and end our families' hostilities, then isn't that a great outcome? After all, that's the goal you're really after.'

'But it *wouldn't* end it, would it? Your father and grandfather would be happy, but my father wouldn't.'

It was true… 'You and I don't have to buy into any of that nonsense, though.'

'Until a week ago you *had* been buying into that nonsense. And now you want me to believe that you don't?'

'I can't believe I'm saying this.' He reached out and took both of her hands, gripping them tightly. 'You've forced me to see things differently, and I like your way of seeing things. I…' he hesitated over the word but held her gaze nonetheless. '*Love* what you're trying to achieve.'

Her mouth fell open.

It was almost a declaration—he was aware of that. But she was so fearless and he suddenly wanted to be brave too. Brave for her. 'We might not be able to achieve the ultimate ideal outcome, but we can temper the situation, improve it. Isn't that enough? Especially if it also means Christian and Siena can be together?'

She pulled her hands from his and raked them back through her hair.

'I don't want to say goodbye to you, MJ. I want to explore what we have. I think it's special.'

'I want that too.'

'With the necklace, I can reconcile my family to all of those things.'

But she didn't throw herself into his arms. Instead her eyes filled. 'The only way to end our families' feud is to get rid of the thing that's been at the heart of all the trouble—the Ananke necklace. As long as it lies between us, there won't be peace, Nikos. There'll always be the perception that one family or the other has the upper hand. It'll continue to breed hate and resentment, no matter how hard we try to mediate that.'

'But—'

'I will *not* bequeath that legacy to my children.'

A burn started up at the centre of him.

'People who value things higher than people will never find happiness, and they won't find peace. I want nothing to do with the necklace, Nikos. It's a curse, and I refuse to have it as part of my life.'

CHAPTER TEN

MJ SHOWERED. SHE felt dirty, tainted, but it wasn't the kind of taint that hot water and soap could wash away.

She'd hurt Nikos.

She hadn't meant to, but it didn't change the fact that she had. It didn't mean she wasn't breaking her own heart as well. Covering her face with her hands, she forced herself to breathe through the weight settling on her chest.

Stop moping. She needed to move, needed to try and dispel some of the agitation that had her in its grip.

Slipping down the stairs, she let herself out of the back door and deliberately strode away from Vasillios's mansion. She didn't want to run into the older man again. Not while he was in a temper. And she had no appetite for accidentally overhearing a conversation between he and his grandson.

Her hands clenched. She could imagine the older man's *triumph* when Nikos told him about the deal she'd made with him. Vasillios had broken her great-aunt's heart. Why should he get everything he wanted now?

Planting herself on a boulder, she glared at the spectacular view of blue sea filtered through the grey-green leaves of olive trees that marched down the slope to a rocky headland. After a moment, she huffed out a laugh. Closing her eyes, she focused on her breathing, on draining the negative emotions from her mind.

One thing the older generations had unwittingly taught her was that, in holding on to such negative emotions, the only person she'd truly hurt would be herself. She might have no say in what was done with the Ananake necklace once she gave it to Nikos—*if* he found Siena—but she could at least break that cycle of bitterness in her own life.

Eventually she started to breathe more easily. Vasillios hadn't got everything he wanted—he'd lost the love of his life through his own actions. And Aunt Joan hadn't been blameless either. She could have ended Vasillios's animosity at any point. They'd both chosen their pride over declaring their real feelings.

Aren't you in danger of doing the same?

She rubbed a hand across her chest, but couldn't shift the ache beneath her breastbone. She concentrated on getting one good breath into cramped lungs and then very slowly shook her head.

Nikos might be able to reconcile his father and grandfather to Christian's and Siena's relationship if the Ananke necklace was once again in the Constantinos fold, but he'd never gain her father's acceptance of the situation. Not on those terms. Which meant her greatest fear would be realised—her father and Siena would become estranged—and the thought broke her heart.

Even if by some miracle an uneasy truce was brokered, the peace between the two families would always be fragile. For as long as the Ananke necklace remained in one or the other's possession, fighting could break out again at a moment's notice. She dropped her head to her hands. She wanted no part of that.

Not even for the man you love?

Very slowly her head came up. She stared at the horizon. In her peripheral vision she saw birds twitching in the trees, fluttering from branch to branch, but inside her everything had stilled. She *loved* Nikos.

Of course she did. It made perfect sense. After their initial rocky start, they'd worked together as a team. He'd kept his word and hadn't tried to shake her off or lose her. For heaven's sake, he'd even brought her here to his grandfather's island. Nikos was honourable to the core. And reasonable—he'd listened to her side of things and had seen the justice of what she wanted to achieve, even as he remained sceptical that she could pull it off.

He hadn't tried to take advantage of her fear of dogs—he hadn't belittled her or made her feel less. Instead he'd been kind and understanding, and had done everything to help her feel safe and secure. *Of course* she loved him.

She glanced skywards, kinking an eyebrow. 'And I'm in Greece, so of course the gods are laughing at me.'

I want to explore what we have.

Nikos's earlier words played through her mind and her eyes filled. So did she. But for that to happen would mean him choosing her over the necklace. *That* was a contest she had no hope of winning.

Footsteps sounded in the undergrowth and she hastily dashed the tears away before swinging round. Nikos strode towards her, his eyes turbulent and his mouth set in a hard, straight line. Her heart thundered and she had to wrap her arms around her knees to stop from leaping to her feet and throwing herself at him.

'I saw you walk this way from the library window.' He gestured at the boulder. 'May I?'

She shuffled over and he thumped down beside her. It was clear things hadn't gone well with his grandfather. Not that she could ask him about it.

Citrus and sandalwood filled her senses. She breathed it in and held it close for a moment, before breathing out again. 'I'm sorry I was so hard on your grandfather, Nikos. I should've been gentler, kinder.'

'He should've been more reasonable. But when it comes

to the past and your great-aunt he has no reason or rationality.' He placed the diary in her lap. 'He refuses to read it—said it'd be full of lies—and told me to give it back to you.'

She ran a hand over the cover. 'Well…at least I tried.'

'I shouldn't have brought you here. I'm sorry. I'd hoped that meeting you would soften him, give him a different view of things, but I miscalculated the strength of…'

She aimed for levity. 'My charm?'

His lips twitched but settled back into a straight line a moment later. 'His stubbornness.'

'He's had fifty years to brood on his sense of injury. That sort of thing can't be overcome overnight.' She stared at the diary. 'I'm sorry he won't read this, though. I thought it might bring him peace, but…'

'But?'

The way he stared at her made her feel like a goddess. She dragged her gaze back to the horizon and tried to control the racing of her pulse. 'Can you imagine how confronting it would be to discover that what you'd thought was true—and was the reason for all of your life's decisions—had been a lie?'

'The regret would kill him, not bring him peace.'

She opened the diary to the final pages and read aloud.

"'Vasilli, if you ever read this, I want you to know that I loved you to the end of my days. Not a single day passes that I don't think of you, that I don't wish you were here by my side. Not a single day passes that I don't wish I'd answered you differently when you accused me of being unfaithful to you all those years ago.

"'But how could I have been unfaithful when I never saw any man except you? I thought you knew that. In my pride and my hurt, I thought you should've known that. I wanted you to fight for me. When you didn't, I thought you no longer cared. And then you married so soon after…

"'I kept the necklace so you wouldn't forget me.

I couldn't bear the thought of you giving it to another woman. If I'm honest, I thought you would come after me, and that once we were face-to-face again we would be able to patch things up. By the time I realised that was never going to happen, too much time had passed and it felt as if our fates were sealed. We should've fought harder for one another, my love. We were a pair of fools. But I want you to know that in my dreams I have danced with you every night for the last fifty years.

"'Adieu, my dear Vasilli, from your ever devoted Joanie.'"

Nikos dragged a hand down his face and swore softly.

She closed the diary. 'The regrets would be great, but wouldn't those words gladden his heart?'

'Only if he had the courage to believe them.'

That was true. She forced herself to straighten and shake off the sadness settling over her.

'Can I read it?'

She blinked when Nikos gestured to the diary, but she passed it to him without a word. He'd treat her great-aunt's words with respect. Besides, as both she and Siena had read it, it only seemed fair that Nikos and Christian should have the opportunity too.

Pulling in a breath, she tried to smile. 'Your grandfather must've been happy, though, when you told him you might be able to win back the Ananke necklace.'

A tic started at the base of his jaw. 'I didn't tell him.'

What? If he hadn't told his grandfather about the necklace… Her heart thudded so hard she could barely think over the pounding. Did that mean that maybe she did have a chance? That maybe Nikos would choose her over the necklace?

Or was that just wishful thinking?

'I didn't exactly get the chance to tell him. He demanded an explanation for why you and I were travelling together, and when he found out that Christian and Siena might already be engaged...' He grimaced.

It was clear the two men had exchanged words, but Nikos could've calmed his grandfather down with that single revelation—that he was in the process of winning back the Ananke necklace. Yet he'd chosen not to.

She shouldn't read too much into it, but her foolish heart leapt with hope anyway. She fought to keep the expression on her face even. 'Did you want to head back to the mainland this afternoon?'

'We wouldn't make it before nightfall. We'll leave in the morning as planned.'

MJ was already at the jetty the following morning when Nikos strode down from the house. She took in his long-legged, lean-hipped stride and had to look away, her hunger for him taking her off-guard. They'd eaten together last night, but his grandfather hadn't shown his face again. They'd spent an oddly restful evening in the living room, Nikos working and MJ reading.

This morning, a maid had brought a breakfast tray to her room with a note from Nikos saying he wanted to leave within the hour.

'My grandfather did some digging,' he said without preamble. 'Christian and Siena are in London.'

'London?'

'Apparently they never left.'

He handed her a scrap of paper. Scrawled across it was the name of a London medical clinic. MJ fought a sudden desire to laugh. Siena had been seeking treatment at home all this time. She pressed the slip of paper to her chest. 'How soon...?'

'We should be in Athens by ten, and we've a one o'clock flight from there to London.'

'Perfect!' It took everything she had not to throw her arms around his neck. 'And, Nikos?'

He swung back from where he'd jumped on deck, his hair ruffling in the gentle breeze. 'Yes?'

'Thank you.'

He held out his hand to help her on board. 'Any time, MJ. Any time.'

And she knew he meant it.

MJ pulled to a halt outside Siena's room and ran a hand down the front of her shirt.

'What's wrong?' Nikos asked, instantly alert.

He'd been watching her carefully since they'd left Athens, and his concern warmed her all the way through.

'Don't you want to go in?'

'I need to go in. I have to assure myself she's okay. It's just…' She bit back a sigh. 'I'm starting to wonder if I should've left it all well enough alone and trusted her.' She had no idea how her sister was going to react to seeing her so unexpectedly, and the thought made her stomach churn. Standing out there delaying the moment wouldn't help matters, though.

'I have your back, MJ. You know that, don't you?'

She did. And it helped. Pulling in a breath, she sent him a smile and forced back her shoulders. 'Here goes.'

Not giving herself a chance to think any further, she knocked on the door and then strode into the room. Siena reclined in a hospital bed, pillows piled up at her back. There was colour in her cheeks and a sparkle in her eyes. She wasn't hooked up to a multitude of machines or with a variety of tubes protruding from her arms as MJ had feared. The relief nearly knocked her off her feet.

Siena's face lit up. 'Jojo!'

MJ raced over and hugged her. Gently at first, but then with the same fierceness that Siena did her. Eventually she eased back and held her sister at arm's length, scanning her from head to toe. 'You're okay?'

'As good as new, I promise. One of Christian's best friends is a doctor here and he agreed to see me as a favour. They did some super-minor surgery and my results are great. I'll be released in a day or two. I probably could've gone home a couple of days ago, but…'

She broke off, reddening.

'But you were hiding out.'

'We just wanted a little peace…some calm before all hell broke loose.' Siena squeezed her hand, her eyes pleading. 'You can understand that, can't you?' She held up her left hand. An engagement ring sparkled on her finger. 'And hell *is* going to break loose.'

'I'm very happy for you both. Congratulations.' She fought the lump in her throat to squeeze Siena's hand and smile at Christian, who'd been sitting in the chair beside Siena's bed, but had risen at her entrance.

Siena's smile faltered. 'Jojo?'

'I'm happy for you, Sisi, but couldn't you have sent me just one text to tell me you were well and getting the treatment you needed? You had to know how worried I'd be.'

'I was afraid if I did that you'd search all the hospitals in London. And I wasn't ready to share our news with anyone.'

'How could you have been so inconsiderate?' Nikos burst out from behind her. 'MJ nearly made herself sick worrying about you. She thought you were in serious danger!'

Siena's eyes widened. 'From Christian?'

'From your health!' he roared. 'She thought you might be dying!'

Oh, whoa. *Wow.* Before MJ could try and calm him, Christian bristled. 'You can shut it right now, Nik. You don't get to speak to my fiancée that way, you hear me?

Siena's had surgery and she needs to rest. The last thing she needs is anyone upsetting her.'

With a muffled oath, Nikos swung away and stalked across to the other side of the room to stare out of the window.

'I'm sorry, Jojo,' Siena whispered. 'I thought when Freddy told you I was in a clinic in Switzerland that it would set your mind at rest.'

To be fair, it had eased it. But it hadn't dispelled her fears completely.

'And I'm so glad you're here now.' Siena gripped her hand. 'We need your help. Neither of our families is going to approve of the match—everyone is going to be against us marrying—and no one smoothes ruffled feathers like you. And—'

'No.' MJ stood from where she'd been sitting on the side of the bed and tugged her hand from Siena's. 'If you love Christian, you fight for him. You'll always have my support. You're my sister and I love you. But this is your fight—yours and Christian's.'

Siena's mouth dropped open. 'Is this because you're angry with me?'

The accusation made MJ blink, but then she nodded. 'I guess I am angry with you. You hurt me more than you know.'

Siena's gaze dropped. 'I'm sorry. I—'

'But I'll get over it, and that isn't what this is about anyway. You said I always come to your rescue, and it's true. I do. I'm sorry, but you don't get to pick and choose when to stand on your own two feet and then abdicate responsibility back to me when it all feels too hard. That's not how being a fully functioning adult works.'

'But...'

When Siena didn't continue, MJ soldiered on. 'I'm also sorry if I made you feel like some kind of sticking plaster because I was missing Mother.' Her heart pounded all the way up into her throat. 'I didn't mean to make you feel like that.'

Siena gave a sob and Christian put an arm around her shoulders. It was odd to see someone else comfort her sister, but they looked right together.

She made herself smile. 'What happened between Aunt Joan and Vasillios Constantinos happened fifty years ago. You'll just have to show everyone that's all in the past. My advice, for what it's worth, is act with integrity, treat everyone with as much consideration and generosity as you can and try to keep your tempers when other people lose theirs. If you can manage to not fly off the handle and act in a reasonable and rational manner, then—'

'That's the problem, though, Jojo!' Siena burst out. 'It's not really in the past at all!'

What was she talking about?

'Oh, Jojo, *our parents*!'

She went cold all over, recalling Nikos's warning that she didn't know the entire story. She turned to glance at him now, but he didn't turn towards her, didn't meet her gaze, and that made her go even colder. 'What about our parents?' she demanded, swinging back.

'Father had an affair with Tori Constantinos.'

MJ's breath jammed. She took a step back. *No!* Surely not? It…

The room spun. The ongoing hatred… Dear God, it made perfect sense. Why had their father kept this from them? Her temples pounded and her eyes burned. Why hadn't *Nikos* told her?

'When Andreas found out…'

Siena broke off to grip Christian's hand with both of her own.

Andreas? Nikos's father? 'Go on.' MJ's voice didn't sound as if it belonged to her.

'He phoned mother…' Siena's voice wobbled. 'And told her. Told her where their assignations took place, told her that's where her cheating husband was right at that current moment in time. That's where mother was driving to, Jojo, when she had the car accident that killed her. She had the accident because she was so upset.'

What?

'Father and Andreas…they hate each other even more than Aunt Joan and Vasillios did. Do you now see what we're up against?'

MJ had to brace a hand against the wall to stop from falling. Siena threw off her covers as if to come to her, but MJ shook her head. 'None of you touch me.'

A sob caught in Siena's throat that found an echo in her own chest. Christian gestured her to the chair he'd been sitting in, but instead she moved to a chair on the other side of the room, one away from everyone else.

All this time, Nikos had known, and yet he hadn't…

Her chest splintered as if a spear had been thrown through it. She tried to focus on Siena's words rather than the sense of betrayal that threatened her composure. All of this time, Nikos had known and yet he'd kept it from her.

Don't. Not yet.

She forced up her chin. 'I'm sorry, Siena, but you're wrong.'

Tears spilled down Siena's cheeks, but she shook her head. 'It's the truth, Jojo. I know it's shocking, but—'

'It wasn't a man's voice on the phone that day.'

From the corner of her eye, she saw Nikos freeze. She did what she could to block him out.

'It wasn't Andreas who told Mother about the affair. It was Tori.'

Christian's face twisted and his hands clenched. 'That's a lie!'

'You were at art class,' MJ continued as if Christian

hadn't spoken. 'And I was having a cooking lesson with Mother. Alice was busy signing for a delivery, and Mother's hands were sticky with cookie dough, so when the phone rang I answered it while Mother washed her hands.

'When she came to the phone, she listened for bit and then yelled at the person at the other end, said they were lying, before slamming the receiver back down. And then she grabbed her car keys and told Alice to finish helping me make the cookies and left.' She pushed her hair from her face with a shaky hand. Clenching it, she dragged it back into her lap. 'It was the last time I saw her alive.'

'You're lying!' Christian's eyes had gone wild. He stared from MJ to his brother. 'Father told me he was the one who called Diana…and how he regretted it, how he wished he'd kept the information to himself.'

'She's not lying, Christian.'

Nikos's words made her want to lie on the floor and sleep for a very long time. Apparently he knew the *whole* truth.

'Father's the one who lied,' he went on.

'Why?'

'To protect Mother. He loved her. She'd rung Diana in an attempt to break up the Mabels' marriage so she and Graham could be together. There was no chance of that happening, though, once Diana had the car accident. In taking the blame for it, Father hoped she'd stay with him rather than give up on their marriage.'

Christian fell down into his chair. Siena pressed a hand to her mouth.

MJ stood and started for the door, emotion boiling, thrashing and whipping at her.

'Where are you going?'

The panic in Siena's voice barely touched her. Still, she turned to meet her sister's gaze. 'I'm going home.'

'But you can't. We—'

'I can!'

The force of her words had Siena's and Christian's jaws dropping. Not Nikos's, though. But every single muscle he had tensed and she hated that she was so attuned to him. So attuned when he'd *lied to her*!

She thumped a hand to her chest. 'I gave you all the best of me—the *very* best. But that doesn't seem to have had any impact on you at all.' She met Nikos's eyes. 'It doesn't seem to have *mattered* to you at all.'

He'd gone grey beneath his tan. She hoped he felt one-tenth as sick as she did.

'I'm taking a time-out. I want some...*space*.'

While she didn't exactly spit out that last word, it emerged with an edge she couldn't temper.

'Oh, Jojo.' Siena hiccupped. 'Please...'

All this time Nikos had known!

'I'm tired of everyone's petty grievances—the way you all deliberately nurse and feed your sense of injury, and all of the wailing, bitching and moaning. I've had enough of it. *All of it!* You can sort it out on your own, because I'm out. I'm not having a bar of it any more.'

And with that she strode out of the door before she started crying.

Nikos made the mistake of following her. She could feel him even before he spoke. 'Let me take you home.'

Not on her life...

Seizing his arm, she hauled him into a thankfully empty waiting room.

'You knew.' She dropped his arm. She could only whisper because a lump had lodged in her throat. Speaking hurt her, but words bubbled up anyway. 'All this time you knew about the affair between my mother and your father and you never told me.'

He dragged a hand down his face. 'God help me, MJ.

I'm sorry. So sorry. At first I couldn't believe you didn't know and then…'

She spread her hands, forcing her eyes wide in mockery. 'And then what? You didn't think I had a right to know? Didn't think I'd want to know?'

'Hell, MJ!' He paced the length of the room and then swung back. 'At first it didn't seem my place to tell you. It seemed a cruel thing to do.'

Anger dissolved the lump in her throat. *Cruel?* Heat scalded the backs of her eyes and burned a hole through the middle of her heart. She refused to let a single tear fall. Not here. Not now. Not in front of *him*. 'You slept with me, but all the time you kept this huge secret from me? I can't even…'

She folded her arms to hide the way her hands shook. 'Was this about revenge after all? Was me promising you the Ananke necklace not enough?'

Crimson stained his cheekbones. 'No! I never wanted revenge on you. I *never* wanted to hurt you. I wish to God I'd done things differently. I wish I could turn the clocks back.'

But he couldn't. And why should she believe him anyway? She'd laid herself bare to this man, but he hadn't done the same. She was a fool. A bigger fool than even her Aunt Joan.

'I care about you, Marjorie.'

Very slowly, she shook her head. 'I don't believe you. Someone who cared for me would never have lied to me the way you did.' She forced her chin up. 'What an idiot I've been. I should've recognised it from the first. Everyone else did.'

'Recognised what?'

The words croaked from him. His face was haggard, his spine and shoulders sagging as if they'd lost the ability to hold themselves up. He looked as sick and wretched as she felt. Maybe he was sorry. But it didn't change the cold, hard facts. What had happened aboard the yacht had obviously meant a lot more to her than it ever had to him.

She enunciated the words clearly. 'I didn't recognise that you're exactly like your grandfather…and your father…and my father.'

His head rocked back, his eyes going wild. He opened his mouth.

'And now maybe I am too. Thanks to you.'

He bent at the waist then, bracing his hands on his knees as if she'd dealt him a body blow.

'I'll see myself home, thank you, Nikos.'

She swept past him and didn't look back.

CHAPTER ELEVEN

'Ms Marjorie Mabel to see you, sir.'

Nikos shot out of his chair. *MJ? Here?*

She'd not answered a single one of his calls, texts or emails yesterday. He knew he needed to give her time, but the guilt had torn at him. And knowing how much she was hurting had slashed him inside out.

He deserved to be dying a thousand deaths, not *her*.

He had to find a way to make things right. He had to find a way to make her see that he'd never meant to hurt her. 'Don't keep her waiting, Giles. I—'

'He hasn't kept me waiting, Nikos.'

MJ emerged from behind his assistant and Nikos's heart thundered in his ears. He rounded the desk to take her hands. Giles left, closing the door behind him.

Damn it! She looked pale and wan. Dark circles stretched beneath her eyes like bruises. 'How are you?'

She raised an eyebrow and he winced. 'Sorry, that was a stupid question.' He led her to a chair and took the one opposite, not relinquishing her hand. 'I can't tell you how good it is to see you, MJ. And I know I don't deserve it, but will you give me a chance to try and explain?'

She bit her lip and glanced away, pulling her hand from his and folding in on herself. He recognised the misery and found himself on his knees in front of her. 'Marjorie, please. I swear I never meant to hurt you. I'd rather cut off my own arm.'

Her eyes widened at whatever she saw in his face.

'What you've been trying to do—wanting to bring an end to the feud.' He pressed a hand to his chest. 'I admire it with all my heart. I want to make that happen too.' Nausea churned in his gut. 'If you now hate me with the same savagery as the past generations have hated each other...'

Bitterness filled his mouth and coated his tongue. He didn't know how he'd bear it. To know he'd taken something so beautiful and destroyed it...

'I don't hate you, Nikos.'

She gestured to the seat opposite, and he forced himself to take it.

'Why did you keep the truth from me? Why did you lie?'

He scrubbed both hands through his hair. How the hell did he explain it to her?

Start at the beginning...

'I didn't know about my mother and Graham's affair until after your mother's car accident. My father bundled the entire family off to the Devon house.'

'Away from prying eyes,' she murmured in a monotone.

'Their fights—' He broke off, breathing hard, not entirely sure how to describe them. 'I'd never heard anything like them before, had never witnessed anything so *raw*. I didn't know what to do, didn't know how to help.'

All he'd wanted to do was put his family back together. He'd come to hate Graham Mabel with every atom of his being that summer. He'd blamed the man for everything. It'd made sense when he'd been fourteen, but now...

He let out a long breath. 'I didn't know grown men— tough men like my father and grandfather—could cry. But my father cried...and he begged my mother to stay. He begged her not to abandon her family. He told her he'd take the blame, that he'd tell Graham he'd been the one to ring Diana, if only she'd stay.'

Two deep furrows carved themselves into MJ's brow. 'And she let him?'

His head felt too heavy for his shoulders. 'I think a part of her still hoped that, if your father never knew she'd been the one to reveal the truth of the affair to Diana, there'd still be a chance for them, but...' He dragged a hand down his face. 'She was in shock, traumatised. She was never the same again. She sure as hell wasn't thinking clearly.'

MJ rubbed a hand across her chest.

'She agreed to stay. And she tried, she really did, but the guilt ate at her.' He was quiet for a moment, his heart thumping. 'She tried to take her own life. It was only my grandfather's quick thinking and knowledge of CPR that saved her life.'

Understanding dawned in her eyes. 'That's why you feel you owe your grandfather such a debt.'

He shook his head. Not in denial, but it wasn't the full truth either. 'I've always loved my grandfather. He's been good to me.' But there was no denying that, because he'd saved Nikos's mother's life, they'd all felt a deeper debt to the older man.

'After her suicide attempt, I confronted my father and told him I knew the truth. I wanted him to tell Christian the truth too—that it'd been Mother not him who'd told Diana about the affair—but he refused. He swore me to secrecy; made me swear not to tell a living soul—not my grandfather and not my brother.'

Her frown deepened and she leaned towards him. 'You were only fourteen. It's not fair to ask a fourteen-year-old to bear that kind of burden.'

It hadn't felt particularly onerous until he'd met MJ. He'd wanted to protect his fragile mother from gossip and scandal, and he'd wanted to help his father save face. But once he'd met MJ... 'I'm sorry I didn't tell you. I should've at least told you about the affair, even if I couldn't tell you the whole truth. But...'

She glanced up.

'I was afraid that, once I started, I'd reveal everything.'

'Who to betray—me or your father?' She pulled in a breath and let it out again in a slow whoosh. 'I'm glad I wasn't in your shoes, Nikos.'

'I know how betrayed you felt yesterday, MJ.'

Her gaze dropped.

'And in that moment I hated myself. If I could do things over, I'd tell you everything.'

'My own father should've told me.' She stared at her hands and grimaced. 'I feel I was unnecessarily harsh to you at the hospital and I'm sorry.'

'Don't you dare apologise.' His voice shook from the force of his emotion. 'You're the one person in this whole sorry mess who doesn't need to apologise to anyone.'

He hesitated. He deserved her animosity and revulsion, but... 'You don't hate me.'

She glanced up.

'And you don't hate my father.'

'I don't hate anyone.' One slim shoulder lifted. 'How can I hate Tori, Andreas and Father when they've all paid for what happened back then a thousand times over? What happened was dreadful, but none of them would've meant for my mother to die. I can hardly imagine the guilt and regret they've all carried since then. No wonder our fathers never remarried, Nikos.'

The depth of her empathy, and her ability and *willingness* to forgive, astounded him. Shamed him. For years he'd mindlessly hated her father and great-aunt because of the pain they'd inflicted on his family. But his family had inflicted just as much pain on hers in its turn.

'And I can see how badly you feel too, Nikos. But you

should never have been put in this a situation in the first place.'

'How do you do it?' he burst out. 'How can you be so forgiving and tolerant of other people's weaknesses? How do you do that and still manage to care about everyone so much?'

'You make me sound like a saint.' She sprang to her feet. 'I'm not! I feel angry with everyone sometimes.' She flung out an arm and paced about the room. 'I have to fight the urge to not shake everyone, and their preoccupation with dwelling on drama and the ill feeling and being double-crossed and feeling ill-used…. I want to yell at everyone to just *get over it*!'

She slammed herself back into her chair. 'The truth is I spent a lot of time with Aunt Joan. What she and Vasillios allowed to happen between them horrified me. If only they'd had the courage to swallow their pride they'd have won *everything*. I swore to never make the same mistake.'

Most people refused to take risks because they were afraid of the consequences. MJ was the opposite. She took risks because she refused to live a life of regret.

'I'm demanding everyone be the best damn person they can be, and I'm not sure that's fair, let alone possible.' She blew out a breath and met his gaze. 'But I still can't help feeling it's necessary.'

An ache stretched through him. He didn't know if it was possible either. But they could make a start on improving things, couldn't they? That was better than nothing.

Her face lost some of its light, as if she'd read his scepticism. 'I have something for you.' Reaching into her handbag, she pulled out a parcel and held it towards him.

He took it in numb fingers, pulled off the plain paper packaging and lifted the lid of a wooden box. His breath bunched beneath his breastbone, every muscle clenching when he saw what was nestled there. *The Ananke necklace.*

'The lawyer wouldn't let me take it until I'd signed a declaration to say I was bringing it directly to you. I wanted to give it to you personally. I wanted to thank you for all you did, for all of your help and kindness. You kept your word and fulfilled our bargain to the letter. I'm very grateful.'

She was going to leave, and if he didn't find the right thing to say he might never see her again! He shot to his feet. 'This can't be goodbye, MJ.'

She rose. 'We'll see each other around, of course, and—'

'I want to keep seeing you. I want to date you.' He wanted to kiss her again.

She set her handbag and jacket on the seat of her chair before glancing at the necklace he held. 'You're planning to use that to buy your family's acceptance of Christian and Siena's engagement, aren't you?'

He nodded. He couldn't see any other way round it. 'But it can buy acceptance for us too, MJ. We can work this out.'

She strode to the window and stared out of it for several long moments before turning, her hands pressed to her stomach. 'Let me give you a hypothetical situation, Nikos. Let's just say, for argument's sake, that I love you. Which, for the record, is true.'

Her words electrified him. Before he could say anything, she continued.

'And let's say you love me too.' She held up both hands. 'Please don't answer that, as either answer will break my heart.' She dragged in a breath that made her whole body tremble. 'And let's say we married and had three adorable children…'

'You want three children?'

The smallest of smiles touched her lips. 'Three sounds like a nice number.'

That smile faded. 'Less nice, however, is if one of the children adored their maternal grandfather, heard our family's history from his perspective and sympathised, while another one heard it from his paternal grandfather and sympathised with that perspective instead. The two of them then start fighting over which of them should inherit the necklace.'

She raised her chin and met his gaze. 'Who do we give it to, Nikos? That kind of thing splits families up. *That's* why I won't have the necklace in my life, even if it means walking away from you.'

She gathered up her things, paused and then very quietly slipped a smooth pink pebble onto his desk. 'Goodbye, Nikos.'

He stared at the pebble and had a swift memory of her bending down on their Greek island to pick it up.

He opened his mouth, but what could he say?

She walked through the door without halting. Walked away from him. And it was as if every good thing he'd ever known had been taken from him.

He flung the priceless necklace across the room and lowered himself onto his chair, closing a fist around the pebble.

MJ walked through the door of her Chelsea flat and halted. Turning on the spot, she searched for…*something*…but she had no idea what.

Whatever. She had a feeling it couldn't be found here anyway.

She had a feeling it couldn't be found anywhere.

'Marjorie Joan Mabel, what have you done?'

Tossing her handbag on the hall table, she tried to rub warmth into her arms, her hands moving briskly up and down, but she barely felt them. She'd gone numb all over.

'And, if you're going to start talking to yourself, it might be an idea to get a cat so the neighbours don't think you're an absolute loser.'

A warm and cuddly cat in the flat might be comforting.

But the thought of cats had her thinking of dogs, specifically Seth and Rufus, Nikos's dogs in Devon. Which, of course, had her thinking, yet again, about Nikos.

She dropped down to the sofa and hugged a cushion to her chest. Had she really just walked away from him? She held the cushion at arm's length.

'Am I demanding too much? Am I being just like Vasillios and Aunt Joan and Tori Constantinos?'

She threw the cushion to one side and dropped her head in her hands. Was she letting her hatred of the feud and all of the fighting between their two families skew her judgement? Nikos was right. Between them, they *could* improve things. Wasn't that a worthy goal, something to be celebrated? Why couldn't that be enough? Why couldn't she be content with that?

But she couldn't be satisfied. It wasn't enough.

The cold, uncompromising relentlessness of that thought dropped down on her, a guillotine blade severing any hope of finding a way to make a relationship work with the man she loved.

For as long as one or the other of their families had possession of the Ananke necklace, the possibility of new hostilities breaking out remained. She'd made a promise to herself and to Aunt Joan to have nothing to do with either.

In her heart of hearts, she knew she was making the right decision. That didn't stop her heart from feeling like a dead, black weight in her chest, though. She hadn't known the price she'd have to pay would be so high.

Curling up on her side, she drew her knees to her chest and stared unseeingly at the room as the shadows lengthened, her eyes burning and her throat aching.

'What did you want to see me about, MJ?'

Her father had *that* look on his face—the 'I don't want any more lectures about your sister' look.

It had been less than a fortnight since she'd last seen him, and in that time it appeared nothing had changed for him. While for her it felt as if her whole life had been turned upside down.

Well, this should be fun.

She closed the office door behind her and squared her shoulders. 'This would've been better said in the privacy of the family home, but as you insisted you had no time to see me out of hours, and to make an appointment with your PA to see you during business hours instead, I'm not going to apologise for it.'

'If this is about Siena—'

'I've given the Ananke necklace to Nikos Constantinos.'

He stared as if he didn't understand the words she'd just uttered. And she didn't give him time to gather his scattered wits.

'I also know what happened between you and Tori Constantinos eighteen years ago—that the two of you were having an affair.'

She sat without being invited and watched the colour leach from his face. A part of her ached for him, but mostly she just felt numb.

'MJ, I...' He swallowed.

'You destroyed the Constantinos marriage.' Not single-handedly—Tori had had a hand in that too—but it was a fact, plain and simple.

'And now you hold me responsible for your mother's death.'

The words dropped from him. She saw his guilt then and her heart burned. She reached across the table as if to touch him, but the expanse of desk was too wide. 'No.' She shook her head. 'No.'

His chin came up and his eyes flashed. 'Then why else would you punish me and give the Ananke necklace to a member of *that family*?' He spat the words, investing 'that family' with as much loathing as he could. 'There are things you don't know, MJ, things that would change the way you—'

'I know you hold Andreas responsible for Mother's death. You think he rang her and told her about the affair, told her where you and Tori met. Told her that's where the two of you were that afternoon, the same afternoon she had her accident. I know that you think, if she hadn't been so distraught, she'd not have had the accident.'

'It's true! Andreas...'

She shook her head.

He leapt up. 'It is! And—'

'I answered the phone that day.'

He stared at her as if her words made no sense.

'I know I was only nine, but I remember. I remember everything about that afternoon.' It was the last afternoon she'd spent with her mother. It was burned on her brain. 'It wasn't Andreas who called, Father. It was Tori.'

His mouth worked but no sound came out. He lowered himself back to his chair as if any sudden movement would shatter him. 'But, when I accused him, Andreas didn't deny it.'

'What would you have done in his shoes? You'd destroyed his marriage—he wanted to strike back. And he wanted to protect Tori.'

'But why would Tori...?' He swallowed and very slowly nodded. 'She wanted to leave Andreas. She wanted me to leave your mother.'

'Were you in love with her?' Had he loved her as fiercely as she did Nikos?

'I...yes.' He dragged a hand down his face, looking haggard and old. 'Your mother was my best friend, MJ, but we'd married young and...' He spread his hands, helplessly mute. 'With Tori, I had never known passion like it. The adultery was unforgivable. I should have confessed all to your mother immediately. But I didn't. And when she died...' His mouth firmed. 'I didn't deserve happiness after that.'

'What a mess you all made of it.'

For once her father didn't argue, but he thrust out his jaw. 'Nikos told you all this? Made you feel guilty so you would give him the necklace?'

'Nikos is a decent man. He actually tried to protect me from the truth. It was Siena and Christian who told me.'

His mouth worked. 'What the hell is Siena doing with Christian Constantinos?'

'Siena's last test results weren't good.'

He straightened, his gaze sharpening. 'Dear God.'

'She went to ground and I couldn't find her. I offered Nikos the necklace in exchange for helping me find her.'

'Why did you not tell me of this?'

'I told you repeatedly to ring her!' She shouted the words, surprising them both. 'What if that fight was the last conversation you ever had with her? How would you have felt? *Have you learned nothing from the past?*'

He shot to his feet. 'Is she—?'

'She's fine.' She worked hard to get her frustration back under control, forcing herself back into her seat. 'Christian took her to a private clinic. She's responded well to treatment. By the way, she and Christian are engaged. So here's your chance to finally act well and make amends.'

Disbelief overturned his relief. 'A union between the Mabels and the Constantinoses can never happen. It won't work. I forbid it. It'll end in disaster and—'

'It's going to happen whether you like it or not.' She rose. 'If you don't want to tear our family apart, I suggest you find a way to make it work.' As she spoke, she strode to the door. She turned when she reached it. 'Or we lose.' Her gaze collided with his. 'You need to decide what matters more to you—this feud or your children.'

And then she left. She'd already lost, but it didn't mean Siena and Christian couldn't find happiness.

If worst came to worst, Siena and their father would never speak to each other again... The vision of being torn at Christmases and birthdays rose in her mind. Her stomach churned. It was the likeliest outcome. As much as she hated to admit it, it was probably what the future held.

Unless everyone found the strength to act as their best selves.

Ha! As if that had ever happened between the Mabel and Constantinos families.

MJ had done her best to set out the facts as starkly as she could, to make sure everyone knew what was at stake. She had no other bright ideas now for how to heal the rift. She'd failed.

When she finally got home she let herself into her flat, kicking off her shoes and letting her handbag slide off her shoulder to land on the floor beside them. Falling down to the sofa, she grabbed the cushion and held it at arm's length. She *really* needed to get a cat.

'Do you think, if I asked him, Nikos would emigrate to New Zealand with me? Somewhere far, far away from all of this trouble and strife...'

She shook her head. 'Me neither.' A lump lodged in her throat. Clutching the cushion to her chest, she concentrated on breathing through the waves of pain that tried to swallow her.

CHAPTER TWELVE

NIKOS SPENT THE best part of the following week trying to erase the time he'd spent with MJ from his mind. While he might never have met a woman who'd affected him as much, their time together had been ephemeral, fleeting—a brief moment of perfection, neither permanent nor durable. It wasn't something they could build on. She'd made that very clear.

He buried himself in work, and in the evenings he read Joan's diary. It made him feel closer to MJ, but it didn't lift the heavy weight that pressed his heart flat, sapping his energy and draining all enjoyment from his days.

On the sixth day he gave up the pretence. He strode around his office and swore—his office in the city, rather than his office at home, because whenever he worked from home now he found himself continually waiting for MJ to burst in, and being disappointed when she didn't.

Damn it all to hell! MJ had told him she loved him. He could try and hide from the truth, but what good would it do? He loved her back, body and soul. Every second was an agony of missing her, aching for her and craving her.

He swore again. Louder this time. He knew how much she'd be hurting. She didn't deserve that pain. In this whole sorry mess, she was the only person who'd acted with integrity. She didn't deserve a broken heart. She deserved a medal!

Then give her what she wants.

He rested his forehead against the cool glass of a window, not noticing the busy cityscape below or the distant view of the iconic dome of St Paul's Cathedral. What MJ wanted was impossible. How could he give her what she wanted while remaining true to his family, and without tearing his family apart?

His mother's betrayal with Graham Mabel had shattered his father. For God's sake, his grandfather had saved Tori when she'd tried to take her own life. Both men deserved peace, not more upheaval and trauma.

As long as either one of our families owns the necklace, there will be no peace.

He could hear MJ's voice in his head as clearly as if she stood in the office with him. The scenario she'd presented him with—of their feuding children—had truly horrified him.

Of course, it was a hypothetical situation. Who knew if such an eventuality would ever come to pass? But, for as long as their families continued to squabble over the necklace's ownership, the possibility remained. His hands fisted. Was this the legacy they'd now pass onto any children Christian and Siena might have?

Acid burned his gut. MJ had been right to want to banish the necklace from her life, from all their lives, but he couldn't see a way to make that happen.

Unless…

He froze. Unless he could bridge the many gulfs that lay between the Constantinoses and the Mabels.

His heart pounded. The odds weren't in his favour. There wasn't any point in fooling himself about that. But what was the alternative—let MJ go?

No!

If there was the slightest chance of winning MJ's heart, and giving her the future she so desperately wanted, then anything was worth a shot. He clenched and unclenched his hands. He might not succeed, but…

If he didn't at least try, then he didn't deserve her.

And he wanted to deserve her. More than he'd ever wanted anything in his life.

Seizing the phone from his desk, he rang his grandfather.

'Have you talked sense into that fool brother of yours yet?' the older man demanded. 'I won't—'

'I've rung to tell you that I have the Ananke necklace.'

Silence greeted his pronouncement, but he heard his grandfather's quick intake of breath.

'MJ gave it to me. It's mine, fair and square. I even have a signed contract to prove it.'

'You…but… I never thought I'd live to see this day! Nikos, you make an old man very happy and—'

'But unless you agree to read Joan Mabel's diary I'm going to give it back.'

'How dare you? I'm your grandfather. You cannot give me ultimatums—'

'I'm not even going to discuss this with you, Pappoús. I'm emailing the scanned diary pages to you right now. I'll ring back in five days and hope to find you've read them.'

He ended the call and then tapped his fingers against the warm walnut of his desk. Pressing the intercom, he ordered his PA to make an appointment for him to meet with Graham Mabel.

She hesitated. 'Graham Mabel, sir?'

'That's right. For as soon as it can be arranged. And an appointment with the lawyer Bayard Crawford. And cancel all of my appointments for this afternoon.'

'Yes, sir.'

His mind raced to the next task—Siena and Christian. Grabbing his coat from the back of his chair, he strode from the office. He'd go and see them in person.

Ten days later Nikos strode into MJ's office, not giving her PA the opportunity to announce him.

MJ glanced up from her computer and her jaw dropped. *'Nikos!'*

Everything inside him protested at her pallor, at the dark circles under her eyes. Had she lost weight? She needed to look after herself!

He planted himself into the chair opposite. 'Can you call your PA off, please, MJ? Tell her she doesn't need to call security to have me thrown out?'

'It's okay, Lucy.' She nodded to her PA. 'Mr Constantinos and I are…'

His heart beat hard.

A smile touched her lips and it lightened everything inside him. 'Old friends.'

God, he loved this woman! She might look tired, she might look worn thin, but her smile told him she was glad to see him. It didn't hold even the faintest edge of resentment or bitterness.

She turned back to him, lifted her hands and let them drop. 'This is a surprise.'

His heart burned. While there might not be any resentment in her smile, it wasn't pain-free. She hid it well, but he'd come to know her heart almost as well as he knew his own. He yearned to replace that pain with joy.

'What can I do for you?'

She was trying to be business-like and professional, but the way her gaze momentarily dropped from his, the way her chest lifted as she pulled in a steadying breath, told him she was having as hard a time as him at reining in her emotions.

'I've missed you,' he found himself murmuring. 'I wanted to see you.'

She swallowed. 'Nikos—'

'I *needed* to see you.'

Her eyes flashed then. She laid her hands flat on the desk. 'I didn't think you were cruel or selfish. This can't happen, Nikos. I've explained why. I understand that you might not agree with me, but I've told you how I feel and you have to respect that, accept that.'

'I will always do my best to accept and respect the way you feel, MJ, but I don't have to necessarily accept how other people feel or act if I think they're wrong.'

Her brow pleated. 'You think I'm wrong?'

No, he thought her magnificent. 'I think your reading of our situation is spot on.'

A tiny light in her eyes died. She moistened her lips and nodded.

He reached into his pocket, pulled out the box containing the Ananke necklace and set it on her desk.

Her nose wrinkled. 'What on earth are you doing bringing *that* into my office?'

He almost laughed out loud. Any other woman would've fawned over the necklace but not MJ. 'I think your reading of our situation is spot on, but I don't think anyone else's is.'

Her gaze flew back to his. 'What does that mean?'

'It *means*,' he said with deliberate emphasis, 'that I've bullied, cajoled, blackmailed and harangued every member of our respective families until they've seen sense.'

Her eyes went wide. She shot to her feet, her hands gripping each other in a white-knuckled clench. 'Including my father and Siena?'

'Yes.'

'How…? But…? Why haven't I heard about any of this from either one of them then?'

He stood too. 'From all accounts, you've been keeping a low profile these last couple of weeks, haven't been seeing anyone.'

She opened her mouth, closed it and shrugged. 'I haven't been feeling all that sociable.'

'MJ, I—'

'So that means…' She pressed the heels of her hands to her temples, frowning. 'Oh, Nikos, I never wanted you to estrange yourself from your family! I know how much you love them, how protective you are of them, and how you want to save them from further pain and suffering. I understand that and—'

'The only way I can truly protect them, and any future generations, is to bring this godforsaken feud to an end once and for all. And to do that we need to get rid of this.' He pointed to the necklace.

Striding round the desk, he took her hand. 'Come.' He led her to the sofa on the other side of the room. 'I have much to tell you and I also need your signature.'

'My signature?' She sat but glanced back at her desk. 'I don't want that damn necklace, Nikos, so don't even think about giving it back to me.'

This time he did laugh out loud.

'I mean it. I—' She broke off and bit her lip. 'Though, if you do give it back, I guess I can finally donate it and we can all be rid of it.'

'I told my grandfather that unless he read Joan's journal I'd do exactly that and give it back.'

'I—' She shook herself. 'What did he do?'

'He read the journal.'

She rubbed a hand across her chest. 'Was he okay afterwards?' She leaned towards him. 'Please tell me it helped him to find peace.'

It took all of his strength not to take her face in his hands and kiss her.

She touched his arm. 'It hasn't hurt your relationship with him, has it?'

He pressed his hand over hers, grasping that small warmth to himself. 'No, we're good. You don't need to worry about that. But it did send him on a hell of a journey—made him question all he thought he knew. Regret, shame, anger have all been part of that journey. But your great-aunt's final words to him…' He paused, recalling the expression in his grandfather's eyes when he'd spoken to Nikos about it. 'They didn't just bring him peace, MJ, they brought him joy.'

Her lips curved in a smile that could have made a man's heart beat a path out of his chest. 'I'm so glad.'

He'd never seen his grandfather joyful before. Pleased and satisfied, yes. Proud, determined and angry, yes. But never joyful. It had been a gift.

'The thing is, MJ, I started to realise there was a flaw in this plan of yours to donate the necklace. The fact is, the power would always remain with the party who did the donating.'

She glanced at her hand on his forearm, his hand resting on top of it. She squeezed gently and then pulled her hand back to her lap. 'I don't mind if you donate it. I can reconcile my family to that.'

She'd try to, but a shadow would always remain.

Some of the light went out of her eyes when he remained silent. 'You want to keep it.' The words were flat, dull…lifeless.

'You misunderstand me.'

She raised an eyebrow.

'I don't want to keep the necklace, but if I went ahead and donated it that'd merely remove the object of all the resentment, not the resentment itself. If we truly want to fix things, we have to address the heart of the problems. If donating the necklace is the wisest course of action for our families, and I think it is, we need everyone to agree to it.'

Her eyes widened.

'We need to reconcile my grandfather to your great-aunt, and our fathers to one another. The journal worked its magic on my grandfather. He signed the contract I have here.' He pulled the folded contract from his top pocket and set it on the coffee table.

Hope flared in her face. 'And now you want me to get my father's signature.'

'I already have your father's signature, and my father's.'

Her mouth fell open.

'And Siena and Christian's,' he added. 'Obviously the pair of them didn't need much convincing—especially not after I presented them with the prospect of our children fighting over the damn necklace in twenty years' time.'

She waved a hand in front of her face. 'You have *my father's* signature?'

He unfolded the document and showed her.

She ran a finger over her father's name, and then his father's signature. 'How did you do this?'

'You did half the work, I believe. I made an appointment to see your father and told him what you wanted… told him I wanted it too. He said he would sign, just like that—no arguments, no wheeling or dealing—but I wanted more from him than just a signature.'

She glanced up. 'You wanted him to apologise to your father.'

Her perception shouldn't have surprised him. 'It was the only hope I had of getting my father to agree to all of this.'

She swallowed. 'How did my father take that?'

'He was quiet for a long time, stared out the window with his back to me, and then he told me you'd had a long talk with him and that he now knew it wasn't my father who'd rung Diana that day, but Tori.'

'And so he apologised to your father…in person?'

He nodded.

A breath whooshed out of her. 'Then I'm proud of him.' She glanced back at the signatures. 'Your father obviously accepted his apology, so I'm proud of him too.'

'I don't know what passed between them, and I suspect

they'll never be best friends, but they'll present a united front when Christian and Siena officially announce their engagement. When they attend any future family functions, they'll pass a few polite pleasantries rather than veiled threats.'

She stared at him with wide eyes. 'You accomplished all of this?'

His heart started to hammer. She'd made herself vulnerable to him, had told him she loved him. He trusted her—would trust her with his life, his fortune and his heart—but saying it out loud scared the hell out of him.

Be braver, Nikos. She deserves it all.

'I love you, Marjorie.'

She stared, and then shook herself, as if she hadn't heard him properly.

'Before I met you I'd thought it impossible our families would ever stop fighting. But what I discovered is, what's truly impossible is living without you.'

She leaned forward, searching his face.

'I've never met anyone like you.' He pushed a strand of hair behind her ear. 'I've always liked how you look—my body always comes alive whenever we're in a room together—but it's your view of the world that captured my heart. You refuse to hold grudges and you believe the best of people, even when they give you no reason to, and you face your fears.

'You are so terrifyingly honest and—' he gulped '—I want to give you the world.' He hoped to God she still felt the same way about him. He traced a finger across her cheek. 'I realised that, if I had to move heaven and earth to be with you, then that was a small price to pay.'

Wonder crossed her face. She touched a hand to his cheek. 'You really love me?'

'Heart and soul.'

'You really trust me—a Mabel?'

Did she seriously think the feud held any weight with him now? 'With my life, with my fortune and with my heart.'

MJ was almost afraid to breathe in case she should wake up and discover this was all a glorious dream. If it were a dream, she didn't want to wake up!

'Can I kiss you now?' His voice was a growl of need that raised every fine hair on her arms and had a shiver travelling a delicious path down her spine. In answer, she pressed her lips to his. Firm but gentle hands immediately caressed her face, lips caressing hers with a reverence that had tears pricking the backs of her eyes. Those lips firmed, and he deepened the kiss until she was breathless and clutching his shirt.

Heedless of the fact she would rumple his clothes, he pulled her into his lap. She ran her fingers over his face, down his neck and along his shoulders. *Mine.* This man belonged to her, body and soul.

'MJ.' Her name was dragged from his throat. 'Unless you have a lock on your office door…'

She contemplated continuing to play with fire—it felt like an age since she and Nikos had scaled the heights together—but there were still things to say. And, when they made love again—and she hoped that'd be soon—she didn't want any interruptions or intrusions. She wanted to focus on him and only him.

She gazed into his beloved face, touching her fingers to his jaw to bring his gaze back to hers. 'I love you, Nikos.'

Joy—pure, glorious and more freeing than anything she had ever experienced—poured into her in a crystal flow of brilliance and she saw the same emotion in his eyes. She couldn't temper her smile, and she didn't try. 'You did all of this for me.' She gestured at the document, now abandoned on the coffee table.

'I know I should say that I'm glad the feud is over for

my father and grandfather's sakes, for Christian and Siena's sakes too, but all I cared about was making it possible for you to be in my life.'

Her heart leapt and swooped with his every word.

'When you walked out of my office after presenting me with the necklace...'

He broke off, shaking his head. 'I thought that was it. I thought there was no hope for us. But I couldn't forget you. I didn't want to forget you. I knew what we had was worth fighting for.'

'And so you applied yourself to finding a solution to an impossible problem.'

'Not impossible. Just challenging.'

She threw her head back and laughed for the sheer joy of it. 'You slayed my dragon, Nikos. You leave me breathless.'

'*Have* I slayed it?'

In answer, she reached across and signed the document.

'You didn't even read it! MJ, that's appalling business practice and...'

She touched her fingers to his lips. 'I trust you with my life, with my fortune and with my heart.'

His eyes darkened at her words. 'This isn't a proposal, Marjorie, because we've known each other properly for less than a month, but I want to build a life with you. I want to live with you, work beside you and be the father of your three children.'

Her heart pounded and her breath quickened. 'As it isn't a proposal, I won't say, *Yes, please*, and set a date for the wedding. But I will say I want all that and more.'

They kissed again. When they eased apart a long time later, she found herself laughing. 'Do you remember the day I stormed into your office and you asked what would happen if you kissed me? Well, I think you have your answer.'

His eyes gentled. 'I wouldn't have believed this possible back then.'

'Happy?' she whispered.

He trailed his fingers across her cheek. 'More than I ever thought possible.'

His edges blurred as her eyes misted over. 'Do you think we could ever find that little Greek island again? Do you think we could go there to hide away from the rest of the world once in a while? You could teach me to sail and we could go skinny-dipping.'

His smile speared straight into the centre of her. 'How about I buy it for you as a wedding present?'

She wrapped her arms around his waist and nestled against his chest, her lips curving up, her heart pounding in gratitude and happiness. 'Sounds perfect.'

He pulled her closer and pressed his lips to the top of her head. 'It does indeed.'

EPILOGUE

Christmas Day, three and a half years later...

'CAN I GET anyone more Christmas pudding?'

MJ's voice rose above the general hubbub. The long dining table was scattered with their now-empty plates and half-filled wine and water glasses that sparkled in the glow from the overhead chandelier. The discarded casings of the gaily coloured Christmas crackers lying abandoned between the dishes added a festive touch that made Nikos smile.

Much head shaking ensued, along with groans of how full everyone was and how they couldn't possibly fit another bite in. Nikos grinned at his wife presiding at the other end of the table. They'd married three years ago. They'd meant to wait until after Christian and Siena had tied the knot, but their siblings had yet to set a date.

MJ's words from three and a half years ago came to him now. *I'm thinking of all the Christmas dinners we'll share if Siena and Christian marry.* She'd evidently seen into the future, had seen all that was possible. He should never have doubted her or her vision for a moment.

Even now he found it hard to believe, had to pinch himself.

He was the luckiest man in the world.

Theirs was the luckiest family in the world.

'Why don't we adjourn to the living room?' he suggested, lifting his two-and-a-half-year-old son from his highchair. Paulo had arrived six months after his and MJ's wedding. 'The fire's been lit, MJ has organised nibbles and the good port has been brought up from the cellar.'

That last had grins spreading across his father's and grandfather's faces, while Graham rubbed his hands together in anticipation.

Siena came over, swooping in to lift Paulo from his father's arms and smacking a kiss to his plump cheek.

Paulo bounced his excitement and Nikos groaned. 'Lord, Siena, don't shake him up like you did last year.'

'Cross my heart. I've no intention of wearing my nephew's regurgitated dinner this year.'

He took nine-month-old Diana from MJ's arms. 'I hope you're not wearing yourself out.'

'Absolutely not.' She reached up and kissed his cheek. 'A fact I'll prove to you later when our guests have either gone home or retired for the night.'

Their gazes caught and clung. It wasn't what he'd meant, but her murmured words had licks of flame heating his blood. Their desire for each other hadn't waned in the last three-and-a-half years. If anything, it had grown. Eventually they blinked themselves back and followed everyone into the living room.

Once everyone was seated, staring lazily into the crackling flames of the fire, their beverage of choice clasped in their hands, Siena said, 'It's time to do MJ's gratitude list.'

On their very first Christmas together, when conversations had still been stilted among certain family members, MJ had insisted that everyone name three things they were grateful for that year. And she'd gone first.

She'd said she was grateful she'd found a once-in-a-lifetime love with Nikos; grateful that she and her family had weathered a tough time and had emerged stronger and closer than ever; and she'd said she was so proud to be a part of the Constantinos family, with its strong traditions and family ties.

But she hadn't stopped there. She'd said how much she loved living in the Grosvenor Square house, that she was grateful every day for her health and for having a job she loved. She'd said she felt blessed that both her families, old and new, were able to come together to share this very special day.

And a strange thing had happened as they'd listened to her. Rather than focusing on the negatives, everyone had made an effort to focus on the positives. They'd started listing things that had happened throughout the year that had brought them joy, and it had broken the ice. The Mabels and the Constantinoses had started to laugh and smile together.

MJ had been the force that had drawn them together, and that first Christmas she'd been the glue that held them together, because everyone had wanted to make amends to her. Her father for having lied to her, Siena for having caused her so much worry, Christian and Andreas because she'd revealed the truth that had mended their father-son relationship, and Vasillios because she'd given him back his beloved Joanie.

They'd exerted themselves that first year because they'd wanted MJ to have the Christmas of her dreams. And now, somehow, it was easy. Somewhere along the line, they'd become a family.

With his arm around MJ's shoulders and his daughter on his lap, Nikos listened as his flawed but wonderful family listed all the things they were grateful for.

'And now I have an announcement to make,' Graham said when everyone had had their turn. 'I've made the decision to retire. Andreas and I have several fishing and golf trips planned for the coming year, and I realised that's what I want to be doing at this time of my life—not going into the office every day. I'd like you to take over the reins of Mabel's, MJ. I can't think of anyone better to lead us into the future.'

MJ leapt up, her eyes shining and hands clasped beneath her chin. 'I'd *love* to step into your shoes. It'd be an honour, but only if you're sure.'

'I've never been surer of anything,' he said, kissing her cheek.

'As we're making announcements,' Andreas said, also rising to his feet, 'I've one of my own. I've decided to move in permanently with Graham.'

MJ's jaw dropped. She swung to stare at Nikos, who could only shake his head. When had his father decided this? She swung back. 'But this is your home!'

'Now don't take on, MJ,' the older man said, patting her arm. He'd moved out temporarily when his rooms were being refurbished and Graham had offered him lodgings in the Mabels' Knightsbridge residence. 'You have a growing family—' he glanced fondly at his grandchildren '—and Graham and I find we rub along together rather well. We have our bridge club and the wine society and…' He trailed off with a shrug. 'The arrangement suits us both.'

Not only was romance possible between their two families, but friendship apparently was too.

She bit her lip. 'Well, if you're sure, but you know there'll always be room for you here.'

'And at the Devon house,' Christian said, glancing at Siena.

Siena nodded, taking Christian's hand. 'As we seem to be making announcements, I guess we should tell you we've finally set a date. Christian and I are planning a summer wedding.'

Much hugging and excited chatter followed this news.

Once they were all seated again, Nikos pressed his lips to MJ's temple. 'Are we going to share our news too?'

'You're having another baby!' Siena shrieked.

MJ happy-danced in her seat. 'I'm three months' pregnant and as healthy as a horse.'

More squeals. More hugging.

'So you're going to have the three babies you always wanted.' Siena sighed happily.

'Um, not quite,' MJ murmured, her eyes starting to dance.

Nikos straightened. Had she changed her mind? Did she want more children? They could have as many as she wanted!

'It appears I'm pregnant...*with twins*.'

He stared. 'Did you just say...?'

'Twins, Nikos.' She pointed at herself and Siena. 'It runs in the family. Tell me you're over the moon?'

With a whoop, he swept her up in his arms and swung her round. When he set her feet back on the ground, he kissed her with a thoroughness designed to leave her in no doubt of his feelings on the subject.

'Oh!' She clung to him, swaying slightly, her cheeks turning pink. 'Wow. So I guess that's a yes, then.'

Everyone laughed.

'Okay, that's it.' He settled her gently on the sofa with a cushion at her back and lifted her feet to a padded footstool. 'You're putting your feet up for the rest of the day. If you want anything, one of us will fetch it.'

Her father came across with a fresh glass of sparkling water. 'All of this...' he gestured around '...is because of you, my darling girl. I can't thank you enough.'

'Your father is right,' Andreas said, coming up beside him and handing her a plate of the choicest delicacies from among those on offer. 'Is there anything we can do to make things more perfect?'

MJ cocked her head, a smile spreading across those delectable lips. 'What would make things even more perfect was if we were to make a family group on the morrow to the Victoria and Albert Museum to see the Ananke necklace.'

That too had become a family tradition.

'Done!' the grandfathers said in unison.

'And then it'll be lunch at ours,' Graham said, raising an eyebrow at Andreas.

'Absolutely,' Andreas agreed.

'Oh, it sounds perfect.' MJ sighed. She tugged Nikos back down to the sofa beside her. 'Doesn't it?'

'The most perfect thing in the world,' he agreed, curving his arm around her and drawing her against him. She was the most perfect woman in the world, and she deserved every good thing the world had to offer. And he meant to make sure that she received it all—every single day.

* * * * *

FINDING FOREVER ON THEIR ISLAND PARADISE

THERESE BEHARRIE

MILLS & BOON

For my husband,
who's always given me the gift of love.
For my sons. You are, and for ever will be, enough.
And for my readers. Please remember that
you are always, always worthy.

CHAPTER ONE

'LIFT YOUR JAW off the floor, darling,' Morgan Simeon's grandmother said in a clipped tone. 'It won't help us if he thinks you're attracted to him.'

'I'm not—'

But Edna had already turned, disappearing into the house at a faster pace than most seventy-year-olds. Edna had been an athlete for years, and her training hadn't stopped when she'd had kids or grown older. Maybe that had been for this very reason. Edna wanted to run away from her granddaughter after a snarky remark, leaving said granddaughter to deal with a millionaire tycoon who held the fate of a very special wedding in his hands.

Shaking her head, Morgan focused on the millionaire tycoon.

She'd been taken aback the first time she'd seen Elliott Abel. That had been a week ago, when her grandmother had first called Morgan for help. Pictures on the internet had shown her how attractive Elliott was. As were all the many women she'd seen pictured on his arm.

Not that that was relevant.

She didn't know why she'd expected him to be unattractive. Perhaps because she'd seen the headlines on those news articles written about him before she'd seen him.

Furniture Tycoon Expands 'Crafted' Empire!

Elliott Abel: The 'Crafted' Furniture Man
From Furniture to Millionaire: the Story of the Ev-
eryday 'Crafted' Man

They'd really honed in on the furniture thing, which made it seem as if there was nothing else interesting about him. And then she'd seen his picture and wondered why the hell journalists neglected to mention that he was a *hot* furniture man.

Much hotter in person.

Now he stood at the end of the path leading to her grandmother's house. Fitted blue jeans, a white T-shirt and matching sneakers adorned his beautiful body. He had a broad chest and shoulders; sculpted biceps; a narrow torso; thick, muscular thighs; and feet that were probably just as attractive.

She'd seen picture of him in suits, tuxedos, but never this casual. Never this...*normal*. He seemed out of place, yet he was clearly comfortable. If her grandmother had stayed long enough for Morgan to reply, that was what Morgan would have told her.

She hadn't been staring because she thought him attractive—well, yes, she did, but that didn't matter. She hadn't done anything about finding someone attractive in ages, and she wasn't going to start with the man threatening to ruin her grandmother's wedding.

No, she had been staring because he seemed so ordinary. But she wouldn't be fooled into believing that.

'Mr Abel,' Morgan said, moving forward. 'Thank you for meeting with me.'

His gaze fell on her almost lazily. 'I thought I was meeting Edna.'

His voice was deeper than she'd expected. It didn't fit the casual look of him. Seemed more appropriate to the bespoke suits of the best quality she'd seen in those pictures.

'I'm Morgan Simeon. Edna's granddaughter.'

'Cavalry.'

It wasn't a question.

'Yes,' she replied softly. 'And you'll find that I'm a much fiercer opponent than she.'

His eyes went dark and there was a flicker of...*something* in their gold and green depths. 'Your grandmother and her friends have been giving me a hard time from the moment I arrived on the island.'

'Only because you're threatening her wedding.'

'No,' he said sharply. 'Not threatening her wedding. Doing the job I was asked to do.'

And there it was. The confirmation to her suspicions.

Elliott Abel, the 'Crafted' Furniture Man, was not the 'son' in Abel and Son Development. That had been clear from her research. But Morgan hadn't been able to find out whether Elliott was still invested in his father's business. Apparently not. He wanted to do what he'd been asked to do and leave as soon as possible.

She could help him with that.

'Your job will go much quicker if you allow my grandmother to get married at the estate before you start development.'

'How would delaying construction by a month make things go quicker?'

'You'd have fewer obstacles.'

'Obstacles have never stopped me before.'

A light shiver went down her spine. A warning, she thought. This man was used to getting what he wanted.

It wasn't the first time she had dealt with someone like him. The people who hired her were often drunk on their own power. And by power she meant money. Heaps and heaps of money that made her clients accustomed to the kind of life she would never understand. Including treating those with less money as if they had less value.

'They will now,' she assured him. 'The people here love me. They love my grandmother even more. If we ask them to co-operate with you, they will. And if we don't...' She shrugged.

He narrowed his eyes. 'What are you saying?'

'I'm saying that if you plan on developing an estate you'll need construction workers.' She lifted a finger. 'People at the harbour to help bring materials onto the island.' Another finger. 'Your general day-to-day needs covered: coffee, food...the same for your workers.' A third, fourth and fifth finger. 'Not to mention the co-operation of the people who are refusing to move out of the estate.'

'Everyone's signed their agreements,' he said tightly. 'Most people have already moved out.'

'Enough people for you to get started,' she agreed, 'but not enough for you to finish. I can think of at least four people who haven't even moved their stuff yet.'

'Your grandmother and her friends.'

'Hmm...' She shoved her hands into her pockets. 'So—a month?'

He didn't respond for a while. When he did, his tone was low, easy. But that shiver went down Morgan's spine again and she braced herself for his rebuttal.

'I see why your grandmother recruited you. You're cunning.' He angled his head slightly. 'But if I allow this you'll ask for more. Maybe Edna and her friends will want to remain in their houses. Maybe others will. In the end, we won't rebuild, and you'll get everything you want.'

'Wow. The furniture business must be much more cut-throat than I thought if that's what you think.'

He lifted his eyebrows but didn't comment on the fact that she knew who he was.

'I'm not looking to cheat you, Mr Abel. My grandmother has been planning her wedding for the past year—well before your father announced his intentions for the estate. She only wants a chance to see those plans come to fruition.'

She deserved to, too. After Morgan's grandfather had died Edna had been crushed. She'd moved to Penguin Island to get away from memories that hurt too much. The move had been meant to be temporary, but Edna had fallen in love with the island. She had worked through her grief, made new friends, and five years ago had met a man she wanted to spend the rest of her life with.

Morgan had been young when her grandfather had died, so she didn't remember him much. But she did remember the summers she'd come to Penguin Island. Her grandmother had taken care of her and her sister and brother, and for a while Morgan hadn't had to worry about them or her parents. More often than not her parents had gone on their own vacations during those times. When they'd returned, they'd been happier, and there had been more laughter and affection in her house than before.

She owed her grandmother a lot for that reprieve. For helping to create the happiest memories of her childhood. She would do anything to give Edna a measure of that happiness, even if it meant going toe-to-toe with a tycoon.

'You mean that,' Elliott stated, his eyes searching her face.

'I do. And I'd be happy to sign something to that effect.'

Elliott folded his arms. She tried not to notice the way his biceps bulged under his T-shirt. Instead, she focused on the fact that *this* was the millionaire tycoon she'd been expecting. Not normal or casual, but a man with folded arms, a knitted brow, and beautiful features drawn into hard lines.

Beautiful features?

She ignored that.

'Delaying things by a month doesn't work for me,' he

said, his deep voice almost a rumble. 'I promised I'd ensure things move along smoothly. Delaying is not smooth.'

'Things are delayed with developments all the time.'

'Not in my experience.'

'Which is limited, isn't it?'

His lips thinned. 'Yours isn't?'

'No, actually. I work with property developers all the
time.' She turned, taking in the estate. 'In fact, I intend on
making sure all the houses look presentable for my grandmother's wedding. The videographer is—' She stopped
when she realised he wouldn't care. 'Look, the houses
here can be repaired. Some need more work than others,
but they have good bones.'

'The experts on our team believe differently.'

'Because it's in their interest to do so. And to tell your
father—a man with ample money, I'm assuming—that
he'll have to knock things down and rebuild them to be
profitable.'

'You don't think so?'

'No.' She paused. 'And I think the work I want to do
will go a long to making your work easier.'

'You want to renovate these houses before the wedding?'

She laughed. 'Heavens, no. Although I absolutely could.
No,' she said again, with a shake of her head. 'I just want
the outside of them to look good. If they do, we can take
a couple of pictures, put them online, and get some interest for when the estate is ready for…whatever it is you're
planning.'

And to tie her entire proposal up with a neat little bow,
she smiled.

Elliott blinked.

Morgan Simeon… He still couldn't get the way she'd
said her name out of his head. A husky little whisper that

had made him feel inappropriate things. And the smile turned her from a moderately attractive woman into a knockout.

No, that wasn't true. There was nothing 'moderate' about her. And it had nothing to do with how she looked.

It was her confidence. Her shrewdness. This woman who'd arranged a meeting under her grandmother's name had come prepared with a plan that would get her exactly what she wanted. She was the type to always know what she was doing. She was smart, she had a killer smile, and was playing him like a fiddle.

He didn't like it—even though parts of his body had taken an uncomfortable interest in her.

'You're good,' he said. 'Better than your grandmother. That's not an insult,' he added, when her spine straightened.

'It sounded like one.'

'Your grandmother made it personal. You've realised it's business.'

Her smile didn't fade, but her brown eyes, so open before, went sharp. 'Is it?'

There was that shrewdness again. It hit him harder than it should have because he hadn't expected it. She'd obviously looked him up. Knew that the company was his father's and his brother's and that he wasn't a part of it.

Something twisted in his gut, but he ignored it. Easily. After all, he'd been ignoring that twist for a long, long time.

He took a small breath, keeping his gaze on her, because he had a suspicion she'd seen the inhalation for what it was. An attempt at controlling his emotions. An indication of his irritation at her having the upper hand before he'd even arrived. His frustration that he'd been playing catch-up throughout their conversation. His anger that his brother

Gio had asked him to take control of this project when he *knew* this wasn't Elliott's area of expertise.

Now Morgan seemed to know it, too.

He didn't know what he disliked more: the fact that he felt so lost, or that this woman knew it and was using it to her advantage.

There was a shimmer of respect beneath his emotions, he could admit. People rarely went head-to-head with him these days. It was one of the perils of being the person in charge. He had his trusted circle at work. People who would tell him the truth. But even they tried to present honesty softly.

'Elliott, have you considered that perhaps the warehouse isn't coping with orders because of our delivery guarantee? Some items take longer than others. It's just not feasible to have such a short timeframe with the number of orders we get.'

That had been the most recent issue Karlene, his COO, had brought to his attention. She'd been with him since the inception of his company—well, his empire now, he supposed. They'd expanded into most of Africa already, and turnover was ten times more than it had been when they'd first started making a profit.

Who would have thought that custom furniture made of high-quality material and sold at relatively affordable rates would become so successful? He'd hoped, of course, and been determined to make something of himself...to feel capable.

He'd sought that feeling for a long time. Had only truly found it when his professional gambles had paid off. Before that it had been as if he were constantly walking on shaky ground. One wrong step and he'd go crashing down.

Echoes of that feeling had followed him the moment Gio had called, begging Elliott to go to some small island he'd never heard of and take charge of a project he had no experience with. They were louder now, after talking with Morgan, and he refused to hear them. Simply *refused* to allow himself to go back to feeling like a helpless kid.

'You said you have experience with property developers,' he said. 'How?'

She didn't seem concerned by his bluntness. 'I'm what they call a property expert. And by "they", I mean me—because that's what I call myself.'

She took a card from her back pocket and handed it to him. It was warm, and he tried not to think about the fact that it had been clinging to her butt. Her butt was of no consequence to him.

Feeling warmer than he had seconds ago, he studied the card. It had her name and contact details on it, along with her title: Property Expert.

'I appraise properties based on the owner's needs and tell them what can be done to meet those needs,' she continued.

'Would you do that for *my* needs?' he asked, and froze. That hadn't come out the way he'd meant it to. It had somehow sounded suggestive. Seductive. Neither of those were possible—he didn't even find her attractive.

Liar.

'I'm not sure what you mean,' Morgan answered slowly. 'What *are* your needs, Mr Abel?'

Arousal beat from a primal place inside him right to between his legs.

Okay, he finally admitted. Maybe he *was* attracted to her.

'Stop calling me that,' he said tersely.

'It's your name.'

'My name is Elliott.'

'Would you like me to call you Elliott?'

He nodded.

'Fine,' she agreed, unperturbed. 'What are your needs, Elliott?'

He'd thought that would be better. He'd been wrong.

Elliott, stop.

Yes, he silently answered that voice in his head.

He would not think about his needs.

He would not think about her needs.

Although he'd bet he could meet them.

He'd bet he could meet her needs for a long, long time.

Elliott.

'What do I need to do for the estate?' he questioned. 'Hypothetically. If I chose not to demolish and rebuild, what would I have to do?'

'Hmm…' It was all she said for a few minutes. Then, 'Well, I can actually answer that pretty thoroughly. I've spent a long time thinking about it.'

She pushed her hair back, straightened her shoulders. She'd shifted into professional mode. He had no idea how he knew it—or why he found her just as appealing as when she was relaxed.

'There are structural issues with a number of the houses, yes, but they don't need to be demolished—only repaired. Most of the changes I would suggest are superficial. Updating décor, making the estate look more cohesive… That last thing is what I plan to do for the wedding.' She folded her arms. 'I've consulted on estates that have needed much more work than Flipper Estate. And, now that I think about it, I'm sure the work that needs to be done here could be done in a month.'

And just like that, he came up with his own plan.

'Great. Then that's what we'll do.'

CHAPTER TWO

MORGAN'S EYES NARROWED. 'Excuse me?'

'We'll renovate the estate together. Instead of tearing down and rebuilding, we'll fix and redecorate. It'll be done by the time the wedding comes along, and you and I will both get what we want.'

There was a beat of silence before Morgan threw back her head and laughed. It exposed the column of her throat. Silky brown skin Elliott saw himself licking. The husky sound didn't do anything to rein in his desire, nor did the way the sound somehow *sparkled*.

He'd never been this distracted during a business meeting—and that was what this was, despite her personal motivations. Despite his. He was going to convince her to do this. And when he succeeded Flipper Estate would be the only place tourists wanted to stay when they came to Penguin Island.

It wasn't what his brother had asked of him. But Elliott wouldn't be able to do what Gio had asked—at least not for a month. He'd been on the island for a week, and he'd already encountered more obstacles than Gio had prepared him for. Each obstacle had made him feel increasingly helpless. But this... This idea... He could make it work, and he'd be doing it his way. He'd save his brother and his father's company time and money, and he'd get back to his own life in a month.

Back to pretending you don't have a family at all.

'You're serious?' Morgan said, laughter fading. 'You *can't* be serious.'

'What about this makes you think I'm not serious?'

'It's ludicrous, that's what.'

She began to pace across the pathway, stopping just before her feet hit the grass. Which meant she had all of a metre to do so. He wondered if she was getting dizzy from spinning so quickly.

'I'm here for the wedding. I can't take on a project this big.' She cast a look over him. 'And apparently hold your hand while I'm doing it.'

'I thought you were an expert.'

'I *am* an expert. And it's my expert opinion that this is ludicrous.'

'Morgan,' he said, as if saying her name wouldn't trip him up, 'this is the deal. You help me with the estate and your grandmother's wedding goes on as planned. We'll pay for every change that needs to be made, including what you want to do for the wedding video. Edna's getting married in the estate garden, correct?' She nodded. 'Well, we'll absorb the costs for whatever needs to be done to make the garden wedding-ready.' He'd take care of that bill himself. 'Do we have a deal?'

She stopped. Looked at him. 'You're blackmailing me?'

He offered her a benign smile. 'Only because you tried to blackmail me first.'

She pursed her lips. Put her hands on her hips. And, although he couldn't be sure, he thought she tried to hide a smile.

'Touché.' She sighed. 'But can I at least have some time to think about it? Speak with my grandmother?'

'Of course. Call me when you're ready.'

Morgan nodded, her dark brown eyes flitting over face. 'You're not what I expected, Elliott.'

With those words, she turned around and disappeared into her grandmother's house. He stared after her, then turned himself, and made his way back to the house he was staying in.

It was perched on top of a hill overlooking the beach and had the most breathtaking views. But those views were nothing in comparison to actually being on the beach.

He walked across the sand to the path that led to the house, the ocean crashing a short distance from his feet. The sun lowered at the horizon, casting a gorgeous orange glow across the sky. There were only four or five people ahead of him, two or three behind, and that was puzzling. There should be families with children shrieking. Adults with drinks and snacks. People on dates or lazy walks. There should be laughter and happiness and an energy that made everyone grateful it was summer.

There was none of that.

It wasn't the first time he'd noticed the island was struggling. A lot of the houses around where he was staying stood empty, though they shouldn't be. Not in summer, and not with those views. Some of the beachfront commercial properties were empty, too, boarded up with 'Closed' or 'For Sale' signs.

He didn't know the history of Penguin Island, but it wouldn't surprise him if his brother and father had bought Flipper Estate *because* the island was struggling. It was exactly like them to try and save an entire island. Elliott supposed there wasn't much else they could do after everything they'd already achieved.

Still, reviving a dying island was a little over the top.

What his father and brother's intentions were wasn't his concern, though. He was only here to do what he'd been asked. And now that he'd formulated a plan to do it, he felt better about agreeing. He no longer felt as if he was floundering, driven by guilt to help the family he'd distanced himself from, and the resentment that they'd asked him at all had gone down to a simmer. He could live with a simmer.

His own business could survive without his physical presence for a month. He'd known that when he'd said yes to Gio. Their father would be back at work by then, and Gio would have hired someone to help him run things while their father had to take it easy. In the meantime, Elliott would work on this and look after his own business as often as he could. Which would be enough now that he had Morgan on his side.

She was a force of nature. Sneaky and smart. But she wouldn't push him off balance again. Yes, she'd had a tactical advantage during their first meeting, but she'd be a fool to think that would ever be repeated. She was no fool. Enticing, beautiful, sharp—but not a fool. He would do well to remember that.

And all the while to forget the attraction dangling from an invisible hook between them.

'I'm not sure about this offer,' Morgan told her grandmother. 'I had his feet to the fire, yet somehow, he ended up unscathed and *I'm* the one with the burns. Imagine how sneaky he'll be during the deal.'

Edna finished making tea and brought their mugs to the couch, where Morgan sat. Her kitchen, living room and dining area were all spread across a large open space. Apart from the kitchen island, the designations for each of the rooms were created by her grandmother's own furniture.

A four-seater table marked the dining area. It stood to the left of them, near windows that offered a glimpse of the ocean. The couches they were currently sitting on, along with the television cabinet and the coffee table, formed the living room. The kitchen was just beyond them.

All of it would have been stunning if her grandmother hadn't insisted on such drab décor.

'He won't accept your offer if you don't agree to his terms,' Edna said, her voice sharp, though her expression was strained.

Morgan reached out and squeezed her hand. 'Don't worry about it, Gran. Your wedding is going to be perfect. It'll be exactly as you imagined it.'

'Thank you, dear.' Edna patted her hand. 'But I don't want you to spread yourself too thin. You've already agreed to help with the preparations for the wedding.'

'Which includes making sure the estate is beautiful enough to appear in the video.'

'Oh, this video business is getting on my nerves.' Edna reached for her mug with a huff. 'I know Stanley's son is a famous videographer, but the pressure he's putting us under to make sure everything looks good enough to be "worthy of his name"…' She rolled her eyes. 'I don't *want* it to be worthy of his name. I just want nice memories of my day.'

It wasn't the first time Edna had complained about this. Morgan knew that, because the first time Edna had complained Morgan had offered to take on that part of the preparations. She'd been sure two weeks would be enough time to do the painting and the landscaping, so she'd told her team she'd be unavailable for that time before the wedding.

Now two weeks had turned into a month. Her business wouldn't suffer too much for it, since most of her projects at home were in the end stages, and she'd apologised to her clients, telling them she'd still be available virtually should they need her. Then she'd taken the first flight to Penguin Island to help her grandmother with the Elliott situation.

She only hoped her parents and siblings would survive her absence, too.

They're adults, Morgan, she told herself sternly. *They can handle themselves.*

Her parents had always been adults, though, and that hadn't ever been true for them.

'I'm going to do it,' she declared, making the decision.

'Morgan—'

'I'm not going to let him spoil your day!' she exclaimed over the inner voice that asked her what the hell she was doing.

If she kept busy she wouldn't be thinking about her family at home. Her grandmother needed her more than they did and, since she couldn't physically split herself into two, she had to be here now. There was no point in worrying about them.

'Are you sure?' Edna asked, hunching her shoulders.

Whenever she did that, Morgan noticed her age. The wrinkles on her hands and around her eyes. The way time had taken her previous straight posture and curved it slightly.

Yes, she'd made the right decision. Her grandmother needed her more than her parents did. More than her siblings did. 'I'm sure.'

'Thank you, darling.'

'Of course, Gran.' Morgan smiled. 'And maybe afterwards you'll finally admit I'm your favourite grandchild.'

'Morgan.' Edna frowned. 'Every time you say that I think the others will hear.'

'It's true, though.'

'It is not.'

But Edna winked at her, making her laugh. Making her even more certain of her decision.

Now she only had to tell Elliott.

CHAPTER THREE

ELLIOTT LIFTED A hand to knock at Edna's door, but it opened before he could do so.

'Elliott,' Edna said with a nod when she saw him standing there.

'Good morning,' he replied in the same tone.

They had only been polite in the last week, though an edge had lined every conversation Edna had had with him. It didn't seem to be there any more. Did that mean Morgan was going to accept his offer or deny it?

'Morgan asked me to come.'

Edna nodded again. 'She's inside. Good luck.'

He watched her go past him, wondering about her words. Her shoulders were straight, her feet bare, even though the rest of her was dressed warmly. There had been a chill in the air that day. The ocean was making it worse, with mist and fog hovering over its surface, spreading its fingers out towards them.

'It's too cold to walk barefoot,' Elliott muttered.

'Yes.'

A voice came from behind him. He turned to find Morgan standing in the doorway, her eyes on her grandmother's retreating figure.

'But she goes for walks in the rain like that, too. It's part of her ritual, no matter the weather.'

'No shoes?' Elliott asked, looking for Edna. The fog

had swallowed her up entirely now. 'She's asking to catch a cold.'

'Hmm…'

He turned back. Narrowed his eyes.

'It's nothing,' she said, then seemed to change her mind. 'You almost sound concerned.'

'What if I am?'

'It would be unusual.'

'Why?'

Morgan shoved her hands into her jersey's pockets. It was long, pockets aligned with her thighs, so the movement didn't quite seem right. But it was enough to get him to look at her.

Two days ago, when he'd first seen her, he'd been too surprised to spare more than a casual thought for how she looked. Then, she'd worn black trousers and a sleeveless black top. Functional and appropriate—which, now that he thought about it, was probably what she'd intended. But today she was casual.

It broke his brain.

How could her tights cling so wonderfully to her legs? Long, *full* legs that gave him visions of them wrapped around his waist. Her jersey was much bigger than her right size, yet it did nothing to hide the lush curves of her body, especially when she put her hands in her pockets, dragging the material down, tight over her chest. It highlighted her breasts, which were…bigger than he remembered.

Did she mean to torture him?

'You haven't seemed that concerned about my grandmother's well-being before,' she said in that husky voice of hers.

He blinked. He wasn't there to ogle her; this was business. Not to mention that she was right. He *hadn't* been all that concerned about her grandmother. A wave of guilt crashed at the shore of his consciousness and he shifted uncomfortably.

But there was nothing he could do about it now.

'Can I come inside?'

Morgan studied him, then nodded and gestured for him to enter. As she closed the door, Elliott took a look at the place. He'd seen the basic design in the blueprints Gio had forwarded him, had even seen a few of the empty houses when he'd done his inspection days ago, but he'd never been inside an occupied one.

It had life. When someone lived in one of these houses it had life. Although the décor in this one was an odd choice. The indigo walls were too dark, the furniture and carpets too heavy. But the cups on the coffee table to one side; the plants on every spare surface of the house; the photo frames and paintings on the walls; the throws on the couches; the dishes in the kitchen cabinets—that was all life, all living, and it made him see what was so appealing about developing spaces that would result in other houses like this.

'Coffee?' she asked.

'Please.'

He contemplated the couch, but went to the kitchen instead. It felt wrong to sit down while she was working.

Strange. He'd never thought something like that before.

He cleared his throat. 'Can I help?'

'Not with the coffee,' she answered, her back to him.

His eyes skimmed over her. The jersey covered her butt, but left most of her thighs on view. His first impression of them had been correct: they were magnificent. He thought about how they'd feel in his hands, around his waist...

'Elliott?' Morgan looked over her shoulder. Her hair was pulled away from her face today, with a ribbon of some kind that made the waves of it flutter down her back. 'Did you hear a word I said?'

'Yes, of course.' He paused, searching his mind for anything she might have said. When he came up with nothing, he cleared his throat again. 'You want me not to help with the coffee.'

'And then I pointed to those biscuits over there and asked if you could plate them.' She turned with two mugs, placing them on the kitchen island. 'But clearly that request must have short-circuited your brain.'

It wasn't the request.

To distract himself, he moved to where she pointed, finding a glass container with what looked like chocolate chip cookies inside.

'Plate?' he asked.

'The cupboard above you.'

There was something that sounded amused in her voice, but he didn't look at her. Wouldn't give her the satisfaction of seeing that he was distracted, or any idea that his distraction was because of her. She was turning him into someone he didn't recognise—or perhaps someone he recognised too well. Someone he'd worked hard to leave behind.

He gritted his teeth, put the biscuits on a plate and added the plate to the island with the coffees. She had cream and sugar waiting for him.

'Black,' he said, with a quick shake of his head.

She nodded and pushed one of the cups towards him. Relief flooded his body. She hadn't handed it to him. Which meant he wouldn't look like an idiot, trying to avoid touching her fingers. And he would have had to. His awareness of her was too dangerous…too insidious to risk a careless touch.

When he met her gaze she was watching him, her eyebrows high, her brown eyes wide open. Had he noticed how rich they were before? How they looked like a thousand-year-old bottle of brown liquor, the finest there was, something owned by an emperor or a queen or someone equally important? When they were open like that he imagined falling into them, into the depths of them, and drowning. Getting drunk on her.

His skin prickled.

He clenched his jaw again, resisting a harsh exhalation.

'I take it you've come to a decision?' he asked. His words had been snippier than he'd intended. He could tell by the way she straightened, though her gaze was still curious.

'I'll do it.'

The relief that came now was more powerful than that he'd felt before. And it was joined by a faint buzz of excitement…of anticipation.

'I'm pleased.'

'I thought you might be.'

'Why?'

'Because you're getting exactly what you want,' she answered, her expression puzzled. 'And you're getting it from me.'

It took him a second to focus on the less dirty implication of her words. 'It seems you're good at your job.'

'Thank you.'

She said it the same way he imagined she'd say, *I know*.

'You're not upset that I looked you up?'

Her puzzlement deepened. 'Why would I be? I looked you up, too. It's only fair that you do the same with me. Although I probably won't like how deep a dive you've probably done.'

'Skeletons in your closet?'

She snorted. 'I'm an open book.'

Was that why he kept asking her questions? Was he trying to figure out how her brain worked? Could he sense that she'd answer all his questions? Simply tell him everything he wanted to know?

It was all to get ahead of her, he told himself.

Even though he knew he was lying.

'Now that you're willing to help,' he said briskly, 'I assume we won't be encountering any "obstacles"?' She shook her head. 'In that case, I'd like to ask you something.'

'What?' she asked suspiciously.

'Has the island always been this quiet?'

Her eyes flickered. 'No. Penguin Island used to be…' She shook her head. 'Busy. Bustling. People used to go to the penguin sanctuary. The beaches used to be packed. There were many more restaurants on the beach than there currently are, and people couldn't get a seat without a reservation.'

He'd done his research and had found a story in the papers detailing as much. It had been on page eight of the paper, which in itself had told him that people no longer cared about the island as much as they used to.

It was a sad situation, since Cape Town had once been considered Penguin Island's mainland and Capetonians had made their way to the island whenever they could. But somehow things had tapered off. The penguin sanctuary had started losing its funding. More and more of the animals had been moved to a sanctuary in Cape Town. Soon, only long-time visitors had spent their summers on the island. People had begun losing their jobs, and because of it Penguin Island was now losing its residents.

'It's still an amazing island,' Morgan continued fiercely. 'It has everything Cape Town has to offer, but with more peace. The people here deserve better.'

She sounded deflated. An impulse rose up, nearly spilled out of his mouth. He clamped his teeth. Took a moment to regroup.

He wasn't about to make this offer because of *her*. Because she was sad that the island where her grandmother lived—where people loved her—was struggling. He was doing it because it made financial and logical sense.

Calibrated now, he nodded. 'Do you think there are enough people available here to work on the estate revamp with you?'

Morgan stared.

And then, when she was done staring, she stared some more.

'You want to hire people from the island to work on the revamp?'

'If there are enough people available.' He dipped his head. 'Are there?'

She thought about all the places that had closed in the last couple of years. The ice-cream parlour down the road from Flipper Estate. The café a short walk across the beach. The two beachfront restaurants that had closed within months of each other.

Every time something like that happened her grandmother would call to tell her. Not because of the loss of business, but because of her friends who had lost their jobs. What Elliott was proposing would be huge for those people. She couldn't quite believe it.

'Why don't you believe it?' Elliott said, sounding affronted.

Oops. Had she said that last part out loud?

'I do.'

'Sounds like it.'

She snorted softly at his dry tone, then pushed her coffee aside, squared her shoulders. 'There are enough people available. But most of them won't have any experience.'

He leaned back against the kitchen island, folded his arms. Her eyes flickered to his biceps. She couldn't figure out her fascination with them. They were big, and obviously muscular, but not so defined that they looked artificial. She didn't understand that description. Nor did she understand her compulsion to reach out, run a finger over the veins she saw there...cover both arms with her hands and squeeze.

She reached for her coffee, taking a huge gulp and biting back her wince at the heat.

'We'll leave the work requiring specialised knowledge to experts. But I'm assuming a lot of it is mainly manual labour, which most people can do.'

He looked expectantly at her.

'That's true,' she said.

She reached for a biscuit, sank her teeth into it.

'And you'll be there to supervise.'

'Me?' she answered after she'd swallowed. 'What do you mean?'

'You said you'd take the lead with the renovations.'

'No, I said I'd *help* with them. As in, help you figure out what needs to be done where. Maybe draw up some plans for the interior design.' She took another bite. Chewed. Swallowed. 'I did not say I'd take the lead on a project I know next to nothing about, stepping on the toes of the professionals you've hired and taking up my time.'

An eyebrow lifted. Her stomach did a cartwheel. She bit into another piece of biscuit, because his sexiness was stressing her out. Not to mention what he was asking of her, which was much more than she'd thought she was agreeing to, and exactly what she'd been worried about when she'd told her grandmother about it.

But he was offering work to people she cared about. People who needed the money.

'I guess we didn't understand one another,' he said.

She took a breath. 'No.' She finished her biscuit and took another. 'But I'll do it.'

'Are you sure?' he asked mildly. 'Because there are only three biscuits left.'

She stopped chewing. 'What are you saying?'

'You've seemed a little…obsessed.'

'I'm stress eating. But I can stress eat and negotiate at the same time.'

The side of his mouth lifted and, man, oh, man, did it do amazing things to his beautiful face. It was a terrible time to focus on it when she had only the day before noticed it somewhat disinterestedly. But now her brain was all *Look at his brooding eyebrows! His full lips! Those cheekbones! His perfectly crooked nose!*

If she'd been interested in dating at all, she probably would have been interested in dating him. But relationships weren't for people who were always holding their families together. She'd learnt that the hard way, a long time ago. A relationship had distracted her, and she hadn't been there when her sister had needed her. Their parents had had to step in, and the anxiety that had caused for both her and Hattie had been…

Well, Morgan hadn't cared for it. Since then, she'd made sure no one would experience it again. At least not because of her choices.

Which was why deciding to help her grandmother had been tough. But her grandmother was family, too, and Morgan had made sure her siblings knew she was still reachable by phone. Hopefully there wouldn't be an emergency that required her presence. If there was, Penguin Island was a two-hour flight away…

She exhaled. Briefly considered stuffing the rest of the biscuit into her mouth. The only thing that stopped her was the way Elliott was staring at her.

Oh, yes. Elliott was still there.

At least she wasn't thinking about his beautifully crooked nose any more.

'I didn't mean to stress you out,' Elliott said. 'Nor did I think we were negotiating.'

'Of course we are.' She set the half-eaten biscuit down. 'You'll have to talk to your team. Make sure they're okay with me taking the lead. Arrange for a meeting so that I can speak with them, too.'

'You wouldn't trust what I tell you?'

'I don't think so, no,' she answered honestly. 'Somehow, in every conversation we've had, you've come out ahead. You're someone who manages to do whatever it takes to *be* ahead. And you're so skilled at doing it that the person you're doing it to doesn't realise what's happened until it's too late.'

His mouth twitched, but he only said, 'This coming from the person who tricked me into meeting with her, then ambushed me?'

'It was hardly an ambush.'

'You're not really the right person to make that call, are you?'

They stared at one another. It wasn't quite a challenge, but it might as well have been. Each second increased the tension. And the increased tension made her heart beat faster. Her skin grow clammier. She felt as if she were in a sauna and someone was incrementally turning up the heat. She'd collapse soon if she wasn't careful.

She was nothing if not careful.

'I'm good at what I do, Elliott. But I can't be good if the team I'm working with doesn't trust me. *That's* why I want to meet with them. If they trust me, they'll trust that I'll be able to manage the untrained people we're bringing in, and the project will go a lot smoother.' She paused. 'If we do this right, Flipper Estate could draw in tourists. Tourists with money they can spend on the island.'

She didn't continue because she didn't have to. He would know that if people started staying at the estate, spending their money on the island, the economy would be reinvigorated. If that happened, the island could invest in its tourism industry again. The sanctuary could reopen. The activities that had died off would come back, more people would want to vacation here, and Flipper Estate would pay for itself in half the time she imagined Elliott's family had banked on.

And, yes, all of that would mean higher employment rates for the people who'd lost their jobs.

She had to consider that Elliott had thought about this, too, since he was hiring some of those people for this job. She'd judged him as shrewd and uncaring, but perhaps she wasn't being fair—though the green and gold storm of emotion in his eyes tried to convince her otherwise. Maybe he was shrewd, but not totally uncaring. Either way, she found herself holding her breath until he spoke.

'I'd like the names of everyone you'll want to put forward for the work. We'll need the admin sorted as soon as possible—though we might have to start before everything is finalised.'

'That won't be a problem.'

'I can arrange for a meeting at the end of the week. I still have employees trickling in.'

'Sure.' She bit her lip. 'Thank you.'

He nodded. 'I take it our negotiation is complete?'

'My grandmother's wedding remains a priority.'

'I have no doubt about that,' he answered dryly. 'If you need anything to achieve that, even if it doesn't actually pertain to the project, you know where to find me.'

Not totally uncaring, indeed.

Pleasure bloomed inside her, but she stamped it down. *No pleasure. Only business.*

'Thank you,' she said firmly.

'We have a deal.'

He pushed himself off the counter and offered her his hand. After a beat, she took it. His hand was much larger than hers, rougher, too, as if he personally made the furniture his company 'Crafted' sold. It sent a shiver down her spine, but she told herself it wasn't erotic. It was concern.

She was worried that she'd just made the biggest mistake of her life.

CHAPTER FOUR

WHEN ELLIOTT HAD first arrived on Penguin Island he'd thought it quaint. The main road—creatively called Beach Road, since it ended at the beach that made the island's perimeter—formed a cross that divided the island into four. Two of the quadrants were mainly residential areas, where the houses ranged from the most beautiful beach homes to more dilapidated ones, worn by the salt of the ocean. The third quadrant was reserved for the now-closed penguin sanctuary, which was the wildest beach of the island. He was currently in the fourth quadrant, that held the harbour and the main town.

Somehow, quaintness had turned into wonder.

It was the kind of place that didn't entirely feel like part of South Africa. The cobblestones were more suited to an English town, as were the narrow paths between the stores, with more people walking than using cars. But the colourful storefronts were one hundred percent South African, as was the energy. It held a friendliness, a welcomeness that he'd never experienced before in the travelling he'd done in his life. He could smell the ocean from here, too, and if he kept perfectly still he could hear the faint wash of the waves against the shore.

The paths weren't busy this morning, despite the fact that they held the heart of the town. The grocery stores, the pharmacies, the doctors' offices and the dentist.

The closer he got to the harbour, the more touristy the places became. A coffee shop, a restaurant and a gift shop, all with penguin-themed décor—and, in the case of the gift shop, merchandise. And there were enough empty buildings that it felt almost ominous.

An uncomfortable feeling settled in his chest. He tried to identify its source. It took time, but eventually he realised it came from the conversation he'd had with Morgan. She'd made him feel almost responsible for reviving the town by telling him the renovation of Flipper Estate could be more than simply that. That it could draw tourists into the town. She'd all but said that it could lead to an improved economy, and there had been hope in her eyes as she'd envisaged a future where the islanders had work again…

Yeah, that had made him uncomfortable.

He didn't want to be responsible for an economy. Hell, he didn't even want to be responsible for the renovation, and he was doing that for his *family*.

Although, to be fair, he hadn't wanted to do anything for his family in a long time. He was content with being the outsider. The son who only visited his parents on special occasions. Doing more than that tended to make him feel small. Reminded him of the kid he used to be, who wanted nothing more than his parents' unconditional love and approval.

He wasn't a kid any more, and he knew he'd never get either of those things. Stepping in for the Penguin Island project was a favour to his brother, who he had a decent relationship with. A cordial one, at least. And, fine, he was also doing it because his father couldn't work immediately after his heart attack.

But helping out didn't mean he was that kid again. Helping out was the kind of thing even a 'special occasions only' son did. Plus, Elliott was helping on his own terms.

He hadn't told his brother about those terms yet—about any of the changes he was planning, really—but Gio had other, more important things on his mind. He wasn't worried about one project when he had several others he was handling by himself.

'Elliott. *Elliott*.' A peppy voice sounded from behind him. 'Why aren't you moving?'

He turned, looking for the voice and finding it lower down than he expected. He adjusted his gaze to see big brown eyes blinking up at him. Morgan. Her long, wavy hair drifted to her face from her ponytail and she pushed it back, irritated.

Charming.

What? No. It wasn't charming. Why would he find it charming? That irritation? That tiny movement? Why would realising she was shorter than he remembered be charming, too? Why would it make his body ache?

It wouldn't.

Good thing he didn't find *her* charming either.

'Distracted,' he said in a short tone.

Seemed he always spoke to her in a short tone. What was wrong with him?

'Hmm...' Even that sounded peppy. 'Shall we go inside?'

He gestured for her to lead the way.

Everyone working at the coffee shop they were meeting at greeted her by name, asked about her family, and only then acknowledged his presence. Because of it, he learnt that she was the oldest of three siblings, that she doted on her niece, and that her entire family would be in town for the wedding, just over three weeks away.

'I'm sorry about that,' she said when they were finally seated. 'I haven't been around for a while.'

'Why not?'

She blinked. 'Oh. I... I've been busy.'

The way her eyelashes fluttered, the way she frowned, told him that wasn't the truth. Or maybe it was, but it wasn't the whole truth. He shouldn't want to know what the whole truth was. He *didn't* want to know.

'Maybe if I hadn't been so busy I'd have seen what was happening here,' she continued, so softly he would have thought she wasn't speaking to him if it hadn't been for her next words. 'My grandmother told me about places closing, people moving away... I don't know why I didn't put it together.'

'You were in denial.'

She met his gaze. 'Is that meant to make me feel better?'

'Yes.'

She smiled then, highlighting the bright red she'd painted her lips with. She'd done some other things to her face, too. Her eyes were sharper, which was probably why he'd noticed them earlier. There was something different about her cheeks as well. He knew make-up was responsible for all of it, but he couldn't figure out what exactly she'd done.

'You have an odd way of comforting people, Elliott.'

'I wasn't—'

He broke off. No point in denying it. He had been trying to comfort her. His cheeks grew warm, but he knew it couldn't be a blush. A blush would mean he was embarrassed. Self-conscious. He was neither.

'I've had an idea,' she said briskly, as if she were aware of his inner turmoil and wanted to move on. 'To boost the estate's profile once we're done.'

He nodded. 'Go on.'

'My grandmother's soon-to-be son-in-law is a well-known wedding videographer. He has a huge social media following, and has shot a few celebrity weddings, some politicians, a couple of millionaires...' She picked up a sugar sachet and began to fiddle with it. 'He's doing his

father and my grandmother's wedding, too—hence their
demands for how the estate should look.'

'You're doing it for *him*?'

She gave him a look. 'My grandmother doesn't care
about how the houses in the estate look. She loves living
there. It's home to her. Although she *is* getting married in
the garden, which is objectively stunning, so maybe she
does care?' She tilted her head. 'But I don't think she would
have asked me to redo the facades of the houses if there
hadn't been some pressure from Gerald to make sure the
venue was "worthy of his amazing name".'

She rolled her eyes and took a second sugar sachet, hit-
ting it against the first. Was she pretending it was Gerald's
head? Maybe she was pretending it was Elliott's. After all,
he'd been as much of a pain in the neck as this Gerald.

Again, he told himself that he didn't care. But his mind
refused the lie this time. He *did* care. He cared that he'd
been short with her, and that she seemed to think he was so
cold and unfeeling that he wouldn't care about her grandmother's health—that her perception of him was that he'd
do anything to get ahead.

It made no sense when he'd actually cultivated that
image. Not only with her, but with the world. When he'd
left the needy child he'd once been behind. The child who'd
been desperate for his parents' attention. Who'd wanted
to be treated as well as his genius brother. He'd purposely
put a barrier between his emotions and everyone else's, in
business and his personal life, and it had suited him perfectly fine. Hell, it had turned him into a success.

But you have no real relationships because of it.

'That was a little bit of a rant, wasn't it?' she asked,
biting her lip.

He focused on her again, his gaze lingering on her lips.
He'd been distracted, had made her feel uncomfortable
because he hadn't been paying attention, and now he was

staring at her. Because a particular part of his body had taken note of her lip-biting.

He shook his head. 'It's fine.' He took a breath. 'Your idea…?'

'Right.' She put down the sugar. 'What if we get him to post the wedding on his social media? We can ask everyone on the island to share it, using a hashtag like *romanceisland*, and get Penguin Island trending?'

'Get everyone's attention?'

'The right people, too,' she agreed. 'The kind of people who would hire a wedding videographer like Gerald. If he can get footage of the beaches, the forests, the town… This place is beautiful, Elliott. There's no way people won't be tempted into getting married here. And with his shots of Flipper Estate they'll know there are gorgeous modern homes to rent for their guests. The garden is beautiful. We can build an altar, or a floral arch—something to signal that *this* is where they want to declare they'll be spending their lives with the person they love.' She leaned forward, pressing her hands into the table. 'It could be amazing.'

He stared. Because her idea was good. Great, really. It would do everything that she said, and quickly, too. People with money wanted the exclusivity of being the first to do something. He knew, because he'd fallen into that trap more than once and was vaguely ashamed of it. If she was right, people would be trying to secure the island for their weddings quickly. She'd probably considered that, too.

It *was* a great idea.

But mostly he stared because of her. Because she was beautiful when she was passionate. It kicked him in the gut, and he had to cling to his breath so the air didn't escape his lungs.

'You hate it,' she said, slumping over.

'No.' He cleared his throat when the word came out hoarse. 'No, it's good. Brilliant.'

'Brilliant? Really?' She picked up the sugar sachet again. 'Someone should tell your face.'

'My face?'

'You look like someone just informed you of a close friend's passing.'

Considering he felt as if he was grieving—for his sanity and for the version of himself who didn't get distracted by attraction—that made sense.

'That's not a reflection of my feelings on this issue.' *Only about you.* 'Your idea really is good. But it means we *have* to be done by the wedding.'

'I know.'

'That's just over three weeks.'

'I know that, too.' The sugar sachets returned to their rightful place. 'You said the meeting with your team is tomorrow?' He nodded. 'Once we have them on board, we'll need to meet with the people we're hiring for the construction work. We'll need a bigger venue, so we should probably use the Town Hall. The big building on the hill,' she clarified, nodding her head in its general direction.

'Won't booking that take time?'

'This is Penguin Island,' she said with faint amusement. 'If the mayor approves, we'll have it. For tomorrow night, too.'

'Of course we will.'

She smiled. 'The joys of a small town.'

'What do we tell them?' he asked, ignoring the slight racing of his heart.

'What we've been saying all along. It'll be hard work in a short time frame. We'll explain exactly what needs to be done and how we intend on doing it. If you can get the paperwork ready by tomorrow, we can have everyone sign it.'

'I can do that.'

'Good.' She sat back. 'We'll be ready to start the day after tomorrow, and then it'll be full steam ahead.'

'You're good at this,' he said, without thinking.

The words were true, but if he'd given himself a chance to consider them he would have tried… Well, not to say them. It felt revealing. He wasn't sure how or why.

But then her expression softened. Grew vulnerable. There were a thousand secrets in her brown eyes when she met his gaze, and when she smiled, it seemed sad.

'Thank you.' Even her voice sounded raw. 'I've had a lot of practice at fixing things.'

And that practice had hurt her.

He had no idea how he knew that, but he did, and he was getting ready to avenge her when she shook her head.

'We should talk to Mayor Henderson about the Town Hall.'

All business now, he saw. 'Tell me how it goes.'

'Oh, no,' she said with a snort. 'When I said "we", I meant you.'

'He doesn't know me.'

She wrinkled her nose. 'That's probably for the best.'

CHAPTER FIVE

THERE WAS A reason Morgan didn't date any more—and that reason began with the mayor of Penguin Island. He hadn't been mayor back then, of course. Back then he'd been a confident, cool, charming boy who'd given Morgan her first kiss. Been her *almost* first lover.

She'd lost her judgement, just like many other people did when they were young and naïve.

Most of those people didn't have parents to look after, though. Two younger siblings to take care of.

'You have history with Mayor Henderson,' Elliott stated.

It *had* been a statement, but it was as if his voice hadn't told his face. His eyebrows were raised, not for the first time during their conversation. In disbelief? Surprise? Judgement?

She didn't care.

Don't you?

No, I don't, she told her traitorous inner voice.

'We had a thing once upon a time.'

The brows lifted higher. 'You and Mayor Henderson?'

'He was just Thaddeus Jerome Henderson the Third when we dated.' She snorted at the look on his face. 'Yeah, I generally feel that way when I think about that part of my life. So I try not to.'

Elliott didn't reply, but he looked at her. Really looked at her. As if he could see into her soul. As if he could draw out her secrets, have them reveal themselves to him, and then he'd have some magical power over her.

It felt as if he was using a measure of that power now. The way his eyes searched her face, met her gaze, lingered. She held her breath, clung to her secrets, and knew it was silly.

Pointless, too, apparently, because he said, 'He hurt you?'

'No.'

Quick, simple denial. She should have left it at that. She didn't.

'I hurt him.'

'I have no doubt about that.'

'What does that mean?'

'Nothing.'

His denial came as quickly as hers had, but it didn't feel simple. Not in the least.

'Look, we dated one summer when I was in my early twenties.'

Why was she explaining this to him? Why couldn't she *stop*?

'Half of the time we spent here, the other half back home in Cape Town, and it was…' She exhaled. 'Exactly what you'd expect from a relationship when you're young and stupid.'

For a while, 'young and stupid' had been glorious. Morgan had been a young adult, but Thad had been her first boyfriend. Her first relationship. He hadn't been the first person interested in her, but before that she'd been too consumed by her family responsibilities. Too haunted by the ghosts of the past.

When her parents had had Morgan, they'd been only sixteen and seventeen. Morgan had always refused to repeat their actions, so she'd stayed away from dating, from flirting, from anything that could potentially lead her down her parents' path.

It had been easy, since she'd had her siblings to look after. They were five and eight years younger than her, and the adjustment to having a bigger family had been hard for her parents. So Morgan had learned how to help. She was the older sister; of course she would help take care of them.

The year Morgan had dated Thad, her sister Hattie had ended up pregnant at seventeen, just like their mother. Her brother Rob had had his sullen teenage feelings amplified by a learning disability diagnosis. And Morgan...

Morgan had been tired.

Too tired to maintain the defences she'd tried to put in place to prevent a relationship with Thad in the first place.

It had only been Morgan who'd come to the island that summer. Hattie had been too far along in her pregnancy, and Rob had had a series of assessments he still had to work through. She hadn't wanted to come, but her grandmother had insisted. Edna had called her parents, said heaven knew what to them, and they'd insisted, too.

Morgan had agreed because of the tiredness. Because everyone had been okay with her cutting the usual time she spent visiting her grandmother in half as a compromise. Because her parents had seemed relatively calm about everything they were being left with.

And then she'd come, and Thad had charmed her, and she'd been young and stupid—hiding the relationship from her grandmother, as if Edna would have cared that her twenty-two-year-old granddaughter had a boyfriend. Rendezvousing with him in secret to keep anyone from seeing them.

When she'd returned to Cape Town, Thad had followed, and she'd lost track of herself. Sweet, innocent kisses had become passionate, desperate touches. Touches had led to caresses. To things Morgan had never imagined herself doing.

But she'd stopped them before she could make the kind of mistake she'd avoided her entire life. And that same night Hattie had gone into labour. Something Morgan had only discovered *after* her niece's birth, since she'd turned her phone off.

Her stomach churned.

This was exactly why she didn't like thinking about it.

'Any tips?' Elliott asked now, his voice gruff, short.

It tended to be at times. She couldn't be sure, but she thought it had something to do with his control. When he felt as if he didn't have it, or when he was clinging to it.

But that didn't make sense in this context. The last few minutes had been about *her*. What did he have to control in that?

Maybe she'd thought wrong.

'Compliment him,' she said softly. 'He likes being flattered.'

'You don't seem the type to indulge a man's ego.'

'Because I haven't done it with you?' She laughed lightly, aware of the tension growing in the air. 'You're not the type of man who wants me to indulge his ego.'

A single eyebrow lifted. She felt as if she'd been dropped into a pool of hot water.

'That's confident,' he noted.

'Yes.' Needing something to do, she gestured for the bill. 'Since you're not here because Abel and Son Development is your company, I assume you're doing all this for your family. Yet you haven't really commented on me doing this for *my* family, which I've been open about. Usually, people try to find some kind of common personal ground, even in business. The fact that you haven't means you prefer to keep people at a distance, which doesn't exactly play into the whole ego thing. So, yeah,' she ended, 'I am confident.'

He didn't reply. Her heart began to pound, but she urged it to remain calm. She meant every word. Didn't regret saying it either. So the intensity in his eyes, the way he clenched and unclenched his hands, shouldn't bother her.

Then he exhaled.

'Morgan, I don't know—' He cut himself off and shook his head. 'You're—' He didn't finish that either.

'Don't hurt yourself, Elliott,' she said, amused. 'I promise to keep the mind-reading part of myself to a minimum. Now, I have some things to do before our meeting with everyone,' she went on, shifting the conversation to a subject he'd be more comfortable with. 'Assuming you can get Mayor Henderson's approval.'

'I'll get it,' he said easily, though still gruffly.

Easy, she warned her body when it shimmied at the sound of his voice. With the power of knowing she'd done it to him. *You don't even know that it's because of you.*

But, even as she told herself that, she knew it was.

She had some power over him.

And, heaven help her, she wanted to discover the extent of it.

Mayor Thaddeus Jerome Henderson the Third was an idiot.

Not within his position. The mayor—who had insisted that Elliott call him Thad—had been professional, courteous, even helpful. Elliott had managed to secure the Town Hall for their meeting, and Mayor 'Call-Me-Thad' had asked if he could be there.

'You're doing a great thing for this community,' Thad had said, threading his fingers together and laying his hands on his desk. 'If I can offer my support in any way, you'll have it.'

Of course Elliott didn't want Thad's support. He and

Morgan were managing things just fine. But that thought had been tainted with personal feelings…emotions he didn't care to examine. So he'd turned that part of himself off and looked at the situation objectively.

Thad's support might not mean anything to Elliott, but the islanders who had been without jobs—who might have blamed the mayor for not doing anything about the employment situation—would be grateful. Politically, Thad would be subtly implying that he was responsible for finding them work.

Smart of him. Elliott could admit that. He wasn't upset about it—he would have done the same thing in Thad's position. But that smartness was clearly isolated to his professional choices. In his personal life Thad had ruined a relationship with Morgan. He'd hurt her—and that made Thad an idiot.

And, yes, Morgan had said she'd hurt Thad, too, but break-ups were like that. Not that Elliott would know. He made sure all the people he dated knew what to expect up front: no attachments, no emotional connections. They got to enjoy each other's company, and that was it. Most of the time it worked. So these…these *feelings* Morgan awoke in him were as unwelcome as they were strange.

The jealousy that had him now calling a perfectly reasonable man an idiot was a good example of that.

That had started the moment she'd told him what had happened between her and Thad. He'd tried with all his might not to let the way her words had affected him show, but he didn't think he'd succeeded.

As a man who prided himself on his control, he didn't appreciate that. But his control was intact once again. So when Morgan had called to ask if they could walk to the Town Hall together, he'd agreed.

Spending time with her was an unavoidable aspect of

their working relationship. He had to get used to *that*, and not his inappropriate feelings for her.

'Hey,' she said now, bounding down the path of Edna's house, her dress flying behind her. 'Thanks for walking with me.'

He nodded.

'I thought it would be good for us to arrive together. Show a united front or something?' She shrugged as they started walking towards the beach that would take them to Beach Road. 'That might be silly. But I figured since I wanted to run some of the décor choices by you, we'd use this walk productively either way.'

She continued telling him about the colour scheme she was thinking of. Suggesting that she use one of the houses as a real-life mock-up, so he could see everything. And she talked about getting her grandmother's friends to start moving out, and her grandmother, too.

Edna had always planned to move out—back to Cape Town with her fiancé, who was currently there, finalising everything for their move.

'But of course she's giving me a hard time, because she's worried you'll go back on your word.' She gave Elliott a look. 'I told her we could trust you, but I don't think she bought it. I should probably do something about that…but she'll get the chance to see you're serious. We'll have done plenty of work before we get to her house. There's time.'

He studied her as they walked down the tarred road that led to the beach. There were houses on either side, some in disrepair, others well-kept, with tidy gardens and swing sets.

'You're nervous,' he noted. 'Why?'

'Nervous? I'm not nervous.' She bent and picked a flower from someone's garden. Twirled it a few times between her fingers before popping it behind her ear. 'What makes you think I'm nervous?'

'You haven't stopped talking since we left your grand-mother's house.'

'That's not true.' Her eyes went wide. 'It *is* true. I'm sorry.'

'No, it's okay. It's…cute.'

He felt her go still rather than saw it, and his cheeks grew hot. Where had that admission come from? Yes, he'd *thought* it. Had been entertained by her constant stream of chatter. By the fact that she'd revealed a quirk. He was impressed that despite all their talks, their negotiations, she hadn't revealed the quirk earlier. Maybe she hadn't been nervous then. But she *had* been stressed, he thought, remembering the biscuit-eating. Another little charming quirk.

Cute? Charming? He needed to get a grip, and fast.

'Sorry,' he muttered. 'That was—'

'Nice,' she interrupted. 'It's nice to hear what's going on in your head. Sometimes I feel like I'm…'

'Like you're what?' he asked when she didn't finish.

'I'd rather not say.'

'I'd rather you did.'

She sighed. 'Sometimes it feels like I'm talking to a robot. You barely give me any reaction, and when you do it's…controlled. Or muted. Like you're keeping yourself from feeling, or something.'

He almost stumbled. Only pure determination kept his feet moving. One foot in front of the other. Left, right, left, right. He found himself mentally saying those words, re-peating the instructions over and over again as he walked, as his feet sank into soft sand and he dropped down to take off his shoes.

How had she known that? She'd spent less than a week with him, but she'd already seen through to the core of him. There were people in his life who'd known him for longer and hadn't seen it. Or if they had, they hadn't said anything. Not even his brother, who'd known him before...

Before he'd made the decision to stop allowing his emotions to get the better of him.

'I didn't want to say it,' she said when he straightened. Her shoes were already in her hands, and she was watching him worriedly. 'I didn't want to upset you.'

'You haven't upset me.'

'You seem upset.'

'Impossible. I'm a robot.'

'No, I didn't mean—' She exhaled. 'You're reacting now,' she said. 'It's muted, but I can see that you're upset. And I'm sorry.'

There was a thickness in his throat. An irrational anger coursing through his body. Because he *was* upset, and he didn't want her to see it. And he hated that his emotions had affected her. He hated that her precise and sharp observations had made him feel raw and naked.

'You see too much,' he said eventually, walking again. 'You talk too much, too.'

She gave a light snort. 'I'm sorry for the first thing, though it makes no sense for me to apologise. It feels right, though, so that's what I'm doing. And, yes, to the second thing.' Seemingly deciding he needed a change in topic, she continued. 'I hid it from you earlier today. I knew it would scare you off.'

He almost laughed.

The desire to do so surprised him into not laughing. The confusion kept him from doing more than shaking his head. The effect this woman had on him was...impossible. Almost a decade of predictability when it came to his emotions, and now he was on a rollercoaster in a matter of minutes.

'I am nervous,' she said, changing the topic again.

For him, he thought. *Again.*

'This is important, right? It's important for your team to respect me, to think I'm capable, to be willing to work with the islanders. And it's important for the islanders to see me as more than just Edna's granddaughter—the little girl with pigtails who used to walk on the beach with her two younger siblings. Never laughing, always serious.'

'I don't believe that.'

'What?'

'The never laughing part.'

As if proving his point, she laughed again. At the same moment the wind rustled through the curls she'd pulled behind a colourful headband. Whipped through the skirt of her white summer dress. He caught a glimpse of beautiful brown thighs. Thick and luscious. Not for the first time he pictured them wrapped around his waist. It was becoming an obsession.

'I was a serious child,' she said with a shake of her head, drawing him out of his own thoughts. 'My parents...' She trailed off. 'There was a lot to think about when I was younger.'

He looked at her face, saw the struggle there. Wanted to ask. But that was hardly fair. He refused to say anything personal to her. And even though he knew she was dying to ask, she never did. She respected his boundaries, so he would respect hers.

So heaven only knew why he blurted out, 'My brother is a genius.'

He stopped walking. So did she. She was watching him now, her face filled with puzzlement.

Of course it was. He'd just blurted out an inane piece of information with no context. A personal piece of information, something he never spoke of. *Never.*

'A genius?' she repeated. 'Is that something your mother told you? Because it's sweet, but not worthy of that kind of proclamation.'

His lips curved, his amusement faint but there. He looked down, trying to figure out how to explain. He couldn't not explain. Not when he'd brought it up in the first place.

'No, he's an actual genius. He went for IQ tests. Evaluations. Ended up going to university at fifteen, finishing at eighteen, and then helping my father run his business.'

Increasing production and turnover by two hundred per cent in five years.

He didn't add that part, though it was etched in his brain. When his father had started what had then been Abel Property Development, the company had been moderately successful. Then Gio had begun to implement his plans, and moderate success had turned into significant success.

His parents had framed every newspaper article. There had already been walls in their house dedicated to Gio. To his awards, his degrees. The newspaper stories had joined them. And by the time Elliott had turned eighteen, ready to go to university himself, with good grades, he'd already felt like a failure.

'Elliott…' Morgan breathed as she came closer. 'I'm sorry for the pain that caused you.'

He stiffened. 'I didn't say it did.'

'You didn't have to.'

She lifted her hand, and for a second he thought she was going to touch him. But she stopped, making an awkward gesture instead. A hand spread in front of her body. He grunted.

She studied him, then angled her head and started walking again.

He waited for her to say something. Anything. So he could get angry and cling to the anger instead of this… this stickiness on his skin. This rippling in his blood. It was as if he'd been challenged to a fight and his body was preparing to defend him.

It wouldn't do. It simply wouldn't do.

And *now*, of course, she refused to speak.

'Why aren't you pushing me?' he asked curtly.

'You don't want to talk about your personal life. That's fair. Now,' she said, redirecting their conversation for a third time. 'Let's talk about the mock-up house. Here's what I'm thinking…'

CHAPTER SIX

THE TOWN HALL meeting went better than Morgan had expected. Most of Elliott's team had been stand-offish at first, but once she'd begun to tell them about her plans, divided into specific phases over the next few weeks, she'd seen some of them relax. By the end of it she was sure she had the support, if not the confidence, of most of them.

She knew the confidence would come—as would the support of those she hadn't yet managed to convince. She was good at her job. They would see that and know her participation wasn't a fluke.

Well, they didn't have to know that her participation, especially the way it had come about, actually was a fluke.

The islanders who'd been approached for the construction work had been present during her speech, too. She'd welcomed them, but waited to address them in her plans, wanting Elliott's team to know she was aware of the uneven dynamics. None of the islanders had seemed to mind. They were too grateful for the work and eager to do what needed to be done—including waiting fifteen minutes while she spoke solely to the team.

During those fifteen minutes she'd seen Thad slip into the room. She'd sensed his surprise at seeing her, but she'd ignored it—and him—until she'd turned to the islanders' group. Then she'd given him a slight nod in greeting, and walked the islanders through what would be happening for them in the next few weeks.

When the meeting was done, she struggled not to let her relief and her exhaustion show. There were too many people who'd remained behind…too many people approaching her with questions or comments. She couldn't show them how she was feeling. It would undermine everything she'd worked so hard for. So she sucked it up, and did what she had to do, until there were only two people left.

Thad and Elliott were both leaning against the wall next to the door, so she would have to pass them to leave. It felt like a metaphor of some kind—or not a metaphor, a *punishment*. In punishment for all her awful deeds, the universe had decided to force her to interact with the man she'd nearly slept with and the one she was considering sleeping with.

What?

No. No, she was *not* considering sleeping with Elliott.

She shut down her instinctive response, which was to admire him as he leaned there, looking mouth-wateringly good in jeans and a T-shirt. It seemed to be his uniform, and after seeing him in it so often she thought that it did suit him after all. He didn't need fancy clothing. He drew enough attention simply by being himself.

Morgan!

Right, this was getting embarrassing. She had no idea where it was all coming from, but it could return there without her acknowledgement.

She took a breath and went to deal with her punishment.

'Hey,' she said as a general greeting, and then she looked at Thad. 'How are you?'

'Good,' he answered, offering her a small smile that reminded her of why she'd fallen so hard. 'I didn't expect to see you here.'

'Yeah. I'm taking the lead on the construction work at the estate.'

'Elliott didn't mention it.'

She looked at Elliott. He only offered her a raised brow. It had more of an effect on her than Thad's smile ever had.

'Should he have?' she forced herself to ask Thad.

'No,' Thad said, straightening. 'No reason to, is there?'

He shook his head and put his hands in his pockets. He looked at her, eyes searching her face, before he gave her a half-smile.

'I'll see you around, Morgan.'

He disappeared before she could reply.

Morgan waited a few minutes, then followed. She felt more than saw Elliott's presence as he walked beside her. In silence, they took the same path they had on their way to the Town Hall.

'You haven't seen Thad since you broke up?' he asked.

She'd known he would ask eventually. 'We've seen each other around town over the last decade or so. It usually goes about the same as it just did.'

'He fawns over you.'

It was a comment, not a question, and she laughed before she could help herself. '*Fawns?* Good heavens, Elliott, if that's fawning, then what you've been doing with me is—'

She cut herself off before she could finish that. It was the best thing to do. Especially considering his expression, which had been tight and blank at the beginning of their conversation and was now stormy and blank. Contradictory combinations, but true.

She couldn't read *why* his face was tight or stormy. There was no anger, no frustration, *nothing* behind the surface. Not even the muted expressions she could usually see on him.

It left her feeling frustrated, but that didn't matter. He

obviously didn't care whether she could read him or not. If he did, he wouldn't continue to keep his feelings under lock and key. Which was a stupid thing to be angry about. They were his feelings; he could do whatever he wanted with them. Control them. Mute them. Hide them. Reveal them to her when he shouldn't so she could understand why her relationship with the island mayor ended and why seeing him now was so awkward.

Wait—that last part was about *her*. Although, to be fair, she hadn't told Elliott any of the details about her relationship with Thad. And she never would. She was pretty sure about that.

They were walking in silence now, down Beach Road and through the main town. Without the anxiety of the meeting she could enjoy the surroundings more than she had on their way up. She loved the charm of the town. The sidewalks and its faded paving. The busy shops now that it was the end of the day. The restaurants and café owners and their regular dinner patrons.

She waved back to those who waved. Touched a lamp post every time they passed one. Stared at the benches with their dark brown, almost black wood and their golden plaques with the names of people in town who had donated towards getting them made.

She couldn't remember seeing anything so sentimental in Cape Town. Perhaps in churches, or national gardens, but in a main road of one of the main areas? No.

It was part of what made Penguin Island special. The intimacy of it. The fact that someone could read a name on a bench and someone who lived there would come along and tell them about that person.

'He feels guilty,' Elliott said softly.

It took her a moment to realise he was talking about Thad.

'Neither you nor I live here, but we've come up with a

plan to get a significant number of the island's people employed. There are likely people who feel betrayed that their mayor can't help them feed their families. And now that something's being done about it—something that might lead to more employment opportunities down the line—he can look good.' He paused. 'He feels guilty about that, too.'

She angled a look at him. 'He told you that?'

'Some.'

'Liar,' she accused. And when his mouth curved, she laughed. 'But it's very likely true. How astute of you.'

'I have my moments.'

She was about to reply, but he took the wind out of her sails.

'I wanted to say thank you,' he said.

Her head whipped to the side. They'd reached the beach, and he was looking ahead at the waves. She bent down to take off her shoes, used the movement as a moment to compose herself.

'What for?' she asked eventually.

'You could see that I was uncomfortable during our conversation earlier.'

As he was now, she thought.

'You changed the subject, more than once, to account for that.' He cleared his throat. 'So—thank you.'

He gave her a curt nod, then bent to take off his own shoes. She pursed her lips to keep from smiling. But when he straightened she was smiling anyway.

'On a scale from one to ten, how painful was that for you?'

He narrowed his eyes. 'Not nearly as painful as that question.'

She laughed. 'An apology isn't necessary,' she said, sobering. 'Though I appreciate it.' At his questioning look, she clarified. 'I understand your personal life is out of bounds.'

'As long as you also understand that it has nothing to do with you,' he replied stiffly. 'My personal life is complicated.'

'Hmm...'

'Hmm?'

'Hmm,' she confirmed. 'I've researched you, remember? I've seen pictures of all those women on your arm. Maybe it isn't complicated. Maybe *you've* complicated it.'

Something dark lit in his eyes. 'You're jealous?'

'Jealous?' She snorted. 'Please. I'm not interested in a man who thinks "fawning" consists of an awkward conversation back and forth.' She'd already walked ahead before she realised he'd stopped. She turned. 'What?'

The darkness was still in his eyes, shimmering right at the surface like a monster in a lake. It was just as dangerous, too, she thought. One wrong move and she'd be snatched and dragged under.

But then he blinked and it disappeared. He began to walk again, ignoring her question.

'You're not the only person with a complicated personal life, you know,' she said after a while.

'You're more open about yours.'

'Am I?' She glanced at him. 'Besides knowing how many members my family consists of—and that I once dated Thad—what do you know about me?'

When he didn't answer, she nodded.

'Exactly.'

For all her talking, she really didn't share details of her life. How had he only noticed that now?

Because he'd thought he knew about her. He'd thought knowing that she had younger siblings, a niece and a grandmother she clearly adored constituted knowing *her.* Same went for her past with the mayor.

But he didn't know what kind of relationship she had

with her siblings. She might adore her grandmother but not approve of Edna's fiancé. Thad might have been the love of her life, and something had happened to break them up.

As he looked back on it, he thought the fact that he hadn't noticed had been partly because of her. She talked so cheerfully, so openly and confidently, that simply listening to her drew people in. Created a false sense of intimacy that made them believe she was exactly who she presented herself to be.

But that was a trick. Something to prevent people from looking further. He knew that because he did the same thing. He could see through her facade now. Through that satisfied expression on her face to the pain just beneath.

She *seemed* satisfied that he didn't know her, but she wasn't. Why?

Then she looked at him, narrowed her eyes and stuck out her tongue.

He couldn't remember the last time someone had stuck out a tongue at him. Probably when he'd been a kid. And it sure as hell hadn't had *this* effect on him. Making him acutely aware of his blood, his skin. Both hot, heavy...

He had the sudden impulse to run into the ocean to cool down. It was an inappropriate reaction to someone so silly. Especially after what he'd been thinking. But he'd been completely taken aback by her sticking out her tongue. Not only because of the effect it had had on him, but because it...*charmed* him. Beneath his more sensual physical reaction, something twinkled and sparked. Something he'd never known existed. A lightness that seemed precious. In need of protection.

The strangest part of it all was that it made him want to smile. And that was more dangerous than anything else this woman had made him feel.

'You're upset,' she accused now. 'But you can't get upset because I pointed out something that's true.'

'I'm not upset.'

'You look upset.'

'I'm not upset.'

'You *sound* upset.'

He grunted, and tried to think of something that would stop this back-and-forth. 'You're proud of the fact that I don't know much about you.'

She frowned. 'I wouldn't say "proud".'

'Satisfied?'

'Satisfied,' she agreed after a beat.

Instead of fighting the urge to smile this time, he allowed his lips to lift and found it easier than resistance.

'You're smiling.'

He stopped smiling.

'No!' she moaned. 'No, I'm sorry. I didn't mean to—' She broke off on an exhalation. 'You have a nice smile.'

That lightness exploded in his chest.

He took a breath. 'Thank you.'

Her cheeks lifted as her mouth curved, making her eyes crinkle, but not dimming their sparkle.

She had a nice smile, too.

'Okay, since I'm changing the subject so well these days, let me point out that you also seem satisfied at keeping things from me.'

He couldn't deny that. 'Yes.'

'Why?' she asked. 'Why are we so happy to *not* share things? Surely we should be opening up to people. To be healthy or whatever...'

She kicked out a foot. Sand sprang from her toes and she grinned, absolutely delighted by such a small, simple thing.

His heart skipped.

Just a little—barely noticeable.

He noticed.

'It's too painful,' he answered honestly, surprising himself. 'To talk about things means confronting them. It's easier to ignore them.'

'Is it?' She snorted a little, her joy of only a few moments ago fading. 'I've always told my siblings that ignoring a problem won't make it go away. And I believe that.' She paused. 'I guess I'm a hypocrite, because I ignore my own problems and hope they'll go away.'

'But you don't ignore theirs?'

She angled her head in acknowledgement. Something about it made him want to know more.

'They haven't yet discovered that you don't take your own advice?'

She crossed her arms, hugging her waist as if she were getting cold. But despite the ocean breeze and the time of day it was still warm. There were only a few stragglers on the beach in the distance, and that felt like an injustice.

People deserved summers on Penguin Island. To feel the sun on their skin during the early evening, its heat only a kiss. To see the blue sky mixing with red and orange as if it were an artist's canvas.

People deserved light breezes. To see them fluttering through Morgan's skirt, her hair, making her look like a summer goddess.

He wanted to worship at her feet.

No.

No, he agreed, affirming that cautioning mental voice. She was making him fanciful. Foolish. He didn't do foolish. He did logic, and success, and when it was necessary seduction. As she'd pointed out, he had dated a *lot* of women. They'd all known what to expect, and he'd ensured the experience was pleasurable.

None of them had doubted his abilities beforehand, which made the fact that Morgan did smart a little. He wasn't bad at flirting or seducing. He was just bad at it with *her*.

Which was exactly why seducing her was out of the question.

'No,' Morgan said finally. 'They haven't yet. I don't... I think they don't think about me as a person very often.'

It had taken a long time, and when her answer had come it had been so soft it might have been carried away by the wind if he hadn't been so attuned to her voice.

She was smiling, but it wasn't one of her bright, sunny smiles. It was a contemplative one. A sad one.

'I didn't mean to make you...' He faltered.

He didn't know what to say. The last time he'd felt so lost had been when he'd gone to see his father in the hospital. Gordon Abel had been sleeping at the time, and it had been disarming to see the man Elliott had sought approval from his entire life looking so weak.

Something had shifted inside Elliott on seeing that, and he'd left the hospital five minutes later.

Before his father could wake up and see him.

Before his mother and brother arrived.

He'd had no desire to spend time with his family when he was feeling so confused.

'It's not you, Elliott,' Morgan said now with a soft sigh. 'I've been ignoring my feelings so long that when they catch up to me I...' She lifted her hands, then shook them in the air as if they were wet.

'You keep absolving me from taking responsibility for things,' he said.

'I do not.'

'You do. It's a kind, innocent thing to do.'

'Innocent?' She stopped walking. Put her hands on her hips. *'Innocent?'*

He stopped walking, too. 'It was meant to be a compliment.'

'Not from you. You mean it's naïve.'

'Not coming from you,' he said. 'Coming from you, it's innocent. I mean it.'

She snorted at him, like a bull letting out a warning, and he almost laughed. But then she began to walk again—stomping, really—and the insidious claws of insecurity gripped him.

Slowly, deliberately, he extricated each one. He'd run away from that feeling with his family, and he wouldn't welcome it back with Morgan.

'Stop,' Morgan said.

He obeyed before he realised her voice had come from behind him; she'd stopped again. He moved towards her, but she lifted a hand.

'No, stay there.' She took a breath. 'I shouldn't have said that. It was rude.'

'You shouldn't have said what?'

'That you saying "innocent" meant naïve. I attribute things to you that I shouldn't. I've done it more than once.'

'Morgan,' he said on a sigh. 'Why does it feel like we're navigating a minefield every time we talk?'

'Do you want the real answer to that? Or the one that's going to keep everything the way it is?'

His heart began to pound, but he said, 'The real answer.'

'Because of the attraction we're ignoring.'

CHAPTER SEVEN

WHAT WAS SHE DOING? *What was she doing?*

The simple answer was something stupid.

She tended to do stupid things when she slowed down enough to listen to her emotions. They made her feel uncomfortable. Made her think about the choices that had brought her to this point in her life. Made her aware of how tired she was of taking care of her family when they hadn't asked her to. Not directly, at least.

'Something stupid' could describe her entire relationship with Thad. And now she was repeating it with Elliott.

'What are you saying?' Elliott asked, that darkness rippling over his face again.

'Nothing.' She shook her head. 'Nothing. Forget what I said.'

'No.'

'No?'

He closed the distance between them. 'No.'

He didn't kiss her, but she knew he was going to. Why else would he be standing so close to her, with barely a whisper between them? She shivered, but it had nothing to do with the weather and everything to do with how aware she was.

Of her body. Of her feet against the sand, the breeze fluttering her skirt, her hair, the mist of the ocean teasing her skin.

Of his body. Of the tips of his toes touching hers, his hands almost trembling at his sides, his eyes intense, aroused, and focused entirely on her.

Of the sun slowly crouching behind the ocean at the horizon.

Of the waves crashing so close to their feet.

Of the privacy they had now that even the last few people at the beach had disappeared.

She tried to remember why stupid was bad. Dangerous. Instead, she said, 'Touch me.'

He obeyed. Slowly he wrapped his arm around her waist. She rested her hands on the biceps she'd admired from a distance, kneading his muscles, feeling a thrilling rush of power because she could. She could smell him—a musky scent mingled with the salty air of the beach—and she closed the distance between them so their bodies were flush.

Now her breasts were pressed against his chest, her stomach against the firmness of his. And at the base of her stomach she felt his hardness against her, too. Heat travelled low, settling between her thighs, making her long to pull him to the ground, push him onto his back and straddle him.

Her eyes lifted. He was still looking at her, with a hooded stare that made her feel hotter. His tongue slipped between his lips, as if he could already taste her there, and her core turned into lava as she imagined what it would be like if he did taste her.

Elliott seemed to agree, because now he was leaning forward. Her lips parted in response and his gaze dipped to it. He leaned even closer...

Then he stopped.

'What?' she choked out.

'You want me to do all the work?' His voice was hoarse,

seductive. 'How will I know you want this if you don't take some initiative?'

She pulled his head down and kissed him.

Her stomach swooped. Dropped down to the pits of the earth at the contact. Soft and hot, the kiss was like the feel of a roaring fire after being out in the snow. There was something calming, something reassuring about it even as it heated her. Never before had she been so aroused by a simple meeting of lips. Never before had something so sweet made her body prickle, her nipples harden, her centre ache.

She pulled back in surprise, but his hand slid into her hair and brought her back to his mouth. His other arm still encircled her, pulling her in tightly, securely, and she felt safer than she had in a long time.

Even though she knew she wasn't safe.

Even though she knew what they were doing was dangerous.

He was threatening everything she'd thought she knew, everything she wanted to uphold, and it made no sense for her to feel so…so *right* in his arms.

The thought left her head when his tongue swept into her mouth. He tasted of nothing discernible—and everything she craved. Her arms went around him, pulling him even closer than before. She wanted to be a part of him— no, she wanted him to be a part of *her*.

Another dangerous thought.

An *intimate* thought that came from passion and lust and nothing that she understood.

She loosened her grip on his body but didn't let go. Instead she ran her hands over his body. Over the hard muscle of his back, the broad shoulders and narrow waist. She lingered there, lifting on to her toes so he was positioned between her thighs, then squeezing his butt to bring his hardness to her core.

She shivered as he traced a path over her curves. He stopped at her thigh, digging his fingers into the plushness there before he shifted and rested his hand on her behind. His free hand played with her hair, and his tongue... His tongue played a game with hers. A slow, erotic, pleasurable game that she'd never played before.

It coaxed, it teased, and then he was touching her hip, her waist, and finally her breast. She moaned in approval, waiting for the wave of desire that would drown her when he teased her nipple, but it didn't come. He'd stopped.

Her eyes popped open. She lowered herself back onto her feet, ready to protest. *Why? Why are you stopping?* But the battle on his face kept her from asking.

When he didn't speak, she asked, 'Are you okay?'

'Me?' He huffed out air in a half-laugh that held no amusement. 'I was about to ask you the same thing.'

'You're the one who stopped.'

'We were about to do something stupid.'

Something stupid.

She stiffened, though she knew he was right. She'd thought it herself, hadn't she? But it was different when he said it. Somehow she'd given him the power to hurt her. So carelessly, too. He'd evaluated the situation—*her*—and thought it was stupid.

No, that wasn't true. She was deliberately misunderstanding him. But it didn't matter. A little balloon of hurt had still popped in her chest, stealing her breath, leaving her feeling...

Alone.

The feeling echoed in her mind, in her body, and its intensity told her that it didn't only apply to her situation with Elliott. She felt alone in her family, too. She'd never thought it before, never given herself the chance to feel it. But it was true, and she closed her eyes, letting the pain of realisation wash over her before she squared her shoulders and faced Elliott.

'I didn't mean to upset you,' he said slowly.

She could hear the angst in his voice and it softened her. 'You haven't upset me. I *am* upset, but it isn't you.' *Not only you, at least.* 'You were right to stop. This… It shouldn't have happened. You're right.' She blew out a breath. 'If my grandmother asks, I'm late because we wanted a debrief after the meeting.'

'She'll ask?' Elliott frowned. 'No. Surely not.'

'She will,' Morgan said with certainty. 'But on the off-chance that she doesn't, let's stagger our return and hope my grandmother has learnt to respect boundaries since I last saw her. Doubtful, but what's life without hope?'

Ignoring all the ways they'd managed to complicate their relationship in less than thirty minutes, Morgan began to walk back to the estate.

'Oi, you!'

Elliott stopped. He recognised the voice, but it couldn't be addressing him. Edna Smith hadn't once called him by saying, *Oi, you!* Still, he stopped. Turned. Saw her storming towards him.

It shouldn't have been as intimidating as it was. But he knew that Morgan's warning was about to come to fruition.

Mentally, he tried to prepare.

And failed.

'What did you do to my granddaughter?'

He opened his mouth to recite the words Morgan had told him to say, but stopped when he realised they wouldn't fit.

He tried to adjust. 'I'm not sure what you mean.'

'I'll clarify,' she told him, almost kindly, but he didn't miss the sharpness that was present, too. 'Morgan came home later than I expected from the Town Hall. When I asked her about it, she refused to tell me the truth.'

'But she did tell you something?' he asked.

Edna nodded.

'How do you know it wasn't the truth?'

'She said you wanted a debrief after the meeting.'

'Yes.'

'She looked too shaken up for that to be true. Why did she look shaken up?'

Because I messed things up.

To Edna, he said, 'The meeting was taxing.'

'I thought it went well.'

'It did. But it was trying for her. She was nervous about getting my team's support, and the islanders' respect.'

Edna harrumphed. 'They respect her.'

'As an employer?'

'*You're* their employer.'

He tilted his head. 'I believe that's the kind of thinking that she was nervous about.'

Edna narrowed her eyes, but there was no retort. He nodded, satisfied that he'd made his point, and waited until she figured out how she wanted to harass him next. What he really wanted to do was leave and do what he had come to the estate to do: check on Morgan's progress with the mock-up house. But leaving would be rude, and he wouldn't insult Morgan's grandmother that way.

Except it wasn't only Morgan's grandmother. Behind Edna was Joyce, Edna's best friend, and behind Joyce her other friends, Clarice and Sharon.

An involuntary shudder went down Elliott's spine. He'd only met them once, but that had been enough. Now he avoided them whenever he could.

He had no idea how he'd got himself into this situation.

Because you wanted to see Morgan.

He didn't need to be on site today. Morgan had assured

him she had things handled. But he wanted to show her that he trusted her. He wanted to show everyone else that, too. Besides, he had his own company to run. He'd chosen a great team who could manage without his physical presence, but he still had emails to work through and virtual meetings to attend. And he needed to do that now, while he wasn't needed at the estate.

But he *wanted* to see her. To assure himself that he'd blown their chemistry out of proportion. Everything that had happened the day before must have been a fluke—especially that kiss.

That *phenomenal* kiss.

He had never in his life experienced intimacy so potent. It had only been a kiss, but he'd wanted to tear her clothes off. More worryingly, that kiss had made him think about more than just a physical relationship. Which made coming to see her now a stupid thing to do.

'Leave him alone,' Joyce said mildly. 'He clearly doesn't want to tell you anything.'

Wisely, he didn't comment on that.

'But I'll tell you,' Joyce went on.

'You will?' both he and Edna asked.

'They kissed,' Clarice said. 'Joyce told us earlier.'

'*I* wanted to tell them,' Joyce almost growled.

'I could tell you were going to make it a whole thing and it was just going to drag out,' Clarice told her. 'So, *did* you kiss?'

That last part was addressed to him. But why was Clarice asking for confirmation when Joyce already sounded so confident? It might have nothing to do with him. Maybe Clarice simply didn't trust Joyce to tell the truth and was looking for confirmation. But that was unlikely. What *was* likely was that someone had told Joyce they thought they'd seen Morgan and Elliott on the beach, kissing, but they couldn't be sure, and now they were looking to him to respond.

All of this was his own speculation, which he would never voice out loud because it would give them exactly what they wanted.

'Why are you convinced Morgan's state has something to do with me?' he asked instead.

Sharon shrugged. 'Who else would it be?'

'Thad? He was at the Town Hall last night.'

Edna gaped at him. 'She *told* you about Thad?'

Uneasiness crept over him. 'Yes. Why?'

'She hasn't told anyone about Thad. Not even me.'

'But—' He took a moment to recalibrate. 'How did you know what I meant, then?'

'Oh, that girl was Frenching our mayor all over town that summer,' Sharon said, rolling her eyes. 'She thought she was being covert, but she wasn't. She's actually really bad at it.'

'Which is how we know you two kissed,' Joyce interjected.

She studied him, still waiting for him to confirm. His lips twitched, but he managed to keep them in a line, refusing to give in to the feeling of amusement that had come at her attempt at trickery.

'You don't know for sure what upset her, then?' he asked lightly, though it wasn't really a question. 'I think I'll take my leave.'

He nodded a greeting, then began to walk back to his house. He couldn't go to the mock-up house now—not with those women watching him. They'd probably follow him, peppering him with questions he didn't want to answer.

Questions he *couldn't* answer.

He *was* the reason Morgan was, as her grandmother had put it, 'shaken'. And it shamed him. Angered him. He was becoming too invested in Morgan. Now he wanted to go and see her to make amends for... For whatever it was called when a kiss rocked the very foundation of a professional relationship.

And now he had to worry because he'd told Edna and her friends about Morgan and Thad. There was likely a reason she hadn't told them. But why had she told *him*? Surely that meant she was feeling the connection between them, too? She must be; she'd been the one to bring up their attraction in the first place...

This was precisely why he hated personal relationships.

He'd spent almost half his life feeling this kind of uncertainty. His parents had never quite adored him as much as they had Gio. He'd done whatever he could to try and get them to. But nothing he did had been enough. He'd seen that early on, and still he'd tried. Always hoping that maybe this time they'd see him. Really see him. But that hope had been futile, and it had come with the anxiety of wondering if *this* would be the moment he'd been waiting for. The anxiety of wondering if he was doing enough.

It had taken their non-reaction at him getting into the best university in the country on a full scholarship to realise that nothing he could do would ever be enough for them. Not when Gio was the standard to live up to.

So he'd started creating his own standards. Started focusing on the things he could control—unlike his parents' affection and pride. He'd chosen each relationship with care from then on, never getting close to anyone so he'd never again have to flounder as he had with his parents.

Morgan was threatening all of that—and he wouldn't allow it.

CHAPTER EIGHT

MORGAN TRIED NOT to be annoyed. Yes, she had told Elliott that the mock-up house was almost complete. Yes,
she'd expected him to see it in person. But she hadn't ex-
plicitly *told* him to come, and she shouldn't expect him
to read her mind.

She still did. Because her expectations when it came to
him were unreasonably high. She didn't know why—and
she didn't like it. Having high expectations almost always
led to disappointment. She had experienced that over and
over again, growing up. She'd managed to set them aside,
realising that they hurt more than helped when it came to
her parents.

Don't think about it, she told herself, but it was too late.
A wave of memories had already washed over her.

Her mother crying on the phone to Grandma Edna,
asking for help with Morgan. Her father standing in the
corner, looking helpless and angry.

Her mother shaking her head at the end of the call.
'She says she can come for a while, but it's not a permanent solution.'

'Why not?' her father had barked.

'Because she lives on an island! Because we're Morgan's parents, not her!'

'So let Morgan live with her on her island.'

Her mother had disagreed. 'We can't do that. We *are* Morgan's parents.'

'What's that going to matter if we can't take care of her?'

Her father had pushed away from the counter, stormed out of the kitchen, and Morgan had run from her hiding place in the passage to her bed. She'd been there barely a minute when her mother had come in and cuddled her.

She'd been three at the time. She should have been too young to remember it so vividly. But perhaps it was so vivid because of the vow she'd made to herself that day, as her mother's arms came around her.

Morgan had promised herself she would do everything in her power to make sure taking care of her would be easy for her parents. She'd entertain herself when her parents had to study for their exams, she'd eat whatever she was given, even if it made her stomach hurt, and she'd be the best damn daughter any person could ask for.

And she had been.

Things had become easier a year or so after that conversation. Grandma Edna had made some calls and got Morgan's father a stable job at a shoe factory, where he'd quickly climbed the ranks. Morgan's mother had finished school and received a scholarship to study full time, but had got a job anyway.

By the time Hattie had come along the financial situation hadn't been as dire and her parents had been less stressed, although they'd still been young and trying to get their lives back on the track having Morgan had diverted them from. And so Morgan had helped with Hattie, and then with her brother Rob, and things had been a lot easier for everyone.

Or so she'd told herself. Because at some point she'd stopped expecting her parents to tell her she no longer had to be Hattie and Rob's third parent. Or her own parent, for that matter.

She exhaled. Shook her shoulders. Tilted her head from side to side to stretch out the muscles.

'Preparing for a fight?' a soft voice asked from behind her. 'I come in peace, I assure you.'

How could something as simple as his voice make her feel so prickly? And then she turned, and her stomach swooped again almost as intensely as it had when their lips had touched three days before.

Three days. This man had waited three days before coming to see her.

She had no right to feel betrayed, but she did. She had no right to expect anything from him—and *he* had no right to have this effect on her.

He wore his uniform of T-shirt and jeans again, and this time the shirt was white. It made the brown of his skin look rich, full. It clung to his arms, his chest, his torso, and highlighted his strength.

Or maybe she only felt that way because she'd felt his body. Run her hands over those arms, that chest. She hadn't had the luxury of touching him everywhere yet, not in the way she wanted to.

She took a breath and let it out slowly.

Yes, Elliott was attractive, and she was attracted to him. But her reaction was unreasonable. She needed to control herself.

'I didn't see you there,' she said in a measured voice. 'It's been a long day and I was trying to stretch out my muscles.'

The lie slid smoothly from her tongue. Despite it, she thought Elliott knew the truth. His gaze was intent on her, searching. Then it abruptly shifted, taking in the room behind her.

This one had been one of the easier ones to fix, which

was why she'd chosen it as the mock-up house. The biggest problem had been some holes in the walls, but those had been easily plastered. The rest of the changes had been superficial.

The walls of each room had now been painted in a shade of white, beige or blue, which matched the handwoven rugs on the floor. The dining and coffee tables were both a light-coloured wood, beautiful and natural—courtesy of "Crafted."

She hadn't asked, but Elliott had offered his company's services and these had been the first pieces to arrive. Along with a ladder shelf that she'd decorated with books and plants, they tied everything in the room they were currently in together.

There were other things she'd added—paintings on the walls in the living room, flowers in the kitchen, candles and cushions in the bedrooms—but those were minor, their purpose to round out the rooms. She'd worked with the interior designer on Elliott's team, and she thought the outcome was close to what Abel and Son Development had wanted when they'd first hired the designer. Morgan had run everything by Elliott, and she'd been feeling pretty confident about it all.

But that confidence was slowly dissipating with each passing second of silence. Part of her was offended. She hadn't expected him to drop to his knees in awe, but *some* reaction would have been better than nothing.

There you go, expecting again.

As annoying as it was, that voice in her head was right. In this situation especially, where Elliott was essentially playing the role of her boss, she needed to have no expectations at all and accept his response. Although that was not very realistic, because even with paying clients she had expectations. She followed their brief, checked in with them multiple times during the process, and she expected them to like what she did. So maybe she was overreacting.

Or maybe he's broken your brain.

This was exactly why she avoided relationships. They took up too much mental space, too much emotional space, and she had enough of her own baggage to fill up those spaces.

'It's amazing,' Elliott said, saving her from that thought.

'Yeah?' She exhaled in relief, as if she hadn't just told herself to get a grip. 'You like it?'

'It's amazing,' he repeated. 'It looks modern, yet some-how retains the traditional feel of the estate.'

'I've kept some of the original pieces.' She pointed out the paintings, the carpet, a throw. 'Minor, but they have enough personality to influence the room. Plus, your fur-niture is gorgeous. If you could have a few pieces in each of the houses and things pick up, it'll drive a lot of busi-ness to Crafted.'

He angled his head slightly, a frown knitting his brow.

'It's worth considering,' she said. 'These houses are going to act like the best showrooms. People will be able to see your pieces in a home setting, interact with them... Think about how often people hesitate over buying some-thing like a chair because they're unsure of its quality. And if they're impressed—which, of course, they will be—they'll buy from you. The best showroom,' she said again. 'Although maybe the costliest, too.'

'I'm not worried about that.'

'Of course not, Mr Tycoon,' she said, rolling her eyes. Then she took a proper look at him. 'You're worried about something else?'

He clenched his jaw, then relaxed it. 'It's fine.'

When he didn't offer more information, she sighed. 'I don't know why I still try.' At his questioning look, she shook her head. 'Forget it.'

'No.'

'Are you sure?' she asked mildly. 'Because you're not going to like it when I elaborate.'

He simply watched her.

She took it as a sign to continue.

'I get it. You're private.'

'As are you,' he interjected. 'We've covered that, haven't we?'

'I'd be a little less private if you were too.' She shrugged. 'That minefield you talked about? This is a part of it. There are so many things we can't talk about. I feel like an explosion might go off at any moment during our conversations.'

'You'd prefer us to be more open about our lives?'

'I'm not asking you to give me your entire history. Just…' She trailed off. 'No, it's fine. I'm sorry. I shouldn't have… There are things in my life I don't want to talk about either. Forget I said anything.'

He folded his arms. Studied her.

She did everything in her power not to shift. Not to show him how disturbing it was to have the intensity in his eyes directed at her so completely.

'I don't know if my father and brother would allow my furniture in the houses,' he said, shifting his gaze.

She almost sagged at the reprieve.

'And I don't know if I want to ask.'

'Why not?' she asked.

When he looked at her this time his expression wasn't muted. It was sad. Angry. Embarrassed. There were a multitude of emotions she couldn't read, too. She only felt them deep in her chest. Her heart ached. At *him*; at his vulnerability. It was as if he had confessed his deepest, most protected secret.

Maybe he has.

She blew out a breath—stealthily, she hoped, because

she didn't want him to think he was affecting her. And she didn't want him to feel bad about it.

'The dynamics in my family aren't easy,' he said carefully. 'If I ask, there's no guarantee they'll say yes.'

And so he wouldn't ask, she realised, and wondered what they'd done to make him feel this way.

'I'm sorry,' she said softly. 'If it makes you feel any better...'

'Yes?'

'No, I've got nothing.'

He stared.

She wrinkled her nose. 'That's pretty ridiculous, Elliott. My family is tough, too, but I'm pretty sure they'd help me with my business if I asked.'

'Morgan...'

He looked so offended that she laughed. And then she couldn't stop laughing. Because his family was ridiculous, and the fact that she'd told him that was even more ridiculous. She hadn't said anything remotely comforting when she really should have.

That sobered her right up.

'I'm sorry,' she said. 'No wonder you didn't want to tell me. I handled that horribly.'

But he was smiling.

The first time he'd smiled it had been nice. A small smile—one he hadn't even noticed he'd been giving. Now he was fully present. Now his smile was wide, genuine, disarming. It changed his face from scarily handsome to unbelievably handsome. Softened the frown lines; curved the usually straight lips.

If she were a warrior princess in need of a deadly weapon, she'd take him along with her and tell him to smile in front of all her enemies.

'You handled it fine,' he told her gruffly, the smile fading.

It was like the sun going down on a cold day, leaving only ice behind.

'It affirmed something I thought was only in my head,' he said.

'I can't be the first person who's done that.'

'You're the first person I've told,' he said simply.

It wasn't simple. It was significant. Hugely significant. It added another layer to their relationship. Another complicated, confusing layer that would no doubt take up a lot of Morgan's time and energy as she tried to figure it out.

Oddly, she didn't mind. Not in that moment, anyway. In that moment she could only think about how honoured she was that he'd share something so deeply personal with her. He *had* told her a secret, and it was one he hadn't told anyone else.

But she couldn't show him that. If she did, she'd be making a big deal of it—and that would be the last thing he'd want. It would be the last time he told her anything, too. So she'd joke.

'Do you want me to kill them?' she asked.

'What?'

'You heard me,' she said, feigning seriousness. 'I'm good at solving problems. I can make your family disappear like *that*.' She snapped her fingers. 'Just say the word.'

His lips parted, brow furrowed, and he regarded her in silence with a faint look of suspicion on his face.

She snorted. 'It's a joke, Elliott. I'm joking. I am not a murderer, nor can I order hits on people.' She narrowed her eyes. 'Unless that's what you want me to do?'

This time she laughed at his expression. Because he was annoyed by her, but he was also amused—and he didn't know what to do about either. Seconds later, though, he shocked her by laughing, too. A soft, deep chuckle that had her skin turning to gooseflesh. She grinned so hard she felt as if she'd been turned into stone with a smile on her face.

When he stopped laughing, he returned her smile. A slight curve of his lips, nowhere near the smile of earlier, but her heart flipped.

'Thank you,' he said, shoving his hands into his pockets. 'I needed that.'

'You're very welcome.'

In her head she played around with what she wanted to say next. Decided to go for it even if it affected the easiness that had settled between them.

'They don't have to know. About the Crafted pieces, I mean. If you really want to do this we'll sneak in the furniture.'

'I don't "sneak".'

'Oh, I know. Crafted is a big, well-established company. It doesn't deserve to be sneaked in, blah-blah-blah.' She said it lightly, hoping he'd understand where she was coming from. 'I just meant that if you wanted to do it we can, and your family doesn't have to know.' She looked around. 'Do they know about these pieces?'

'No, but they were donations. If we did this in all the houses Abel and Son Development would have to buy the furniture. Which makes "sneaking" nearly impossible,' he added dryly.

'So, donate more.'

'I can't donate what it would take to furnish an entire estate.'

'Why not?'

'My board of directors would have something to say about that.'

'They didn't have anything to say about these pieces?'

'Too few pieces to care about.'

Her eyes narrowed. 'You're lying...'

He frowned. 'They don't care about a few pieces of furniture.'

'I'm sure that's true, but I don't think it's relevant in this particular conversation.'

'You can't possibly—'

'*You* donated them,' she interrupted. 'You own these pieces, don't you?'

He exhaled sharply. 'Fine. Yes. They're mine. I bought them.'

'You bought your own pieces?' she repeated thoughtfully. 'For this house?'

'No.' He looked to the sky, then back at her. 'I've been buying pieces since the inception of the company. It…motivates me. Every time we make a significant sale, I buy something. If the sale is big, I buy something big. If it's small, I buy something small.'

'So you have a warehouse full of your own company's furniture?'

He nodded stiffly. And was that…? Was that a blush on his cheeks? It was! The faintest pink against his brown skin.

Instead of teasing him about it—it would be cruel to make fun of him when he was embarrassed, though it was hard to resist—she said, 'Mine's decorating.'

'Your what is decorating?'

'My reward, I guess. For making my company a success. My house is pretty empty. Deliberately. I bought this big old house that was essentially a blank canvas. The roof was leaking when I first got it, the paint was peeling in most of the rooms, and the tiles were cracked. But the plumbing was intact, the water pressure was amazing, and the kitchen was big and modernised. I have no idea why,' she added, 'considering the rest of the place was a mess. But when I first saw it I knew it was mine. So I bought this broken house and I've been fixing it up ever since.'

'You literally live with the success of your career?'

'No, I live in a disaster area.'

'Surely your house is complete by now?'

'I appreciate your confidence in the success of my company, but I've only just managed to fix the walls, repaint them, and retile. The roof wasn't part of my deal with myself—the leaking was excessive, and it would have ruined whatever I did in the house anyway—so I had that done before I moved in. The rest will take time.'

'But your company *is* successful.'

'I'm doing the renovations myself. What I *can* do, anyway. The tiling I've had to outsource, but I can replaster walls and paint, and I did those things first. My bedroom is pretty perfect, because I sank a lot of my attention into it, but the rest... It needs more time, and I don't always have it.'

'Why not?'

She'd braced herself for the question, and since he'd been honest with her she said, 'I spend a lot of time with my family. I help my younger sister take care of my niece. And my younger brother is still at university. He sometimes needs help with his assignments because of a learning disability.'

'I'm sorry,' he said softly. He must have seen her confusion, because he continued, 'Your parents? I didn't realise they'd passed away.'

'What? Oh, no. No, they're alive.'

'Then why—?'

A knock cut him off. Elliott looked at her questioningly, but she shook her head and shrugged.

He strode to the door then, opened it—and she saw his jaw drop. Her feet were already moving, her brain urging them forward, since Elliott never showed that much emotion so easily and it must have been an emergency.

She nudged him and he stepped back, and her own jaw dropped.

Because in front of them were roses.

Rows and rows of roses.

CHAPTER NINE

HE WAS BEING FRAMED—and it didn't take a genius to figure out by whom.

Elliott was mildly horrified at the number of flowers in the garden. How had Edna and her friends even managed to find so many roses on the island? They'd filled the small front yard, leaving only the path free. Morgan would have to walk through the roses to get to the road—which was, he would admit, romantic. But he hadn't had anything to do with it.

Morgan seemed to realise it, too.

Her bemused expression quickly changed to humour, and then she turned to him, grinning. 'I told you.'

'Told me what?'

'My grandmother.' Morgan put her hands on her hips, staring at the flowers again. 'She can't help herself.' With a shake of her head, she looked over her shoulder. 'What did you do?'

'I don't know… She ambushed me, like you said she would, but I didn't tell her anything you and I didn't agree on.'

He thought back to the conversation and winced. It was too much to expect her not to notice.

'What?' she asked.

'I…' He swallowed. The nerves tangled with his tongue, and it took him longer than he would have liked to answer. 'She said you were upset after the Town Hall meeting, and I might have implied that the reason for it was Thad's presence.'

She faced him now, her usually cheerful expression neutral. 'Implied?'

He sighed. 'Said. Outright.'

'You told my grandmother that I was upset because of Thad?' She didn't wait for his confirmation. 'You decided to shift the blame off yourself by telling them about my ex-boyfriend, whom I have personally never told her about?'

'In my defence,' he said weakly, 'I didn't realise she didn't know about Thad. Or rather, that you hadn't told her.'

'What does that mean?'

'They all knew. Your grandmother and her friends,' he clarified. 'You're very bad at sneaking around. Apparently.'

'My grandmother *and* her friends?' She snorted. 'You *were* ambushed.'

'Yes.'

'Don't sound so relieved. You're not off the hook yet.'

But she was smiling. At him. He had never experienced something so warm and light as her teasing. Or something as precious and as pure as her opening up to him. *He* was responsible for that. He'd let her into his head, his hurt, just a fraction, and she'd trusted him in return.

It felt too impossible to be real. Too *good* to be real. His actions were progressing a relationship with someone he actually cared about. That had never happened before—largely because he'd never allowed it to. Not after his actions had done nothing to change things with his parents. But they were changing things now, with Morgan, and it made him feel…hopeful.

The very thought had tension thrumming in his veins.

He ignored it and watched as Morgan stepped off the

veranda onto the path, lowering herself to her haunches and playing with the petals of one of the flowers.

'I know this isn't real, but it's beautiful,' she said softly.

The soft undertone of disappointment made him desperately wish it *was* real. 'I'm sorry.'

She straightened. 'Don't be.' Then she tilted her head. 'You didn't tell them about what happened between us?'

'Of course not. But—'

'But…?'

'Joyce seemed to know that we…' He trailed off. Cleared his throat. 'Kissed.'

'What?'

'I have no idea how she knew, but she told me—well, actually, Sharon told me. Or was it Clarice?' He shook his head. 'The point is, they had the information. Which I did not confirm.'

She pursed her lips. 'So, they heard a rumour that we kissed, confronted you, and you told them about Thad, which I hadn't told them about.' She heaved out a breath. 'They want us to be together.' He shook his head. She lifted her brow. 'Really? You don't see that in all of this?' She waved her hand over the flowers.

'Perhaps it was meant to be a simple gesture.'

'Oh, no. Those women do not do "simple". I bet you they're planning our wedding, because they think we've had both a physical connection because of the kiss and an emotional connection because I confided in you about Thad. We'd better be careful. They'll be watching us.'

'No, they won't,' he managed to say over the intense desire to ask her if they did, indeed, have a physical and emotional connection.

'Hmm… You're right. They probably sent one of the neighbourhood kids to ring the doorbell.' She looked around. 'They wouldn't dare show their faces now. Too worried we might murder them. And even if they did show,' she continued with a huff of air, 'they'd hunch their backs over, walk really slowly, and make themselves seem like innocent old ladies. But the joke's on them! We all know that isn't true.'

He stared. 'They *do* that?'

'Oh, you sweet summer child. Yes, they do. It's a ploy to make you feel bad for not doing something they want you to do. It's fool-proof, too. You can't trust it, but you'd be a terrible person to ignore it on the off-chance that it *is* true.'

Now that the surprise had worn off, Elliott remembered that he'd already been victim to that ploy. Edna had done it after their first meeting. She'd risen from her chair slowly, as if her body was aching, and walked back to her car taking double the time he now knew she needed.

He should be upset about it—and the multiple other times she had manipulated him—but he wasn't. In fact, he felt reluctant amusement.

'They grow on you,' Morgan said with a soft sigh. 'You realise they have good intentions, so even when you're mad at them you're okay with being swept into one of their houses and handed a fresh batch of biscuits.'

'Biscuits would have been preferable.'

She smiled. 'So boring, though. And less aesthetically appealing, for sure.'

He walked down the steps but didn't breach the space between them. She was looking at the flowers again. There was a light flush of pleasure on her cheeks, and again he wished that he *had* done this for her.

He wished he hadn't spoiled their kiss with his careless words. He'd thought about it after his encounter with Edna, and now he saw that maybe Morgan hadn't been upset by the kiss itself, but by the way he'd handled it.

He had to apologise.

He cleared his throat. 'The other day,' he started. 'On the beach…'

She looked at him, eyebrows raised.

'The kiss,' he clarified.

'Yes?'

'I didn't think it was stupid.'

'You said it, though.'

'Well, it *was* a stupid thing for us to do. There should be boundaries we don't cross. This project is important and…'

He trailed off. Was he really going to do this? *Say* this? He continued before he knew it, because she was looking at him with soft brown eyes and she had a power over him he would never understand.

'It wasn't stupid for me to kiss you.'

'I can't tell what the difference is.' Her voice was low. Husky.

'You can.'

She pressed her tongue into her cheek. 'Hmm…'

He took a tentative step closer. When she didn't move away, he took another step. There was barely a breath between them now, but again she didn't walk away. She only lifted her eyes, challenge, curiosity, interest clear in her gaze.

'I don't take risks in my personal life, Morgan. I don't like feeling…' *Unwanted.* 'Vulnerable.' Both were true, anyway. 'I don't have experience with relationships. Real ones,' he added, since she'd already brought up the women he'd dated. 'Everything about this feels real. Too real,' he said with a frown.

A piece of her hair fluttered over her forehead. He focused on that. The slight curl of it…the tiniest fuzz around its edges. Slowly, he lifted his hand, gripped the strands between his index finger and thumb, and gently put it back behind her ear. It promptly flew to the front again. He smiled.

'When you say things like that…when you do things like this…' She nodded her head, so he'd know she was talking about his actions with her hair. 'You take my breath away.' Her hands gripped the front of his T-shirt. 'I don't like feeling vulnerable either. The last time a man made me feel that way I almost lost...' Her voice faded. Her fingers tightened.

'I don't want you to lose anything,' he whispered.

'I know.' Her gaze met his. 'Maybe that's why I feel like I'm gaining something with you instead.'

His heart filled. Overflowed. With what, he didn't know. He wasn't sure he wanted to find out. But he knew that honesty had brought them here. Vulnerability. Things he'd viewed as enemies since they'd done nothing but hurt him when he'd tried them with his family.

But they'd brought him this closeness with Morgan. Literally and figuratively. Both seemed of the utmost importance. Although literal closeness took precedence now, because he could see the faint dusting of freckles on her right cheek. There were none on her left, and it fascinated him. As did the sparkle in her eyes. Every time he looked at them he came up with a better description for their colour. Today they looked mahogany. Full, deep, rich...

The colour would make the most beautiful piece of furniture. A desk, he thought. He'd make a desk of this exact colour so that he could be reminded of her eyes, of her, whenever he sat down to work.

'What are you thinking about?' she asked quietly.

His eyes dipped to her lips. They were somewhere between pink and red, reminding him of a tart fruit, and their creases formed a pattern he wanted to memorise. An impossible task. An illogical task. He wanted to take it on, nevertheless.

'I'm thinking I'd... I'd like to kiss you.'

She smiled. 'What are you waiting for?'

He immediately lowered his head and kissed her. Drank her in as if she was a potion that would give him eternal happiness. He savoured it. The taste of her tongue…the feel of it teasing his. Heat scattered through his body, sending nerves prickling as she deepened the kiss.

His hands settled at her waist, his fingers digging into her skin.

Touching.

Claiming.

Wanting.

She groaned, pulled him in closer, her hands fisting his shirt before they moved to his stomach. His muscles tensed beneath her warmth, beneath her exploration, and for a moment he lost his breath. He pulled away, chest heaving, and she blinked up at him.

'Too much?'

'Not enough,' he growled, and lifted her.

Her legs went around his waist, her mouth fused with his, and he walked up the steps, back through the door. Or he tried to. He got up to the second step and his foot caught, and then they went tumbling down to the ground.

He angled his body to shield her from the worst of it. The good news was that it worked: she landed on him. The bad news was that he took the impact from her and from the ground. His breath was stunned out of him, and it took him a long while before he could respond to her panicked words.

'Elliott? *Elliott?* Are you okay?' She was kneeling next to him, frantically patting his body—he assumed to check for injuries.

'Morgan,' he managed. 'You're touching me.'

'Of course I'm touching you. I'm checking for—' She stopped, before catching his face between her hands. 'You're talking! That means you're okay, right? I didn't kill you?'

He huffed out a laugh, pushing himself up as he did so. 'You didn't kill me. Only my pride has died.'

'*Your* pride?' she asked. 'I'm the one who made you fall.'

'No, my foot caught.'

Come to think of it, his ankle felt a little unpleasant. He lowered it to check on it, felt a twinge in his back, too.

He groaned. 'Clearly not in my twenties any more,' he muttered.

'You're not?' She blinked. 'If I'd known that, I probably wouldn't have made out with you.'

He opened his mouth, even though he didn't know what he was going to say. But she rolled her eyes and gave a small laugh.

'Don't look so concerned. It was a joke. Now, put your arm around my shoulders and let me help you up.'

He obeyed, wincing a little when he put weight on his ankle.

'We need to get you to a doctor.'

'No,' he said. 'I can feel it isn't that bad. I just need to ice it.'

She didn't look convinced, but she merely said, 'I'm assuming you walked here?' At his nod, she pointed to a green car in the driveway. 'That's mine. I'll take you home, get you what you need, and then leave you to languish in the not so badness of yourself.'

Despite the pain, he snorted.

Didn't that seem to be the general gist of his experience with Morgan?

CHAPTER TEN

MORGAN HELPED ELLIOTT to his couch, and only then did she allow herself to look around.

Old Mr Barnaby had lived in this house when she was growing up. He'd been a sour man who'd hated children. To him, 'child' had referred to anyone under eighteen, so Morgan had never really interacted with him.

He'd died by the time she hit her early twenties, and the house on the hill that she'd personally believed to be haunted had stood empty.

By the time she'd become an adult, settled in her career and able to appreciate the beauty of its structure, the house had been bought. No one knew by whom, as still the house had sat empty. When the *For Sale* sign had finally disappeared Edna had called Morgan, speaking in excited tones about the possibility of someone new moving to the island.

Of course that excitement had faded once they'd discovered the house had been bought by property developers—Elliott's family, not Elliott, so she felt less bad about judging it.

There was a part of Morgan that had thought the house would be a ruin. Mr Barnaby hadn't exactly seemed the type of person to keep things clean and tidy. Besides, the house had sat empty for years.

She had been wrong.

The house was sleek and modern. Natural light streamed through the windows and glass doors, reflected by the white tiles, white walls, the white roof with its wooden panels.

The couch in the living room faced one of the glass doors, overlooking the ocean, and to its left was an electric fireplace. To its right, furniture had been arranged to form a dining room with the most gorgeous table she had ever seen. It was large, oak, and had three chairs on one side, a bench on the other, and chairs at both heads of the table.

She resisted the temptation to examine it, and instead looked at the kitchen, just beyond the dining area. It was white, again, though the appliances—all top of the line; she could tell by how complicated they looked—were black.

There were two staircases on either side of the front door, both leading to upper passages with a glass railing that overlooked the open area below. She could see three or so doors on each side, and imagined they disappeared into modern bedrooms.

She turned to him. 'This is going to be a problem.'

'What is?'

'Getting you up those stairs.'

'There's an elevator.' He tilted his head to one side, where she saw a hidden door she now knew to be an elevator. 'Goes directly to the master bedroom.'

'Wow.' She plopped down onto the couch beside him. 'This is some house, huh?'

He shrugged. 'Do you like it?'

She looked around again. 'It's…nice.'

'Nice?' he repeated with a grim smile. 'Small word, so much meaning.'

She snorted. 'No, I mean it. It's nice.'

He merely looked at her.

'But,' she continued with a roll of her eyes, 'it feels cold. I think that's because the man who used to live here kidnapped children from town and ate them, so I guess my opinion comes with baggage.'

He stared for a second, shook his head. 'Sometimes it's hard to know when you're being sincere.'

'I'm sorry.' She thought about it and winced. 'My mother hates it. I don't do it often, but when I do, I really lean in.'

'You do do it often.'

'With you, yes. And, no, I don't know what that means.'

His lips curved. It seemed to come easier now. Because of her? she wondered.

Yeah, yeah, she knew she was crossing a line. She didn't need the cautionary voice in her head to tell her so.

'I like it.'

Listening to that cautionary voice now, she didn't climb onto his lap and begin purring. Instead she made a sound of acknowledgement and looked out of the window. It was evening, with the sky shifting from light blue to navy, the ocean dark but still visible.

'Do *you* like the house?' she asked softly.

'No.' His answer came quickly. 'It reminds me of—' He exhaled abruptly. 'It used to feel cold in my house when I was growing up, too.'

It had clearly been difficult for him to say.

'I'm sorry,' she offered.

'Don't be. It's done.'

'But it's not.' She took his hand. 'It's never really done, is it? My…' She hesitated, then told herself it was too late to hold back. 'My house now is the opposite of what I grew up in. It's…calm. I know that's a strange way to describe a house, but—'

'I understand.' He tightened his grip on her fingers. 'Your life sounds busy. Helping your siblings.'

'Busy. Chaotic. More so when I was growing up because I was so young.'

'Where were your parents?'

'They had me when they were teenagers,' she said with a light snort. 'It became almost natural for me to step in when they needed me to.'

She'd just told herself it was too late to hold back, but she was still doing it. To protect herself, she realised. Not so much from Elliott—although that was certainly a factor, and one she didn't think she could manage to think about right now—she was protecting herself *from* herself. If she told him the truth, what she'd buried in a hole deep inside her would come out. She wasn't ready for that.

'If you're looking to make a place that doesn't feel like your house growing up, it's an easy fix.'

His frown deepened, but he didn't push. In fact, he indulged her. 'Tell me.'

'Make the place feel warmer. Furniture would be an excellent start. Get some Crafted pieces.' She paused. 'Do you know how often I use Crafted for my clients?'

'Really?'

'Really,' she said, looking around. 'I've used other furniture providers, too, but it doesn't feel the same.'

She looked at him and saw something burn in his gaze. She quickly turned away.

'Then I'd recommend painting the walls. Maybe even the ceiling. No, those wooden panels look gorgeous against the white. Leave that. But definitely paint these.' She pointed to the walls. 'If you change them from white to, say, a cream or a beige—something softer—it'll help things seem less harsh.'

She turned around, tilting her head from left to right as she considered it.

'If you add some colour it would make things seem more homely, too. A painting here...some cushions. Maybe fresh flowers every now and then. I hear there are roses available at the estate.'

She was smiling as she turned back to him, but stopped when she saw his face.

'What?'

'I can't do any of that.'

'Right, of course. This isn't actually your house.'

'No,' he said mildly. 'Doesn't mean I can't be impressed at how easy this comes to you, though.'

'My job? Yeah, I would hope so.'

He shook his head. 'You're good at seeing solutions.'

Seeing solutions?

She *was* good at that. She did it for her siblings. Helping Hattie raise Georgie…helping Rob with his learning disability. She stepped in when her parents needed help with the house, or with a dinner party they were throwing, or anything they called on her for. She was doing it now with her grandmother's wedding. With the estate. Hell, with the entire island.

She'd always known that she was good at stepping in when she was needed, but for the first time she saw how that had translated to her professional life. Her entire business was solution-orientated. Someone didn't like their house? She would fix it! Someone needed to transform a property so it could be rented? She could do that! Someone needed help figuring out who to market their property to? She knew what to do!

Her entire life was built around a skill that sometimes she wished she didn't have.

No, that wasn't true. She enjoyed her job. She liked helping people. It was just that the expectation that she *would* help—at least in her personal life—made her feel… trapped.

It was the first time in her life she'd acknowledged it— and it made her hate herself.

'I've said the wrong thing.'

It was more an observation than a question. Elliott had

been watching Morgan closely. He'd seen the way her lashes fluttered. The way her expression had drawn tight. The way she'd opened up to him and then, after his comment, snapped shut.

He hadn't meant to make the observation out loud either, and now he felt like a lumbering giant who'd been given a precious human artifact and was struggling not to crush it in his hands.

But Morgan only smiled. A fake smile that didn't reach her eyes and made him long for the earlier version of her. The one who had smiled easily, whose laughter had lit up her entire face. He had robbed her of that—robbed himself, too. But he understood it. It was more familiar to him than whatever had been unfolding between them before.

He used that knowledge to bolster himself. To soothe the ache he hadn't given permission to take root in his body.

'It has nothing to do with you,' she said. 'I just…'

She gave him a shaky smile. Again, so different from the ones she'd given him before.

'Come on, let's get you upstairs. I'll give you permission to boss me around once we get you settled in bed.'

In other circumstances he would have enjoyed this. Hell, a mere hour ago he'd thought he'd have the opportunity to get her to a bedroom. It wasn't even in the realm of possibility now.

She dealt with him almost clinically.

She decided, once she had him seated on the bed, that he'd feel better after a bath. So she ran him one, then helped him to the bathroom, telling him firmly that he could take it from there.

He did as he was told, and the minute he sank into the warm water he sighed in gratitude. The knots in his body eased, and the aches he'd felt subsided to a dull throb. When he was done, he tied a towel around his waist, testing his weight on his ankle. It still hurt. It would probably take anti-inflammatories and ice to get it to a manageable level of pain.

He'd told Morgan where they were, and since he heard sounds coming from his bedroom he figured she was already there, sorting everything out.

He limped out through the door. Morgan had obviously heard him coming and turned.

'Right, so I've got your pills—'

She stopped. Stared.

It was a completely disarming stare. Her lips were parted, her eyes wide. And in them he was able to see a mixture of surprise and…desire. Lust, really. Hot and wild and completely unencumbered by whatever had caused her to withdraw before.

He had never been a vain person, but he couldn't help the way his posture changed. His chest puffed out, his shoulders pulled back, and his spine straightened. The hours he spent in the gym, trying to relieve the stress of his workdays, trying to forget the pain of the loneliness he refused to dwell on, were finally doing more than simply helping his mental and emotional health.

He was tempting this woman.

His woman.

His woman?

Where the hell had that come from?

But it didn't matter when she was looking at him like that. When she was walking towards him. He didn't move, didn't even breathe, too scared he might do something to mess things up again.

She stopped steps away from him. 'You're doing this on purpose,' she said.

'What?'

'Tempting me.'

'Tempting?'

'Oh, don't look so smug,' she said crossly. 'You're well aware—'

And then she stopped, her eyes dipping down. At the same moment he felt cool air over his body. His *entire* body.

His towel had come loose.

He swore silently—because, contrary to what she believed, he didn't want to seduce her. Well, he did, but not like this. He didn't want to worry about what was going on in her head when he kissed her, teased her, claimed her.

He quickly bent to retrieve the towel before his body betrayed his imagination. When he looked back at Morgan she was looking at the ceiling.

'Are you done?' she asked in a small voice.

Great. He'd embarrassed her.

'Yes. I'm sorry. It wasn't intentional.'

'Are you sure?' She quirked her brow. 'You came out of the bathroom wearing nothing but a towel and then it "magically" fell to the ground...'

There was a beat of silence.

'I didn't have any clothes.'

'That's what they all say,' she replied dryly. 'For the record, there are easier ways of showing me...that.'

Heat stirred in his body, but it quickly cooled when he saw that she'd covered her hand with her mouth.

'I didn't mean to say that,' she said, the sound muffled.

He only looked at her. Then, when her cheeks pinkened, he gave a quiet laugh.

Her gaze jumped to his, accusation bright. 'Are you *laughing* at me?'

'I wouldn't dare.'

She tilted her head, then stuck her tongue out before slipping her arm under his and helping him to the bed. He kept a hand firmly on his towel this time, not even letting go when he sat down.

'Let me get you some clothes. Please,' she added.

He resisted the urge to smile again as he told her where his clothes were, and she left him to get dressed. He did so slowly, trying to figure out why things were so confusing between them. It didn't help when she returned with a sandwich and a cup of tea.

'Eat,' she commanded. 'When you're done, take the pills.' She pointed to the glass of water and pills on his bedside cabinet. 'You don't have an ice pack in your fridge, so I put ice in a plastic bag and wrapped it in one of your dish cloths. It'll have to do for now. I'll get one on my way into town and bring it for you tomorrow. No point in coming back later, when you'll be fast asleep because of those pills.'

Confusion gave way to something stronger, though he could still feel it. The foundation of whatever wave of emotion had crashed over him.

She had driven him home, helped him inside. Run a bath for him, got his clothes ready. Made food for him, got him medication. She had taken care of him—*was* taking care of him—even though he'd said something to upset her earlier.

'Why are you doing this for me?' he asked.

She blinked. 'What do you mean? You hurt yourself.'

'I would have managed.'

'Why should you have to if I'm here?' she asked, brow furrowing.

'I've always managed.' He knew his reply was terse, but she was making all this seem small, when it wasn't.

Her eyes flickered. 'Yeah, well, sometimes you shouldn't have to. Especially on this island. You'll always have help here.'

CHAPTER ELEVEN

MORGAN SHOULD HAVE known once she told her grand-mother about Elliott's fall that it wouldn't be a secret for long.

When she pulled in front of Elliott's house the next day her car was one of several. Dr Sam's car was right in front, followed by Sharon's. That meant all her grand-mother's friends would be there, since Sharon was their designated driver.

Plus her grandmother herself.

Edna had insisted on coming with Morgan that morning.

This was all her fault. Elliott probably hated her.

She turned to Edna. 'Behave when you get inside, okay?'

'What does that mean?' Edna demanded. 'I always be-have.'

Morgan looked at her.

Edna looked back.

After a while, Morgan sighed. 'Fine, you always behave. There definitely haven't been any times when you've said inappropriate things or intervened when you want things to go your way.'

Edna's jaw dropped. 'How long have you been keep-ing *that* inside?'

Morgan put a hand over her mouth and blushed. She

hadn't meant to say that. It had rolled off her tongue without a thought.

'I'm sorry.' She dropped her hand. 'I don't know where that came from.'

'Keep it up,' Edna said after a moment, patting Morgan's thigh. 'If you do, you'll be able to tell your parents to step up in no time.'

With those words, Edna got out of the car.

Morgan stared after her, then hurried to follow. Her grandmother was in the house before Morgan could ask her what she meant, and then they were swarmed by people, all demanding the details of what had happened the previous day.

'Edna told us Elliott fell,' Joyce said, a hand on her chest. 'Was it because of the flowers? Did you push him?'

'I did not push—'

Clarice didn't give Morgan the chance to finish.

'Of course she didn't push him. She was quite happy about the flowers. Accepted them with open arms.'

Morgan glanced over and got a wink in return. Had Clarice seen what had happened the day before? There was no way. Morgan was absolutely sure there had been no one lurking in the shadows. Not to mention the fact that Clarice wouldn't have been able to resist helping if she'd seen Elliott fall. She hadn't been there. So she must be taking Morgan's side because she could tell Morgan was outnumbered.

Morgan accepted the help with a smile, and immediately diverted the conversation. She did not want to tell them the truth about Elliott's fall. She had been purposely vague when her grandmother had asked.

'Where is Elliott?' she asked. 'I thought you'd have asked *him* all these questions.'

'He's upstairs with Dr Sam,' Sharon said. 'He said he felt light-headed.'

Morgan pursed her lips. 'How long after you arrived did he say that?'

'Oh, not long. Maybe fifteen minutes?'

'Uh-huh.' Morgan forced herself not to laugh. 'How long ago was that?'

'Another fifteen minutes,' Joyce said. 'Dr Sam must be doing a thorough job of examining him. Either that, or the fall was more serious than either of you let on.'

'Hmm.' Morgan didn't think it was either of those options. 'I'd better go upstairs to check.'

'You do that, dear,' Edna said. 'I have some biscuits in the car,' she told her friends. 'I thought one of you might have been making him some food.'

'So did I!' Clarice said. 'I didn't make lasagne, because I thought Joyce would be making butter chicken and I didn't want to overwhelm him with food.'

'I did bring my butter chicken,' Joyce replied. 'But I also brought biscuits. I'm not an amateur.'

Morgan left them in the kitchen with a smile, before pressing the button for the elevator.

When the door opened Edna exclaimed, 'There's an *elevator*!' and the topic swiftly changed to the house.

Morgan was still smiling when she knocked on the bedroom door. There was a long wait before anyone answered, and then Dr Sam opened.

She was five or so years younger than Morgan's grandmother, her countenance kinder. She walked with the confidence of someone who knew what she was doing, and the grace of someone who didn't hold that knowledge over people's heads. She was one of seven doctors on the island, one of two GPs, and she breathed a sigh of relief when she saw who was at the door.

'It's only Morgan,' she called over her shoulder, then gave Morgan a smile. 'I'm so glad it's you. The others

have been stressing my patient out. His blood pressure was
much higher than I would have liked it to be.'

'You checked his blood pressure?'

'He was feeling light-headed.'

'I'm pretty sure he only said that because he was trying to escape my grandmother's friends,' Morgan said as
she walked into the room.

Elliott didn't say a word, only watched her from the bed.
He was wearing track pants and a T-shirt, and somehow
still managed to look put together. Come to think of it, the
only time he hadn't looked put together had been the day
before, when he'd come out of the bathroom.

She really didn't want to remember him coming out of
the bathroom. She didn't want to think about how won-
drous he'd looked. His shoulders, chest, biceps...all gleam-
ing with the faintest hint of water. His body had looked
as if it had been crafted with the sole intention of making
her fall to her knees.

She had thought that the day before, too, and it had been
as alarming then. And that had been *before* his towel had
dropped and she'd caught a glimpse of his—

No.

She refused to think about that again, or to rehash the
dirty thoughts that came with it. She was just going to
make sure he was okay. Then she was going to work—and
keep working—so the image of his glorious body, and one
part in particular, faded from her mind.

'It's higher than I'd like, so I'd suggest keeping him
calm,' Dr Sam said, unaffected by the tension crackling
in the room. 'I'll be back later to check it again—if that's
okay, Elliott?'

Elliott grunted.

'I'll take that as a yes,' Dr Sam said with a smile. 'You'll
have to excuse me now. I have other patients. But, Elliott,

please take the pain medication when you need it. And call me if things get worse.'

'Thank you,' Elliott said.

She nodded, then gave Morgan a kind smile before leaving the room.

The tension turned up a notch. Before it overtook them, Morgan spoke. 'Is…everything okay?' She tilted her head towards the door Dr Sam had left by. 'You're going to live?'

'Yes.' He waited a beat. 'It's a mild sprain. It'll heal within two weeks, and the other aches and pains will fade sooner. I have medication. I need to elevate the ankle and keep it iced.'

'That's good news. About it being mild.' She cleared her throat. 'I…um… I brought you an ice pack.'

'Thank you.' He studied her. 'I need to stay off my leg for at least a week.'

'I figured.'

'The timing is inconvenient.'

'There's never a convenient time to sprain your ankle,' she pointed out.

'I meant—'

'I know what you meant,' she interrupted. 'You're worried about the project without your presence. But it'll be fine.'

Briskly, she outlined what would be done in the next week, all the things that would continue without his physical presence.

'You're taking a lot on your shoulders,' he commented when she was done.

'That was always going to be the case, your sprained ankle or not.' She shrugged. 'I'll keep you updated at every step. We can do daily check-ins. I'll even show you our progress via video chat, if you like.'

'I'd appreciate that.'

He spoke gruffly. Something was clearly bothering him. She waited, but he didn't elaborate.

'What about the wedding?' he asked eventually.

'What about it?'

'Won't this affect your work on that?'

'My work for the wedding is to make sure the wedding venue is ready. Which basically means that I'm already doing it by doing the work on the estate.' She tilted her head. 'Is that what you're worried about? That all this is keeping me too busy to help with the wedding?'

'I don't want you to make sacrifices for me.'

She thought about what he'd asked her the day before. *'Why are you doing this for me?'* What he said now was an echo of that—which, in turn, was an echo of something else.

It must have something to do with his family. Based on what he'd told her about them, he didn't know how to handle it when people cared about him. Or rather, when people *showed* him they cared about him. So now he was bracing himself for her to hurt him in some way because he thought he was making things difficult for her.

She didn't know how to tell him that that ship had sailed a long time ago. From the moment Grandma Edna had called Elliott had been making things difficult for Morgan. Things had only gone downhill from there. She was fixing up an entire estate, for heaven's sake, hoping to boost the economy of the island while she was at it. 'Difficult' was the minimum of how she'd describe what was happening.

And still she stayed.

Maybe she shouldn't.

Maybe she was giving him false hope by staying.

By doing that was she telling him that she'd always be around, even when he treated her poorly? Not that he *was* treating her poorly. It was just…that was how things had started with her family. Her constant support had become the reason they constantly expected it—and never appreciated it.

Was she teaching Elliott to treat her the same way? And would that eventually lead to the hurt he was expecting? From her? *For* her?

'I'm not making any sacrifices for you,' she said now, a little primly. She was trying to keep the tangle of emotions out of her voice. 'I have things managed at the estate, which means I have them managed for the wedding. My part in it, anyway. The rest of the wedding is being handled by the four women downstairs—who, for the record, have already planned each of your meals, including teatime treats, for at least the next three days. They'll probably rejoice when they hear they might be getting to help you for weeks.'

He winced.

'They'll behave,' she told him. 'My grandmother promised.'

'You believe that?'

Her lips curved. 'No. But what can you do? Now, while I have you, I've had an email from…'

Purposefully, she delved into business. There wasn't really anything urgent she needed to discuss with him, and he seemed to know it. His gaze flickered to hers, narrowing, but it went back to normal seconds later and she pretended she hadn't seen it. Slowly the tension eased from his face.

Relief unspooled in her stomach, but seconds later a sinister kind of tightness curled around her heart and squeezed.

Somehow in all of this she had taken responsibility for Elliott's emotions. For making him feel better. She didn't know how that made *her* feel. Especially since she was now dealing with the realisation that she was unhappy with the way things were with her family.

Surely she needed to work through that before she opened herself to a new relationship? Did she even *want* a relationship? Was that what Elliott wanted?

There were too many questions, too many layers to whatever was happening between her and Elliott. This was why she didn't examine her feelings. She'd rather keep busy, not work through anything, and be just fine with her life.

Maybe she should put some distance between her and Elliott.

'I should probably go,' Morgan said after a short bit of silence. 'Can't slack off with the boss out.'

'I'm not your boss.'

'Aren't you?' she asked casually, though really it was a serious question that didn't only refer to work.

His brow knitted, but he didn't comment.

'You'll be okay?' she asked. He nodded. 'Do you want me to come over later?'

That's not distance, Morgan.

Elliott shifted before she could examine that thought. Something about the movement bothered her. It wasn't that he was in pain—she'd seen him deal with that, and it wasn't like this. But she couldn't ask him about it without veering into territory she'd already breached by asking him if he wanted her to visit later.

'No,' he said finally. 'You don't have to come.'

I want to.

The words almost left her lips, but she snatched them back, telling herself to take the win. But as she dragged herself to the door it didn't feel like a win. She looked over her shoulder, saw Elliott leaning back against the pillows, eyes closed, his posture more defeated than she'd ever seen on him.

Although everything inside her told her to go back, to

shake it out of him, she walked out. Went to her car. Drove back to the estate. Started to work. Refused to think about him. And failed.

CHAPTER TWELVE

THIS LAST WEEK of Elliott's life had been unlike any other.

He'd had more people in his house than he actually knew on the island. Someone had always been popping in to check on him, bringing some form of food or entertainment. The fridge and freezer were packed with enough meals for, he suspected, the next century, and his living room now held a number of magazines and board games he'd never heard of.

The more he'd told people he could read or play games on his tablet, the more they'd waved off his suggestions. He'd stopped trying to tell them he had enough food, too. That had come after he'd said it to Sharon and she had laughed out loud and said, 'You never have enough food on Penguin Island.'

She'd promptly dished him up another plate of her admittedly brilliant chicken *alfredo* and told him to eat.

After day two of this invasion, he'd told himself to accept it. Nothing he said was going to change what the people of Penguin Island were doing for him. And once that resistance had gone away, he had finally been able to examine his emotions about it all. He supposed one of them was bemusement. Why were all these people being nice to him? They barely knew him. He was an outsider; he didn't deserve their kindness.

It made him think of how Morgan had helped him in

those first few days. He hadn't deserved her kindness either, but she'd given it to him. Things had changed since then. Now when she called him, she did the bare minimum of checking in before immediately shifting to business. The project seemed to be going well, and he clung to that. The sooner it was done, the sooner he could leave the island and pretend the last confusing month had never happened.

Still, every day he missed Morgan. More than he had any right to. He'd told her not to visit—because he'd seen on her face that she didn't want to—and yet every day he wished she would.

It happened on the Sunday.

Edna knocked on his door, bright and early. This wasn't unusual; she'd been bringing him brownies every day since she'd discovered he liked them. It had bothered him at first—he had come here and threatened her wedding. But she seemed to have put that aside, probably because he had built the entire estate project around the event, and now she was dedicated to taking care of him. After he'd thought about that it had still bothered him, but somehow…less.

That morning though, Edna looked fierce as she entered his house. She usually knocked before letting herself in. Crime here was nearly non-existent, which was only one reason he left the door unlocked. It was the easier option. Otherwise he'd be walking to the door every hour at least, and that would prolong his recovery even more.

'My granddaughter has something to say to you.'

Elliott put down the cup of coffee he'd been drinking. He shifted, for the first time seeing an exasperated Morgan behind her grandmother. He folded his arms and leaned back on the couch.

Morgan quirked a brow at him. *Really?* it said. *You're encouraging this?*

He wanted to say he was unaffected by it, but he wasn't. His body immediately reacted to that eyebrow. The hair on his skin prickled, his blood heated, and he had to look at Edna to try and get other body parts under control.

He thought he'd stopped wanting people who didn't want him.

He breathed in at that, but Morgan was speaking, saving him from exploring it further.

'Elliott, I am sorry for not coming to see you this week,' she said, in a tone that sounded as if she was reciting the words. 'I should have abandoned all the work we need to get done so my grandmother's wedding can continue and offered you my company instead, reassured your ankle that it's doing an excellent job at healing.'

But it clearly wasn't a correct recital, because Edna poked Morgan in the stomach.

'Ow!' Morgan exclaimed. 'Why did you do that? You said I had to apologise, and I did.'

'That was not an apology,' Edna scolded. 'The man has sat here pining for you for a week and all you can offer him is sarcasm?'

'I wasn't pining,' Elliott interjected with a frown.

'Of course you were, dear.' Edna waved a hand. 'It was obvious to everyone who came here this week. We all thought Morgan would come to her senses, since she's been pining, too, but no. Apparently the two of you need me to intervene.'

'I was *not* pining,' Morgan said now. 'And even if I were—which I was *not*,' she assured Elliott, 'it isn't your place to intervene, Gran. I thought we'd gone over this?'

'Ha!' Edna exclaimed. 'We've not been over it. You let it slip and then apologised. But now that you've said it again, I'm forced to believe it and act on it.' She bowed her head in mock humility. 'I shouldn't have forced you to come here, Morgan. Please accept my apology.'

With that, she walked out through the front door. There was no mistaking the turning of the key in the lock.

Morgan looked at him. 'You gave her a key?'

'I did not,' he replied grimly.

Silence followed as they both stared at the door. Eventually Morgan walked to the kitchen. She looked striking in the black and white monochrome. She wore a bright red dress with hundreds of little flowers on it. The dress was scooped at her neckline, revealing the faintest of cleavage, and fell to her knees. Her hair was tied back with a white ribbon, a bow at the top of her ponytail, and her sandals had white straps with a sparkling circle between her two front toes.

He couldn't believe he was studying her in such detail that he had noticed the sparkling circles between her toes.

No, that was a lie. He could believe it. He wanted to know every detail about her. And as she stood in the kitchen, making his world brighter with her red dress, he wondered if it was a metaphor of some kind.

Was she there to change his world? To add colour to something he had, for the longest time, believed to be dull and bland? Or was this a warning? A sign to slow down or a sign of danger? A warning about what she would do to him?

'I hope you don't mind if I help myself to some coffee,' Morgan said, interrupting his annoying thoughts. 'It's been a pretty eventful morning, as you can imagine.'

'I can.'

'Can you?' She cast the question over her shoulder. 'Edna woke me up at six this morning—the one day I'd actually managed to sleep to six, mind you—and demanded I tell her why I've been avoiding you. She did not take me pulling the blankets over my head as an answer. In fact, she pulled the blankets *off* me, and demanded to know, once again, why I've been avoiding you.'

He didn't know what to say for the longest time. Then, 'There's cake. Brownies. Biscuits. Help yourself.'

'It's eight a.m.'

'You've been up since six, arguing with your grand-mother. That makes it equivalent to at least noon.'

She gave a small laugh. 'You know what? I actually haven't eaten this morning, so I'm going to take you up on that offer.' She walked to his fridge. 'Have you? Eaten, I mean?'

'Yes.' Idly, he laid a hand on his stomach. 'That's all I do these days.'

'Are you implying that you look different from when I last saw you?' Her eyes skipped over him. 'I assure you, your stomach is still as it once was.'

It wasn't, and he was fine with it. But it was immensely pleasing that Morgan had looked at him in that way.

He tried to shake it off. His entire adult life people had looked at him *in that way*. He shouldn't be preening be-cause Morgan was.

He shouldn't be, but he was.

Because Morgan was different.

'Can I at least get you another cup of coffee? A brownie?' she asked.

'If you must.'

'I'm not asking you to sacrifice your life,' she said with another laugh.

'I've already resigned myself to a slower recovery be-cause of all the sugar I've consumed.'

'Generally, I find sugar *aids* recovery,' she offered help-fully. 'Are you…?' She cleared her throat. 'Are you feel-ing better?'

He nodded. 'Dr Sam is happy. She thinks I could be back on the ankle by Wednesday.'

'That's great.' She sounded relieved.

'Anything new at the estate?' he asked, as her relief tightened something inside him.

There wasn't, but still she talked him through their

progress. She showed him pictures, videos, asked him for confirmation on a number of issues. She told him about how Edna's soon-to-be stepson had agreed to post the video on his social media and seemed fine with their plan to use his fame to lift the status of the island.

'I'm sure his father had something to do with that,' Morgan added, 'but we won't question the ways of the gods. Also, Thad has got a group of volunteers together. I mentioned the arch idea to him and he kind of jumped on it. So now they're building one for the garden. It might also turn into an altar of some kind… He cleared it with my grandmother, so honestly I didn't ask too many questions.'

'Thad?'

'Yeah,' she said with a faint smirk. 'You were right about him feeling bad, I think. So now he's being overly enthusiastic about how he can help.'

'He's been around the estate a lot?'

'Popped in once or twice.' She brought him a fresh cup of coffee and the brownie she'd heated, before settling at the kitchen table with a plate of food herself. 'Mostly to check in on the islanders. For their morale, I suppose.'

'How has that been?' he asked slowly. 'For you?'

She pierced a piece of pasta rather forcefully. 'Fine. He's been perfectly respectful.'

'He usually isn't?'

'No, it's not that. I just…usually avoid him.' She ate for a bit. 'And he avoids me, too. It's been awkward between us since…' She exhaled. 'Since we broke up. You saw.'

'Yes.' And because he couldn't help himself, he said, 'Tell me.'

She lifted her head, looking at him. Indecision creased her face, pursed her lips. Her eyes searched his, seeing things he probably didn't want her to. Then her expression softened, and he felt something akin to a key unlocking in his chest. Warmth rushed out, as if it had been locked behind that door, the pressure building, until finally it had been let out.

'I think I loved him,' she said before he could process what was happening to him. 'I was young and… I was tired.' She exhaled. 'There was a lot going on at home at that time. My sister was pregnant at seventeen, scared and still so innocent, even though she'd made a decision that would change her entire life. My brother had just been diagnosed with his learning disability and he was angry, like only a teenager can be. I'd been spreading myself thin, trying to manage it all while working on my degree, and my parents…' She shook her head. 'Anyway, I was feeling particularly vulnerable when I came to the island that year, and Thad was Thad. Charming, sincere, handsome. He made me the centre of his world and it was the most romantic thing.'

She pushed around the leftover pasta on her plate, before very deliberately eating a few bites. When she'd finished chewing them, she continued.

'It wasn't a healthy relationship. We were hiding it, for one thing, because we—no, because *I* didn't want anyone to know. And we didn't talk about anything real. It was all fluff and giddiness. And…and physical stuff,' she said in a shaky voice. 'I'm sorry. I don't know why that was so hard for me to say. I'm an adult. It's stupid.'

'Not stupid,' he growled.

The sides of her mouth quirked up. 'No, probably not.' She lifted a shoulder, dropped it. 'I hadn't had a physical relationship before him. He was my first kiss…my first touch.' Her cheeks pinkened. 'You get the point.'

He grunted now, because he did get the point, and he was insanely jealous that Thad had got to share something so precious with her.

'One night, we…um…got to a point when…' She cringed. 'No, you know what? This is stupid. I'm just going to say it. We almost had sex, but I chickened out. I was terrified of getting pregnant. I didn't trust that the condom wouldn't break. I wasn't on hormonal contraception, and I wasn't going to destroy my life or a child's life because—' She broke off on a gasp. 'That's awful. Oh, no…' she moaned. 'That's an awful thing to say.'

Elliott had no idea what to do. He'd never been in this position before, where someone had shared something so intimate with him. And it clearly was intimate. Even from where he sat, he could see the faint trembling of Morgan's body.

He wanted to go over, pull her into his arms. He didn't know if he should. If he *could*. Would he be crossing a line if he did? Was it the right thing to do? He'd failed too many times, his instincts letting him down. He didn't want to do the wrong thing now and make Morgan feel worse.

But something stronger than instinct urged him up. He made his way to her slowly, so she'd see him coming—and also because he had no choice with his leg—and stopped right at her side. She tipped her head to look up at him, her eyes open and vulnerable and looking for reassurance. And so he did what he wanted to do. He opened his arms, put them around her, and brought her close to his body.

The height of the kitchen chair elevated her so that she fitted snug against his chest. She relaxed into him. Made a cute little sound that might have been a sob. He was too terrified to check. Everything about this moment felt precarious. What if he shifted and things collapsed? What if she pushed him away…told him that this wasn't what she wanted? That *he* wasn't what she wanted?

For half his life he'd been made to feel that way—and it had broken him. He could finally admit that now, with Morgan in his arms, and that terrified him, too.

'I'm sorry,' she said after a bit, lifting her head. 'I shouldn't be so emotional.'

'Don't apologise,' he replied. 'I'm honoured that you would share that with me.'

She smiled, but bit her lip. It was probably inappropriate to find that sexy, but he did.

'Thank you,' she said.

'You're welcome.'

'Do you want me to help you back to your seat?'

'No.'

His heart was beating faster, speeding up the natural rhythm of his breathing. He knew it was because of her, because of her smile, and because of the softness she was staring at him with.

He sat down next to her, not wanting to take a chance. But she was eating again, and he didn't think it was because she was hungry. Was he making her nervous? Should he have gone back to the couch? Given her space?

'The day that happened,' Morgan said suddenly, pushing her now empty plate aside, 'my sister went into labour.'

She turned to face him, her elbow sliding onto the counter. She rested her head in her hand.

'She tried to call me but I'd turned my phone off. I'd wanted to be…free. To pretend I didn't have all those responsibilities. And I… I missed my niece's birth.'

'Why are you blaming yourself?' he asked, searching her face.

'Who else should I blame?'

'Blame implies wrongdoing. You did nothing wrong.'

'I *ignored* my sister's call.'

'She made it to the hospital?' he asked.

She nodded.

'Your niece is healthy?'

Another nod.

'And you adore her.'

A soft smile curved her face. 'Without question.'

'Which is why I didn't pose it as one,' he said dryly.

She snorted.

'Everything turned out fine, Morgan. It makes no sense for you to feel guilty.'

Morgan became so still a feeling of alarm went through Elliott. But he could see her chest rising and falling quietly, as if she'd decided her breathing was bothering him.

'Feelings make no sense,' she pointed out eventually. 'It's been eight years, and I still feel the embarrassment of breaking up with Thad because I was scared of what would happen if I stayed with him. And the guilt of missing Georgie's birth will always be there.'

He frowned. 'You're punishing yourself.'

Now she stiffened. 'I am not.'

'Okay…'

'Don't just say "okay" because you don't want to argue.'

'Okay.'

She shook her head. 'You're infuriating.'

'Yes,' he acknowledged. 'But so are you.'

'*Me*? What did I do?'

'You can't see that your break-up with Thad was inevitable. If the physical side of your relationship was the only thing keeping you together it would have ended anyway.' He continued before she could object. 'As for the situation with your sister—you are not her parent. You aren't responsible for her.'

She was shaking her head before he finished. 'You don't understand—'

'I understand complicated family dynamics.'

'Not mine. I don't have a personal life, Elliott. None. No friends, no steady relationship since Thad. I go to work, I go home, and I wait. I wait for my family to need me.'

She put a hand on the counter. Not quite a slam, but close enough.

'I bought a house that needs work because it gives me

something to do, but it's not something so consuming I won't be there for them.'

His heart cracked. Warmth oozed from it. Sympathy, frustration, anger—and more. Something deeper. He didn't examine it since she wasn't finished.

'And my job...' She squeezed her eyes shut and took a deep breath. 'I've had several people approach me with projects that would take me out of Cape Town...'

'You turned them down?'

She nodded. 'I was afraid I wouldn't be there when they needed me.'

Punishing yourself for not being there once. He didn't get a chance to say it.

'I've sacrificed so much for them.'

'Why?' he asked.

She blinked. 'What do you mean, why? They're my family.' Then her lashes fluttered as her gaze came to rest on him. 'Maybe you *do* understand that. Otherwise, why would you be here on the island at all?'

CHAPTER THIRTEEN

IT MIGHT HAVE been a little sneaky, but Morgan was worried she'd shared too much. Her emotions were finally freeing themselves from the hole she'd dug for them—for *Elliott*. It felt as if they'd been waiting for this moment all week. It must be part of the reason she'd been struggling to sleep.

Every night she would tumble into bed, exhausted, but her brain would go through everything she needed to do the next day. Over and over and over again. Until she looked at her clock and saw it was some early-morning hour. The anxiety of not sleeping would keep her up for another hour, then she would eventually fall into a restless sleep minutes before her alarm went off.

And everything would start all over again.

She hadn't been able to pinpoint the exact cause of her insomnia. Of course she was juggling multiple things at once, with higher stakes than any of her other projects, so it made sense for her to be struggling. But she'd also been fighting the urge to visit Elliott. Probably because she'd known the minute she saw him she'd tell him her every secret.

And now things had shifted in their relationship. She could feel their new intimacy in her soul, upsetting her equilibrium. The only way she knew how to handle it was to coax his secrets out, too.

It was sneaky, as she'd thought, and she wasn't proud of it.

'I know what you're doing,' Elliott said.

'I have no doubt that you do.' She sighed. 'Come on, let's go sit on the couch. You can't be comfortable like this.'

He didn't say anything as he hop-shuffled back to the couch, with her hovering at his side, ready to jump in if he asked for help. He didn't, and they both sat down. Their bodies were close together, but it was too late for Morgan to shift without drawing attention to the movement.

And still he wasn't saying anything.

She began to regret that she'd pried—or tried to, at least, since prying would mean that she'd actually asked a question. She hadn't. She'd made an implication about his family, but that was it. She'd wanted to shift the focus, hoping to make herself feel better, and now it was—

Her thoughts stopped when she felt an unfamiliar warmth at her hand. She looked down, staring blankly at their entwined fingers. And then she paid attention to her body. There'd been a spinning in her chest that had stilled once he'd made contact. Now that spinning was in her stomach. A soft tightening and releasing. Not uncomfortable, but alarming.

'I've wanted to do this since I came into the kitchen,' he said softly. 'I've been thinking about it since then, too. Going back and forth about whether it's the right thing.'

She couldn't stop staring at their hands. More at his than hers, caught by the swells of his knuckles, the dusting of hair, the strength that seemed impossible to tell from a hand and yet was somehow there.

'I don't think you've done a single thing that hasn't been right since I came to this house,' she replied. 'Except maybe siding with my grandmother this morning.'

'I got this, didn't I?' he asked, squeezing her hand.

She laughed. 'Touché.' A beat later, she asked, 'Why would you doubt your instincts?'

He didn't answer; she didn't push. Not when his face looked the way it did. Raw. Honest. Had she thought his expressions unreadable before? Muted? She was a fool. Or perhaps merely uneducated in the enigma that was Elliott.

She wanted to change that.

She hadn't planned on acting on that thought, but before she knew it her free hand was cupping his face.

Their eyes held. And then he turned and kissed the palm of her hand.

It stole her breath, that simple contact. It felt more intense than the kiss they'd shared at the beach. Even when he'd carried her to the house it hadn't felt like this.

'My instincts have led me astray,' he admitted quietly. 'With my family. My parents, specifically. They always seemed to care more about my brother than me. Everything Gio did was more important. I tried...' He pulled away from her, letting go of her hands, and rubbed a hand over his jaw. 'I followed my instincts, trying to get them to notice me. Excelled at sport. Worked hard at school. Nothing I did could measure up to my genius brother.'

'I'm so sorry.'

He shook his head. 'It's fine.'

'No, Elliott,' she said with a shake of her head. 'It's not fine. Not when they made you feel...' She trailed off, unsure whether he wanted her to say it.

'That was why I was so confused when you took care of me,' he said roughly. 'I'd done nothing to deserve your kindness.'

Her heart broke for him. For the young boy who'd thought his actions would dictate how his parents treated him. Who, because those actions had never been enough, didn't think *he* was enough.

'You don't have to do anything to deserve kindness, Elliott. Although in this case you have.'

His eyebrows lifted.

'You're the reason my grandmother can have her wedding here. You've employed a good number of people on the island. You've even come up with a way to help the island succeed after your departure.'

'That last thing was you.'

'Us,' she insisted. 'I wouldn't have come up with the idea if it hadn't been for you.'

He didn't reply to that, but the silence that spread between them was easy. They didn't touch one another again, and she was happy with that. It gave her a chance to settle. This morning had been a lot. She was desperate for...

She wasn't quite sure. Sanity? Stability?

'There have been so many people in my house,' he grumbled.

And then it hit her. She was desperate for levity.

'Oh, man, that must have freaked you out.'

'They touched my things,' he said in a low voice. 'Opened my fridge. *Talked* to me.'

She pursed her lips, but the laugh slipped out anyway. Once she'd started, she couldn't stop. His face was priceless. He was *disgusted* that people had talked to him. People he barely knew...who barely knew him. These people had come into his house, touched his things, opened his fridge, and *talked* to him.

Maybe disgusted wasn't the right word. Confused was probably more accurate. But it didn't matter. Not when she was already laughing harder, apologising in huffs of breath.

After a second his lips twitched. His eyes crinkled. And then he was laughing, too. The tension in her shoulders was released, the knot in her belly eased and, strangely, a wave of sleepiness washed over her. But she resisted it, enjoying her freedom instead. Finally, they stopped, but lightness was still in the air.

'It's been an experience,' he muttered, with a twist of his mouth.

'I can imagine.'

'Will it keep happening after I get back on my feet?'

'Yes. I'm sorry, but it's true! This community is...' She threw her hands up. 'They care about people. And now that you're part of it—'

'I am *not* part of this community.'

The dark way he said it sucked some of the lightness out of the air.

'They'll always see you as part of the community now. You're giving them jobs. Potentially saving the island they love.' She shrugged, no longer able to resist the tiredness. 'Plus, you're a good person, Elliott.'

Letting her tired brain take over, she curled onto her side, resting her head on his lap. He froze, but then slowly began to stroke her hair.

'You say nice things because...' He hesitated. 'Because you care about me?'

'Yeah,' she answered, stifling a yawn. 'But that doesn't mean I'm wrong.'

She fell asleep before she could hear his reply.

CHAPTER FOURTEEN

ON ELLIOTT'S FIRST full day back, Morgan handed him a clipboard with a long list of everything that would now be his responsibility.

'We're in it now,' she said with dark amusement, and proceeded to inform him that all the rental houses in Flipper Estate had been booked by wedding guests.

Most of the structural work on the estate had been completed, though there was still some way to go on some of the houses that had more damage than the others. They'd be cutting it close in fixing those by the wedding, but Morgan was confident they could do it. The estate aesthetic was coming together, with all the renovated houses painted a pretty blue and white. And the garden was, without a doubt, the most magnificent thing he'd seen.

It was a medium-sized open space, not unlike the gardens back home in Cape Town, enclosed by a silver fence partially obscured by trees. His attention was immediately drawn to the big oak tree on his left as he entered the garden. Its thick crooked branches exploded in leaves, casting shadows over a significant portion of the garden. Flowers sprang up all over—red, yellow, white—bringing colour to an otherwise sea of green.

He hadn't visited the garden until now. Technically, it wasn't a part of the renovation, so he hadn't seen the need. That had seemed particularly true when he'd thought it more likely he'd bump into Edna or any one of her friends there, since it was the wedding venue.

Elliott was aware of the shift that had brought him to the garden today, but he wasn't interested in doing any more than acknowledging it. What had happened between him and Morgan the previous week had been... Well, it *had* been. No point in thinking about it further.

Liar, an inner voice whispered.

Fine. He'd thought about it. About her trusting him enough to tell him about her family. About her fears. She'd even said she cared about him, and his heart had expanded to double its size. Which meant he was finally feeling full again, after his family's rejection had halved his heart in the first place.

Perhaps it wasn't that he didn't want to examine it, but rather that he had no idea what to do now that he had.

'You don't like it?' Morgan asked from beside him.

Slowly, he turned. 'I do.'

'So why are you frowning?'

He looked back at the garden, eager to shift the blame to something other than his emotions. Conveniently, his eyes rested on Thad. The mayor was working with a group of about five people on a wooden altar. Not far away, another group was constructing an arch of some kind. Elliott had seen them on his initial scan of the garden, but he hadn't realised Thad was there.

'What did you tell him when you broke up with him?' he asked quietly.

If she was surprised by the question, she didn't show it. 'That I wasn't ready for a relationship. And I certainly wasn't ready for what we were about to do.' She moved in front of him. 'Are you planning on defending my honour?'

'Do you want me to?'

She tilted her head, eyes twinkling. 'I kind of do, yeah.'

Then with a small smile—and a resulting leap of his heart—she shook her head.

'Come on, we have more important things to do than talk about my ex.'

She stalked past him and he followed with a smile of his own, before being thrown into the deep end with work.

The next two weeks passed in a blur. They worked day and night on the estate, where everyone was putting in more than their fair share of effort to try and get it done on time.

Whenever Elliott could spare a moment, he checked in on his own business. He attended virtual meetings while walking from one house to another; answered client phone calls in the middle of painting a room; soothed employee tensions at the warehouse as he helped carry furniture into houses.

Things were busier than they had ever been for him, and he didn't mind it a single bit. Because in between all the craziness was Morgan.

They shared looks when something ridiculous happened. Talked about it as they walked into town to get lunch. They joked about the work, and about the wedding, because laughter was the only way to manage the pressure.

Sometimes late at night, when the last of the workers had finally left, they shared a beer on the porch of one of the houses. Those nights were his favourite, because she'd talk about her work then. About projects she'd done, or projects she would do once the wedding was over. He loved to watch her as she talked. As she *sparkled*. Because this was her passion.

She'd turn to him without fail and ask him about his own work, and he'd tell her. Share with her things he never had before.

'You're proud of what you've done,' she remarked one night, smiling at him. 'As well you should be.'

'I... I am,' he replied, surprised that he could admit it. Surprised that he hadn't admitted it, even to himself, before.

These surprises were becoming more frequent with the more time he spent with Morgan. She complimented him so easily, pointed out things he did well. She also pointed out things he didn't do well, but it never sounded condescending. Never as if she was comparing him to anyone else.

Whenever he had those thoughts, he realised how much his youth still affected him. Some part of him had been indoctrinated never to acknowledge his successes, to keep on pushing because they were never enough.

He'd been giving his brother only the vaguest of updates, and whenever Gio prodded, Elliott wouldn't reply. Because deep down he was afraid he'd made a mistake by going in this direction with the estate. What if things didn't work out the way he intended? Should he have just done what Gio had asked him to do? Gio was, after all, a genius.

But then Morgan would say something nice to him, or her excitement about the progress on the estate or the wedding would spill over onto him, and he'd feel better. He had no idea what to do about it. He'd never had a relationship like this. Where there was more than superficial commonality or physical attraction.

Although the physical attraction was certainly there. He thought about it all the time, in fact. And worried that acting on it would spoil whatever they were building.

'Are you ever going to tell me why you're doing this?' Morgan asked one night, a week before the wedding. It was Friday, everyone had gone home, and they were sitting on the porch of the house they'd just finished. 'We've talked about all kinds of things, but you haven't said a word about that.'

He swirled the contents of his bottle, looking up into the

night sky. If he sat perfectly still he could hear the crash of the ocean. With Morgan at his side, he felt…content.

Content? Not once in his life had he ever used that as a description for himself. There was always more. Always ways to expand his business. Always another person to charm—which was a very loose way to think about what he'd done with women in the past. The point was that 'more' had become his way of life.

But that happens when you don't think you're enough.

He took a swig of the beer, swallowing it down along with the emotion that thought awakened. 'My father had a heart attack.'

Her head whipped to the side. 'What? Is he okay?'

'He's fine. It could have been worse.'

He stilled. How would he have felt if his mother had called to tell him the heart attack *had* been worse? He couldn't answer. Hell, he barely knew how he felt about it now.

'The doctor wants him to rest, which means no work.'

'So you stepped in?'

'My brother called to ask me if I would.' His fingernail worried the label of the beer bottle. 'He never asks for anything. I… I couldn't say no.'

'Because you're a big ol' softy beneath that hard exterior,' she teased, but quickly sobered. 'And because families are complicated and you didn't know how to say no.'

He was constantly amazed at how well she knew him. Constantly annoyed, too. He muttered a curse.

She gave a soft laugh. 'What was that for?'

'You.'

'You *swore* at me?'

'Not specifically.' His exhalation made him sound like a bull. 'You see things other people don't.'

'Oh, yes, that clarifies the swearing thing,' she said

wryly. 'Go right ahead and defile this new house with your dirty words.'

Slowly, he turned his head. 'You're worried about the house's innocence?'

Her gaze met his. 'My own, actually.'

She could have said *Take off your clothes* and it wouldn't have heated him as much as those words did. Or was it because of the way she was looking at him? Because of the lazy desire in her eyes, as if she was turned on but couldn't be bothered by it?

He could change that. He could bother her if she let him.

He didn't even care that these thoughts were dangerous—the kind he avoided whenever he was around her. The kind he *fought* whenever he was around her. He'd come to accept that sexual tension would be their constant companion. That the cloud of lust following them would always be threatening to burst into a thunderstorm of seduction.

It was in the looks he caught her aiming at him when he was working. The way she sometimes tilted her head, bit her lip. The power of it triggered something primitive inside him. Made him want to pull off his shirt, beat his chest, roar.

The only way to make it abate was to touch her whenever he could. When she asked him to pass her something he grazed her fingers, eager to feel their softness. He touched the small of her back when she went through a door ahead of him. She never complained, touched him, too, and on those days he'd dream of her. Of touching her, licking her, doing wicked things to her. And then he'd wake up sweating and aroused, unable to sleep for the rest of the night.

'I only take innocence when it's offered,' he all but growled.

Morgan's brows rose. There was no judgement in her

gaze, no reprimand. Only curiosity, amusement. *Fire.* 'Are you propositioning me?'

'That's not what "offered" means.'

'Hmm...'

She set down her beer and stood, turning to him. Nothing about the movement was hasty or alarming, yet his heartbeat sped up. His muscles tensed. It was a ridiculous reaction to someone hooking their thumbs around the straps of their denim dungarees. But he'd been staring at her in those dungarees for weeks. She wore them whenever she painted.

'It's an unspoken rule that if you're going to paint a house, this is what you wear,' she'd said when he had commented on it. 'It makes no sense, since it's not really comfortable, but I don't make the rules.'

But she altered them. Her dungarees were sometimes made of a flimsy material that clung to every curve and dimple of her body. She only wore a sports bra underneath, from what he could see. Probably underwear, too, though he never looked long enough to figure that out. He didn't want to get caught, for one thing. For another, he was afraid of what imagining her without underwear as she stood beside him every day would do to his brain.

His body.

'We've been avoiding this,' she said conversationally.

'Yes.'

'You sprained your ankle last time.'

He grunted.

'But that isn't why we've been avoiding it, is it?'

'No,' he replied, setting his own beer down. He stood now, too, but didn't walk any closer.

'It's a terrible idea,' she informed him, but took the tiniest step towards him. 'It will muddle things.'

He took a step forward. 'Yes.'

'We might not come out unscathed.'

'There's no "might",' he contradicted. 'We won't.'

The vulnerability on her face all but jumped at him. It slammed into his chest, his heart, and that traitorous organ told him it didn't want to come out unscathed. He was in love with her, and he wanted something to show for it. *Her* heart, he realised, but he shut that thought down, looking at her face again.

'Don't do anything you don't want to.'

'I...want to,' she said softly. 'With you.'

He'd asked her to offer—and she was. He knew what it cost her, too. She'd stopped things from progressing with Thad because she'd been afraid of what it might lead to. She hadn't dated much after him because she was afraid of the cost. She was sacrificing those fears for him. If he'd had any chance of resisting her before, he didn't now.

He closed the space between them. She was trembling when he did. His body demanded that he take her, take his fill. Show her just how much he could make her tremble now that he had the chance.

He wanted to touch every part of her body. To kiss her mouth, her breasts, lower. He wanted to lick, to taste, to feel her writhing beneath him.

But he knew that wasn't the way to go. He wanted to make this mean something. And while their passion, their insatiable thirst, would do that, too, he could tell that wasn't what she wanted.

He'd give her what she wanted.

It might kill him, but he would.

He lowered his head, taking his time as he studied her face, illuminated under the full moon. Her eyes held desire and trust, her lashes fluttering as he made her wait for the kiss. There was a blush on her cheeks. Her mouth was open, and warm breath heated his lips. He inhaled, felt that heat move to his heart, settle there in a way that had nothing to do with sensuality and spread.

With each heartbeat it reached further down his body. He ached for her. Chest, arms, torso. He was already aroused, had been from the moment she'd stood up, but when that heat hit between his legs he pulled her even closer, relishing her gasp.

He slid his hand over the small of her back, then cupped her butt, tilting his hips forward. Another gasp, this one inches from his lips because he'd moved closer. She gave a little moan—a protest, he thought, because he still wasn't kissing her.

But she would have to wait.

If he was going to torture them he would revel in it. Revel in the way her chest heaved against his, the press of her plush breasts, the tiniest pulse as she shifted her hips against his. The movement was so small—barely there— as if she didn't want him to notice she was trying to soothe the ache she must feel, too.

He smiled.

'Masochist,' she accused softly.

'Never before,' he said, adding a second hand to her butt. His body was screaming at him, unhappy with the restraint controlled by his mind, which his body had officially declared its enemy. 'It's you.'

'I'll bring you much more pain if you don't kiss me.'

'Kiss *me*,' he commanded.

The last thing he saw before her lips met his was her smile. Then he closed his eyes, sinking into the pleasure of finally, *finally* kissing her. Her mouth was warm and soft…familiar yet entirely unknown to him. A mountain or a forest he passed every day but never explored.

He explored now. He moved his tongue against hers in a battle they would both win. Took in every shiver that came with a certain angle, every moan when he changed the depth.

His hands moved, too, away from the curves they'd

enjoyed until now, moving on to the rest of her body. He traced the arch of her back, his fingers lingering on her ribs before sliding up. His thumbs and forefingers formed a semi-circle under her breasts, but he hated the roughness of the denim beneath his touch, and groaned in protest.

He had no idea how she knew what he was protesting about, but she reached up, undid the buttons of her dungarees and let the material fall open—all without breaking the kiss.

He leaned back to look. She wore a crop top. Red and sleeveless, it stopped above her belly button, skimming the loveliest skin he'd ever seen. He dropped to his knees so he could get a better look. Stared in awe at the brown skin that reminded him of sand when the sun hit it just right. He traced the slight white lines of stretchmarks peeking out at her waist, where the dungarees were still held up by her hips, and he looked up so he could tell her how beautiful she was.

Her gaze was open, soft as she watched him. As she smiled a smile that travelled to his heart, settling in the heat that had been there from the start. She reached out, cupped his face, and they stayed like that for a while. Him on his knees…her staring down at him. It was something he'd always remember. He knew it in his soul. It was as if someone had taken a picture, capturing the intimacy, the specialness of the moment.

And then she reached for him, and he stood, and their mouths met again, and all the slowness of before disappeared. They kissed as if it was their final day on earth. Eager, desperate, wanting to memorise what was happening because it would likely never happen again.

Even as he had that thought he pushed it away, kissed her deeper. She gripped his top and he moved back, throwing off the offending item before pulling her top off, too. He stared at her. The sports bra she wore today flattened her breasts, and his fingers itched to pull that off, too. But there was something beautiful in the simplicity of it. And breasts were breasts—even when they were flattened.

He kissed the curves he could see, and then she was running her hands down his chest, her nails lightly tickling him, and he bit his lip, feeling the arousal of it hit him in the gut. He'd had enough. He wanted to be doing more than this.

He picked her up and pushed her against the door. Felt the air leave her body as she absorbed the impact.

'Morgan,' he said, chest heaving. 'Are you okay?'

'Yes.'

'You don't sound okay. You sound...out of breath.' He shook his head. 'I'm sorry. I shouldn't have—'

'Are you listening to yourself right now?' she interrupted. 'You're out of breath, too. Because we're...you know...'

He did know. But he had to make sure.

'We can stop,' he told her, searching her face. 'We can stop any time you want.'

'I know that. We won't have sex,' she said a little shakily. 'I... I'm not...'

'Morgan.' When she looked at him he lifted a hand, brushed her brow, her cheek, her lips with his thumb. 'I only want what you want to give me.'

'I want to give you everything.'

It was so simple, his heart ached.

'I just...'

'I know.' He kissed her forehead. 'Show me what you can give me.'

Her eyes filled with gratitude—and then with a need so fierce he felt it fill cracks inside him.

And then she did. She showed him.

And he tumbled even harder in love.

CHAPTER FIFTEEN

MORGAN HADN'T EVER brought anyone to this place.

It was special to her, and unknown to so many. Which was strange on an island as small as this. But the teenagers who lived on the island only knew of the so-called 'private' beaches that everyone knew about. The lookouts that were supposedly hidden but were actually common knowledge amongst everyone who had grown up there.

None of them had felt the need to explore as if they were desperately seeking peace. Shelter from a chaotic family.

The path was a short distance away from the estate, towards the edge of the island. The beginning of it was obscured by trees and branches, and a few meters up a collapsed tree lay over the path.

'Are we allowed to be here?' Elliott asked quietly at her side.

He was more relaxed than he'd ever been since they'd met. Which was unsurprising, considering what they'd just done at the house.

She gave an involuntary shiver at the memory of his clever hands, his extraordinary mouth. And her heart swelled at how sweet and respectful he'd been about her reservations.

She felt stupid for still having them. For being thirty years old and still having hang-ups about sex. She was well aware that birth control worked. That it was possible to have safe sex. But she didn't feel secure enough to risk it. It made no sense, and yet she clung to it—just as her twenty-two-year-old self had. Except then the man she'd been with had stiffened, grown colder, and made her feel like she'd led him on.

It had taken this experience with Elliott for her to fully realise that *had* been how Thad had made her feel. Because Elliott hadn't. He'd followed her lead, assuring her that whatever she was comfortable with was all he wanted. And so she had given. And received. More than she had with Thad, because Elliott was more dedicated to her pleasure than Thad had ever been.

It was probably unfair to compare them. But since she'd only been with two men in this way—the few dates she'd managed to go on over the years never having got past a kiss—being unfair was natural. Necessary, even, for her to stop blaming herself.

Why did she always blame herself?

'Morgan?'

She turned her head. 'Yes?'

'Are you okay?'

'Of course.' She blinked. 'Why? Don't I look okay?'

'You were distracted,' he told her. 'You look…fine.'

A compliment? She bit her bottom lip to keep from smiling, then said, 'You're worried about us being here?'

'"Worried" isn't the word I'd use.'

'Well, most people seem to share your…hesitance, when coming here. Not many people know about this place.'

'I wonder why,' he muttered darkly, before battling through the branches of the collapsed tree.

She had done it on purpose. All so she could see him struggle. When they returned, she would show him the way around the tree, and tease him when he asked why they hadn't taken that route before.

It was immature and silly of her, but she needed that.

There seemed to be a dark cloud following her around. Far enough away that she didn't have to pay attention to it just yet—and there were more important things to do… the estate, the wedding—but as soon as those distractions were gone, that cloud would burst, and everything she'd been running from would rain down on her.

The drizzling she'd experienced every now and then with Elliott wouldn't compare. And that worried her. Because that drizzling… It had messed with her head. What would a full-blown rainstorm do to her?

It didn't help that her family would be arriving this week. Her mother had called her the day before, her excitement for the upcoming wedding clear. Hattie had been messaging her in the same vein.

She hadn't heard much from her father and brother, though that wasn't surprising. In fact, she preferred it. She didn't have to pretend that things hadn't changed in the last month. That *she* hadn't changed. They had, and she had, but she had no idea how that would look when she went back to her real life.

You control it—not them.

She stepped into the clearing as that thought came, and pushed it out of her head. This wasn't the place for those kinds of thoughts. Instead, she breathed in, her lungs expanding further than they had in a long time.

Peace.

She closed her eyes, opened her arms, and let herself be. Elliott stopped next to her and she heard his sharp intake of air. Joy spread through her, as if she had birthed this piece of nature and done something impressive.

And then she opened her eyes.

They were standing in front of a waterfall. A small one, about four metres high, with a steady fall of water that filled the stream below. The water was clear enough for her to see the pebbles beneath it, the fish swimming in it. She had never followed the stream to see where it led. The mystery of it was far too enjoyable for her to solve it with knowledge. Besides the sound of the water and the faint crash of the ocean, the chirps and squawks of nature, it was quiet.

That quiet crept around the tension she carried in her soul, kneading it until it was flat and smooth. With an exhalation, she turned to Elliott. 'What do you think?'

'It's magnificent.'

The reverence in his voice made her want to do a happy wiggle.

'No one else knows about this?'

'I'm not sure.' Carefully, she made her way over the moss-covered stones to the edge of the stream. 'I found this the first summer I came to visit my grandmother. I haven't heard anyone talk about it, and no one has ever been here when I have. If other people know about it, they're content to keep it a secret.' She shot him a look. 'Which now includes you. You take this to your grave.'

He followed her, his mouth curved. 'You're adorable.'

Adorable?

'You're taking my reference to your death pretty calmly,' she replied, pretending it hadn't affected her at all.

'I wouldn't have come with you to this secluded place if I was worried that you'd kill me.'

She let out a huff of laughter. 'Fair point.'

His gaze stayed on hers, skipping from amusement to... to something she didn't understand. Something intense, searching.

'What?'

'You're okay with what happened back at the house?' he asked quietly.

'I am.' Now she searched *his* expression. 'How about you?'

'I'm fine.'

He said the words so quickly she might have thought he was lying if not for the ghost of a smile on his face. She snorted at it. At the arrogance that smile showed. The confidence.

Although, to be fair, he deserved it.

The thought brought a hot flush to her body. Reminded her that she was clammy from the walk up and—other things. But there was the stream…just there. They were alone. And there was no point hiding her body after what they'd already done.

She kicked off her shoes and began to take off her dungarees.

'What are you doing?' he asked, eyes widening.

'Undressing.'

'Undressing?'

His mouth opened and closed as if he was mouthing the words to a song he knew by heart.

'I promise I'm not seducing you,' she said with an amused smile. 'Not again, anyway.'

'Not purposely,' he answered darkly.

She stuck her tongue in her cheek. 'I'd like to cool off in the stream. You can turn around if you want to.'

'I don't.'

It was a growl.

Electricity charged the air.

Was this how she'd die? Electrocution?

She considered it. What had happened at the house meant the chemistry they'd been ignoring since the night she'd fallen asleep on him was finally out in the open. They could do this. Share more intimacy. Her body ached for it. For him.

But there was a part of her that acknowledged they'd been ignoring the chemistry for a reason. They were working together. Stakes were high enough that they had to put their personal feelings aside. But beneath the working together stuff, beneath even the physical attraction, was growing a solid friendship. She didn't want to ruin that most of all.

For these few weeks she'd felt close to someone. The only person she'd ever shared that feeling with was her grandmother, but there were things she couldn't even share with Grandma Edna. For the first time she was talking about her family. About helping her parents, taking care of her siblings.

It was a relief to speak honestly about it. To share the facts and sometimes even her feelings. Not talking about it had been her way of shielding her family. She hadn't wanted anyone to think poorly of them. Not even herself.

She had got to know herself better after talking with Elliott. And she knew *him* better, too. His favourite colour, favourite food. The days of the weeks he most dreaded and most loved. What his typical day back home looked like.

She'd pulled all that information out of him carefully, deliberately. He wasn't used to talking about himself. But those mundane things had laid a foundation for the more important things. Like the fact that he was stepping in to this project because his brother had asked. Because his father had had a heart attack. It was complicated and messy—just like her own situation. She understood his position better than anyone because of that. But it also meant she knew a relationship between them would be near impossible.

Unless things changed.

Unless *they* changed.

Unless they acted on those changes.

Her heart cracked. Just a little, but enough for her to notice it. For her to realise that her feelings for Elliott wouldn't matter if they intended on returning to their old lives. She didn't know how things would look for her...

for him. It made her desperate. Desperate for this moment with him.

She pulled down the straps of her dungarees, letting them fall to her hips. In one quick movement she took off her top. Her bra followed. Then she shimmied the dungarees down over her hips. Kicked them off. Repeated the movement with her underwear, slower.

All the while, she looked at him.

Met his gaze.

Waited as his eyes followed her movements. As they glowed with the fire of desire when they rested on her face.

She knew what he saw. Her naked body, responding to him. Knew that it turned him on, too. An emotion she didn't recognise thickened her throat. Not knowing what to do with it, she turned, stepping into the stream, walking until the water deepened just beneath the waterfall.

The coldness distracted her mind, her body for a minute, and she relished the relief of it. She held her breath, sank beneath the water and stayed there until her lungs tightened. When she came back up she faced Elliott again. He was still standing there. Still watching her.

'Are you coming?' she asked hoarsely.

He grunted, but made his way down to the stream. Her eyes followed him, taking in the strength of his shoulders, his arms, his legs. He pulled off his shirt, his jeans, his underwear. She heard herself exhale, though the sound was faint beneath the thudding of her heart. He was the most beautiful man she had ever seen. His chest was broad, dusted with a scattering of dark hair that disappeared at his abs but reappeared at the base of his stomach, leading to his—

She swallowed. They'd kept some of their clothing on at the house. Their heat and passion had been too fast, too delicious to bother with complete nudity. At least, that was what she'd thought. Now she wondered if she'd been protecting herself. Looking at him like this, fully naked and aroused and beautiful, she knew she loved him. Not because of his body—although it was a work of art—but because of who he was. Because he'd chosen to share himself with her, despite how vulnerable it made him feel.

When she'd stood in front of him naked she'd felt that vulnerability, too. Sharper than ever before. It had been... overwhelming. Scary.

And he'd chosen to feel that way for her.

He must have sensed something was happening because he made his way to her slowly, leaving space between them when he stopped.

'Morgan?' he said, his voice husky, the word a question.

She closed the distance, her mouth fusing with his before she could talk herself out of it. His arms wrapped around her, pulling her against him, and he kissed her with the same urgency, the same need she'd come with to him.

It was a while after that when they lay on the rocks, staring up at the midnight-blue sky with its stars twinkling down on them. Morgan had never felt so sated. So fulfilled. So...scared.

They hadn't made love, but had done almost everything except the act. And it had been an expression of her love. If things had been different—if they'd been in a relationship and this had been intentional...if they'd been anywhere but on the island—she would have had sex with him.

Because she trusted him.

Because she loved him.

But they weren't in a relationship.

They'd just fallen into what was happening between them. The island had become an alternative reality, where their happiness was more important than what had always kept them from experiencing that happiness before.

It was a fantasy.

Fantasies never lasted.

CHAPTER SIXTEEN

'WHAT ARE YOU thinking about?' came her quiet question.

Elliott couldn't tell her. He couldn't say that touching her had awakened things in him he hadn't realised existed. That kissing her had filled him. That sharing the intimacy they'd just shared had shifted things so completely he didn't know how to move on, how to move forward.

But he couldn't lie to her either.

'You,' he said, playing with the wet strands of her hair lying across her chest. 'Us.'

'Yeah?' She lifted her head, resting her chin on his chest. 'How's that going for you?'

He could hear the teasing in her voice, and the raw emotion he'd seen on her face in the stream had disappeared beneath a mask. Things must have changed for her, too. If he'd had the courage, he would have asked how. But he didn't. He was a coward, unable to face situations that were difficult. He'd done it with his family; he would do it with her. He knew that.

But for now there was this. Them. And he'd cling to the moment for as long as he could.

'It's good,' he answered.

Her expression softened and she pressed a kiss to his chest. 'You're awfully charming, Mr Abel.'

He snorted. 'Only you would think that.'

'Hmm...'

She lay back, on the rocks this time, and for a while there were only the sounds of the waterfall, the animals, the ocean. Despite his promise to himself earlier, his mind spun with thoughts. What would happen when they left this place? Would they go back to who they'd been before this night? Or would they become something he didn't recognise?

It's not good,' she said, her voice clear. Her meaning clear. 'You're worried.'

'Aren't you?'

'I'd be a fool not to be.'

And you aren't a fool.

There weren't many things about Morgan he didn't like. But one of them would certainly be how clearly she saw him. And how obscured her view of herself was.

'It wouldn't be your fault,' he said quietly. 'If things… changed.'

'Wouldn't it?'

He straightened, looked at her. Her hair was spread over the rocks, curling wildly, glowing faintly in the moonlight. She'd put her clothes back on, but her dungarees were pulled down to her waist, so that he could see the red crop top. She was as beautiful like this as she had been naked and vulnerable before him.

His heart begged him to reconsider, making him realise he'd already decided to push her away. But it was for the best. He'd rather hurt her now than down the line, when she realised he could never be what she wanted.

The wind rustled. He looked at her again, this time noticing her nipples had pebbled underneath her top and her skin was gooseflesh.

'You're cold,' he said.

'You're scared,' she replied.

Oh, he *did* hate how clearly she saw him. But he wouldn't deny it. 'You are, too.'

'Worried…scared,' she confirmed. 'You've turned me into someone who thinks about her life. I haven't done that. Not in a long time. And now I want—' She broke off. Sat up. Wrapped her arms around her legs. 'What I want doesn't matter.'

'It does.'

'No, it doesn't. I have a real life to go back to. Spending nights with you under the moonlight isn't real.'

'But it could be.'

Why had he said that? It had leapt from his lips, directly from his heart, and now she was looking at him with wide eyes. Wide, *hopeful* eyes.

Then she shook her head. 'No, it can't be. What happens when we go back? My family…they still need me. And yours…' She trailed off, looking at him. 'I don't even know how to answer that, Elliott. And doesn't that mean we're bound to fail?'

No.

But he wouldn't say it. He wouldn't give her hope again, only to witness it being snuffed out. As it had to be.

'You're right,' he said roughly. 'It's not because of you.'

'Why do you keep saying that?'

'Because you don't see it.'

'See *what*?' she snapped. 'This started because of me. Right from the moment I tricked you into meeting with me that first day.'

'This is what I mean. You take responsibility when you shouldn't.'

'If I don't, who else will?'

She stood, tied the straps of her dungarees. Elliott vaguely recalled the beginning of the night. When she'd untied them and everything had felt beautiful and hopeful.

He'd spoiled that.

No, he thought. He couldn't believe that if he didn't want her to believe it.

'I know why you think that,' he said quietly. 'You've been responsible for your family for as long as you can remember. But that doesn't mean you should be. Your parents are adults. Your siblings are, too.' He paused. 'Maybe it's time you let them take responsibility for themselves, Morgan.'

'Really?' Her tone was sarcastic. 'I did that once, remember? My sister was hysterical and my parents were—'

'Morgan,' he said again, 'you don't owe them your life.'

'That's what you don't get!' she exclaimed, throwing up her hands. 'I do. I *do*. My parents' lives changed because they had me. They sacrificed so much. So I...' She folded her arms, shivering in the wind that had gone cold. 'The least I could do was make it easy for them.'

He'd known what her situation with her family was, but he hadn't expected this. A guilt that made no sense, and yet was perfectly sensible when it came to her. When it came to family. She hadn't expected to tell him either, it seemed, because her eyes widened and filled.

Instinctively he stepped forward, his arms open. She stepped back, shaking her head.

'I'm sorry,' she hiccuped. 'I just...' She shook her head again, more vehemently. Then, deliberately, she inhaled. Blew out air. Squared her shoulders. 'We should probably get back.'

He followed her wordlessly, down the steep decline that forced his focus to the path. When she led him around the fallen tree she'd previously led him through, he didn't comment. If it had been a couple of hours earlier he would have. He would have asked her about it. Likely been teased about it, too.

But a couple of hours earlier things had been easier between them. Inside himself.

She hadn't meant to reject him. Still, it stung. Reminded

him of all the times in his childhood when he'd followed his instincts and been pushed away despite that.

Because of it?

He took a breath. No, this wasn't about him. If Morgan had known what he was thinking—if she had been thinking clearly—she would have told him that, too. He knew that as well as he knew that his own issues were blinding him. That they were the reason he couldn't be with her in the first place.

How could he know that and still be so helpless to stop it?

Not helpless, a voice that sounded alarmingly like Morgan's echoed in his head. *Unwilling.*

Unwilling?

He was immensely grateful that they'd arrived back at the estate then, because the scene in front of him demanded all his attention.

'Morgan!' Edna pushed through the small crowd of people who'd been standing outside the house he and Morgan had been working on. 'Morgan, thank goodness you're all right!'

'Of course I'm all right. I just— *Ow! Gran!* Why did you *do* that?'

'Because you didn't come home!' Edna emphasised each word with another poke to Morgan's chest. 'You didn't come home, you didn't leave a message, and you weren't answering your phone.'

'I'm a grown-up!' Morgan exclaimed, shifting so that his body was in front of hers.

She was using him as a shield.

It would have amused him if he hadn't been afraid Edna would start poking him, too.

'A grown-up lets the people around her know that she's okay!'

'Honestly, Gran, what did you think? There's virtually no crime around here. And I was with Elliott.'

Edna's eyes narrowed to slits as they rested on Elliott.

'Elliott,' she growled. 'What were you doing with my granddaughter?'

He had absolutely no answer for that.

'It better have been something sexy,' someone said from behind Edna. 'I think Edna would be able to forgive you if it were something sexy.'

There was a long pause as everyone in the crowd—people he knew and didn't know—watched them expectantly.

'I could,' Edna said a beat later. 'I could forgive you if it were something sexy.'

'The *people* on this island—I swear!'

With those words, Morgan stormed off.

They all stared after her. Then, slowly, people looked at him.

'No,' he said.

He had no desire to share what had happened with these people. Even if he did feel more connected to this community than he had anywhere before.

The thought stayed with him throughout the short drive home—as did thoughts about Morgan. Memories, good and bad, of everything they'd shared tonight. They distracted him. Twirling in his head. Mocking him. Teasing him. So much so that when he parked in his driveway he didn't realise there was another car there until it was too late.

By then his brother had already seen him.

CHAPTER SEVENTEEN

MORGAN WENT THROUGH variations of what she would tell Elliott when she saw him that morning.

I overreacted.

I shouldn't have said what I said.

I'm sorry we can't be together.

The last one was what she really wanted to say. She *was* sorry. After everything they'd been through—particularly everything they'd shared the day before—all she wanted was for them to be together. But it was impossible.

He'd made her see that her issues ran deeper than even she had thought. She'd had no idea she'd been making herself smaller because she felt guilty. She'd had no idea the real reason she'd helped raise her siblings was because she'd wanted to make it up to her parents.

It wasn't right, and it wasn't healthy. She could recognise that. But it twisted her insides. She hadn't been able to sleep the night before, trying to think it through. When it had become clear that wouldn't be possible she'd tried not to think about it at all—and had ended up thinking about Elliott instead.

She'd hurt him, even though they both knew they had no future together. They both wanted one, though. That much was clear. If things were simple, if the world were an easier place, that would be enough.

Why couldn't that be enough?

Her phone rang, distracting her. She opened it to find a message from Elliott, telling her he wouldn't be coming to the estate that day. Her shoulders stiffened, her stomach tightened, but she sent back an acknowledgement—a thumbs-up emoji, because she had no words—and began on the finishing touches of one of the last houses they had to do.

She wasn't angry at him for not coming. She understood it on a personal level. But they still had to work together. She'd hoped he'd manage to set aside his feelings so that they would be able to complete the project. And fear that he might not was the reason she hadn't wanted them to give in to their desires. Part of the reason, anyway. The other part was that she'd always known giving in would bring them to this. Sad, broken, without even the friendship they'd forged over the last weeks.

Every instinct told her this was her fault. She had been the one to make the first move the night before. She'd taken off her clothes at the stream, offered herself to him. But he'd accepted her; offered her the same. It hadn't been easy for him, and still he'd done it. And he'd told her it wasn't her fault. That they'd both made the decision and that meant they shared the responsibility.

Was that true for her family as well?

She straightened, leaving the carpet she'd been putting down half unrolled. *Could* she apply this to her family? No, that didn't work. Her siblings hadn't asked Morgan to look after them—Morgan had made that decision. In the same way her parents hadn't asked Morgan to make their job easier. Morgan had made that decision, too.

Oh.

Oh.

She *had* made those decisions. The situation with her family was what it was because *she'd* crafted it that way. She'd assumed responsibility because of her own feelings. But, in the same breath, they'd allowed her to. It might not have been an intentional decision, but her parents had encouraged Morgan's obedience, accepted her help.

It was trickier with her siblings, because that was all they'd ever known. But her parents? That situation was a little simpler. And if she was assigning responsibility for decisions more fairly, it had been her parents' decision to have her. They had chosen to go through with the pregnancy. They had chosen to raise her. She would always be grateful for their sacrifices, but perhaps...perhaps her gratitude could be shown in another way.

After decades, maybe she could finally stop trying to make up for her birth.

Maybe...maybe she didn't have to.

'Morgan?'

She whirled around, clamping her hand over her chest as she tried to calm her heart.

'Elliott,' she said, her knees going weak at the sight of him.

That was just because of the shock, she was sure.

No, it's because you love him.

'I'm sorry.' He shoved his hands into his pockets. 'Didn't mean to scare you.'

'No.' It was a quick response. As if responding quickly would allow her to escape that thought. All her thoughts. 'It's not your fault. I was distracted.' She cleared her throat. 'I thought you weren't coming,' she accused softly.

If he hadn't come she could have pretended her feelings for him had been amplified by the moonlight. She wouldn't have had to see his handsome face, all stormy and closed off from her—and yet still so breathtaking. He was wearing T-shirt and jeans again, and they moulded to every muscle she had admired, touched, the night before.

She'd lain her head on his chest, heard his heartbeat, and felt closer to him than to any other person. She'd kissed him, tasted him, shared the sweetest intimacy with him.

Physical intimacy. Emotional intimacy. It was because of him that she was realising things could be different with her family.

She was standing on the precipice of a new life. If he hadn't come she could have pretended she didn't want that life to include him.

'I...' He stepped through the door, and for the first time she saw that he wasn't alone. 'This is my brother—Gio. Gio, this is Morgan. She's been co-ordinating the estate revamp.'

It was as if someone had cloned Elliott, with a few key differences. His brother was shorter, stockier. He had a beard, lighter eyes, and he wore glasses. But he was just as handsome as his brother, and much less still.

Gio walked forward, smiling politely at her, and offered his hand. 'It's nice to meet you, Morgan.'

Morgan took his hand, her eyes flickering to Elliott. He was watching them with an unreadable expression on his face. 'It's nice to meet you, too.'

'Hard to believe that this is the first time we've inter-acted, considering you're running point on this project.'

The words put her back up. 'Technically, your brother's running point. I've worked with many project managers, and Elliott's one of the best.'

It wasn't a lie, but from the corner of her eye she saw Elliott stiffen.

Gio frowned. 'With all due respect, you're hardly quali-fied to make that evaluation.'

Her brows rose. She looked at Elliott. 'You didn't tell him who I am?'

Elliott grunted.

She sighed. 'Mr Abel—Gio?' Gio nodded. 'Gio, my name is Morgan Simeon. I'm a property expert. Which means I—'

'Morgan Simeon?' Gio interrupted. 'Why does that

name sound familiar?' His eyes widened. 'You worked on the Lando Project.'

'Yes, I was responsible for that.'

'It's amazing. Some of the best work I've seen. Which I'm sure you know is a compliment, coming from me.'

Cocky, this brother. But, since she did know it was a compliment, she smiled. 'Thank you.'

'How did Elliott manage to get you here?'

Her smile faded at the incredulity in his voice. 'Happy coincidence. Now, I'm sure you have questions. And I'd be happy to answer them. But, as I told you, your brother's been responsible for most of the work.'

As if he'd been waiting for that moment, Gio began firing questions at them. Well, at her. Despite her suggestion that he ask his brother, Gio chose not to. And Morgan soon grew tired of it. She diverted the questions to Elliott, and he—grudgingly—answered.

His answers were good, though there were times when she wanted to interject. She resisted the temptation. If she did that she would undermine him, and Gio had just started actually directing his questions to Elliott—just as grudgingly as his brother had begun to answer them earlier.

At the end of it, Gio folded his arms. 'I'm impressed, E. If this pans out—and it seems like it will—you'll have saved us time and money. No small amount of either.' Gio studied his brother. 'But if you'd answered my emails I wouldn't have had to fly all the way here for this conversation.'

'He's humble,' Morgan said when Elliott's expression closed up. 'And emails wouldn't have given you a chance to speak with me and inspect the work yourself.'

Gio smiled. It was a nice smile. An easy smile. Elliott's was neither.

She preferred Elliott's.

She preferred Elliott.

'I haven't seen as much as I'd like to,' Gio said slowly, 'but what I have seen has impressed me. You wouldn't by any chance be interested in a job, Ms Simeon? I could make you a lucrative offer.'

'You'd have to do more than that to get me to give up the business I've built my entire adult life,' Morgan said with a huff of laughter. 'But I'm flattered.' She became aware of Elliott's gaze, hot and intense, focused directly on her. 'I'll give you my card, Gio. Maybe we can find a way to work together minus the part where you become my boss.'

She handed him one of the cards she kept in her wallet and then pretended to see a message on her phone that required her attention. She made her excuses, claiming that she needed to check on something in the garden, and hightailed it out of the room.

Minutes later, her brain caught up with her legs. She'd walked further than she intended. Past her car, past the houses she needed to check on, past the garden she'd claimed to be going to. She was almost at the beach when Elliott caught her up.

'Morgan.'

He wasn't out of breath when he said it, which was, frankly, rude since he must have run. She'd *walked* and she was breathing faster than usual.

'Why are you here?' she asked. 'Your brother must want you to show him the estate.'

'You lied.'

'I did not.'

'You told him I was responsible for the estate.'

'You are.'

'No, I'm not.'

When she didn't reply, he reached out and caught her wrist. He let go as soon as she stopped.

'We did it together.'

'I'm trying not to take responsibility where I don't have

to,' she said. It felt as if she'd tossed the words in the air, not caring where they fell. 'It's not important for your brother to know that I helped you with this. It *is* important that he knows about *your* part in it. You've played a huge part, Elliott. The time and money he's saving is because you decided to renovate instead of rebuild.'

He didn't answer. Only stared at her with a deep frown. His brain was spinning. She could all but see it in his eyes. It stung, as she remembered the time when she hadn't been able to read him. Now he was like her favourite book.

She started walking again.

'Morgan,' he growled. 'You can't say something like that and walk away.'

'Yes, I can.'

He jogged up to her side, and then sped up and stopped ahead of her.

'Stop.'

'No.'

'Morgan.'

'Elliott?'

'Morgan.'

She stopped. 'I don't want to talk about this.'

'Why not?'

'Because you don't see yourself. Or you hide yourself. Either way, nothing I say is going to change that.'

Emotion flickered in his eyes. It softened her, and so she walked until she was in front of him and cupped his face.

'You're kind. Thoughtful. Someone with power who chooses to help those without it. You're smart. You've built a successful company from scratch. You did all of that—' she pointed in the direction of the estate '—on your own terms. Why you don't see how capable you are...' She shook her head, dropping her hands. 'I don't even have to answer that. I know why. I saw it back there with your brother.'

He exhaled. 'He's the smart one.'

'Elliott,' she said, resisting the urge to smack him. 'Just because your brother's smart, it doesn't mean you aren't! People can have the same qualities.'

'Not in my family.' He shoved his hands into his pockets again. The same thing he'd done back at the estate. It meant he was feeling vulnerable, she realised. 'You were either my brother, or...'

'You weren't good enough?' she asked when he didn't finish.

'Or you were me.'

She breathed in carefully, exhaled slowly, even as she was plotting the deaths of all the people who'd made this beautiful, brilliant man feel that way. Words formed in her head, almost spilled from her lips, but she pulled them back. Went through them carefully because she knew whatever she said would have an impact.

'Do you trust me?' she asked quietly.

He gave an imperceptible nod.

'Good.' It *was* good, but that wasn't a thought for now. 'If you trust me, you have to believe what I've said. I meant every word, Elliott. You're a good person. The best person.' *My person.* She swallowed. 'And I see you. I see you for who you are. I see you better than you see yourself.'

He clenched his jaw, looked out at the waves. It was done on purpose, so she couldn't see his face, and she gave him his privacy. Waited until he'd worked through it. Hoped that he trusted her enough to listen.

But when he looked at her she could see the fight on his face. The disbelief. Her heart, already showing signs of wear, crumbled. She didn't want him to feel this way. She wanted him to feel confident. Proud. She wanted him to believe in the mask he showed the world. To believe in himself.

She let out a shaky breath, stood on her toes and kissed his cheek. Then she turned and walked away.

'This isn't fair,' he said at her side.

He'd followed her.

'No, it's not,' she agreed. 'But that doesn't matter.'

'Please.' His voice was gruff. 'Try to understand.'

She stopped. Looked at him. 'I can't understand what I don't know.'

His chest was heaving. Up, down...up, down... In a steady rhythm despite its speed.

And then he spoke.

'You do know. You know what it's like to turn yourself into something because you want your family's love and acceptance.'

The words went off like a gong in her head. It was true; she knew it. Still, it echoed, ringing in her ears until he continued.

'I spent half my life doing that. All it ever did was make me feel...incapable. Not good enough,' he said, using her earlier words. 'Getting my parents' love shouldn't have been that hard. I knew that, and still I tried. Eventually I got tired of it. I refused to let people's opinions affect the way I saw myself.'

'Including mine?'

His eyes met hers. 'Yes.'

She pursed her lips. 'That's fine. Admirable, even. The only problem is that you see yourself the way you believe they see you. No?' she asked when he frowned. 'You let your brother walk all over you. That's not the Elliott I've got to know. And when Gio did eventually give you your due, you didn't accept it. You didn't *believe* it. Just like you don't believe me.'

It hurt, but this wasn't about her. It would never be about her, about them, until he saw the truth. Maybe she'd known that all along.

'You don't have to believe him. Or me, for that matter. Just believe the work you've put into your life over this second half of it. Look at yourself, at your achievements. Look at the warehouse full of your furniture. Look at the estate.' She paused. 'And when you're done, look at me. At us. At the relationships you've built with the people in this community. There's a whole new life waiting for you if you look and *see*. If you stop pushing people away. If you just…' She exhaled. 'If you just believed in yourself.'

This time when she walked away she didn't turn back. And he didn't follow.

CHAPTER EIGHTEEN

'LOOK AT ME. At us... There's a whole new life waiting for you if you look and see.'

Elliott couldn't get those words out of his head. Had she been saying he had the chance at a life with her? If she had been, would that change anything? Would he be able to do what she was asking?

The fact that he couldn't answer told him all he needed to know.

Slowly, he made his way back to the estate. His brother had continued the tour without him, and he found Gio in the garden, chatting with Thad. Elliott paused. Watched them. Tried to figure out how his worlds had collided in this strange, incomprehensible way. He had no answers—it seemed to be the day for it—so he hung back, waited for Gio to finish, all the while thinking about what Morgan had said.

He didn't want to think about what Morgan had said. Her words threatened everything about his life. Because they'd pointed out precisely how carefully he had crafted that life. Throwing himself into work so he didn't have to think about his feelings. Not engaging in any meaningful relationships for the same reason. If he'd given himself the time to think about those feelings—if he'd allowed people into his life who would have made him think about those feelings—he wouldn't be where he was now.

Confused. Hurt. Sad.

But he wasn't that person any more. That little boy who'd felt those emotions all the time. Who'd allowed those emotions to drive him. He didn't want any of that—but he wanted Morgan. And, unlike his family, she seemed to want him, too.

His eyes fell on Gio. Maybe he wasn't being entirely fair towards his family. Gio had asked him to help with the project. Surely he wouldn't have done that if he didn't trust Elliott? If he thought Elliott incapable? He'd complimented Elliott, too. Yes, it had come after some dismissal, but that might have been because Elliott had always allowed it. Encouraged it, in fact.

Over the years Elliott had chosen to let his family think what they wanted. On the odd occasion when they saw one another they treated him like the person who'd been written about in the newspapers. A furniture tycoon. A playboy. And he'd allowed it because it was easier to let them reject that version of him than reject who he actually was.

His brother didn't know who he actually was.

No one did—except Morgan.

Perhaps he needed to change that.

'Elliott?'

Gio was staring at him expectantly. It took Elliott a second to realise his brother was standing in front of him.

'What?'

'We can go.'

Elliott nodded in reply. He drove back to the house in silence. Once there, he unlocked the door and went straight to the fridge. He stared at the meals he'd defrosted. There were plenty more in the freezer. Proof, he thought. It might be part of their generosity as a community, but the people of Penguin Island had gone out of their way for him. Proof that he was a part of something. That he meant something to them.

And they had come to mean something to him, too.

'Okay, this is getting ridiculous,' Gio said.

Elliott turned, surprised to find him hovering a few steps away.

'What is going on with you? You've been distracted since we left the estate.'

'Sorry,' he muttered. Then he thought, *Screw it.* 'Did you mean what you said back there? That you're impressed with the plans for the estate?'

'Yeah.' Gio frowned. 'Why wouldn't I mean it?'

He shrugged. 'I don't know you well enough to know when you're lying.'

'And you think I'd lie about this?' The frown deepened. Gio folded his arms and leaned against the counter. 'This is because of Mom and Dad, isn't it?'

Elliott's heart skipped. He gave a quick nod, and half hoped his brother hadn't noticed.

Of course he'd noticed.

'Yeah, I guess a lot of your stuff is because of Mom and Dad...' Gio exhaled. 'Mine is, too.'

'Yours?'

Gio's brows lifted. 'What? You don't think our parents screwed me up, too?'

He didn't know what to say to that.

'I guess that's fair.' Gio straightened and went to the fridge, taking out one of the meals Elliott had been staring at. 'I haven't really spoken about it. Not to you, at least. You want some of this?'

Elliott could barely keep up with the conversation. He said yes to the question, though he wasn't really hungry, then waited for Gio to say more.

'It's always been a ton of pressure to be the genius in the family.' Gio slid the food into the microwave and pressed 'start'. 'They expected me to act like one. But I didn't know how to act like a genius, only myself, and that didn't seem good enough for them. Ironic, considering acting like myself meant acting like a genius.'

'But they've always been so proud of you.'

'Yeah…' He didn't speak for a while. 'Did you ever know how jealous I was of you? They let you do whatever you wanted. You had a freedom I'd never got and…' Gio's mouth twisted. 'I wanted it. I wanted to be you. You left home after school and you didn't look back. What was that like?'

It took Elliott a second to realise Gio was really asking. Then he said, 'Lonely.'

Gio's gaze didn't leave Elliott's face. For once Elliott didn't care about what Gio saw there.

He wasn't surprised when his brother said, 'You felt the same way about me, didn't you? You wanted to be me.'

'I wanted them to…love me.'

'They do love you.'

'Maybe.' His mind was spinning with Gio's confession. With the fact that he'd made his own. And, since he had, there seemed no point in keeping this next part to himself. 'But not in any way that matters.'

The microwave beeped in the silence. Gio was still watching him. After a few minutes his brother took out the food, shared it between the two plates he'd got out earlier, and took two beers from the fridge.

'How about we talk, brother?' Gio asked as he slid the meal over to Elliott. 'I think we could both do with an honest conversation.'

The morning of the wedding, Elliott woke up early. The last week had been a blur of final preparations. They'd managed to get all the houses ready on time for the guests who were staying there, and Morgan had pulled some strings to ensure the final inspections had been done on time. It had literally taken until the day before, with him, his brother and Morgan burying themselves in work.

Gio had readily agreed to stay and help when he'd learned about the wedding, although Elliott suspected it had less to do with the wedding and more to do with him. That 'honest conversation' Gio had wanted to have had been…illuminating. They'd both told each other something about what they'd felt growing up—not everything, but enough to get an idea—and somehow that had created a bond between them. It was new and tentative, and neither he nor his brother was entirely comfortable with it, but it was there. It was important.

For now, that was enough.

He couldn't believe it. His brother…wanting a relationship with him. Every instinct told him not to trust it. It would disappear, and then what would happen? He'd be hurt again and he'd go back to his old life.

Except nothing would really change in his life. At least not in the life he'd created in Cape Town. If Gio did something to break their fragile bond it wouldn't affect Elliott. He'd go back to running his business. Back to only seeing his family on special occasions. Yes, he'd be hurt— but wasn't a relationship with his brother worth the risk? Because if Gio *didn't* let him down, Elliott would finally have some semblance of a family. And wasn't that what he'd always wanted?

He would have given anything to talk it through with Morgan, but she'd been treating him coolly since the last time they'd spoken. That was fair. He'd pushed her away and she was responding in kind. Fair, he thought again, but not harmless. It hurt. But then, he seemed to be in a place where hurt was inevitable. It scared the life out of him, and yet it seemed hopeful.

Hope. He hadn't experienced that in years. He supposed that was what happened when someone fell in love.

He showered, left a note for his brother, and went to help with the last-minute preparations. The café that had become his and Morgan's unofficial meeting spot every morning was normally closed at this time of day, but today they let him in. Morgan was already there. Seemed they'd opened early for her, too. And they'd given her breakfast. An untouched croissant along with coffee.

He gestured to the server for coffee of his own and went to join her. She didn't look at him. Instead, she kept on staring into the distance. He followed her gaze, saw there was nothing there, and then waited to see if she'd notice him.

It took the delivery of his coffee to draw her out of her thoughts.

'Hey,' she said, blinking a few times as her eyes came into focus. 'How long have you been here?'

'You need a fresh cup of coffee,' he replied, nodding at the server. 'You're nervous.'

'What? No. I'm just…distracted.'

'What's happened?'

'Nothing.' She dipped her finger into the cold coffee, winced, and pulled her finger out. 'Urgh. I really have been here too long.'

He waited.

She sighed. 'It's annoying when you do that.'

'But it works.'

Her lips curved and she shook her head. 'Nothing's happened. I just need to breathe before the day starts.' She paused. 'My family got in last night.'

He searched her face, looking for any sign that they'd done something to upset her. She looked…strained. And distracted, as she'd said. But she didn't seem angry or upset.

'Are you okay?' he asked for good measure.

'I'm fine. No, that's not true.' She immediately contradicted herself. 'I need to have an honest conversation with them and I… I don't know how to do it.' There was a beat. 'Maybe I am nervous, after all. How did you know?'

'I know you.'

He didn't know if that was the right thing to say, considering how things were between them. But she just nodded, looked out of the window. As if what he'd said was true. As if she'd accepted it.

Hope bloomed inside him.

'Honest conversations aren't that bad,' he said.

'Aren't they?' Her tone was dry. 'I recall several of ours being catastrophic.'

He grunted. The server brought her coffee.

A few seconds later, she said, 'Are you talking about you and your brother?'

He nodded.

'You told him? About the stuff with your parents?'

He nodded again.

She bit her lip. 'How did he respond?'

'Well…' He cleared his throat. 'He…he has some issues, too.'

This time she nodded. She ran a finger around the rim of her coffee cup, a smile playing on her face. She was happy for him.

Of course she's happy for you. She loves you.

He didn't know that. He didn't know that at all. And he refused to entertain the thought until he did.

'He asked me to offer you a job again,' Elliott said into the silence.

'He's already offered it to me three times. Your offer makes it a fourth.'

Elliott couldn't blame Gio. Her work on the estate was impeccable. She'd turned viewing several somewhat unremarkable houses into a striking, cohesive experience. Flipper Estate could easily compete with other top-rated beachside estates now, and she'd managed that with straightforward reconstruction and clever design. The garden was a triumph, too, although she'd had little to do with that. It didn't matter. Her contributions made it clear she deserved to be called an expert.

'Will you consider it?'

'Not a job, no. A partnership, maybe.'

'He'll be disappointed.'

'I think he'll survive,' she answered dryly.

She began to eat her croissant, breaking it apart and leaving flakes all over her plate. He waited for her to say something else, but she didn't. That told him just how tense things were between them. Morgan liked to talk. She had from the moment he'd met her. He hadn't realised how much he liked it when she filled the silences until now, when she didn't.

He'd never really cared for small talk, but he found himself doing it anyway. 'Did you like him?'

'Who?'

'Gio.'

She brought her cup to her lips. 'I've liked him more since he's started giving you the credit you deserve.'

'He likes you,' he answered softly, and then continued with something he'd had no idea he'd been thinking about. 'And his fascination isn't only professional.'

Her brow furrowed. 'Are you flirting with me on your brother's behalf?'

'No.'

'No...' she repeated, her eyes searching, seeing too much. She sat back, her hands still around the cup. 'In case it isn't clear, my feelings for your brother are entirely dependent on you. He's been treating you better, so I like him better.' She set her coffee on the table. 'I'm a little offended that you think I might reciprocate whatever fascination he has for me beyond professionalism.'

Up until she'd asked that question about flirting, he

hadn't been aware of his jealousy. He'd watched the ease with which Morgan and Gio interacted and he'd…he'd internalised it. Now he could see that he'd been bracing himself for her to tell him she preferred Gio. That she'd compared him with his brother and found him lacking. The fact that she hadn't—that she'd based her entire opinion of Gio on his treatment of Elliott—told him that she cared about him.

And that he needed to get a grip on his issues.

'I'm sorry. It's…it's not you.'

'I know that,' she snapped. Then she gave a frustrated exhalation. 'But honestly it *should* be about me. You know me better than anyone, Elliott. You know how I feel about you. I wish you'd trust that.'

He was about to reply when Sharon stormed in, eyes wide, chest heaving.

Morgan was at her side immediately, Elliott not far behind. 'What? What's happened?'

'Edna,' Sharon panted. 'She's gone.'

'Gone?' Morgan repeated. 'What do you mean "gone"?'

'She's not at the house and no one can find her.'

CHAPTER NINETEEN

SOMETIMES WHEN MORGAN couldn't sleep, she'd go through the wedding day in her head. She'd think about how beautiful her grandmother would look, how stunning the garden would be, how everyone would gaze upon the couple with joy and celebrate their union of love.

Not once had Morgan considered a runaway bride.

'We'll have to cancel,' Joyce said.

All her grandmother's friends had arrived shortly after Sharon, with assurances that the only people who knew what had happened were those in the room. They'd yet to tell Stanley, who was still peacefully asleep in one of the other houses on the estate, her grandmother having insisted they not see one another until the wedding day.

No. There was no way her grandmother had run away from him.

'We're not cancelling,' Morgan said.

'We have no bride,' Joyce pointed out.

'We have a bride. She's just…not here right now.'

'And do you know where she might be?'

'No,' Morgan replied, 'but I know my grandmother. She would not leave her fiancé at the altar.'

'I don't know, dear,' Clarice said. 'Edna loves drama. Some of her favourite movies are about jilted grooms.'

Morgan resisted the urge to roll her eyes. 'I'd bet an

organ that that isn't what's happening here.' Something occurred to her. 'Has any one of you actually *looked* for her?'

There was a beat.

'Well, not physically,' Sharon said. 'We've all tried to call her, but her phone's off.'

'So when you said "no one can find her" you meant what, exactly?'

A strange sound came from her left. When she turned, Elliott had his hand over his face and was pretending not to laugh.

She narrowed her eyes. 'Find this amusing, do you?'

He held up both hands in surrender, his lips twitching. Now she did roll her eyes, and then turned back to her grandmother's friends.

'I'm beginning to think Grandma Edna isn't the one who loves drama.'

'Excuse me?' Sharon huffed, straightening her spine.

'Morgan,' Joyce said. 'That's just rude.'

'Not untrue,' Clarice added with a sniff, 'but definitely impolite.'

The bell on the door sounded and they all turned with smiles on their faces as if nothing was wrong.

Edna stared back at them. 'What's going on here? You all look insanely suspicious.'

As her friends flocked to her, admonishing her for switching off her phone, demanding her whereabouts, Morgan hung back. She felt Elliott at her side long before he spoke.

'How did you know she hadn't run?'

'She loves Stanley.'

She watched her grandmother laugh and roll her eyes at her friends, her face bright and happy, the most joyous Morgan had ever seen her.

'I think, for her, it's the simplest thing. She loves him.

She wants to be with him. She wouldn't do anything that would mean they can't be together.'

She looked at Elliott now, her breath catching at the look of intensity on his face. Her words replayed in her head, and she realised that maybe it *was* simple. If she loved Elliott she would do what she needed to do so they could be together. He would, too. But she couldn't control his actions—heaven knew she'd tried. Tried to get him to see himself…to see her. The truth was that he needed to see them, too.

She could see them. She could see their future together. And that meant that she needed to make things simple. Which involved facing her worst fears. But she could do it. She *would* do it. For herself *and* for them.

'I'll see you later?' she asked him quietly.

He nodded. She did, too. Then she turned before she could linger. Before she could cup his face, kiss his lips, tell him her plans.

Her grandmother left with her, and they walked back to the estate.

'That was an exciting start to the morning,' Edna commented.

Morgan laughed. 'Not quite what you imagined for the morning of your wedding.'

Her grandmother didn't answer. Morgan narrowed her eyes suspiciously and saw her suspicions confirmed.

'You *wanted* that to happen?' she accused her.

'I wanted some excitement.'

'Your wedding almost had to be cancelled. Why wasn't that enough excitement for you?'

'Oh, I stopped worrying about that the moment I called you.'

Morgan chose not to address that. 'How did you even know your friends would react that way?'

'They love drama.'

'As do you, apparently.'

Edna winked at her, and she couldn't help but laugh.

'You're a hypocrite,' Morgan informed her. 'You nearly had a heart attack when you didn't hear from me the other night, and then you do the same thing to your friends.'

'Yes, well, I'm your grandmother. I have a right to hypocrisy.'

'Is that what you tell yourself?'

'Yes.'

She snorted again.

They walked in silence for a bit, and then Edna said, 'Have you told him you love him yet?'

Morgan nearly stumbled. 'What? Who? No.'

'Darling,' Edna said, in the gentlest tone, 'you do realise that I have eyes in my head?'

She opened her mouth, but her grandmother was still talking.

'I can't remember the last time you smiled the way you do when he's around. You don't ever do things like sneak around and not let your grandmother know where you are. You didn't even do that with Thad,' Edna added. 'Even when you sneaked around with him, you'd give me an itinerary. Fake, but still... I knew where you were.' She paused. 'Where did you go that night with Elliott?'

'Gran...' Morgan huffed in protest, bothered by her grandmother's revelations, but not enough to sacrifice her privacy.

'Fine, fine.' Edna waved a hand. 'Don't tell me. I'm sure I don't really want to know.' She took a deep breath. 'Morgan, you never do anything for yourself. *Never.* Elliott's been helping you with that. You should tell him that you love him.'

'That's... Gran...'

'You think I haven't seen it?' Edna asked, cutting off her stammering. 'I have. I've intervened when I can with your parents, but you've always seemed content with the way things are. And then you haven't been—not in the last few years. So I decided that I would finally accept Stanley's proposal and we'd move to Cape Town. We'd help with Hattie and Rob, give you some space to figure out what you want. But I knew you'd need a kick in the butt, so I asked you to come here. To help me.'

Morgan's jaw dropped.

Finally. Finally it made sense why her grandmother had called her. Edna had never asked for Morgan's help. Not once. Morgan had assumed it was because Edna's life was exactly the way she wanted it. Edna was sharp, smart about her decisions, and she was happy to live with the consequences when things didn't work out.

It was for that very reason that Morgan had jumped on a plane when Edna had called. She'd thought things must be serious if Edna was reaching out to her.

That part was probably still true. Only it was Morgan's life that had needed the intervention.

Also—Edna had spoken to her parents about this?

'Gran,' Morgan said slowly. 'How are you only telling me this now?'

'Would you have listened if I'd told you before?' Edna didn't wait for an answer. 'I'm quite pleased with the way things have turned out. I only meant to get you to the island for a break. I didn't think you would meet Elliott, let alone fall in love with him. That was an unexpected bonus.'

She sounded giddy.

'This is a lot to take in…'

'Oh, don't be angry. I'm your grandmother. I have a right to interfere in your life.'

'I thought we went through this?' Morgan muttered darkly.

'We did,' her grandmother said cheerfully. 'I made an executive decision.'

Morgan couldn't help her laugh. It displaced some of her tension, causing it to flutter through her body. Her stomach felt jittery, as did her heart—which wasn't great on top of the nerves she already had, knowing she needed to speak with her family. But this jitteriness wasn't bad. It was…relief. Someone in her family had seen what she was going through. Someone had *cared*. Hell, her grandmother had decided to move back to Cape Town for her.

It wasn't something she would ever have thought to ask. Grandma Edna had done so much for Morgan already. All those summers Morgan had come to the island, all the times Morgan's parents would call and Edna would fly over immediately to help.

Morgan could see now that she'd tried to relieve her grandmother of that responsibility, too. If she could look after Hattie and Rob—if her parents didn't have to call Grandma Edna—then her grandmother wouldn't see Morgan and her siblings as a burden.

Such nonsense, she realised. Edna would never see her family as a burden—not in the way Morgan had worried they were. It was clear to her now, and she felt silly for not seeing it before.

'Gran—' Morgan started, but her grandmother interrupted.

'There's more.'

'More? How could I possibly survive more?'

'Funny,' Edna said with a glare in Morgan's direction. 'I thought… Well, I've always wanted to give you the house.'

Morgan blinked. 'Which house?'

'My house. I thought I'd bequeath it to you. But then I decided to move back, and the Abels decided to buy the estate…' Edna shook her head. 'There were several factors, really. Eventually I sold it.'

Morgan kept silent. She knew her grandmother. She knew there was more.

'But then I saw you here. How happy you are. I regretted it. So when that nice boy Gio came I asked him for the house back.'

'You asked…?' Morgan blew out a breath. 'What did he say?'

'Yes.'

She stopped walking. 'He said yes?'

Edna stopped, too. 'I told him it was for you, and that you'd worked for free to turn the estate into what it is now, and I said that I'd tell the community to make his life a living hell if he didn't sell it back to me.' Edna shrugged. 'He said yes.'

There was likely more to it than that. Gio was a businessman first and foremost—this was probably something he'd thought about strategically. But it didn't matter to Morgan.

'You're giving me the house? *Your* house?'

'Yes.'

Morgan shook her head. 'Gran, I can't—'

'Yes, you can.' Edna took both Morgan's hands in hers. 'I *want* you to have it. You deserve to be at peace. And I've never seen you more at peace than here, so I bought back the damn house for you.'

'Well, at least let me pay—'

'Morgan, I don't need the money. Your grandfather left me more than I expected, and I've been smart with it over the years. Not to mention that I'm moving in with Stanley. The money I have left is more than enough to keep me going until I don't need it any more.'

She squeezed Morgan's hands before dropping them.

'Now, I believe it's time for me to get married. Let's go, dear. You'll make me late.'

Helplessly, Morgan followed her grandmother.

CHAPTER TWENTY

ELLIOTT HAD NEVER pictured his own wedding day. He'd never thought he'd get married. But since he was more inclined to such fanciful thoughts these days, he imagined this was the kind of wedding he'd want, too.

They'd set up the altar and the arch beneath the oak tree, and pinned flowers to every available space of the arch, creating the most stunning backdrop of white against the brown and green of the trees. There were white chairs in rows and rows, extending from the altar further into the garden. The flowering bushes added to the summery feel of the wedding, their bright colours a happy contrast to the simple white of the wedding décor. It was beautiful, and romantic, and the buzz from the rows and rows of guests— the only thing Elliott thought he might *not* want at his own wedding—added to the atmosphere of anticipation.

The groom stood at the altar, handsome in a navy-blue suit and not showing any nerves. But then, Stanley was a steady sort of guy. The few times Elliott had met him he'd been courteous, patient. It was clear that he adored Edna, and that she adored him, and Elliott imagined this was a dream come true for both of them.

He wouldn't quite describe Stanley's son, the famous videographer, in the same way. When Gerald had walked into the garden he'd exclaimed his pleasure. Then he'd barked instructions at his team, begun filming, and now wherever he went a nervous energy followed. Not his own, but the energy of those around him, including whichever guests he happened to be near.

Elliott was eager to see how that energy did around Morgan. Her relentless cheer and no-nonsense attitude were likely a match for Gerald.

Elliott caught himself smiling at that thought. The moment he realised it, he stopped. His brother was sitting next to him, towards the back of the garden. What if Gio saw him *smiling*? At *nothing*? No, that wouldn't do.

Unfortunately, that only made him think of what Morgan would say if he ever told her what had gone through his head. It made resisting a smile harder, and he was grateful when music began to play to indicate the entrance of the bridal party.

Several bridesmaids came through first, one of whom reminded him so much of Morgan that Elliott did a doubletake. But when he did, he saw that the woman wasn't as tall, with shorter hair dyed pink. Her features were different, too: her nose smaller, eyes bigger, mouth wider. She was obviously Morgan's sister, and the flower girl, who shared her mother's pink hair and big eyes, was Morgan's niece.

None of that mattered when he saw Morgan. She was wearing a dress in a colour that fell somewhere between purple and blue. It formed a V at her breasts, was cinched in at her waist, then fell sleekly down her legs, opening on one side to reveal a beautiful brown thigh. Shoes in the same colour as the dress adorned her feet, a silk strap hugging each calf and stopping right below her knee. Her hair was curled, tied in a ponytail at the nape of her neck, though some strands had broken free and were fluttering across her face.

He'd always thought her beautiful, but today she stunned the breath right out of him. And when she caught his eye, and gave him a coy half-smile, he thought he might never breathe easily again.

'Tell her,' his brother said at his side.

Elliott waited until Morgan was standing at the front with the rest of the bridesmaids before he asked, 'Tell her what?'

'That you love her.'

His head whipped to the side as Gio stood—along with everyone else—for the bride. It took him a moment longer to stand, but he did, and tried to focus on Edna. He couldn't. Though she looked beautiful and happy, he kept glancing at his brother, hoping for an explanation. And when it seemed clear he wouldn't get one, his eyes rested on Morgan.

He did love her. From the moment he'd seen her in front of her grandmother's house he'd been caught by her. Since then she'd tortured him, challenged him, teased him. She'd made him into a better man. He could easily see himself walking down the aisle right now, stopping in front of her and getting down on his knee.

The urge was so compelling that every muscle in his body clenched, as if to stop him from doing just that.

He was tense for the remainder of the wedding. At one point, his brother nudged him in the ribs.

'Relax,' he said under his breath. 'You're scaring the flower girl.'

Elliott looked at Morgan's niece who, despite the hundreds of other people in the garden, was somehow looking at him. When she saw him return her gaze she grinned, showing off a mouth full of various-sized teeth.

His lips curved. 'She's fine.'

His brother sighed, but didn't say anything.

Elliott made an effort to relax after that, for the sake of that stupid new and fragile bond between them. He didn't know what the rules were, so he wasn't sure what the implications would be if he ignored Gio. His heart thudded, and a familiar voice inside told him to throw it in. To stop caring.

It's too hard. You don't even know if it's going to work out.

But he ignored it. It took all his power, but he ignored it. Because it *was* worth it.

Having someone to sit at his side at a wedding was worth it. Having that person tease him. Having that person be family. He'd shunned relationships out of fear, but never considered what that fear had cost him.

His eyes rested on Morgan and he knew what he had to do.

Except he wouldn't get the chance until later that night.

The celebrations began as soon as the ceremony had ended. Canapés and champagne were brought out as the couple had pictures taken, some alone, some with their guests. Every time he managed to get close to Morgan someone whisked her away, and he was left talking to a stranger, discussing something he didn't care about but trying not to show it because he was being polite.

Gio seemed to be having a ball, which was a confusing learning experience. Elliott hadn't realised his brother was so sociable. He'd only ever seen Gio working. It might be that Elliott just hadn't ever got to see Gio in his off time, but he had a feeling it was more that Gio didn't *get* much off time. He was beginning to think Gio's call for help hadn't only been for the company. Maybe Gio had called him as a show of trust—and in a first step to a better relationship and life.

Maybe Elliott would ask him.

Eventually, after hours and hours, the celebrations died down. There were still stragglers in the garden, drunk and happy—his brother included—while others had migrated to the beach. Elliott made sure Gio was okay, then began his search for Morgan. She was nowhere to be found, and nor were any of her family members, whom Elliott had met at various points during the wedding. His opinion of them had finally helped him understand Morgan's words about Gio.

'My feelings for your brother are entirely dependent on you.'

Her family seemed like nice enough people, but his judgement was based on Morgan's opinion of them. Since he wasn't sure what that was, he'd wait until he was before drawing any final conclusions.

In a last-ditch effort to find her, he went to the secret waterfall.

She was sitting on one of the rocks, staring at the water.

'Are you okay?' he asked, near enough that she could see him.

Her head whipped up, but she didn't seem surprised. She rested her chin on her knees.

'I think so.'

Slowly, he made his way to her side. She somehow managed to look even more beautiful than earlier. Her hair was untied now, falling in curls around her face. It reminded him of the last time they'd been at the waterfall together. But now, with the moon shining down on her, as if it had anointed her, he wanted to fall to his knees in worship.

Instead, he sat down, waiting for her to speak.

'It's trending,' she said quietly. 'Hashtag *romanceisland*. On social media. Gerald shot a video and posted it. A bunch of us reposted it, with the same hashtag, and then more people shared it because it's Penguin Island.' She smiled. 'We got *romanceisland* trending. It's a promising start.'

'It'll continue.'

'You sound awfully confident about that.'

'I am.'

'Why?'

'You,' he said simply. 'You did this. You won't fail.' He paused. 'I also know that Gio has invested a significant amount of money into marketing the estate. He'll make good use of this attention.'

'Isn't Gio just full of surprises?' she muttered under her breath.

'What does that mean?'

She didn't reply immediately. 'He sold my grandmother's house.'

Elliott's body tensed. 'I'll talk to him.'

'No,' she said, dropping to her knees. 'It's not like that. He sold it to *her*.'

'He…what?'

'He sold the house back to her for reasons that remain unclear but I'm sure are strategic. And she…' She blew out a breath. 'My grandmother gave the house to me.'

He stared at the waterfall, his brain working. Why hadn't Gio told him this? What was his plan here? He didn't think it was anything nefarious. Especially since apparently, Gio knew what Elliott's feelings for Morgan were. Had he done this for Elliott? And, if so, what was the end game?'

She squeezed his knee. 'It's a good thing.'

He looked down at her hand and took it. 'Is it?'

'I think so.' Her voice was shakier now, but she tightened her hold. 'I think… I think I'm going to move to the island.'

He didn't know how to reply. It didn't matter. She kept talking.

'I haven't been able to stop thinking about it since she told me this morning. But it's the right thing to do. I haven't talked to my family yet, but I'm going to—' she sounded resolute '—and I think some distance might help us all figure out how things will go from now on.' She looked at him. 'Am I...?' Her lashes fluttered. 'That's okay?'

He squeezed her hand tightly. 'If it's what you want, then it's more than okay. It's right.'

She let out a long breath. 'Why is making these decisions so hard?'

'You're changing your life,' he answered. 'That's hard.'

The waterfall was all they heard for a while, then she angled herself towards him. 'I saw you with your brother today. You two seem to be getting along well.'

'We are.' He allowed himself a small smile. 'It's...nice.'

She laughed. He wished he could bottle the sound and take it with him. Whenever he was having a bad day he'd shake it, uncork it, and let it shower over him. Give him the good feeling he had every time he heard it.

Good heavens, what was this woman *doing* to him? Turning him into a sap because he loved her...

'You what?'

He looked at her. Her eyes were wide, lips parted.

'What's wrong?' he asked.

'You just said I'm turning you into a sap because you love me.'

'I did not.'

'Yeah, you did. It was under your breath, and quite frankly it didn't sound super-complimentary, but I heard it.'

So now he wasn't even in control of what he said.

He exhaled. 'It's true.'

She stared at him. Then she started laughing again. And if he'd thought she deserved worship before, watching her throw back her head now, exposing the long, smooth column of her throat, and hearing the infectious sound of her laughter would require sacrifice.

He supposed that was what love was. Sacrifice. Sacrificing his fears of rejection. Sacrificing the lonely life he'd created for himself and his feelings of unworthiness.

He loved Morgan, so he would believe her when she told him he was worth her love. And because of that he would work every second to get to the point when he didn't have to believe her any more.

When he only had to believe himself.

Abruptly, the laughter stopped. She turned fully to him, her gaze searching. 'You love me?' she whispered.

He brought her hand to his lips. 'Yes.'

'I love you, too.'

His world shifted on its axis. But he didn't feel unsteady. The opposite, in fact. He felt as though things were finally right. As though his world, which he'd never been comfortable in, had settled.

'Thank you,' he managed to say through his emotions.

She laughed. 'You're not meant to thank me, Elliott. You're meant to say "I love you" back.'

'I already have.'

'So say it again.'

'I love you.'

Her lips spread into the sweetest smile and she leaned forward to give him the sweetest kiss. Slow, gentle, as if they had all the time in the world for the rest.

When she pulled back her eyes searched him. 'Are you going back?' she asked. 'To Cape Town?'

'I have to.' He frowned. 'I have to see my father.'

'He's not doing any better?'

'He's fine. But I have to see both my parents to...' He trailed off even as he felt his frown deepen. 'I suppose I have to face my ghosts.'

'Hmm...'

'But I'll be back,' he promised. 'For you.'

'No,' she said, shaking her head. 'You have to be back for *you*. You should want to live here, too. What about your job?'

He could hear her fear, so he pulled her closer, lowered

his forehead to hers. 'I want this. You. A life together. I want us to base our businesses here. Fly out when we need to, but come back home to Penguin Island.'

He didn't give himself a chance to think about his next words.

'I want us to get married here. Maybe we'll have children, maybe we won't. But I want it all with you, Morgan. That's the choice I'm making because I trust us. Most importantly, I love you.'

She was kissing him before he'd finished, and he relished it. Poured his heart and soul into it.

And when she pulled away, she whispered, 'Yes... Yes, I'll marry you.'

If he'd known she'd take those words as a proposal perhaps he would have thought about it more. But as he smiled, as he kissed her again, he thought that sometimes things didn't have to be different to be perfect.

EPILOGUE

SIX MONTHS AFTER Edna's wedding Morgan finally moved into her grandmother's house. No—*her* house. It would be her permanent home, her base, though she was keeping her house in Cape Town. It was still a huge part of her, part of her history, and she needed somewhere to stay when she was in town for business. Which would be often.

It had taken months for her to figure out how her business would work with her move, and the result had been lots of travel. But that was fine with her. It meant she could go back to see her family as much as she needed to.

'After everything you've done for us, making this hard for you would be selfish.'

Those were the actual words her sister had said when she'd told her family about her plans. She'd decided not to tell them her feelings on everything—it would only hurt them, and what was the benefit in that?—only that she wanted to move to Penguin Island and wouldn't be there for them so much any more.

There had been a lot of back-and-forth: questions about why and how it would work with her job and her house. She'd been honest. Told them that the island had always felt more like home to her than Cape Town did.

When they'd seemed to accept that, she'd told them she was engaged, which had distracted them for much longer, and eventually, with her family all around, Hattie had told her that.

'After everything you've done for us, making this hard for you would be selfish.'

Morgan had teared up and looked at her grandmother, who had been smiling, and at her parents, who had been tearful themselves. She hadn't understood why, and had felt the familiar desire to soothe their discomfort in some way. But then her mother had nodded at her, her father had, too, and her grandmother had winked.

It was time for her to let go.

Apparently her family agreed.

Of course it helped that Elliott had been there the entire time. And that when he'd met with his family she had been there, too.

His parents had been kinder than she'd imagined, albeit uncompromising. But they'd given Elliott praise for what he'd done for the estate. She'd watched him as he'd heard the words he'd always wanted to hear. His expression hadn't changed, although he'd thanked his parents, and told them about the engagement. And that had been the end of it.

He'd told her afterwards that it hadn't felt the way he'd thought it would. But they hadn't been able to talk about it in detail because then they'd met up with Gio for dinner.

They'd wanted to tell Elliott's parents before telling his brother, keeping the news a secret until they'd left the island. When Gio heard he'd grinned widely, hit his brother on the back, kissed Morgan on the cheek and told her, 'Welcome to the family!'

Elliott's face had brightened, and Morgan had known he'd found the family he wanted. The one he deserved. She fully intended on expanding on that.

'Morgan?'

She whirled around. 'Elliott?'

She was jumping into his arms before he could say anything else. They'd been in touch every day of the last six months, seeing one another a couple of times here and there, but this had been their longest stretch without an in-person meeting. He'd been travelling for work, she'd had to get things ready for her move, and a month had passed. She hadn't expected him today, so jumping into his arms was the only reasonable reaction.

He caught her without missing a beat, spinning her around before setting her down on the ground. She clung to his waist, dug her face into his chest, and felt his warmth settle in her body. He was here, in her house, *their* home. They'd agreed he'd move his stuff in bit by bit, until he'd finalised his own business plans and could settle on the island on a more permanent basis.

In a couple of months they'd be married. And finally, their lives would begin in the place where their relationship had started.

'Good surprise?' he asked, pulling back far enough to see her face.

'Good surprise,' she agreed. 'You can help me unpack.'

He laughed, the vibration reverberating through her body. 'That wasn't what I had in mind.'

'Yeah, I'm sure.'

She rolled her eyes, but she was smiling as she turned in his arms. As he wrapped them around her she looked at the house.

And it hit her.

It didn't matter where they lived as long as they were together.

But it felt damn good to be together on Penguin Island.

* * * * *

COMING SOON!

We really hope you enjoyed reading this book.
If you're looking for more romance, be sure to
head to the shops when new books are
available on

Thursday 14th April

MILLS & BOON®

Coming next month

SECRETS BEHIND THE BILLIONAIRE'S RETURN
Rachael Stewart

'Why have you come home? Now, after all this time?'

Felicity felt Sebastian's gaze on her, burning into her, and for one silly moment, she wondered: was he going to tell her he was here for her?

Like some fairy-tale romance where the hero made his fortune and returned to sweep the heroine off her feet...

As if. She almost laughed aloud at the ridiculous notion and choked on her drink in the process.

'Steady.' He placed a hand on her back, the innocent touch reverberating right through her. 'You okay?'

She hurried to recover, to break the electrifying contact. 'You avoiding the question?'

He gave her a slight smile. 'No. Truth is, now my grandfather's gone, my brother and I can do what we like with the estate. We toyed with letting it go but I figure the old man will turn in his grave to see us return to it.'

She could hear the bitterness, see the smile still playing about his lips adding to the chill of his hatred, and fought back a shudder. She'd never known Sebastian to be cold, stripped of his good humour, his care, his passion.

Was this more the man he was now? A cold-hearted business mogul?

She wanted to ask, but she was only putting off the inevitable, the all-important conversation that they had to have and that wasn't fair...on any of them.

'Sebastian?'

His eyes wavered over her face, his brows drawing together. 'Yes.'

'There's something I need to tell you...'

'I figured as much.'

She wet her lips. 'You did?'

'You look like you're about to confess to some heinous crime.'

'No.' She gave a tight laugh. 'No crime. Only...'

'Only?'

'I'm—I'm a mum.'

'I know.' His smile softened, his eyes, too, something akin to regret lingering there. 'I gathered that earlier. Is—is her father around? I notice you don't wear a...'

He gestured to her ring finger and she snatched it back self-consciously, twisting her hands together. 'No, he is—wasn't.'

Oh, God, why couldn't she just say it? Why was it so hard?

'Can't have been easy bringing her up alone, looking after your gran, especially when she got sick, and then there's this place...' He gestured around him and she couldn't even nod, couldn't even blink.

His eyes narrowed as the silence extended...a beat, two, three. 'Flick?'

Continue reading
SECRETS BEHIND THE BILLIONAIRE'S RETURN
Rachael Stewart

Available next month
www.millsandboon.co.uk